The World
in a
Glass Dome

Anthony Engebretson

GRENDEL PRESS

Published 2024
ISBN: 978-1-960534-22-4 (Paperback)
ASIN: (eBook)

Written by Anthony Engebretson
https://anthonyengebretson.com/

Cover by Just Venture Arts
Edited by Kasey Kubica

Published by Grendel Press LLC
www.grendelpress.com

THE WORLD IN A GLASS DOME

ANTHONY ENGEBRETSON

CONTENTS

Part One
The Store

CHAPTER ONE

THE RADIO CRACKLED WITH noise. Skyler hadn't noticed when she'd lost her station. Even when the music had been playing—Tom Petty, Cheap Trick, Van Halen—it had all been background noise at best. She glanced at the clock: 3:30 p.m. She had been driving for three hours but it all seemed like a blur. Her eyes were glazing, she felt drained; she took a sip of warm Coke, as if that would boost her energy.

She was driving into a tiny town. An old, rusty water tower read "DAYTON." This was where she needed to be.

Skyler rarely ever went this far west. Having lived in Omaha her whole life she was a city person to her core. It was hard to imagine living in a little village like this. So far from any cities—and with so little to do.

Though, it didn't seem anybody actually *did* live here. The town's main street was a small strip with a couple buildings on each side. None of the buildings seemed to be occupied. There was a bar, marked by an old, broken Budweiser sign above the door—a large piece of plywood reading "Closed For Good" over its front window. There was a tiny building with the words "Town Hall" over it next to a church—both of which were boarded up. No grocery stores, there probably wasn't one for miles. The yellowing sign in front of the church read: "God Bless You." There wasn't a soul in sight. Some cars were parked along the street—one of which was an old pickup with an outdated license plate and a missing front tire.

Skyler felt deeply lonely out here. This was a forgotten place. She pictured the people who built the town probably a hundred years ago. Maybe they hadn't expected Dayton to grow into the next Chicago—but they surely had pictured something greater than abandoned buildings, long-dead roadkill on the streets, and the only functioning establishment being a Dollar General a couple miles out of town.

She was out of Dayton almost as soon as she'd entered. Once again, there was only an endless stretch of farmland. Many of the fields were flooded by the excessive rainfall that had been happening all summer and into early fall.

Skyler tried to picture Morgan driving through Dayton. It was hard to imagine someone like her—someone who belonged with people, and in the here and now— in that forgotten place. It made her feel sad.

Her phone buzzed from her purse. Her heart leaped. What if it was Morgan? What if she was calling to tell Skyler it was alright? That she was home again, and where the hell was Skyler? Then Skyler would have to explain that she was all the way out in the boonies, looking for her. Morgan would laugh. Skyler could only imagine what she would say.

"Good lord, Sky. I'm sorry, my phone was off. I just needed to get away from things, you know? Now, get your ass home."

Skyler would laugh too, and she would drive back to Omaha. Morgan would give her shit for months, but her fears would be quelled and her heart settled.

But when she pulled out her phone, her hopes expectedly fell when the caller ID said "Rachel Horne." She threw the phone back into her purse.

It was then that she finally noticed the white noise on the radio. She turned it off, allowing the only sounds to be her tires roaring against the highway. Sometimes, she would drift onto the shoulder of the road, vibrating her car on a rumble strip. The wind was pushing her. The trees and fields whipped about violently.

She passed a tiny cemetery where she could count the old headstones with one hand.

Goddammit, Morgan, she thought, not for the first time. *Where the hell are you?*

Skyler felt like she wanted to slap that woman once she found her. Shake her by the shoulders and ask her what the hell she was thinking. Yet, she knew that if—when—she found Morgan, she would be too relieved and happy to do any of that. She would give her cousin a huge hug and never let go.

Shortly past the cemetery was a small gas station. At first glance, it appeared to be as ramshackle and abandoned as Dayton. But in the front window was a little orange "OPEN" sign and the two gas pumps appeared operable.

This was good. Her gas tank, she noticed, was almost empty.

As she pulled up next to the gas pump, her phone vibrated again. She sighed, this time there were no hopes or delusions about who was calling. When she pulled the buzzing phone from her purse, the same name screamed at her.

"Hello?" she answered.

"I can miss my classes tomorrow," the voice on the other line abruptly said. Rachel's voice was high like Skyler's, but much firmer. "I'll be there tonight."

Skyler rubbed her temples, preemptively soothing the incoming headache. "Rachel, no."

"What do you mean 'no'?"

Here we go, Skyler thought. "I need you to feed Oscar and Nightmare. Maybe take Oscar for a walk."

"I can find someone else to do that."

Skyler's chest tightened. Why did Rachel always have to make things so much harder for her? "Rachel, I don't even know if she's out here."

"Where the hell else would she be?" Rachel's voice blared. But within that anger, there was a trembling desperation. *She's just worried too,* Skyler reminded herself.

"If I don't find her this weekend," Skyler said with more patience than she had, "I'll come home. Then, I promise you, we can *both* figure out what to do next." Maybe their mom would help too, finally show some concern for her sister's daughter. If Morgan still wasn't heard from after so much time, surely Mom could no longer chalk this up to her "just being a brat."

"But what if she *is* out there and you just don't know where to look?" Rachel asked. Skyler flinched. There was that accusing tone she knew all too well. It made her angrier than she wanted to be right now.

"Rachel, there aren't too many places *to* look." She kept her voice as steady as she could.

"Well, I'll be there tonight."

"No!" Skyler burst. She was usually able to put on a smile and keep her temper under control with people. But sometimes, it was impossible to do so with her little sister.

"What is your problem?" Rachel snapped.

"I came out here on a *whim*, Rachel. I don't even know if there's anywhere to stay out here. I might have to sleep in my car." Skyler preferred not to do that. In fact, the idea mortified her. But she had the back seat cozied up just in case.

"I can sleep in my car," Rachel said. "I've done it before."

"Rachel, listen to me…"

"I am!" As if moved by Rachel's fury, the wind pressed against the car, making the metal pop from the pressure. "Morgan doesn't belong to you."

"Grow up." Skyler spoke a little more loudly than she'd intended. She was glad there was no one else in earshot. "This isn't about Morgan belonging to anyone. It's about—" It was about safety. It was about making sure she wouldn't lose anybody else. But Skyler didn't think Rachel would understand or care about that.

"I'm going out there. We don't have to meet up, whatever."

"Don't be stupid. Do you want me to call Mom?"

"I don't give a shit," Rachel snarled and hung up. Skyler tried to call again. After two rings, it went straight to voicemail. She had the urge to throw her phone against the dashboard, restrained only by a sliver of calm.

As she slipped her phone into her purse and regained her composure, she thought about how differently that would have gone had she been Morgan, or remotely *like* Morgan. Rachel would have listened to her then. She wouldn't have even argued. If only Skyler had that rock-steady inability to take bullshit and the confidence to call it out. She tried, but felt like a chihuahua trying to be a wolf. Skyler only had the second-best thing, having someone like that in her life. Someone who could inspire and strengthen her every day. And now that someone was nowhere to be found.

Unbidden, her eyes welled up. She allowed herself a couple minutes to cry. When they were over, she breathed in and wiped her eyes and nose with a tissue from her purse.

Morgan was okay, she told herself. There was no way she wouldn't be.

When she opened her car door, the wind whipped her hair about her face. She never let it grow too long, but it was still lengthy enough to be a pain sometimes. She shut the door again; propelled by the wind, it slammed furiously.

As she began tying her hair into a thick ponytail, she noticed another vehicle pull in and park in front of the gas station entrance. It was a black Jeep. Or, at least, Skyler thought it was black. It was so dirty she was surprised not to see the words "wash me" written anywhere. It had a Minnesota license plate, and a broken back window covered in tape. Part of her was relieved to see *someone* else out here. But it also made her feel deeply uneasy. Who knew what kind of people she would be running into, and she was stout and flabby with no fighting skills to speak of.

The door of the Jeep opened and a tall, thin, pale man stepped out. He was somewhat gawky and geeky looking, not at all what Skyler expected the driver of the vehicle to be. Once he was inside the gas station, she braved the outside again. The wind pounded against her eardrums and her eyes, but her hair at least stayed where it belonged. The smell of wheat was pungent. There was moisture on her forehead and a damp feeling in her clothes. It was unseasonably warm for early fall. Even the wind was warmer than it should've been. A southern warm front to be sure, heightened by climate change. But it was something else too. There was a bitterness to this warmth, a disappointment and discontent that could be felt in the violent wind and seen in the dying trees and flooding fields.

She wanted to be home. She had a life of her own to live. There were bills to pay, a job to go to. She had been able to take off two days for this. She didn't tell anyone why, of course, though her mother probably already knew. She hoped these two days, plus the weekend, would give her plenty of time. But she feared it wouldn't, that she would find nothing, and have to go home and try to live life as if everything was normal.

She realized there was no card reader on the pump. After pumping her gas, she would have to pay inside. What was this, the seventies? The thought petrified her. She hoped it wasn't cash only, she didn't have much. Plus, she felt very conscious of herself and her appearance. Her skin was a light olive color and seemed to get pastier the older she got, to her dismay. Between that and having her father's facial features, she was often mistaken for being fully White. Depending on where she was or who she was with, it was a distinction that sometimes made her feel safe, but also often ashamed, embarrassed, like she was a phony who didn't belong anywhere. She couldn't say who would be on the other side of that door and how they would perceive and treat her. Maybe she was being presumptive. After all, it couldn't be any worse than going into a rich suburb of Omaha. And it was better to go in and get it over with than cause a bunch of trouble by not paying.

She breathed deeply. It was time to channel her inner Morgan.

The smell inside the gas station was that of cigarette smoke and sour garbage. The floors, ceilings, and walls were stained with a dark yellow hue. She had to pee, but didn't want to even *think* about what the toilets would be like here.

The tall man from the Jeep stood near the front window, inspecting a revolving rack full of crappy novelty snow globes. Up close, she realized how ill-fitting his tattered khaki jacket was—the sleeves nearly stopped at his elbows. His jeans also seemed to ride up to his ankles. It was suspicious, how he inspected the worthless knickknacks as if they were valuable artifacts.

She decided to get a bottle of water, but when she went to the display cooler, she couldn't find any. In fact, the cooler was mostly sparse other than a few bottles of pop and some energy drinks here and there. All the shelves in the gas station were mostly barren. It clearly hadn't been restocked in a long time.

Eager to get out as soon as possible, she went to the front counter. The attendant was a middle-aged woman with a sunken face and a name tag reading "Pat." Next to her was a tiny ancient television, playing some equally old show set in a hospital. She thought she recognized a young Denzel Washington playing one of the doctors. Pat wasn't paying attention to it, nor did her sad, hollow eyes look up at Skyler. She was fixated on clipping her fingernails. Behind the woman was a large wall cluttered with posters of different shapes and sizes. Skyler felt queasy looking at them. They were missing person posters. The smiling faces of the vanished plastered the entire back wall, some taped along the shelf of cigarettes.

Skyler had tried not to think much about what she learned about this area. But it all came rushing back.

The day was vivid in her mind. She had been sitting on the couch, reading a book with Oscar nuzzled up next to her. Saturday afternoon, a post-walk routine for them. Morgan plopped onto the armrest without warning; she was so light-footed.

"So, listen," Morgan had said. Skyler remembered being instantly alarmed by the heaviness of her tone. "I'm going to be away for a few days."

She had learned her father was out in western Nebraska, near the town Dayton. How she had heard it, or who from, Skyler never learned. It seemed to her that Morgan had more connections than a drug dealer. She was determined to go out and see him. She had fallen out of contact with her father since her mother had left him, taking Morgan with her. All she knew was that he was a private detective. He had no social media or online presence at all. Sometimes, especially after a few drinks, she would talk about saving up money to hire her own private detective to find him. Though Skyler had been apprehensive about Morgan going out there alone, she had also been thrilled for her cousin.

But shortly after Morgan left, a friend of hers had sent Skyler a text. "You going with Morgan to the Prairie Triangle?"

Skyler had spent the afternoon researching what the Prairie Triangle was. She'd heard of it in passing before, one of those disturbing unsolved mystery things. But she never looked too far into it.

The area between three towns—Dayton, Rembrandt, and Farrington—called the Triangle was infamous because more than a hundred people had disappeared there over the past few decades. Those were at least the reported ones—people who either lived in the area or were last seen out that way. They would simply vanish without a trace, only vehicles and belongings left behind—no blood, no bones, no spooky old house or mass graves filled with corpses. Sometimes, even those investigating missing persons would disappear.

Beyond that, the Triangle was also home to other bizarre phenomena. People were sometimes found wandering along the road with no clue as to where they were going. They reported feeling an urge to get up and start walking, no matter what they were in the middle of doing. To where, they never could say. Sometimes, those very same people would wind up disappearing.

Skyler had immediately called Morgan after reading these disturbing stories.

"The house burn down already?" Morgan had asked.

"No, um, I've been reading a bit about where you're going."

"Weird, huh?" Morgan hadn't seemed concerned. But she never seemed worried about anything, even when there was definitely something to be worried about. Skyler found Morgan's carefree demeanor comforting, but knew not to always trust it.

"Morgan." Skyler had felt it unnecessary to reiterate her findings as Morgan was clearly aware. "I don't think this is a good idea."

"Sky."

"I know..." Skyler had felt helpless, knowing there was nothing she could ever say to change Morgan's mind. She always knew how abandoned Morgan felt, wondering why her father had made no effort to come find or contact her. She wasn't looking for reconciliation, but she wouldn't let him get away with it either. He needed to answer for why he left Morgan at the mercy of her stepdad's wrath and her mother's judgmental cruelty. There was no talking her out of it; she had even quit her job because she couldn't take the time off for the excursion.

"Give Oscar a hug for me," Morgan had said.

"I will. Him and Nightmare."

"You can leave that cat out for the coyotes for all I care."

"Morgan! He's your cat!"

"He's an asshole," Morgan had sneered flippantly. "And keep Rae-Rae out of trouble."

"You know I can't do that."

"Well, try."

"I always do. But you know what my biggest obstacle is? Or 'who' more accurately?"

Morgan had let out her deep strong laugh, a sound that amused and comforted Skyler. "You know I'd never let her get in real trouble."

"You don't call underage drinking real trouble?"

"Oh, hush. Who was the one pounding them at Ashley's graduation party?"

The conversation then turned into a debate on how much wine—and one alleged shot of Fireball—Skyler had drank at a high school graduation party. This led to a discussion of favorite kinds of wines, and how Morgan would buy a bottle of cheap Zinfandel when she got home and they would watch *Grey's Anatomy* while finding her a new job. The conversation melted away all Skyler's anxieties about the Prairie Triangle. It seemed as if everything would be okay.

That had been the last time Skyler heard from Morgan.

The faces on the posters stared back at her. Young and old, different races and genders. Over a hundred people missing. Skyler realized this was why Dayton was so empty. It was why everything was so empty out this way. Those who didn't vanish off the face of the Earth likely left of their own accord, either from fear or from the dwindling of their communities.

So many gone, and Morgan among them. But where were they? There was no way they could all be alive and well...

Skyler breathed in and out, expelling the thought.

She felt someone lingering behind her and glanced to see the tall man. He smelled like cheap deodorant, only barely masking a putrid body odor. She quickly turned back, where the attendant now had her sad eyes on Skyler.

"Um." Skyler suddenly felt taken off guard and forgot what she was doing. Neither the man nor Pat helped. They said nothing, silently waiting for her to make her move. The only noises in the room were the roaring wind outside, the humming refrigerators, and the muted echoes of the television.

"Um... Oh, my gas!" she said, finally remembering. Then she realized with horror that her shoulder felt light. "I, um, left my purse in my car."

Pat frowned at her.

"I'll go get it."

"Forget it," the man behind her said. He gently pushed her aside. Skyler wanted to speak up, call out his rudeness. But she didn't.

The young man plopped a bottle of Pepsi on the counter. "I'll pay for her gas," he said.

"Thank you," Skyler replied.

"It's fine." He didn't look down at her. He slid his card over to the attendant. Skyler realized there was a condescending undertone to this action. It was as if he was saying: *I don't have time for this, it's beneath me. I'll pay for your gas and you can be on your silly way.* The thought made Skyler want to shout at him, but there was something hard-assed and authoritative about the man. He stood at least a foot taller than her, with piercing blue eyes that looked like they would cut into whatever stood in their way. Skyler wondered if he was an FBI agent or something. He appeared world-weary—there were streaks of gray in his billowy black hair—though he couldn't have been older than thirty-five. Yet, he also seemed to have the confidence of a man who thought the world was in his hands.

"So where are you heading?" Skyler asked. She didn't want to make conversation with him. Yet, she felt she had to. People smiled and made small talk to fill the awkward silence, even if it was with someone they clearly didn't want to talk to. It was simply the courteous thing to do.

The man was silent. He reached under his collar and pulled out his necklace, perhaps checking to see if it was still there. The necklace's pendant looked like a rusty old key. When Pat returned his card, he tucked the necklace back under his collar. "Don't forget your purse next time," he said with a passive, unsmiling glance at Skyler.

She stood still as he marched out the front door.

"Asshole," she hissed. He was probably just another self-absorbed, entitled middle-class White guy. Completely arrogant despite having no accomplishments other than winning a butt-chugging competition at some frat party. She regretted trying to be friendly with him at all.

She realized Pat was in earshot and felt immediately embarrassed. But the woman didn't seem to care.

Before leaving the gas station once and for all, Skyler grabbed her phone from her car and pulled up a picture of Morgan. It was her favorite one, a selfie she had taken before she, Skyler, and Rachel went to a Spice Girl's reunion concert. She was in her bedroom, wearing a Union Jack skirt. She had a scandalous half smile and her brown eyes shone bright. Skyler went back into the gas station and showed it to Pat.

"I was wondering if she might've come through here?" Skyler's heart clenched with hope and fear.

"People come and go," Pat said, shrugging. "Only person whose face I remember is the fella who used to bring the gas. Though he disappeared too, few months ago. Have a new guy now."

She got back on the road, cruising five miles under the speed limit. Of course, there wasn't a cop or sheriff in sight; there was nothing but fields, the wind, the road, and her thoughts.

Through this emptiness, something crept into her mind. An intrusive urge. The sudden need to pull over and start walking. To where, she couldn't say. The feeling came, went, and came again. She wished she could distract herself with something, *anything*. She couldn't listen to a podcast or music through her car's speakers. Her over ten-year-old Taurus didn't have that capability. She supposed she could listen to something from her phone and turn it all the way up. But as soon as she reached into her purse, the intrusive urge gnawed harder than ever.

What the hell is wrong with you? she wondered to herself.

Along the road stood a lone building. It was a square brick structure that looked like it had been a general store a hundred years ago. It was in shambles, bricks falling out, a jungle of overgrowth surrounding it, gray-green foliage creeping up its walls. The windows were boarded up, yet its entry way gaped open. Above this entrance was a faded sign. Skyler could barely make out the words: "Mom & Pop's Antiques and Miscellaneous."

The sight filled her with dread, like something was inside watching her from the blackness. Yet there was something inviting there too, almost intoxicatingly so. There was something else—a thought, or maybe more of a gut feeling. It was telling her that she would find Morgan there.

As she moved farther away from the building, these thoughts and feelings began to subside. She gave the old shop one more glance in her rearview mirror and noticed a vehicle parked outside of it.

It was a dusty black Jeep. The same one that rude gas station guy drove.

CHAPTER TWO

Luxury Inn.

She saw the sign as she came over a hill. It was a piece of plywood with the words spray-painted on, sitting on top of a pole that probably had once held a more professionally made sign. It was a crappy little motel, as unluxurious as one could imagine. It looked abandoned except for a blue truck parked outside and a sign at the window of the front office reading "Open." Another flutter of hope tickled her gut. What if Morgan had stayed here? Maybe she even still was there.

As Skyler parked next to the truck, the anxiety she had felt outside the gas station was back. She swallowed it as best as she could, got out of her car, and went inside.

The tiny office smelled like moldy food. Like the gas station, there was a hint of that old cigarette stench. It made Skyler miss the chlorine smell normal hotel lobbies had. The clerk leaned along the front desk. He looked deeply tired, his face pocked and wrinkled. He had a wispy mustache that reminded her somewhat of her father's, which made her feel both comforted and sad. He glanced at her, his eyes as lifeless as cashier Pat's had been.

"Man, that wind," Skyler said, making the polite conversation that was always expected.

The man nodded.

"Does it usually get this windy out here?" she asked.

"Sometimes. You want a room?"

She was suddenly getting serious Bates Motel vibes here and wondered if she would be better off sleeping in her car after all. At the same time, getting a real bed as opposed to her lumpy back seat was far too appealing. "Yeah."

They went through the motions. She paid, he handed her the key. She wanted nothing more than to go to her room and make sure it was doable. But she quickly remembered why she was here. Pulling out her phone, she showed the clerk the picture of Morgan.

"Did this woman come here by chance?"

The man looked at it for a long time before nodding.

"Really?" Skyler's throat went dry. "Did she stay here?"

"Yep."

"When did she leave?"

The clerk shrugged. "One day she up and left without checking out. They finally came a few days ago and impounded her car." He looked at his desk and mumbled, "Far from the first."

Skyler felt sick. She hadn't thought about Morgan's car. Why would she leave without it? Thoughts of human trafficking rings or murderous cults crept into her head.

"Wish I had more I could tell you," the man said. There was a genuine hint of sympathy in his dull voice.

"I—" Skyler felt her voice break. "Where do they go?" It was all she could ask.

"I don't know," the man said. He almost sounded pained, and Skyler realized that he might have lost somebody too. "I get people asking me all the time. Not to mention cops and feds. I wish I could tell them anything. It's a hell of a thing." His tone became bitter. "You know, the main reason I get any business any more is these conspiracy tourists coming out here. Wanting to see the 'Prairie Triangle.'"

She at first wondered how he could be so upset about getting business. But this was his home, and he was living in fear every day. He didn't need people turning the horror he lived into a theme park. She wanted to ask him why he doesn't close the motel and leave. But she held back. His reasons were his own and none of her business.

"Listen," the man said, his voice softening again. "If you just want to go home, I'll refund every penny."

Skyler hesitated, almost every part of her wanting to take him up on his offer. But she shook her head.

The clerk shrugged. They stood in silence for a moment. There was nothing left to say. She thanked him and left the office. Before the door closed, she heard him call out. "I hope you find her."

Her vision blurred as she walked to her room, and tears came soon after. She wanted to call her mom, or even her dad. But above all she wanted to talk to Morgan.

The bed creaked as Skyler plopped onto it—though only after throwing one of her blankets on top. She pulled a container of trail mix from her gym bag. Her appetite was hardly there, but she knew she needed to eat. There likely weren't a lot of places to get a meal out here, so snacks would have to do. Luckily, she had packed plenty.

The room was about as nice as she'd expected. The flowery wallpaper was peeling away and the shaggy carpet was patterned with stains. There was dust coating the bedside table, the dresser, and the bulky old television. She wondered if there were any housekeepers employed here. Or if the clerk did all the cleaning. Or maybe nobody did.

On the bedside table, aside from dust, was a magazine that someone had left behind. It was an issue of *Cosmopolitan* from 2010. She had been a junior in high school the year she and Morgan became best friends. For most of their lives, they'd barely known each other. Their mothers clashed and never took the time to visit each other. It was only after Morgan's parents divorced and her mother took her to Omaha that the cousins started seeing one another more. But they still barely spoke, even when they were going to the same school. There were a couple disastrous Thanksgivings where they sat and watched cartoons together while their mothers bickered back and forth until Morgan's mom couldn't take it anymore and left early. But that had been the extent of their interaction. Skyler used to dislike Morgan. She seemed like a cynical punk girl who would only get you in trouble. Then came that day in choir class, junior year, the group sang some cheesy Christian song—the kind that the choir director, Mr. Fellers, always loved to do. The alto part, Skyler's and Morgan's section, was especially lame and tedious.

"This sucks," Morgan had whispered to her at one point.

Morgan then spent the rest of that class revamping the song with obscene lyrics. It made Skyler laugh so hard, despite herself, she peed a little. And that was where it began. Morgan proved to be someone Skyler could be her truest self with, and who inspired and gave her confidence to be more. Their relationship grew over the years. They became the pair of loving sisters their mothers never could be; the sisters Rachel and Skyler probably never would be either.

The memory of those obnoxious choir days brought a smile to her face.

After her snack, Skyler took a quick shower. The bathroom wasn't as gross as she'd feared. The tiled floors were cracked and the walls above the shower were spotted with black and green mold. But at least there were no cockroaches or anything like that. At least none in sight. As she let the hot water trickle down her hair, she thought about next moves. Visit one of the other towns, she supposed. That thought comforted her. Rembrandt, Farrington—those held possibilities. Those held hope.

But part of her knew they would probably be like Dayton—abandoned, lonely, and fruitless.

From the sadness of that thought, bubbling in the pit of her gut, came that intrusive urge again.

Leave, it told her. *Don't take the car. There's no need for it. Leave. It's what you want to do. It's what you need to do.*

Her heart raced and she felt short of breath. It was as if someone was in the bathroom with her, on the other side of the yellow curtain, watching her. Even when she pulled the curtain back, revealing nothing, she hardly felt reassured. The intruder was still there, hiding behind the steam-frosted mirror.

You're just paranoid, she thought.

Leave, the urge retorted. *You know where to go. You want to go. You'll find what you're looking for.*

She wondered if the stress of the situation had finally gotten to her and she was having a meltdown. Maybe it was a good idea to go home. Just pack up. Maybe see if the clerk was still offering that refund. But as soon as she turned off the hissing water, the urge subsided again. Something told her it would be back.

She dried off, brushed her teeth, and threw on an old Aerosmith T-shirt that used to be her dad's, as well as her favorite pajama pants. As soon as she curled up into her silky blanket, the urge came back.

Leave. Don't take the car. There's no need for it.

Her therapist always told her that trying to repress thoughts and urges only made them worse. Regardless, she tried her best to fight this one back. It was just too strange, too unnatural to try to sit with, or explore, or reason through.

She kept the bedside lamp on while trying to sleep. That presence was still there, watching her from the little green chair in the corner of the room.

You know where to go. You'll find what you're looking for.

Was this her gut instinct trying to tell her something? Her dad would always tell her to follow her gut. Morgan and Rachel certainly set an example in that regard. But it was hard to know if it was actually the right thing to do. Sometimes her gut feelings only led to trouble. Besides, these urges didn't seem like they were coming from inside her head or body.

Leave. You'll find who you're looking for.

If she followed this nonsense whim, would it really lead her to Morgan? *You're just tired and stressed,* she thought.

Leave, said the urge. *You know where to go.*

She couldn't sleep this off, she couldn't even close her eyes for long. Her heart raced, her stomach clenched, sweat trickled down her forehead. What the hell was happening?

Leave.

It was batshit that she couldn't get this urge out of her head. It was even crazier to her that she was hopping out of bed, putting on her jeans, socks, shoes, and jacket, and tying her hair back. She grabbed her cell phone and wallet—but not her keys—and headed out the door. She wasn't thinking about what she was doing. Not even for a second.

She walked across the parking lot, avoiding her car. The urge told her she didn't need it.

It was early evening, the horizon still light. But the world was already dark. She walked along the barren highway, mortified by what she was doing, yet too hazy to consider it though somehow so certain of where she was going.

The wind had died down, and there was a sticky humidity in the air. She was alone, yet she didn't feel alone. It wasn't just that intrusive presence that loomed over her. Everything seemed to be watching her: the trees, the wispy clouds, the vast black landscape. She wondered if there were coyotes or mountain lions out there, stalking her. At least that would explain why everything felt so conscious. Even the dirt and grass beneath her feet seemed to curiously observe her. The dirt, she realized, was also full of shoe prints and scuffs, all heading in the direction she was going.

She walked for a long time. The horizon slowly winked out and only the light from a half-moon showed the way. Though she had taken off her jacket, her shirt and pants were moist with sweat. Her legs were sore and her chest was beating. She took walks all the time, but never like this.

Then she was where she needed to be—or at least where it felt like she needed to be. She recognized the square building with the faded sign reading "Mom & Pop's Antiques and Miscellaneous." Her skin felt cold when she noticed the gas station man's Jeep still parked along the side.

She didn't want to go inside. She wanted to run back to the hotel, jump in her car, and get the hell out of Dodge.

It's okay, the urge told her. *Keep coming. It's okay. She's here.*

Skyler knew better than to listen to this. But she did anyway.

Her phone's light guiding the way, Skyler stepped into the blackness. Immediately, she was overwhelmed by the stench of mildew, feces, and decaying bodies—hopefully animal.

Though the phone light only covered a couple feet, she could see the room well enough. Three rows of shelves filled the long space. To her right was an old desk, covered with cobwebs and dust. There was a bulky cash register with a curved ridge for the number keys and a split flap display perpetually stuck at "050" dollars and "05" cents. Skyler guessed it was from the 1960s. The wooden floor was disgusting, covered in broken glass, litter, and god knew what else. Hundreds of footprints and scuffs had kicked the floor's dust coating away.

The building was stuffy and humid, and Skyler felt swampier than ever. She wished she had brought a bottle of water, fearing she was on the verge of passing out from dehydration. There were occasional noises. Though they startled her, they didn't deter her. She could recognize them as rats scuttling in the walls and bats scratching around in the ceiling; and of course, her own footsteps made the floorboards creak.

She kept moving inward, her pulse throbbing in her throat. That strange presence seemed closer than ever here. But she was beginning to feel less afraid of it. In fact, she felt more intimate with it. The presence was drawing her to the back of the room.

The shelves were mostly empty but for cobwebs and the dead insects snagged in them. But there was the occasional leftover antique. A porcelain baby doll smothered by webs stared at her with hollow eyes. A cookie jar, once in the shape of a black-and-white cat, was shattered along the floor. On one of the top shelves was a sewing machine, black and curved. Skyler wondered if it was from the nineteenth century. She couldn't guess when it was patented or by whom, but it caught her attention all the same. She loved that century and had dedicated—or wasted, as her parents and Rachel claimed—much of her college career to studying it. She was particularly drawn to Victorian Britain. In another circumstance, she would have happily spent hours examining this relic, imagining all the hands that had touched it and what they had used it to create. Ornate quilts? A beautiful dress? Stitching up the tear in a coat? It was clearly one that had been used for personal rather than industrial use.

These fanciful thoughts lasted only a brief, sweet moment before the scratching of bats snapped her back to her situation. Then, the urge had her again.

Keep moving along.

At the end of the room were two doors. Between them was a dark entryway. Somehow, she knew this would take her down to the basement. There, it would have what she was looking for. *Who* she was looking for.

The air became colder as she moved down the bending wooden stairs; cool enough to throw her jacket back on. The smells grew even more rancid and she had to breathe shallowly just to avoid vomiting. She reached the last step with her eyes closed, fearing that—when she opened them—she would see a pile of bodies. On top of which would be...

But upon opening her eyes she saw nothing but rotted wooden boxes and shelves. The floor felt moist beneath her shoes, and the concrete walls were moldy and damp. She could see the black shapes of roaches scuttling away from her phone light.

Oddly though, she felt calmer than ever. In fact, the fear had dissipated entirely.

An old mahogany table sat in the middle of the room. It seemed to be in better shape than anything else down there. Beneath the table, Skyler could clearly see a round object lying on the floor. Without a moment's thought or hesitation she kneeled and picked it up. There was a heaviness to it—not that it weighed a lot or was difficult to pick up, but it felt dense. It was a snow globe, a huge one too, about the circumference of a toddler's head. It was more of a snow *dome* really, the base wider and the dome flatter than the typical variety.

The wooden base had a strange and elegantly carved design. It looked a bit worn, as if it had been touched many times. But the images could still be made out. On each side of the base were strange symbols. They looked like the top part of a flathead screwdriver pointing upward. Between these symbols were randomly placed dots. They looked like stars, a line connecting each of them as if marking a constellation. Skyler didn't know her constellations well; the shape looked like an hourglass with two antennas, one of which had been greatly bent to the side.

The dome's glass was imposingly thick, yet clear. As she looked into the little world inside, the detail and beauty took her breath away. The world mostly consisted of a forest, which covered all of the edges of the dome. At the center was a tack-sized castle, sitting steadily on top of a rocky hill. It was tall, square, and white with a blue arched roof aligned with towers. On its east side was a particularly elongated tower. Its design reminded Skyler of the Neuschwanstein Castle in Germany, which she had always wanted to see. The castle's size compared to everything else seemed odd to her. Usually in a snow globe, the castle would be large, the centerpiece of the whole thing. But here, it seemed to be just another small part of the whole.

At the foot of the castle's hill was a village. It was full of white and wooden cottages, as well as a few brick buildings. Far to the north of the castle were two elevated planes forming a valley. In this valley was a glacier from which a stream formed. Though the stream was so small and thin it looked like a piece of string, it still seemed so real. It weaved through the village and into the forest where it finally stopped at a lake far to the south of the castle. The water in the tiny lake almost seemed to move. It might have been a trick of the eye, but the trees in the forest appeared to sway as if moved by wind. There was a murky haze lingering above everything, as if there were clouds. Skyler felt a sense of vertigo, as if she was on a plane looking down.

Everything was so bright and clear inside the snow globe that Skyler realized she didn't even need her phone light. She turned it off for a moment and slipped her phone back into her pocket.

She shook the snow globe, but there appeared to be no snow inside. *What's the point?* she wondered. Yet deep down, she knew there was a point. For whatever reason, this was more significant than anything.

There was something she needed to do. Why? She didn't know. But the urge to do it was agonizing. Desperate for relief, she followed its command, raising the snow globe above her head and flipping it upside down. As she gazed up into the dome, she felt herself rising. The ascension was brief, and quickly turned into falling. Descending toward the world, the village growing closer by the minute. But she wasn't falling fast, she was lightly floating down like snow. She couldn't scream. It felt like she had no mouth or arms or legs. She wouldn't have screamed if she could anyway; she wasn't scared.

Her descent brought her closer to a little round object in the village square. A well. She was going to fall right into it. She hoped there would be something soft at the bottom. Soon, the pit's darkness became everything, and she was taken into a place where she could see, hear, and feel nothing.

For one brief moment, she was completely gone.

CHAPTER THREE

S HE WAS IN A museum, the art museum at her old university.

Each gallery was devoid of people. She felt alone. Whenever she tried to look at the paintings and sculptures, she couldn't make them out. They were there, but they seemed indecipherable—as if teasing a secret she wasn't worthy of knowing.

Suddenly, voices shouted at her from somewhere else in the building. Yet, as she followed them, wandering room to room, each ranging from vast to tiny, she couldn't find anyone.

A shadow appeared in the corner of her eye. When she turned to look at it, it moved back to her periphery. She turned her head again and again. Each time, it evaded her. When she finally tired of the shadow's game, an unbearable fear squeezed into her. She ran.

It was no longer the art museum but her old home—the big house her family lived in before her parents' divorce. She ran down the upstairs hall, trying to reach her old bedroom door. Dark blue, chipping paint. The voices were all around her. They chanted something, sounding like a cheer at a pep rally. She didn't know what they were saying.

She reached the door and grabbed its handle. It wouldn't turn.

Something clutched her by the throat.

The chanting still echoed through Skyler's head as she awakened.

She was back in the basement, though it was too dark to see anything. Slowly, she realized how uncomfortable she was. The air was moist and freezing. The stony wall against her back was rough and jagged. Her bottom was soaked by the damp floor. Cold, wet droplets gently fell on her face. The smell of rot and musk was stronger than ever.

The chanting finally faded, allowing the soundlessness of the room to set in.

She carefully came to her feet, gripping something hard and slimy on the floor along the way. Repulsed, she recoiled and fell against the wall.

"Shit," she hissed as the force of the wall hitting her back sent a painful wave up her spine.

After the jolting pain subsided, she rose again, using the edges of the wall for leverage. Her eyes were adjusting to the dark, but she could only see more wall in front of her. Perhaps she was in a corner. But as she looked around her, she saw there was nothing but wall, each corner melding into the next in a circular motion.

"What?" Her memory was coming back. She had gone into the basement of the old shop. Then there had been a snow globe. What was she missing?

The cold droplets still fell onto her head. She could see tiny white specks floating down past her vision. Snow. She looked up and saw a bright gray circle from where the snow was falling.

Her stomach tightened, and her heart raced. She was in a pit.

"Hello?" she asked gently. There was no answer. She called out a little louder. "Hello!"

Again, there was nothing but silence. The acrid and stale air barely carried her voice.

"Hey!"

She had been looking for Morgan. This she remembered. Morgan was missing, along with countless others. And now...

"Hello?" she cried, her heart racing faster, tears coming to her eyes. She felt like running, but there was nowhere to go. She was trapped, gasping for air. "Hey!" She screamed it again and again—hoping for someone to hear her—until her voice grew hoarse.

She became dizzy and fell to the ground, onto those slimy objects. As she felt them jutting into her legs and bottom, she realized what they were. Human bones, each in varying states of decay, scattered on the ground. Her blood retreated from every vein in her body.

Rising to her feet, she squeezed herself against the wall, as if it could protect her. She could hardly breathe, her chest heaving beyond control. Her body felt hot and her legs turned to jelly. She fell to the floor, among the bones, again. Squeezing her eyes shut, she tried to imagine what her therapist would say. *Breathe. Center yourself. Something else.* It was hard to think of any of those coping tools she'd learned.

It took a long time for her breathing to steady and the panic to fade. Her mind and body were now calm and thoughtless—at least for the time being. She opened her eyes. There were no more floating specks, the snow had stopped. Examining the walls around her—only the walls, not the floor—she noticed some indentations ahead of her. They seemed to form a stack that went all the way to the top of the pit. It was a ladder.

Without hesitation, she climbed. It was hard to keep a firm grip as she was still shaking. But she held strong and kept looking up, fixing her eyes on the way out. The little circle grew closer with each climb. Bright sky greeted her, filling her with its light as she climbed further. It looked strange. It seemed plain and cloudless and was a silvery gray. There was no sun, no epicenter of the brightness, the light evenly filled the whole sky. It was like looking at a TV screen.

When she reached the top of the pit, she desperately pulled herself up and tumbled onto the hard, uneven, cobblestone ground. After reorienting herself, she looked around. She was in the middle of an old village square. Everything looked like it was from the seventeenth or eighteenth century. Most of the houses were white with brown frames. One of them had a wooden sign above the entrance reading "Jimmy's Pub."

The pit had actually been a well, she realized. She scrambled away from it, getting as far across the square as she could before exhaustion stopped her. When it did, she balled herself up, clutching her knees and breathing deeply. Strangely enough, there was nothing satisfying about the breaths. The air was stale. It was also cool, but not cold. It was the same feeling as being in a garage during a freezing day.

After a few moments, Skyler climbed to her feet, trying to take in her surroundings. The village looked like a Disneyland attraction that had been long abandoned. The antiquated houses were unevenly aligned, some bigger than others. All of them were dilapidated. The only building that seemed to be in decent shape was an important-looking brick structure ahead of her. But her attention was taken by what lingered behind it. Sitting high on a hill was a tall, white castle with a blue arched roof. Next to it was a tower, stretching toward the sky. She was awed, having never seen a castle in person before. It didn't seem extraordinarily large—at least compared to how big she imagined castles to be. But still, it intimidated her. It also felt familiar.

A woodsy smell overcame her—not like an actual forest, but more like a pine-scented candle. It soothed her. She turned and looked opposite the castle and beyond the rest of the village. There she saw the green outline of trees. The pressing urge that had drawn her to the shop suddenly came back and was stronger than ever.

Skyler moved toward the forest. As she passed the well, she noticed a large circular stone lying next to it. A lid, perhaps. There were claw marks along the lid's surface, as if a bear had been scratching at it.

Her path took her down a narrow street. It was barren but for a broken-down wagon along the curb. On the door of each house was a yellow sheet of paper. Most of them were torn or rotted away, but she was able to read one that remained intact:

"STAY INSIDE - ORDER OF MAYOR SHANKS"

This was an actual community, she thought. Or at least it had been. It was a real place where people had lived, played, worked, and apparently elected mayors. She called out a couple of times. Maybe someone was in one of those houses and would hear her. But there was no response, not even the flutter of a window curtain. Where the hell was she? Was this some old town in Europe? If so, who brought her here? And why? The confused panic began building in her gut again. She wanted to get to the forest. She would be safe there, though she didn't know why she trusted that instinct.

Where the village ended, a large field began. It had once likely nurtured crops, but was now overgrown with tangled, brown weeds. At the field's edge was the forest. The trees were lush and green. They almost seemed too perfect, their bright-green needles and choco-late-brown trunks were polished, almost plastic looking.

She couldn't see anything between the trees, only darkness. There was so much danger in that dark place, yet so much possibility. The urge needled into her again.

Come on. You're right there.

Breathing in deep, she let go of any reservations and walked toward the forest, not even thinking about it. She surrendered herself to the stale air resting against her face, dirt slipping inside her shoes and the overgrowth scraping her pants.

"Hey!" a voice boomed from behind her, just as she was nose to nose with the forest's dark entrance

Startled out of her stupor, she turned around to see a lanky shape standing on the other side of the field near the village. Even from a distance she could feel those bright blue eyes glaring into her. It was the man from the gas station. He still wore that grungy khaki jacket and jeans. A large bag was slung over his shoulder and he held a black object in his hand.

"Come here!" the man ordered.

Skyler looked back at the forest. Even this close she couldn't see into the darkness. It was as if someone had turned off the lights.

"Come here!" the man roared again. She wanted to feel relieved that there was another human being. But she didn't like his tone. There seemed a good chance she would be less safe with him than on her own. The trees above her swayed encouragingly in tandem, affirming this thought, though there was hardly any wind to move them.

"What the hell is wrong with you?!" the young man shouted. His voice sounded a little closer and she could hear the crunching of weeds. He was coming toward her. Within the black void of the forest, she actually saw something. It was speedily fluttering toward her. A bird? It looked bulky and appeared to have some difficulty moving. Its flight pattern lilted up and down and back and forth as if the creature were drunk.

It let out the shriek of a drowning crow. The sound sent shockwaves through Skyler's veins, compelling her to let go of the delirious urge. She turned and ran. The young man was close behind her, watching her rush toward him. When he saw what was following her, he began to back away.

The shriek came again, vibrating against Skyler's neck hairs. Then something knocked her to the ground, as if someone threw a sharp branch at her back. It was the creature; its wings beating, slimy talons clutching the back of her head and beak scraping along her skin. She didn't know where her own screams began and the creature's ended. There was a horrible stench.

It felt like centuries before the creature was forcefully pulled from her. She wasted no time clambering to her feet. The creature's shrieks turned pained. Skyler looked to see the man stomping it into the ground. Once it was reduced to helplessly writhing, the man held out the black object in his hand. It was a handgun. He fumbled with it as the creature howled pitifully. Skyler held her hands to her ears, wanting it to end, but the man struggled with turning off the safety. Finally figuring it out, he fired into the creature. With one loud pop, the shrieking ended.

"Fucker," the man mumbled at the gun as he clicked the safety back on.

Skyler crossed her arms and went to his side, involuntarily gasping when she got a good look at the creature. The whole body was green, as if completely overgrown with moss, with black veins trailing around it like vines. It had the head of a raven with bulging green eyes, but the twitching wings of a bat. There was a growth on its chest, which she realized was a bat's head, an oozing black hole in one of the eyes. Above the bat's head were a raven's wings, limply laying along the creature's upper body like a long collar.

"What the hell is that?" Skyler said.

The man didn't answer. His eyes were wide, making him look like a terrified boy. After a moment, he blinked a couple of times and shook his head.

"It must be some kind of..." He stopped, apparently not knowing what to say.

Skyler had a creeping feeling. The world was still, even more so than usual. She looked to the forest. The man seemed to share her feeling as he looked as well. The trees were completely motionless. The air grew rank. The acrid stench wasn't just coming from the dead creature, it was everywhere. Skyler had never been to a swamp, but she could imagine that this was what one would smell like if it had been filled with rotting corpses.

"We need to go," the man said. He retreated toward the village. This time, Skyler didn't hesitate to follow.

When they reached the square, a repetitive thrumming filled the air. It gave both Skyler and the young man a momentary pause. The sound was guttural, boring deep into the pit of her stomach. It was only when she looked up toward the castle and saw its black windows light up that she realized the thrum was coming from the tall tower. It was a bell.

More noise erupted from behind them, from the forest, the rustling of hundreds of leaves and the creaking of wood. Something was coming, or perhaps *hundreds* of somethings. The man began running again, and she followed, going as fast as her short legs would allow. She hadn't run so much since high school gym. But the fear boosted her stamina.

The dreadful thrum of the bell tower continued. It sounded like battle drums. When Skyler glanced up at the castle again, she could make out faint humanoid shapes moving behind the windows.

The man rushed to the tall, stone-and-brick building at the head of the square and pulled its double-door entrance open.

"Come on!" he shouted.

Without thought, she ran into the building where she kneeled and caught her breath while the man slammed the door behind them.

It was a library. The windows helped light up the room, but without sun, everything was dim, like the indoor darkness on a cloudy day or at the break of dawn. From what could be seen, it was a massive and elegant room with tiled flooring and wooden pillars bridging the lower and upper floors. Books were splayed everywhere, large brown and tan volumes collecting dust. They flooded the floor, the shelves, the tables, and chairs, some nearly on the verge of falling from the second-floor railing. At the center of the room was an odd-looking figure. As Skyler came closer, she realized it was a statue. It depicted a slender person with a thin, flowing gown that looked ancient Roman. The statue would have stood six feet tall if it weren't missing its head.

The thrumming continued, reverberating through the building. A loud crash startled Skyler into a scream. She turned to see that the man had pushed over a shelf, blocking the front door. He held his finger against his lips to shush her. She had the urge to throw something at him.

"Come on," he said, running up the wooden steps to the second floor.

Skyler followed, nearly tripping over something along the way. She glanced down at the stone object that had almost felled her. It was the statue's head. The blank eyes of a gaunt, curly-haired person stared priggishly up at her.

There was a steady vibration beneath her feet as she ran up the stairs. At first, she thought it was from the thrumming tower, but this vibration was inconsistent, less rhythmic. It felt akin to a minor earthquake.

When she reached the second floor, she began hearing a wild chorus of howling, moaning, and snarling from outside. With that came a familiar stench—that same damp rot that the bird thing had given off. As the rumbling intensified and the howls grew louder, the stench became worse.

"Hey!" the man hissed, motioning to her from the westernmost railing. He was poking out from between two bookshelves.

She cupped her hands over her mouth and nose and ran to join him in his hiding spot. He kneeled beneath a large window and aggressively motioned for Skyler to do the same. As she did, pressing tight against the wall, the rumbling grew worse than ever. It felt like a stampede was raging right beneath them—*and that stench*. The man peeked up, looking out the window. As he did, his eyes widened and his face paled—that childlike look of fear again. She dreaded the idea of looking for herself, but curiosity overtook her.

Her first thought, peering through the dirty glass, was that the bushes were moving, scrambling across the cobble streets below. But slowly, she registered what she was seeing. These were creatures, their bodies covered in moss and overgrowth that hung from their limbs. Whatever skin of theirs that showed looked sickly, in various shades of a milky green. On many of them, the skin was sagging away, making some of the creatures look nearly skeletal. Thick black veins formed unique patterns across each body.

Most of them humanoid, but some resembled other creatures. A scraggly, green, catlike thing slipped between the feet of its larger counterparts. What looked to be a basset hound—its lichen covered jowls dropping from its skull—snapped its fangs at what might have been squirrels scrambling by. Birds soared and fluttered above. Some creatures appeared to be fused together. Two swampy deer attached at the hip slinked along, followed shortly by a two-headed, four-legged humanoid.

They were all moving toward the castle, which was now bright with activity under the cold, repetitive thrum. The shapes behind the windows stood at the ready.

Skyler noticed one of the creatures standing still among the monstrous flow, which parted purposefully around its body. The creature had an emaciated equine body, with the head and torso of a human—like a centaur. Though the body looked more like a mule's than a horse's. The human part was a man—thick and muscular—its bald head mapped with black veins and mouth covered by a sinewy green beard. His bloated green eyes stared directly at her. She felt a frightened sting in her chest. She wanted to duck and hide, but she was frozen. Yet there was no expression on the creature's face. It was as if he had no real interest in her or the man.

After a long time, the centaur turned back toward the castle and galloped off. It was then that Skyler saw what he really was. A mule's head drooped uselessly below the man's torso like an unnecessary appendage. Its skin tightened against a long, grimacing skull, and whatever was left of its mane was covered in bramble. On each side of the mule's body were two large growths along its ribs—long and thick as muscular legs. It was a man and a mule fused together.

Once the centaur was out of view, the streets were empty. Skyler looked at the castle, where the creatures were climbing up the walls like spiders. Some windows along the castle's second and third floors opened and bright liquid poured out. Some creatures leaped away; others were smothered by the liquid. Their shrill screams rang through the air. The thrum continued. From another window, the shadowy figures within appeared to be jabbing at the invaders with long swords. This was effective enough to cause some of the creatures to plunge to the ground below. Some creatures were attempting to climb the tall tower, but liquid was also pouring from it like bright, creamy waterfalls.

Skyler felt sick to her stomach. Her head grew light and she looked away from the window. Her vision began to fade and her shoulder cramped painfully.

"Hey," said a muffled voice in the darkness.

She felt someone tip up her chin and pour cool liquid down her throat. It was water, which she drank happily, though it tasted unnaturally sweet and metallic. Her vision slowly trickled back, and the first thing she saw was the young man's wide blue eyes, staring at her with an intensity that made her uncomfortable. Outside, she could still hear the sounds of shrieking, smell the rot in the air—all underscored by the never-ceasing thrum.

"Here." The man let her hold the bottle and began sifting through his bag. After a moment, he pulled out a protein bar and tossed it to Skyler. She scarfed it down ravenously, almost eating the plastic wrapper with it. The bar had a chalky cookie dough flavor—absolutely awful—but she wasn't picky at the moment. She chased down each bite with large swigs of water.

"Drink up," the man said, peering out the window. "I'll just refill it when everything's clear."

Refill it? Skyler wondered. "There's water here?"

"The stream."

He glanced at her and seemed to see the uneasiness on her face. "It's clean," he said, returning his attention to the scene outside. "It's clearer than any stream I've seen in our world."

Our world? Skyler didn't quite have her wits back, so she might not have heard him clearly. Or perhaps he had made a flub. After all, it *did* feel like a different world here. But that couldn't actually be possible.

Though the steady thrum continued, the sounds of shrieking and fighting lessened. Eventually, the thrumming came to an abrupt stop. "They're retreating," he said.

Skyler could tell. She could feel the stampede again. She peered out, and sure enough, the creatures were pouring through the streets, their moans sorrowful and bitter. They were heading back toward the forest.

Her heart filled her throat when she saw the centaur, once again staring at them. He seemed to tower, his face locked in that icy indifference. He nodded toward the forest, as if beckoning Skyler to come with. It felt like he stared at them for ages. She just prayed the man next to her was ready to use his gun again. But eventually, the centaur turned away and galloped off with his comrades. Gradually, the thundering faded and the moaning melted into the air, leaving silence. Even the smell gradually dissipated. The world seemed calm again, as if nothing had ever happened.

The man barely allowed the calm to set in before he stood and cleared his throat. "Time to go."

"Wait!" Skyler said, slowly bringing herself to her feet. "Where are we going?"

"The castle."

That made sense. The people there, whoever they were, were clearly enemies of the creatures. Hopefully, they could help her understand what the hell was going on.

"If there's any way of getting back to our world," the man continued, "I'll bet it's in there."

There it was again. "What do you mean 'our world'?"

"The world we come from," he answered impatiently as if he were stating an obvious fact. When she continued staring at him, head cocked in confusion, he rolled his eyes and sighed. "Where do you think we are?"

"Where do *you* think we are?" Skyler snapped back.

He arched an eyebrow, looking at her like *she* was the crazy one. "I thought it was obvious."

"Nothing about this is obvious!" This was a tone she rarely ever used, especially not with strangers. But she felt emboldened.

The man sighed again. "You remember how you got here, right?"

"No!"

"I mean, you remember what you were last doing before you woke up in the well?"

"The well?" Just thinking about it made her want to panic.

"Yes. The well is the entrance, apparently. But I don't think it's an exit."

"I—" Skyler did remember. The shop, the basement... "The snow globe." With the castle, the village, the forest.

He nodded.

"So you're saying, what? The snow globe transported me here?"

"No, I'm saying it brought you into it."

"You mean we're inside the—" That was too absurd to even entertain. Or at least it should have been. "There's no way."

"Why not?" The conviction on his face was unflinching. He wasn't messing with her.

"Because it's physically impossible!" Her voice faded as she said that aloud. What really frightened her wasn't how certain the young man was, but how weak her doubt felt.

"Physically impossible? Did you see those things?" He pointed to the street below. "How is any of *that* possible?"

Skyler felt her skin tingle thinking about them. She could see the centaur's grotesque eyes again, staring right at her.

"You want my advice?" He placed a hand on Skyler's shoulder, but quickly withdrew as if he had touched a hot stove. "Throw whatever you think is and isn't possible out the window."

"How do you know?" It was all Skyler could mutter. She was out of rebuttals.

He frowned and looked at his feet. She thought she almost saw a flash of uncertainty. But the look passed as soon as it had come and he steeled his face. "You've gotten this far thanks to me."

Skyler hadn't thought of that. She had been so close to going into the forest, where all those things were. Would she have stopped if he hadn't been there? What would have happened? The possibilities made her stomach drop.

The man pulled out the key he wore on his neck, checking it before tucking it back under his collar. "I'm going. You'd do well to come along."

To the castle. Yes. There would be the answers.

"Hey, what's your name?" she asked, following him down the library stairs. He looked at her and rolled his eyes in an insufferable way. She couldn't wait to find somebody—anybody—else besides this guy. Still, until then, he was all she had.

"What?" He spoke like she had asked the stupidest question in the world.

"If I am to trust you—to follow you—you can at least tell me who you are."

The man paused, pursed his lips, and then nodded. "My name is Sam."

CHAPTER FOUR

"**S**KYLER," SHE SAID BACK.

Sam nodded. He didn't care about her name. He didn't want her to be here. Why did she have to go and follow him? Now here she was, her own damn fault, stumbling into something far bigger than herself.

It's far bigger than you too, said a voice in his head. *You're fucked.*

He forced the voice to shut up, at least for the time being. Inevitably, the doubts and fears would rev up again. He surprised himself; he never thought he would be so frightened. Certainly, he had anticipated that things would be... unorthodox once he'd reached this part of the search. But everything was moving faster than he'd prepared for. He wanted to scream. To curl up and cry. Sometimes, resisting the urge to do so was like flexing a muscle. Somehow, this weakness he had spent years trying to snuff out still found its way. And he was failing his father, his great-grandfather, his entire family's legacy—or the legacy they had been denied—and the mission he was born to fulfill.

But you're close, he insisted. *It's here. It must be. You found your way here all by yourself. Dad can't claim that, and he'd spent his whole life searching.*

Sam swallowed his shame, painful as it was. "Let's go."

He tugged at the bookcase blocking the doorway. In retrospect, barring the door had been unnecessary. The creatures hadn't been interested in the library or whoever was inside. The old bookcase only budged a couple of inches. It had felt lighter when he pushed it over.

"Here," she said. He'd already forgotten her name.

She pushed while he pulled. It made more headway, but she lost her footing and slipped, causing the bookcase to crash back in place. His patience thinning, he turned to another idea. He pulled his pistol from its holster, flipped the safety off, aimed at the nearest window, braced himself, and fired. The painfully loud pop left a ringing in his ears. She screamed and threw herself to the ground. The window's glass remained intact. Not even a bullet hole.

Impossible.

"What the fuck?" she howled at him, rising from the ground. Her dark brown eyes, which were usually drooped as if she was tired, were wide open, her thin lips curled in a snarl. She looked ready to hit him, her wide shoulders tensed and her fists clenched.

"I'm sorry," Sam said, preparing for her to strike. "I thought that would work."

She breathed deeply and relaxed her body, though her eyes remained wide.

"The window," Sam said. "It's bulletproof."

"Then let's try moving this thing again." She moved back into position near the bookcase. Sam put away his gun, now overcome with embarrassment. He hated her for making him feel this way. She wasn't even supposed to be here in the first place. What right did she have to be so mad at him? He wanted to go and find another way out, leave her in here where she could push the bookcase to her heart's content.

But instead, he got into position and pulled while she pushed. This time, they successfully moved the bookcase away from the door.

⁂

Sam peeked his head out the door, holding his gun at his hip. The square looked clear, but that didn't mean it was empty.

He turned to her. "Hey…" What was her name again? He only remembered it being an odd one.

"Skyler," she said, taking the hint. The twinge of exasperation in her voice embarrassed him again. But hell, how would he be expected to learn her name? There was enough happening. She wasn't even supposed to—

"Is everything clear?" she asked.

Sam looked back through the doorway. "Let's go."

"Okay, *Sam*," she said, putting emphasis on his name.

He took another quick glance at her, expecting to see a smug grin. But she wasn't even looking at him. She was looking out at the village square, nervously popping her fingers against her chin and breathing heavily. Right, there were bigger things at hand.

He led them slowly across the square. The world was still and dead silent. It felt like an ambush was imminent, that at any moment the creatures would come leaping over the roofs. A chill went through his body. The thought of being pinned down by those things—it was too much to think about. He wasn't sure how much of a fight he'd be able to put up with so many coming at them. Hell, even if there was only one, would he be able to shoot it? He'd rarely ever shot a moving target before. He shot an old and lame deer once, the only thing he'd ever killed on a hunting trip. Even *that* had taken him the better part of an hour.

Despite his fears, they reached the stream without any issue. The forest stood across from them. Sam felt like thousands of eyes were staring from within. He was petrified of going any closer to the woods. Yet an urge beckoned him to. He had felt this urge off and on since coming to the Prairie Triangle. This feeling that everything he was looking for was there, deep within that blackness. But he knew the truth. There was nothing for him there but death. What he was looking for was in the castle. It had to be.

He looked down at Skyler, whose eyes were also fixed on the dark forest. She was trembling and twitching, perhaps also struggling with that urge. He handed her his water bottle.

"You fill it. I'll stand watch."

She snapped her attention away from the forest and gaped at him. For whatever reason, the look gave him a small flare of warmth. She reminded him of someone.

"Or I could fill it," he continued. "Then you can stand watch."

He offered his gun to her. Though he held out the butt-end, she recoiled as if he was sticking her up.

"No," she said. "I don't think—"

"You know how to use this?" he asked.

"I—"

"You ever fire a gun before?"

"I tried paintball once."

"This one's pretty easy to use. It's an M1911, standard-issue US military since World War One."

She seemed unimpressed by his gun facts. Saying nothing else, she took the bottle from him and moved cautiously toward the stream. Sam felt relieved. He never actually had any intention of giving her the gun, even if she'd somehow accepted it.

"God, this is clear," he heard Skyler murmur to herself as she kneeled at the shallow, crystalline water and placed the bottle underneath.

He scanned the forest, his gun at the ready. The trees looked so fake, like the artificial trees decorating a sporting goods store. But they must have been real, in some way.

Skyler finished filling the bottle and paced back to him. "Can we go please?"

He snatched the bottle and took a small swig. The water tasted funny, and he knew it wasn't the bottle. Maybe the water wasn't as safe to drink as he'd assumed. But if he recalled correctly, the stream came directly from a glacier to the north, and this had probably been the village's water source. Of course, none of the villagers were left. Regardless, he was compelled to trust it. What other choice did he have? Maybe the castle would have a safer water source.

They headed back toward the square. Along the way, empty houses silently watched them. This could have been a quaint little village, the kind of place Sam wouldn't have minded living in another time in different circumstances. That's exactly what it looked like, a different time—medieval, perhaps? He was no expert in time periods and architecture. He only knew the history that mattered. They had tried to build quite a little society here, it seemed. He wondered where things went wrong. It could've been bad water, but it more likely had something to do with the forest and all the things inside it. Perhaps everyone had fled to the castle and were living there now. But even *it* seemed uninhabited. He looked up at its still, dark windows. It couldn't be uninhabited; he had seen people inside, fighting those monsters. They passed a stone building with the words "Faragó School for the Young" above its door. The name sent an angry chill up his neck.

That proved it then. This was *her* world.

"Maybe we are in some kind of indoor facility?" Skyler's high voice broke the silence, startling Sam.

"What?" He glared down at her.

She was gazing up at the sky like a turkey in rain. "The sky looks fake. It's like a ceiling. Maybe we're underground?"

"I *told* you where we are." Anger was growing in his chest.

She looked at him. "But how do you know?" There was a twinge of pleading in her voice.

Sam's anger slowly evaporated. That question again. Perhaps he needed to be patient with her. She was scared and reaching for any explanation that made sense to her. She didn't know what he knew.

At any rate, how could he be sure he was right?

Because I am. I have to be. It only makes sense.

"Just trust me," he said.

She frowned and looked to her feet, clearly unsatisfied. He felt a little guilty. But all the same, he could never tell her why he knew what he did. It was a long story, a deeply woven history that she had no right to know.

It was only his to know, and his alone.

He had learned about the Prairie Triangle sitting in a library in St. Paul. He spent an afternoon browsing the web until happening upon an article titled: "Top 5 Most Terrifying American Mysteries." The Triangle sat at number one. Sam immediately knew it was worth looking into. So many people vanishing over the course of several decades, yet nothing ever found to hint at where they went.

Theories about what was going on were numerous. Electromagnetic waves affecting brain activity and making folks wander off aimlessly.

Alien abductions or dimensional portals. An elaborate underground human trafficking ring. One pretentious columnist suggested the *sheer* despair from the death of rural America was driving individuals to wander off in search of meaning, or death. Some theorists noted that, at the center point between the three towns of Dayton, Rembrandt, and Farrington—the epicenter of the triangle—was an abandoned antique shop. The people found wandering were often heading toward it. Sometimes, the vehicles of missing people would be found outside it. But any investigations into the building were fruitless.

Why would it, Sam would consider in retrospect? Who would ever blame some worthless knickknack? But it was strange that the investigators didn't feel that urge. Unless, of course, the urge didn't come to everyone. Perhaps it was selective. Not everyone who came to the Triangle was swallowed by it.

What had truly triggered Sam's interest that afternoon was an article from 1996. It was about the shop's owners, Bob and Jodi Johnson. Back in the seventies, the Johnsons had been a young Bohemian couple from Chicago who were desperate for a simpler life. They left the hustle and bustle of the city to start a little antique shop out in the Nebraska countryside. They called it "Mom & Pop's Antiques and Miscellaneous," hoping, apparently, to make it a family business. With their young son Keith, Bob and Jodi lived in a mobile home adjacent to the store. They homeschooled their son and let him help out around the shop.

The article included an interview with Keith who, at the time of the article's publication, had just been released from a psychiatric institution. He detailed to the journalist the fateful morning that had ruined his life. He'd had breakfast and was about to start math lessons with his mother. But first, she had needed to help Bob unpack some things in the shop's basement. Hours went by and she didn't show up for lessons.

The boy grew impatient and decided to go into the shop to see what the holdup was.

Inside, he called to his parents. There was no response. Keith wondered if maybe they had gone out to run errands in one of the towns. But their car was still there. So, as he explained in the article, he went into the basement. He found his mother down there, but not his father. He remembered that she was crying and looked mortified. But when he called to her, she didn't answer. Keith vividly remembered a large round object in her hands, how she lifted it above her head and appeared to be sucked up into it. The sight, of course, terrified him and he wanted to run. But he had instead felt compelled to come closer to the object. It was a large snow globe, and when he looked at its world inside—a forest, a stream, a lake, and a castle—he had felt his mother and father, somewhere in that world. But they were too small, too distant, for the eye to see. Finally, the boy pulled himself together and ran—straight out of the shop and kept running until he couldn't any longer. A sheriff had found him, exhaustedly shuffling along the road.

The article continued with Keith stating he had made peace with his parents' disappearance, which those following the mystery attributed to being the first in the Prairie Triangle. He had also made peace with what he thought he had seen. He even planned to revisit the old place. He, and the article, accepted the notion that what young Keith had accepted had been a stress-induced delusion—or perhaps false memories. But for Sam, it was a revelation.

When Sam looked for more information on Keith, he learned the man had disappeared only months after the article's publication. He also learned the shop remained standing. Any contractors seeking to tear down the building and take that plot of land always lost interest, or encouragement.

The more Sam learned about the Prairie Triangle, the more excited it had made him. Could it be? A lead? After so many years of wandering aimlessly, finding nothing only to come home and face his father's shame, it had to be something worth looking into. The Keith story had brought back all the things Sam's father used to tell him. The glorious, if a little absurd, visions the man would conjure in his more sober days. The promises that, when Sam finally found the secrets their family were entitled to, he would hold a world of his own in his hands.

Then he had come to the Prairie Triangle and found himself drawn to the shop's basement, like no doubt many others before him. He saw the snow globe with his own eyes, and the Society's obelisk symbol along its base. That proved he was right.

"How *do* you know?" Skyler asked again as they reached the square.

Sam sighed. He couldn't tell her anything. Where would it end if he gave her an inch? There would only be more questions. His father, his great-grandfather, the Society, its history—only when all that was explained would she get the truest context. Then she would know everything that she shouldn't.

"Do you want to get home?"

She suddenly looked sick. She nodded.

"Then you need to trust me. I know about as much as you." He felt no guilt about lying; it was family business and hiding the truth was the kindest thing he could do for her. "But if there's a way in, then there has to be a way out, and I'll bet you my life it's in there." He pointed to the castle. "At any rate, it's the only place that seems safe, wouldn't you say?"

Skyler nodded absently, looking through him. She seemed to be trying to get her thoughts together. He couldn't blame her. Even he, having prepared for this his whole life, was a bit stunned. There was so much about this strange little world that he didn't understand. But he understood his mission.

They moved toward the castle. Eventually, the village's cobblestone street gave way to a rocky trail slithering up toward the castle entrance. This gave them a clear view of the entire structure, including the castle's bottom portion. It was windowless, the stone a darker gray than the rest of the castle, forming a kind of rampart. It was covered in uneven rows of steel spikes that curved upward. Sam noticed that, hanging on some of the spikes, were rotting green and black corpses that had once been those creatures. Some were in such a state of decay their bodies were breaking away, bits and pieces of them drooping from several spikes like vines.

"Oh god," Skyler muttered, apparently noticing the same thing.

The windows along the upper floors were pitch-black. The castle seemed so lifeless, even though they had seen people less than an hour ago. Plus, the glass windows looked almost pristine, as if somebody was maintaining them—even if the rest of the castle walls were growing discolored. These windows reminded Sam of the one in the library, how the bullet had bounced off the glass without even leaving a mark.

Glass that will not break, he could hear his father saying.

The castle's blue roof sat beneath the silvery sky. Skyler was right. The sky was very odd looking, like an unnatural screen. Perhaps the world had a little atmosphere of its own, a barrier between it and the larger world outside. At the same time, he had been able to see within perfectly fine. Maybe there was some kind of light scattering or refraction going on, the same reason you can't see the stars during the day. Or perhaps it was the product of forces he couldn't understand—like the creatures from the forest. Or, alternatively, Skyler was right, and they weren't actually in the snow globe. This was just some kind of sick experiment being conducted in an underground facility. Maybe he was wrong about everything. He swallowed that idea away.

The entrance to the castle was blocked by a red door that stood at least three feet taller than him. He tugged at one of the steel knockers. The door wouldn't budge. He pounded the knocker against the thick wood; the banging should have alerted anyone who was inside. But after several moments of waiting, there was no answer. The castle remained as still as the world around it.

"What now?" Skyler asked.

"I don't—" Suddenly he was hit by another idea. He pulled out the rusty key around his neck. His father had passed it down to him, telling him how his great-grandfather had gotten it. It had been given to him by a former follower of Maria Faragó, the aristocratic tyrant who had tried to murder her opponents—especially Sam's great-grandfather—and keep all of the Society's secrets for herself.

He was certain that madwoman had created this world. Why else would the school be named after her? Besides, only a mind so twisted could create such a place.

What this key opened and where had always been cryptic. All that Sam and his family knew was that this key would lead to what had been taken from them.

Unfortunately, the large red door had no keyhole. Disappointed, he tucked the key away.

"Hey!" He channeled his frustration to shout loudly up at the windows. "Hey!"

"What are you doing?" Skyler hissed, tugging at his jacket.

"What do you think?" he snapped back. He hollered back up to the windows. "Down here!"

There was no answer but his echo.

"What if those things hear you?" she whispered.

Sam hadn't thought about that. It was a good point. He should have known better. How was this woman—with her ill-fitting Aerosmith T-shirt and the face of an exhausted child—being wiser than him? He could only imagine what his father would say, and it twisted him inside.

"Let's go," he muttered bitterly, moving away from the door.

"Where?" Skyler asked.

"We'll find another way."

✧

More and more, he was questioning if this *was* the place he thought it was. Maybe it wasn't, and he had failed by ending up here.

Was he going to die here?

This wasn't the time for entertaining these doubts. There had to be a way into this castle, and he was going to find it. The entire structure was sitting on a plateau, its walls right at the edge of a rocky surface. Apparently, they would need to do some climbing. They hobbled off the trail onto a large grassy field that separated the castle and village. It was mostly empty except for some dead trees and two gray hedges in the middle. As they came closer, Sam realized these hedges were gravestones.

One read:

Annabelle

1919

"A baby?" Skyler asked.

He nodded, though he hadn't considered that until she said it. He had been ready to ask whether that was the year she was born or the year she died.

The other read:

Noémie Goddard

1855–1920

We Are All In Your

Children's Hands

"What the hell does that mean?" she asked.

"I don't know," Sam said, though the epitaph strangely unnerved him

"So people have definitely lived here. I mean, they've at least died here. Unless these are fake. You know, just for decoration or something."

"They're real." He felt mostly sure that was true.

"It's odd that there are only two."

Maybe there was no one left to bury anyone else, Sam thought. He figured Skyler might have been having the same idea but she said nothing. She only popped her fingers against her chin. A nervous tick that made her look even more juvenile in his eyes.

One of the dead trees stood only a few clicks away from the gravestones. It looked more real than the trees of the forest. Its rotting, wooden surface was covered in curves, bumps, and crevices; uncoordinated imperfections that only nature could achieve. He had seen other dead trees and bushes here and there in the village as well, not to mention the fallow field near the forest. It was likely these plants had been native to the natural world and brought into this one. Obviously, they weren't able to survive.

Some of the tree's branches had fallen away from it. Sam bent to pick one up. The grass brushing against his knuckles as he grabbed the branch felt rough. It was like FieldTurf from a football stadium. Yet, unlike artificial grass, it seemed somehow alive.

The branch he picked was almost as tall has him, and sturdy. It would make a good walking stick. Skyler looked at him, her thick eyebrow cocked. He wished he had something snarky to say to her, or at least clever.

"Let's go," he said instead.

Walking directly beneath the castle gave them a better chance to see the deadly rampart up close. The curved spikes along it were rusty and grimy. Sam could smell some of the dead creatures strewn about, that rotting stench more pungent than ever. Whenever he glanced back at Skyler, he noticed she was holding her nose. With a gun in one hand and a branch in the other, he didn't have that luxury. He wished he had brought his gas mask, or at least one of his face masks.

Sam noticed an abnormality in the wall. It was a divot of a different shade. As they came closer, he saw it was an arched entryway.

"Jackpot," he muttered. He looked to Skyler, who nodded cautiously at him.

He holstered his gun so he could clutch his walking stick with both hands and began scaling the rocky plateau. Though it wasn't entirely steep, it was difficult to maneuver, requiring a lot of balance and lower body strength. Often, the walking stick was a boon in keeping him balanced. Sometimes though, it was almost a hindrance, an awkward bit of extra weight. He wondered if Skyler would have difficulty keeping up, with her short legs and stocky, unathletic build. Yet, she consistently stayed directly behind him. She was able to hop from rock to rock while he simply stretched a leg or his walking stick to the next rock and pulled the rest of himself up.

⁓

They reached the entryway without any issues. It led them into a dark, cavernous hall. The air inside was cooler than the outside, and even more stifling. It took Sam's eyes moments to adjust—aided by the light from outside—as the short hall led into a round room. It looked like a dungeon with its stone floor and walls. Black splotches that looked like mildew were splattered here and there. The room was empty but for a firepit in the center and a door along the wall. The door was tall, broad and made from a dark steel—making it appear industrial and unwelcoming.

"There were people in here?" Skyler asked, her voice again startling Sam. "I'm sorry," she whispered, apparently noticing his jolt.

"Just keep it down," he muttered.

She was right, though. The firepit was makeshift and might have been recently built. It was just a bunch of smooth stones, likely pulled from the riverbed, piled in a circle. In the middle of the circle was some charred wood. Sam also noticed some claw marks surrounding the firepit. As his eyes adjusted, he realized that marks and gashes like these were all over the room. He also realized, with another chill down his neck, that those black splotches weren't mildew, but dried blood.

Whoever had been in here before didn't leave willingly.

He went to the steel door. The sooner they got inside the castle, the better. The long handle was freezing cold. He tugged and pushed, but the door wouldn't budge.

Shit, he thought, a hum of despair slowly weakening his body. What would they do now? Maybe there was another entrance. But what if there wasn't? Or there was and it was also locked? Would they have to climb up to the windows?

Then he noticed something beneath the handle. It was a keyhole. His breathing grew heavy as he broke the chain that had held the key around his neck for most of his life. He pushed the key against the hole. It wouldn't go in. He wanted to cry out in anger before realizing it was upside down. After flipping it, he pushed it again. It wouldn't quite go in, but... He pushed a third time, jostling the key until finally, it slipped inside. He let out an involuntary grunt of excitement, turned the key, and heard a delicious click. With that, he pulled open the door.

He was greeted by another narrow, dungeon-like hallway. It was so dark he could hardly see a foot ahead. But he wasn't too concerned with that now. He had done it. This was where he needed to be. This was the place that held what his great-grandfather had spent the last years of his life looking for. What his father had spent his entire life looking for. Only thirty-three years old, Sam had done it.

"Let's go," he said to Skyler.

"Just a moment," she mumbled.

He turned to see her sitting on the stone floor, next to the firepit.

"What are you doing?"

"I just need to rest a little bit."

"It's dangerous." He had a flash of resentment. Of course she would be slowing him down.

"Just for a moment." Skyler seemed too exhausted to care what he thought.

"We need to keep going."

But she didn't respond. She slumped on the floor. Not long after, he could hear her heavy, steady breath. She was asleep.

"Goddammit!" he hissed.

He looked back to the dark hallway. *Just keep going,* he thought. *It's her funeral.*

But leaving her behind didn't feel like a serious idea, like anything he would actually do. He could hear his mother tell him: *Help and take care of those you can. I promise there'll be a day when you'll need others to do the same for you.*

What the hell did his mother know? She'd turned out to be insane. To hell with her. Still though, the thought of her voice calmed him. He realized he was pretty tired as well. It had only been the adrenaline that kept him going. Now that he had a moment to stop, the exhaustion was catching up to him. But they couldn't both sleep, not at the same time. Not in this world. He would have to keep watch.

He kneeled and examined the firepit. Though the wood might have been there for a while, it didn't seem too spent. It looked like it had been collected from one of the dead trees, rather than the plastic-looking ones from the forest. He had a lighter but hadn't packed anything else to start a fire. It was chilly in the room, but they were at no risk of freezing to death. Still, the glow would have been welcoming.

Keeping his gun on his lap, one bullet in the chamber, he took small drinks of water and chomped down half a protein bar. Afterward, he pulled out his lighter and flicked it on, watching the warm flame. As he stared at the flickering fire, he thought about his father. What was he doing now? Drinking, no doubt. If only he knew. Sam remembered the last time they had spoken.

They had been in his father's study. A large picture of Sam's great-grandfather, Samael Adamsen the First, loomed over the fireplace, leering down at his brood with a steely gaze. A smaller photo of a smiling young man in a soldier's uniform sat on the mantle. This was Samael the Second, Sam's grandfather. Junior had never had an interest in the Society or his father's mission. If his plane hadn't gone down in World War Two, maybe Sam's life would have been different. Maybe Junior would have taken his family far away from the elder Samael. But fate dealt its hand and Junior's son was raised by his grandfather. Now the boy,

Michael, was an old man, sprawled on his chair and smelling of sweat. Sam hated seeing his father that way. The man was drinking straight from the bottle. Bourbon was his preferred poison. He, as usual, offered Sam none. Sam had gone there to tell him about his hunch—the Prairie Triangle, the snow globe.

But before he could say anything, his father sneered. "Now I know what drove your mother to the loony bin."

"What do you mean?" Sam asked, knowing he would wish he hadn't.

"I spent years of my life raising you to be the best you can be. Did I do anything wrong?"

"Of course not!"

"So why are you failing me?"

Sam heard this spiel plenty of times. But it always hurt as if it were the first time. "But listen..."

"You've given up," his father snapped.

"No, I haven't."

"Enough. Don't bullshit me. I see you moping around, getting fat, working at department stores..."

"I need to make money—"

"Sleeping around with whores."

Sam had clenched his teeth. He hadn't been with anyone in a long time, and never planned on doing so. "I haven't."

"Yes you have. I've seen you running around with them, squeezing every inch of their disgusting bodies. Don't deny it."

Sam kept shaking his head. Casey had been the last, and she hadn't been a "whore," or "disgusting." He resented his father saying that, but he wouldn't argue too much either.

But she had been his last, hadn't she? His father's furious glare shook his certainty. Was there someone he had forgotten?

"A waste of your existence." After this, the old man had become morose. "The existence *I* gave you."

"I'm not—" Sam no longer knew what to say. Conversations with his father always left him deeply ashamed and unsure of himself.

"You have so much to offer," his father's voice had softened as he pointed a swollen finger at the judgmental portrait of Samael the First. "I see him in you." The man in the painting was as tall and slender as Sam with those same bright blue eyes. "Please," Sam's father had continued, and Sam would never forget the quaver in his voice. "Just go. I can't... Seeing you just breaks my heart."

And Sam had left.

Now, staring into the flame of his lighter—Sam delighted in picturing the look on his father's face after all this was done. The pride, imagine the pride. Maybe he would finally quit drinking cold turkey. He often said that Sam was the reason he drank. Would he be happy? Would he finally be able to look his son in the eye and say, "I was wrong about everything"? Sam didn't just want to see his father's pride. He wanted to see the man's shame, his humility. But more importantly, he wanted to see his love. Then, with their purpose achieved—they both would truly be happy. Maybe even more than happy.

He thought excitedly about all that might lay in the castle. It reminded him of what his father often used to say when Sam was younger and he was more sober:

"The old Society held many secrets. And ours will hold them again. The brightest among us used ancient information and technologies to create things world leaders would slaughter millions of their own people to attain. Glass and metal stronger than anything we know, honed long ago. Strong and intelligent machines powered by old technology. But beyond those creations is something greater and older. Something not created *by* us, but given *to* us. The tool that carves worlds."

Part Two
The Castle

CHAPTER FIVE

ORGAN WAS THERE. IN the mom-and-pop shop. Her face was hidden, her slender body hunching in the corner, but it was definitely her. Her arm moved back and forth; she was painting something. One of those incredible paintings of hers that always seemed—to Skyler—to jump off the canvas. Skyler always wondered how Morgan did it.

"They're not that great," Morgan would say. "I just take my brush and throw shit at the canvas. Then it just kind of takes on a life of its own."

Skyler was in another part of the shop, trying to paint too. But she never could paint as well. In fact, no matter how hard she pressed, none of the paint was showing on the canvas.

They were in a dentistry clinic now, in the operating room.

Morgan hummed while she painted, sounding flat and tuneless. She was a better singer than that. She had even tried to start an experimental rock band called Shrimp Piano when Skyler went off to college. It hadn't gone very well. She was a better painter than a musician, but did both better than Skyler, who couldn't even hold her paintbrush tight enough; it dropped from her hands.

She looked over at Morgan's painting. It was so detailed. It depicted a centaur standing before a deep, dark forest. The creature's eyes were green and buggy; it had a mossy beard. It was staring directly at Skyler. It was moving.

Skyler tried to scream at Morgan, to tell her to stop. But her voice wouldn't carry. Morgan kept going. The creature gave Skyler a cruel, knowing smile as it reached a thick arm through the canvas. She wanted to move but felt too weak to take a single step.

The centaur grabbed Morgan by the throat, and all Skyler could do was watch.

ↄ∕ↄ

Once again, she woke up in a dark place where all she could see and feel was cold stone.

Panic began to build. *Not again*. But when she turned her head, she saw a somber, thin face beneath the glow of a small flame. Some of the panic dissipated, a slight relief.

As she rose from the ground, she felt a sharp pain in her neck. The consequence of sleeping on a hard floor. Her side was also sore, as if something had been poking into it for a while. The culprit was in her pocket. Her cell phone. She'd forgotten she had it. She pulled it out—it still worked but only had fifty-four percent battery left.

"Any signal?" Sam asked, flicking off his lighter.

"No," she replied.

"Naturally."

It didn't surprise her either. Wherever this place was, the outside world had no bearing on it.

"How long have I been asleep?" she asked.

Sam shrugged. He flicked his lighter back on, then off, then on again. There was certainly some handsomeness in his wary face—at least in certain lights. He had a kind of gaunt, distinguished look, not to mention those sharp, bright eyes. But those very same eyes and his deathly paleness made him creepy too. Almost alien. She had always been able to appreciate the attractiveness in men—and in anyone, really. But she'd never felt a need to pursue anything. She had little interest in romance or sex. The first and only time she'd ever tried to have sex had been a painfully dull and awkward affair. Of course, it had been college and the guy had no idea what he was doing, despite all his boasting—flopped about on top of her like a captured fish. But in general, she had more interest in doing literally anything else than hitting the sack or being in a romantic relationship with someone. Sometimes, she'd masturbate to relieve stress. But during those moments, she'd imagine traveling around the world, or other exciting things that didn't really involve another person's body parts. She often wondered if she was asexual or aromantic, or both. Morgan sometimes suggested she might be, whenever they talked about it. Morgan was also the only one Skyler knew would never suggest she just needed to "find the right person."

But even if she *had* been more interested in sex, Sam wouldn't have been her first choice. His appearance aside, there was something cold and unpleasant about him. He wasn't even the type she'd want to hang out with at a coffee shop.

"We should get going," he said.

There was that blaring personality again. "Did you get any sleep?"

"No. I needed to stay up in case—"

"Maybe you should get some sleep?"

"So you want to stay up and keep watch?" Sam asked, wearing his skepticism with a humorless grin.

"I could always wake you up if I hear anything."

"You might sooner smell something," Sam muttered. He sat quiet for a moment, staring at his gun. Skyler thought he was going to offer it to her again. She hoped not. Truthfully, she had never been into guns. In fact, she hated them. At the school where she worked, they had to have mass-shooter drills all the time. It saddened her; she'd never had to worry about that when she attended school. But this situation was different, wasn't it? Maybe she would have to learn not to hate guns if she wanted to get through this.

Sam pursed his lips, obviously the last thing he wanted to do was hand over his weapon.

"I can just wake you up," Skyler suggested.

"What if one of those things comes in here and there isn't time to reach over and wake me up?"

Skyler said nothing. Maybe she did need to know how to protect herself here. Hesitantly, she reached over to Sam's gun, but he pulled it away.

"What do you want me to do?" she asked irritably.

Sam observed her for a moment, his eyes sharp, judging. He pursed his lips again before giving in and handing the gun to her. He gave her a brief tutorial, showing her how to turn the safety off and where to look to aim. It was already fully loaded, with a bullet in the chamber. If she needed more than the current clip, they were probably screwed anyway.

When this brief lesson was finished, Sam sat in the dark, quietly staring at her.

"What?" she asked. Sam shrugged. "Do you want the gun back?" He pursed his lips again. "We can just keep going. That's fine. I just figured you needed some sleep."

"I'll be fine." But the heaviness in his eyes suggested otherwise.

They sat staring at each other in the dark chamber. Skyler expected Sam to lean forward at any moment and snatch back his gun. But instead, his eyes slowly closed and his head dropped to his chest.

She took a deep breath. She could finally relax without his leering. On the other hand, now that he was unconscious and essentially leaving her alone, she would have to be even more on guard.

As the silence of the room set in, her thoughts began to creep back. She still had no idea what was happening, where they were, why they were here, how... *if* they would ever get home. The castle didn't seem as promising as it had been. It felt empty. What if they were utterly alone here? She would die without her parents or anyone else ever knowing where she went or what had happened.

Skyler squeezed her eyes shut. Thus far, she had mostly gone through the motions, following Sam's lead. Now that she was thinking again, she wanted to scream, to cry. She looked at the pistol in her hands, imagined putting it to her head and...

She needed to occupy her mind with something else. Maybe singing would help. "Do You Hear What I Hear" was the first thing that popped into her head. It reminded her of Christmas Eve. Some of her best memories were of Christmas Eve—the dinners, the presents, even the midnight church services. Even when she stopped believing, she loved the peaceful solemnity of the ceremony. She remembered one year, she had brought Morgan with her. They both spent the whole night giggling at Pastor Dan's terrible singing. Rachel had tried to be in on it, so she giggled too, and loudly. They had been so noticeable that the pastor gave the whole family a rather cold salutation on their way out.

Her eyes fell on one of those dark stains on the wall, next to a claw mark. She stopped singing. Other people had been in this room, and they'd fallen victim to those monsters.

Was Morgan among them?

No. Morgan was alive somewhere. Alive as she was in Skyler's memory. Two seventeen-year-old girls giggling as if they were twelve. Skyler's mom glaring at them, but her dad barely repressing a smirk.

Dad.

She hadn't thought about his old clinic in a long time. Why had it appeared in her thoughts now? She'd been there so many times throughout her life: hanging out in the lobby, playing with one of the toys—be it pushing beads along a twisty, rollercoaster grid or mastering Bop It—exploring, playing with the dental equipment, roleplaying as a dentist, sometimes pretending to do very serious dental surgery on Rachel. When she was a little girl, the patients thought she was absolutely adorable. Her dad even said that her presence brightened their visits. As she got older and less adorable, she'd do her homework there or fill out job applications. She used to like being with her dad more than her mom, so his office became a sanctuary. For a while, at least.

When she was a freshman in college, he hired an assistant barely older than Skyler. Terra was her name. She always seemed nice enough. But one day, Skyler came to the office. It was closed for the day but she had a key. She had wanted to say hi to her dad, having seen his car there. Maybe she should have minded her own business. His office door had been shut, as usual. But she always used to take for granted that she could just walk right in. The first thing she saw when opening the door was Dad—his head tilted back, mouth open in ecstasy. She saw Terra there too, on her knees. She could still remember how surreal it had all felt, how she felt her blood rush from her body. She must have looked like a ghost, that was certainly how her dad looked at her.

Despite all his pleading, she ended up telling her mother. It soon came out that Terra hadn't been the first young female assistant he'd gotten to have sex with him. The divorce came quick. Her dad left town, and though he often called her and sent gifts, occasionally visited and sometimes apologized, insisting he was changing, she could never look at him the same way. It wasn't simply that he had cheated, lied, and betrayed her mom's trust. It was the disgusting way he'd abused his position and took advantage of those below him. She'd truly thought him better than that.

For a time, her mother became distant to her, as if Skyler was a walking reminder of her ex-husband's betrayal. Rachel had been hit the hardest. She had always been close to their dad, even more so than Skyler. Even after so many years, she was still insistent on blaming Skyler for their parents' divorce and "ruining their family."

The only one who had ever given Skyler compassion during that horrible time was Morgan. Her cousin had given her a shoulder to cry on, reminding her it was going to be alright in the end. She told Skyler she had done the right thing. Her mom deserved to know what happened. The consequences weren't her fault—it was her dad's. Still, Skyler would always wonder if she should have kept her mouth shut.

It sickened her to relive those moments. But in a way, grappling with the darkness of the past was more comfortable than facing the madness of the present. The past was predictable, analyzable, tangible. This was not.

Dread began creeping into her again. She imagined those bulbous green eyes peering in through the entryway. She remembered the centaur, the way it had nodded at her, beckoned her.

Not in a thousand fucking years.

Skyler tried not to think about it. But the more she tried to push the thoughts from her mind, the more she felt things gazing at her in the darkness.

"We should probably get going," said a deep voice. It startled her so much, she let out a yelp. Once she composed herself, she saw Sam staring at her perplexedly.

"When did you wake up?" she asked, letting her heart settle.

"Not too long ago."

Not even a yawn or a stretch. He just popped awake. Powered up like a robot.

"Are you ready?" he said.

"I—"

"Can I have my gun back?"

Skyler felt hesitant. The gun had become a comfort to her, even if she wasn't all that prepared to use it. Overcoming this hesitation, she handed it to Sam.

"Can I have some water?" she asked in return.

He nodded and handed her the bottle. Though sweet and luke-warm, it refreshed her throat. "Conserve it," he said. "I'm not taking another trip to the stream, and I don't know if we'll find any potable water in the castle."

"I know," she replied, making her voice intentionally icy.

She also ate half a protein bar before Sam packed everything away, rising to his feet with the help of his walking stick.

"The door," Skyler said. "How did you get it open?" The last thing she remembered was Sam tugging on it. She'd been too exhausted to pay any more attention. He showed her the key. "Where did you..." She realized it was the same key he had been wearing around his neck. "*That* opened it?" So many implications swam through her head, but she couldn't put words to any of them. "So you know where we are?"

"Yes, and I already told you where."

"You really believe we're inside that snow globe?"

"Yes," Sam said, his voice airy with exasperation.

Skyler's gut churned with anger. He had no right to be annoyed with her. Not about this. "How do you know?"

"Just trust me."

"It doesn't make sense to me," Skyler snapped. "But it makes sense to you. Why?"

Sighing, Sam kneeled. "There are things that are—" He looked up, searching for the words. His hands were wringing the stick. "Well, they are need to know."

"Need to know?" Frustration and desperation was making Skyler bold again. She let them drive her. If she stopped to think for one moment, she would get cold feet. "I'm in this, Sam. I'm in this as much as you are. I need to know."

He glared at her; a look that asked, *Why do you have to complicate this?* But Skyler didn't care. When she didn't back down, Sam softened his glare and sighed again, rubbing the bridge of his nose with his thumb and forefinger as if he wore glasses.

"Okay," he said.

Skyler swallowed, proud that she got her way, but not letting that lower her defenses.

"I—" Sam paused as if trying to find the best words. "I'm with an organization, I guess you could say."

She nodded. Oddly enough, the idea of an "organization" comforted her. The fact that there might be a whole group of people out there who understood... whatever was going on. It gave her a dim feeling of hope.

"It was founded by my great-grandfather. It's called the Society for the Recovery of Lost Artifacts. I know, it's a mouthful. That's kind of the point. It's supposed to sound… uninteresting. Keeps attention away from it. You think that's bad? The one before it had been called the Society for the Preservation of Miscellaneous Artifacts."

"What do you mean the one before it?"

"The Society for the Preservation… The old society had existed for centuries. Before the eighteenth century it had been called the Order of Exceptional Artifacts, though I guess that name had seemed too interesting. Before that, it was called the Order of the Chisel, way back in the Middle Ages. I don't know if it had any other names."

"Order of the Chisel? Why was it called that?"

Sam pursed his lips again, clearly hesitant to explain. "I don't really know. But it was started in Europe around the early crusades—don't ask me which one. The Order consisted of lords, knights, and scholars committed to protecting and studying the tool."

"What tool? Like a physical tool? Like a hammer or… a chisel, I guess?" Sam nodded. "I see." Fascinated as she was with history and all the dry details therein, she still couldn't grasp the relevance of this.

"But not literally a chisel, or a hammer, or any tool we've ever seen. I don't know what it looks like, or how it's used. I do know it's been around for a long time. The Society has records of it dating back to the Assyrian Empire. That's as far back as 600 BC or somewhere around there." Sam was beginning to loosen up. His posture slackening and his eyes widening, he seemed excited to be telling someone a story he'd apparently known for so long.

"Was it a weapon?"

"No. It's a—it's honestly the opposite of a weapon. It doesn't destroy, it creates." He breathed deeply through his nose, tightened his lips, and shut his eyes. He was obviously hesitant to tell Skyler any more.

"Sam," she said. "Please." She didn't know how long she would be bold enough to push him. But she needed something.

Sam looked at her. His eyes softened—she caught a hint of pity there. "It's a—it's... I've been told it can be... It's used to create worlds."

"Worlds? What do you mean?"

"Worlds. Like the world we live in. Like Earth."

"So, planets?"

"No... Well, yes. I'm not sure. But I know you can use it to create living, breathing worlds. Maybe not worlds as vast and diverse as ours. But actual worlds. They are small, though, from what I've been told. They can be small enough to hold in the palm of your hand. But you can also get inside, if the way in is open. Become a part of it. It's... something my father always told me about. My great-grandfather used to tell him about it. I had never been able to quite picture what exactly they meant until... until now."

"So, okay." Skyler paused to gather her thoughts. "So you are basically saying that we are in another world? And it was a world made with this tool."

"I know it sounds unbelievable. I used to have a hard time believing it myself. My father always told me I needed to commit my life to finding it. And I did commit. Mostly. But I could never... I never understood it."

As silence set in between them again, Skyler grew disappointed. She tried to make sense of this explanation. But if anything, it made Sam sound delusional. Still, she couldn't deny that this place was unnatural. Otherworldly. But it still just as easily could have been an underground facility, or maybe inside some revamped stadium.

But there *had* been that snow globe. She had been inexplicably drawn to it. Looking into it she'd felt like she was peering down at a land from high above. Everything had seemed so alive within. And then, as if pushed—goaded by some external voice—she lifted it over her head and…

"The Society," Sam continued. "The previous society, I mean. Preservation of Miscellaneous Artifacts. It fell apart in the early 1900s. This person—Maria Faragó, a member of one of the Society's oldest families—she wanted to keep the tool for herself. Some of the newer members, my great-grandfather included, rebelled against this. But Faragó was a thug. She had many of her opponents murdered. The Society was finished after that. My great-grandfather had to flee to New Zealand, lay low for a long time. Then, one day, Faragó and her followers just up and disappeared. It wasn't until later that my great-grandfather was visited by one of Faragó's most loyal followers. Seemingly loyal, I guess. This follower had betrayed her and brought my great grandfather this key." He held up the rusty old key.

"She said it would help him. She didn't say how. The damnedest thing is that she had contracted something on her voyage and died before she could explain any more; namely, where exactly the tool was being held. All she said was that it was in North America, yet 'not on this Earth.' Maria Faragó had made a new world, one that you can hold in your hands. So after this, my great-grandfather gathers up a few other surviving members of the old Society—they had been hiding all over the world—came back to America, reconnected with old friends, invested, rebuilt his wealth. Then he started the new Society, dedicated to finding the tool…"

Sam frowned, looking like a sheepish little kid who had been caught doing something naughty.

"I shouldn't have told you any of that," he mumbled.

"No, it's fine."

"It's not."

Skyler sighed. She had so many questions yet hardly knew if there was any point in asking them. Then, she thought of one she was eager to ask. "So, there are other members of your Society out there? Are they looking for this too?" She didn't know what she was hoping for. Maybe a sign that the calvary would come at any moment.

The deep sadness that grew on his face shot down that hope. "I guess I told you what I did because you've come this far. That's about everything I know, anyway. But you don't want to get caught up in any more of this, you know?"

Why not? Skyler thought. *I'm already in pretty goddamn deep.* But her boldness was floundering, so she said nothing.

After more silence, Sam took a breath and his mouth formed an O as if he were about to say something. But he quickly squeezed his lips together.

"What?" she asked. Sam looked at his lap. *"What?"* she asked again, the frustration at his aloofness giving her another wind.

"It's not important," he said.

She closed her eyes and let out a hiss.

"Okay," he said, relenting at nothing. "I'm just wondering what you were even doing out here." The question stunned Skyler. As she tried to find the words, Sam shook his head again. "It doesn't matter."

"I—I'm looking for my friend."

Sam looked at her blankly and nodded. Skyler wouldn't have been surprised if he didn't know what a "friend" was.

"Actually, she's my cousin," she continued. "We're very close. She went missing about a week ago."

"So she was taken? By the world, I mean."

"I—" The thought sickened Skyler. "I don't know. I just hadn't heard from her for about a week and…"

"So you came all this way just to find her?" Sam looked genuinely surprised. "Why?"

That seemed to confirm her suspicion that friendship was foreign to him. "It isn't too far. I'm from Omaha."

"But why didn't you just call the cops or something?"

"I did. I reported her missing almost a day after I stopped hearing from her. But they're never much help."

"So what the hell was *she* doing out here?"

"She came looking for her dad."

"He also went missing?"

"No. At least, I don't think so. He's a private investigator."

Sam bit at his thumb, as if gnawing off a hangnail. He nodded.

"Do—" Skyler wasn't sure how to ask her next question. "Is this… I mean, do you think they would be *here*?"

"Your cousin?"

"Everyone. The people who disappeared."

Sam nodded without hesitation. "*We* ended up here. I imagine we've vanished with hardly a trace. It only makes sense."

She looked at the charred sticks lying pathetically in the firepit. Who was to say where *here* was? She knew where, though. Stubborn as she tried to be, she knew. But it was hard to admit it. "So Morgan's here," she mumbled. Morgan would be able to handle herself in a place like this, she knew. But the idea was mortifying.

"It stands to reason," Sam said.

"She's here somewhere. Alone."

"If she's alive."

Skyler felt the blood drain from her face and her gut tightened. She looked at him, and whatever expression was on her face seemed to affect him.

"I'm sorry," he said, looking at his feet bashfully.

"Fuck you," she said, hating him at that moment. The idea that Morgan was possibly… It wasn't a thought Skyler hadn't considered before, but having someone else say it made it seem all the more real.

"I said I'm sorry," he said, his voice growing testy. "She's probably fine—" When he saw that did nothing to relieve Skyler, he threw his hands in the air. "I mean, I don't know!"

Sam quickly seemed to decide it was wiser to keep his mouth shut. The room became silent again, leaving Skyler with her thoughts. She looked at the dried blood around them. They were in a world of death. If anyone who had come here had survived, she would know it by now. Would it be worth going back home if Morgan was gone? She would be completely alone there.

The dark thoughts constricted her and the tears came. She tried to keep her weeping as quiet as possible, but the pain had a mind of its own. She was conscious of Sam sitting across from her, saying nothing. He quietly kept his head down, as if he didn't notice.

Eventually, the tears slowed, and she felt better, or at least more composed. The hope wasn't back, but she at least was in a place where she could ignore the hopelessness for a little bit.

She wiped the last bit of her tears on her sleeve. They had been here long enough, dangerously long enough. There was only one thing to do now that the tears had been shed and the dark thoughts were temporarily at ease.

She looked at Sam and said firmly: "We should get going."

Chapter Six

S AM PULLED HIS LITTLE black flashlight from his bag and clicked it on. The LED lit up the entire room with a white glow. He took the lead as they moved through the now-opened doorway and down the dungeon-like corridor. A feeling of apprehension began to flutter in his chest, that uncertainty and fear of what might be around the corner.

He held his gun in one hand and the flashlight in the other. Skyler carried the walking stick, which stood nearly two-thirds her height. He could hear her heavy breathing at his back. He gritted his teeth thinking about all he had told her. What had come over him? Granted, it had felt good to tell someone the truth he had been forced to keep to himself for so long. But it was a burdensome truth; one that his family took on with both reluctance and dignity. And now, he had implicated an outsider in it all. What would have to become of her once they got out of here? Would she need to join the Society? He could think of only one other alternative; and that, he didn't want to consider.

The hall split into three paths: left, right, and forward. Each one was a continuation of the narrow, stony hallway.

What the hell kind of castle is this? he wondered.

"Let's go right," he said.

Skyler agreed and they moved down the hall. It wasn't long before they reached another three-fork path.

"It's like a maze," Skyler said.

"Let's go right again." He had no justification for this decision. It wasn't his gut, or his brain. He was just choosing right because he had to choose *something*. This hall brought them to a corner where the only option was to turn left. Sam was relieved to have only one choice.

Moving down this new hallway, he noticed a wide stairwell to their left. The thick stone steps led upward toward a landing.

Up. There was promise in going up. He climbed the stairs, not bothering to consult Skyler. If she had any objections, she didn't voice them. When they came to the landing, Sam paused before continuing onto the next set. He shined his light up the stairs and could hardly register what he was seeing. The steps didn't seem to lead anywhere, instead converging with the stone ceiling. It was a dead-end.

"Is that a—a trick?" Sam asked nobody in particular. He rubbed the bridge of his nose. This place was going to turn his hair completely white. Maybe make it all fall out.

Skyler said nothing, pondering the stairs to nowhere.

There was no time to waste. He led them back down, and left, taking them further along the hall.

"Oh my god!" Skyler whispered.

Alarmed, Sam whipped around, pointing his gun and flashlight at her. She shut her eyes and raised her hands to block the blinding glow.

"I'm sorry," she said. He realized she likely didn't see the gun pointing at her or she would have been more frightened. It had been a muscle instinct. He quickly lowered both items.

"Don't do that!"

"I'm sorry," Skyler said again, blinking her vision back. "It's just... These lights." She pointed to the ceiling where a bulb hung from a large base that looked like a silver cheese wheel. "It reminds me of something. Oh! A Tesla coil." For a moment, her eyes glowed with fascination.

"How do you know?" he asked.

"I mean, I'm no expert. But I remember seeing this design before. I'm not sure where, maybe in a textbook."

"What makes you so interested in lights?"

"No. I'm pretty sure I saw this in a textbook, one of my classes on the Industrial Revolution. I was a history major with an emphasis on nineteenth-century Europe."

"Hmm." Sam found this surprising. She hadn't struck him as the type to be interested in that kind of subject. He thought she'd be more... Well, he didn't know. He hadn't thought about her interests or the possibility that she might have any at all. He somewhat envied her experience going to college. He'd only ever been homeschooled by tutors hired by his father. He knew a public institution was no place for him. But still, he often wondered what it was like.

"I wonder if we can turn it on." Her eyes widened excitedly. He felt that strange affection coming back. The interest and passion in her voice and face was rubbing off on him. It made him feel excited too—a passion he hadn't been allowed to have for a long time.

He shined his flashlight along the ceiling down the hall. Every few feet hung another light. They were everywhere. Sam was surprised he hadn't noticed these, as they were only about three feet from his head. He looked back at Skyler, and she at him, the fascination and enthusiasm faded from her eyes. His own excitement dropped. The reality of their situation returned to their minds.

"Let's..."

"Keep going," Skyler concurred.

This was definitely a maze. They wound through the uniformly stone halls, each often splintering into several paths. There were places where it seemed simply like a grid, four points at a time. But then they would reach points where there were only one or two paths to take. Sometimes, they ran into a dead-end and had to double back.

As they moved down a particularly long hall, Sam suddenly felt the floor drop away from him. It sent a jolt through his body, and he instinctively leaped back, knocking both himself and Skyler onto their backs.

"Fuck!" Skyler howled with unmasked frustration.

Sam didn't pay much attention to her anger. His heart was still pounding. The floor before them had vanished, and in its place was a large, rectangular hole. He leaned over and shined the light inside. At the bottom of the pit, several jagged spears pointed up toward him. There was a deep groan as the floor folded back into itself, sealing the hole. It was a trapdoor, blending almost seamlessly into the floor.

Sam exchanged a glance with Skyler, whose eyes were wide with terror. "We need to be more careful," she said, clutching the walking stick for dear life.

He nodded. Yes, it was just one more thing to keep an eye out for.

They came back to their feet and took care to shimmy around the trapdoor. Now Sam was staring at the ground with as much vigilance as he could. It wasn't long before they came across another one, its thin slits barely visible against the dark gray stone. They were able to cautiously slide past it as well. Though the threat was disturbing, Sam considered the exciting implications. This castle was clearly not built to be lived in. Instead, it seemed more like it had been constructed to hide something. He had an idea what that something was. The only question was *where* it was.

They came to a hall that was narrower than the others, the ceiling lower. The musty smell in the air became more pungent. Sam had to start bowing as the ceiling started scraping against his head. He realized there were no cobwebs. He would've expected to see some in an old, decrepit place like this.

"I feel like a kid in a haunted house," Skyler said. "Like at a pumpkin patch or something."

Except those won't kill you, Sam was tempted to say. It had been a stupid comment. But maybe she had only made the comparison to lessen the danger in her mind, or associate it with something positive to ease her. He remembered those Halloween haunted houses. The last date he'd taken Casey on was to one of those things. The haunted house itself hadn't been scary; the most frightening thing was the obnoxious adolescent boys jumping out of the shadows to spook people. But he could remember the feeling of Casey's slender hands around his arm, clutching him tight. He could still smell the perfume in her hair. Life had seemed exciting then. Everything had seemed new. Then, the day after their haunted house excursion, out of the blue, it was over. She said they weren't right for each other, but she wished him the best in life, offering little to no explanations beyond that. He hadn't asked for it either, which he regretted. But it didn't really matter. The fantasy had ended, and he'd had to accept that. He had shuffled back to his father, swallowing the pain and loneliness, letting it strengthen him. To be great was to be lonely. He knew what his purpose was. What he was meant to find.

The next turn brought them to a slightly wider, but still tight hallway. To one side was an entryway leading to a room. This deviation was welcoming, but they would need to exercise caution before entering. He realized he was a bit too careless at corners, rounding them full go, assuming nothing was on the other side. He stood on one side of the entryway while having Skyler stand on the other. He shined his light inside. It was a hollow, square chamber. No furnishings, no decorations. Just stone.

There had to be something. A secret entrance, maybe? He began to move in.

"Wait!" Skyler shouted, pulling him back with a surprising bout of strength.

"Christ!" He furiously stared her down, inadvertently shining the light in her face again.

"The ceiling!" she said, shielding herself from the brightness.

After a steady breath, Sam turned his light back into the room and shined it upward. There were several metal faucets pointing down.

"What the hell are those?" he asked.

"I don't know but I have a bad feeling about this room," she said.

"They almost look like shower heads."

"I think they might let out gas."

"Gas? How do you know?"

"I don't know for sure. But..." Skyler hesitated. "This place, it reminds me of Winchester Mansion. Or no, more like H. H. Holmes's murder castle."

"*Murder castle?*" It sounded like some Disneyland ride, and Sam was already feeling irritated that Skyler would bring up such a benign comparison.

"H. H. Holmes was a serial killer," she explained. "I don't remember how many people he killed, but he was active in Chicago during the 1893 World's Fair. He had this elaborately built 'murder mansion' that he would lure people into. It was full of traps, false stairways, gas chambers. This castle reminds me of that, though a lot bigger."

Sam turned his light to the floor. It had the usual stone tiles. But one of them, sitting close to the entryway, protruded from the ground. Some kind of pressure-activated switch, most likely. This was definitely a trap, and it chilled him to think how close he came to falling into it.

He looked at Skyler. Her face was wrenched in discomfort as she pondered the chamber. Maybe telling her so much hadn't been such a bad idea. Perhaps her knowledge would make her an asset to the Society. Not that it could really be called a society. He and his father were the only ones who had any semblance of commitment to it anymore, and Sam was the only one who wasn't consumed by drunkenness. It was heartbreaking to think about something so old and once so powerful, reduced to a sad shell of itself. It was all because of Maria Faragó and her greed and ambition. But once he found the tool, he would correct everything. He would rebuild the Society. Though, perhaps he would need people like Skyler to help him.

Or maybe he was being stupid. After all, they were caught inside a death trap. Worse yet, they were *lost* inside a death trap. Sam could no longer identify where they were going or where they had already been. If the traps or whatever the hell else didn't get them, they would certainly starve to death or die of dehydration.

If that was how it ended, what would there be to say? His father would die believing his coward son had run away from his responsibility. He could feel eyes watching him, invisible eyes filled with hope but braced for disappointment. They were not just the eyes of his father and his great-grandfather, but all the ghosts of those who had committed their lives to this mission. It fell solely on him to ensure their lives hadn't been without purpose.

His death would be their death. His failure would be humanity's failure.

With each hallway, each corner, he became more disoriented. All sense of direction was gone. Were they heading north or south? Did it even matter? Every turn led either to a dead-end or another hall with endless paths. They kept a close eye on the floor, shimmying around trapdoors or turning to avoid them completely. At one point they came across another entryway, but it turned out to be another gas chamber. Or it might have been the same one from before. Some halls were narrower or wider than others, some areas colder. But in all, it was a uniform dungeon. They were even fooled by two more false stairwells, one going up and one going down. By the second time, he took it with defeated acceptance.

The disorientation was becoming all-consuming. It felt like he was in a dream, floating out of his body, rounding corner after corner in an endless rhythm. His vision was becoming full of noise, a buzzing in his ears, the weight of his backpack on his shoulders both chafing and nonexistent. Each dead-end made him feel emptier.

Run, run, little rat. Find that cheese.

He didn't know how Skyler was feeling; she was mostly quiet except for her steady, heavy breathing. It seemed they were both concentrating on each step or on finding something that wasn't another lifeless hall or a trap.

Keep going, little rat. Seeing you just breaks my heart.

"Hey!" Skyler suddenly said, pointing. He followed where her finger was aimed. Light. Dim and gray, but light nonetheless. It was down a long hall from them, peeking around the corner.

Energized, Sam moved swiftly forward, forgetting the threat of traps. He was starving for the light, not to just see it, but to feel it. As he came closer, he didn't even need the flashlight. When he entered the light, there wasn't much to feel. But it was enough to make him almost want to weep. He was in a large room with massive windows, about the size of a ballroom. Though the light had the vibrance of a cloudy day, it felt so invigorating after the suffocating darkness of the maze. The floor was made up of blue and white marble tile, caked in a light coating of dust. A row of large white pillars lined each side of the room reaching toward a ceiling where there was a vast blue mosaic. It depicted a night sky, stars connected by lines, forming shapes. Constellations. Sam wasn't knowledgeable enough to know which they were, but many of them looked familiar.

Two large staircases converged from the floor, winding toward a second-floor landing. Across from the staircases was a familiar tall red door. Sam sighed ecstatically. After hours of wandering around, they had finally reached the castle's front entrance.

As he rushed farther into the room, he accidentally kicked a small object. It skidded across the floor with an echoing clank. From a distance, he was only vaguely able to make out the shiny object. He moved in closer until its gold color and circular shape were more apparent. A coin. His interest suddenly enflamed, he scooped it up and examined it. On one side was a coat of arms depicting a two-headed eagle. It held what looked to be a sword in one claw and a crown in the other. A larger crown loomed above the bird. On the coin's opposite side was the profile of a man's head. He looked regal, with old-fashioned mutton chops. Sam could make out a couple of worn words next to the head: "AVSTRIAE" and "IMPERATOR." His heart pounded excitedly.

"What is it?" Skyler asked.

"It's Austrian," he said.

He flipped it back to the side with the coat of arms. It had the words "HVNGAR" and "BOHEM" and "REX" surrounding it. He also could make out a year, "1915."

"Austro-Hungarian," he clarified. He searched his memory stores for the name. "It's a gold... ducat."

Suddenly, he was taken back to his leather-bound albums filled with rows of coins, each sorted by time, place, type, rarity. Back to the countless guides and manuals piled up by his bed about coin collecting. The breathless excitement he would feel whenever he would find, assess, and add a new addition to his collection. It had been a hobby his father had not only allowed, but encouraged. It helped Sam be more observant, more curious. It helped him become not just a seeker, but a finder. These, after all, were skills he would need to fulfill his purpose. Of course, he hadn't thought about it that way at the time. All he had thought about were his beloved coins: the stories they told, their delightful beauty, or fascinating ugliness, the small sense of progress, yet addiction for more he would feel every time he found another.

But that child was gone. He would never be able to feel that way again.

He broke from his trance and realized Skyler was looking at him, wearing a muted smile. It was open enough to show her small, bone-white teeth.

"What?" he said.

Skyler shrugged. She still smiled, slightly leaning against the walking stick. Was she laughing at him?

"What?" Anger began building inside him.

Skyler's smile dropped. "I'm sorry!"

He shook his head and looked at the coin in his hand. That brief flare of childlike excitement was gone. Now, looking at the coin made him only feel sad. No, it was no longer his duty to wonder. It was his duty to be a protector of wonders. Hobbies, love, friendship—they were not lasting things. At least not for an Adamsen. His father always told him that.

Sam tossed the coin across the room. He couldn't see where it went. The only sign that it hadn't vanished in thin air was the sound of a faint tinkling.

"What was that doing here?" Skyler asked.

"Who knows." But he did. Maria Faragó, the devil of his childhood nightmares, the target of every practice shot he fired, the murderous witch his great-grandfather had barely escaped, her wealthy and powerful family rooted in the Austro-Hungarian Empire. Whether she was still alive or not, she loomed in this place. Her specter lingered in every crack and crevice, leering at him, a snakelike grin on her face.

But he kept his head up. He wouldn't fear Maria Faragó, or her castle, or her world.

Like all childish things, he put his fear behind him.

Chapter Seven

S HE WAS FED UP with this guy. Navigating his fragile masculinity was too much. She'd seen the way his face had lit up from that coin and thought she would be welcomed to smile along. But obviously she had misread.

"I wasn't trying to mock you," she said as Sam surveyed the red door.

"Forget it," he said. He pushed against the door, but it didn't budge. "Fine."

Sam was the kind of person she felt lonelier with than if she had been alone. He was behind a wall, or more accurately, a scared boy hiding inside a man-shaped pillow fort. Once in a while that boy would peek out. And maybe there was nothing more to him than that. For all she knew, his "secret society" was bullshit. It wouldn't surprise her if that were the case. She was no stranger to habitual liars. In high school, there had been a girl in her class, Tammy, who told all sorts of tales: how she once flirted with Justin Bieber; that she flew out every summer to hang with her best friends Malia and Sasha Obama; and how her aunt worked for Oprah, who always had positive things to say about her employee's niece for some reason. Every liar had their reasons for being that way. Tammy had grown up in a broken home and had few friends at school. She probably made up incredible stories to impress her peers.

Skyler wondered what Sam's reasons would be.

"Here we go," he said. To the right of the door, a silver lever jutted from the ground. He holstered his gun and flashlight and grabbed the lever with both hands, pulling it toward him. It slowly groaned forward. She could only imagine the effect this effort had on Sam's back, which was already buckling under the weight of his backpack. Sounds erupted from the door: the sharp popping of locks and the growling of gears. Some of the gears squealed and creaked, coming to life after a long, long sleep.

When the noises stopped, Sam pushed against the door again. This time, it opened. Cool, stale air from outside crept in. The first thing Skyler saw was the forest, far away yet seeming so close. Its trees stood utterly still, welcoming them back to the outside world. That urge crawled back into her gut. All the time spent in the maze, she had forgotten this feeling. It wasn't as intense as before. It was more like a reminder that the forest was there. It remembered her, and she was always welcome.

Sam stood silently, staring outside. He probably had the feeling too. For a moment, Skyler feared he would succumb to it.

She was almost relieved when he turned to her and spoke. "At least we have another way out." He then added abruptly, "Do you need to use the bathroom?"

"Oh." Skyler realized that she did. She had to pee badly, in fact.

Armed with a box of cleansing wipes that Sam pulled from his magic bag, she went through the door and climbed down into the grassy field between the castle and the village. While she relieved herself, Sam stood guard on top of the trail, thankfully looking the other way. She couldn't see the forest from where she was, but the castle's barbed wall lingered above her. She saw how easily one could get impaled on those spikes if they tried to climb. One bad step and they'd be shish kebabs. It was a sickening thought. She suddenly felt eager to get back to Sam as quickly as possible. When she returned to the trail, Sam told her to go back inside the castle while he went down to relieve himself.

"Do you want me to stand watch?" she asked.

"No." He clutched his gun as if she were going to try and take it from him.

In no mood to argue, she went back inside.

As she tensely paced in the main hall, waiting for Sam to reappear in the doorway, she felt the forest's unblinking eyes trying to get a glimpse of her. To occupy herself, she looked up at the beautiful constellations along the ceiling. There had also been constellations on the snow globe's base, she recalled. Was there a connection?

Finally, Sam reappeared. "I was debating whether or not we should refill at the stream," he said. "But we should be fine for now."

"Yeah?" Skyler asked. "But what if we get lost again?"

Sam frowned for a moment before shaking his head. "We won't." He pulled the water bottle from his bag and sloshed it around. "We should have plenty if we're conservative."

Famous last words. "Maybe it wouldn't hurt. Just to be safe."

"Do you want to go refill it?"

Skyler said nothing.

Sam gave an insufferable smirk that said, *I thought so.* He looked back at the opened doorway. "Maybe we should lock it again. We don't want an open invitation for those things."

"I guess." She shrugged. She was still thinking about the water. She didn't want to go all the way back down to the stream, and obviously neither did Sam. But was it really wise not to?

Before she could think any more on it, he shut the door. The forest was blocked from their sight, but Skyler still felt it watching. He pushed the lever forward. The cacophony of grinding gears and heavy clicks came and went again. Enclosed inside the castle, Skyler felt both safe and constricted.

Sam readied his gun and flashlight and turned to her, his face steely. "Let's go upstairs."

Part of her wanted to meekly agree and follow his lead. But he obviously didn't know what he was doing. They needed a plan. After all, they couldn't afford to get lost again.

"What are we looking for?" she asked.

"I told you."

"But we can't just keep wandering around without any idea of where we're going!"

Sam shook his head and shrugged as if to say their hands were tied. "I don't know this castle, do you?"

"Maybe we should find help."

"I think that's going to be impossible."

"But there are people here," she said. Though, she wondered if that was actually true. "We saw them. At the windows."

"We don't know what we saw," Sam said.

That was hard to deny. But there had been signs of life at one point, at least when the bell started ringing. "The tower!"

"Tower?"

"The big one. When those creatures were attacking and that bell started ringing... It came from there, remember? Someone has to be up there. Maybe they can help us." In her heart, the tower held possibility. At least it gave them a tangible goal, and goals had hope.

He looked at his feet, pursed his lips, and then nodded. "Fine. But if I'm correct, that's on the complete opposite side of the castle."

"We just need to make sure we keep going that direction."

"Fine," he said.

"Okay." Really? That was that? It felt surreal to Skyler, convincing someone to do something. Especially someone as stubborn as Sam. Usually, she felt she didn't have much pull to change people one way or the other. She always felt like she'd be a shit politician.

"Still," he said, "let's go upstairs. I'm not going back in that maze."

Skyler nodded. She also preferred not to return to the dungeon. She just hoped the second floor would be better.

"I hope you're right," he added. She nodded again. She knew she was risking severe disappointment. But the tower held more promise than anything else she could think of. She could only imagine what or who was up there. Maybe even Morgan. Not likely. But who could say that was impossible until she knew for certain?

They went up the stairs. She used the walking stick to support her, sometimes practically pole vaulting with it. Its hollow tap echoed through the room. At the top of the stairs was a landing with three open entryways. They stood side by side along the same wall. Each of them seemed to lead to their own narrow, stone-like hall. She almost wailed at the sight. More mazes.

"Shit!" Sam hissed.

They stood quietly, feeding their nervous habits: Sam rubbing the bridge of his nose and Skyler popping her fingers against her chin.

"I guess we don't have much of a choice," he finally grumbled. "At least we have a point of reference."

"What if we can't find our way back?" she asked.

"Well... Oh!" Sam holstered his gun and flashlight. From the front pocket of his backpack, he pulled out a large red marker. The magic backpack saved the day again. He marked the cragged wall between two entryways with a large, blood-colored X.

"We can leave one of these every few feet. Make a trail."

"Like Hansel and Gretel," Skyler said.

"Yeah," Sam mumbled. "But if there's a witch, I'll blow her god-damn head off."

Skyler almost laughed, but thought better of it. Was that even a joke? It was hard to tell.

"You want to do it?" he asked.

Before she could answer, he tossed the marker to her. She reached out for it, causing the walking stick to fall out of her hands and clatter to the floor. The marker slipped through her fingers, landing next to the stick. After recovering both, she looked up to see Sam glaring at her. The look embarrassed, but also offended, her. What did he have to be so high-and-mighty about? He would've probably been gassed to death had it not been for her.

The thought of the gas chamber made her feel queasy. It reminded her of what kind of place they were really in. The *danger* they were in.

"You ready?" he asked, wearing his impatience on his chest.

She nodded, holding the marker at the ready.

It was tedious, marking an X on the wall every several steps. She also wrote a number under each, to prevent the order from becoming confusing once there were enough Xs, thus rendering their bread-crumb trail useless.

After twenty-one, Sam suggested, "Maybe you could do that every twenty feet or so."

"We don't want them to be too spread out."

Sam snorted in what passed for begrudging agreement.

The halls were as twisted and winding as their downstairs counter-parts. This time at least, there didn't seem to be trapdoors. But they still encountered false stairwells and several dead-ends. Though the goal was to keep going forward toward the tower, the maze still turned them around. More than a few times they encountered one of their Xs. But thanks to Skyler's numbering, they were able to get back on track. She always tried to keep the last number she'd made in her head, rehearsing it over and over, like when she used to memorize information for tests or lines in a play.

After she marked off X number eighty-seven, everything went dark. For a moment, Skyler thought she had gone blind. But she quickly realized the flashlight had turned off.

"What are you doing?" she asked.

"I think the battery's dead." She heard him hitting the flashlight and clicking its button.

She could feel her heart pounding. The darkness was dense, enclosing her; she could practically feel it touching her nose. She feared taking a step forward. What if they weren't alone as they had thought? What if there was something else in here and it was just waiting for them to be at their most vulnerable.

She had to breathe. Just had to breathe.

There was a shuffling sound. It was Sam, fumbling through his back-pack.

"Sam?" she said into the blackness, hoping her voice could break through.

"I have more batteries... somewhere in here."

Then she remembered something. She pulled out her cell phone. She was relieved to see it light up, freeing them from the darkness. Her dog, Oscar, greeted her from the phone's lock screen with his sweet doughy eyes and his golden face with traces of white, holding a ball in his mouth. She missed him so much it hurt. She wanted to see him again, to walk through the door and have him rush in to greet her, his large tail swinging violently and hitting Morgan's cat Nightmare in the face. That cat also always came out to say hello whenever Skyler came home, or at least to say she was hungry. Skyler wanted them both. She also wanted her mom. For the first time in a long time, she had a need to hug her mother—bury her face in those slender shoulders and take in her sweet, cozy fragrance. She even wanted Rachel who would just have to put up with her hug for once. Most surprisingly, she wanted to see her dad. She still didn't know if she could ever look at him the way she used to. But she wanted to see his smile, to hear him tell a dumb joke or badly sing some Rolling Stones song.

With every thought, her heart lifted and sank like a buoy. What were the chances she would ever see any of them again?

She unlocked her phone so the screen could brighten even further. When she did, there was Morgan in her Union Jack dress, her copper skin glowing and her eyes bright.

She held the phone over the backpack to give Sam some light. He glanced at her, his alien eyes glimmering. "Thanks." He snatched the phone from her hand and shined it inside the backpack. "Here we go." He pulled out two small cylinders. "Who's this?" he asked, getting a glimpse of the screen.

"Morgan," Skyler said, holding out her hand for her phone. "My cousin."

"Huh." He swiped to the next picture as if he were on a dating app.

"Hey," she said, holding her hand out for her phone.

He didn't listen. He was looking at a photo of Skyler and Morgan, also from the Spice Girls concert. It was a good one of Morgs, her head tilted back in laughter. Skyler certainly wasn't the highlight of the picture, her little half-hearted smile only made her look awkward. Sam swiped again to a photo of Rachel, Skyler, and Morgan at the concert. They were trying to pose like the Spice Girls. Morgan with her legs and arms up, Rachel kicking toward the camera and her fists at the screen, and Skyler making the least effort. She stayed on the ground with her hands open and a wide smile. They all had failed whatever pose they were going for, but it didn't matter.

"And this other person?" he asked.

"My little sister, Rachel. Can I have my phone back?"

Sam looked at the picture for an uncomfortably long time. His face reminded her of a cat staring into a sink.

"Sam?"

"Oh yeah, sorry." He handed her the phone. "Your sister—"

"Hard to tell we're related, right?"

He turned on the flashlight, its white beam filling the hall.

"You have the same hair," he said, shrugging.

Skyler got that a lot. Same slightly curly brown hair, maybe a similar looking face at certain angles. But Rachel was taller and slenderer, her skin darker, her eyes more striking, oval and bright gold. She also had more personality, more friends, was probably smarter, and certainly had more potential. She wanted to be a dentist one day, like their dad. With her 4.0 GPA and high honors, it was probably going to happen. She had come a long way from the obnoxious little girl who would sneak into Skyler's room to steal makeup and plaster it all over herself. Or the girl who would sneak into Skyler's bed to sleep with her during thunderstorms. Skyler never felt like an adequate older sister. Morgan had been much better suited for that job. Rachel certainly liked and respected their cousin a hell of a lot more, especially now that she basically hated her sister.

"She kind of looks like someone I know," Sam added.

"Yeah?" She felt a bit uncomfortable with the way he'd reacted to her sister's photo. It didn't seem perverted or anything like that, but it was odd.

"Yeah." He tried to say it casually. Skyler decided it would be better to let it go. Rachel wasn't here. *They* were, and they needed to get out. She turned off her phone to conserve power in case they needed it again. With nothing more to say, they moved onward.

The flashlight's unwinking eye against the stone walls brought Skyler back to her childhood. Back to when she was little and Rachel was littler, telling scary stories with their dad. They would be in his den, the lights completely off. The sisters would be huddled together on the couch, giggling with fright while their father told them spooky tales. During those moments, his ridiculous stories seemed more exciting than anything else in the world. She would hold Rachel close in anticipation of the story's climax, which always consisted of their dad roaring, jumping on the couch, and tickling them. The joyful screaming would often lead to their mother coming into the room and saying curtly that story time was over.

Sam stopped and shined the light through another entryway. "Look," he said with such a low whisper Skyler thought someone was asleep in the room. But when she looked inside, there was nobody. The room was empty except for another entryway on the other side. The entryway was at such an angle that she couldn't see much into it, but it seemed to lead to another hall.

"No gas." Sam shined his flashlight at the ceiling, which sure enough, was bare.

Without any apparent thought, he stepped into the room.

"Wait!" Skyler tried to pull him back, but she didn't pull hard enough and ended up getting jerked into the room with him. Beneath his feet came the low sound of scraping stone.

"Shit," Sam said, stepping away from the inclined tile. But it was too late—a sharp metal noise came behind them. Skyler and Sam turned to see the entryway blocked by metal bars. They had apparently shot up from holes in the ground. The doorway ahead was also barred off.

"Shit!" Sam said again.

Skyler felt flushed. She breathed deeply in and out, trying to calm the growing tide of panic.

"There." He kept his voice steady. He pointed the light across the room.

"What?" She couldn't see anything.

"A switch."

Then she saw it. On the wall, next to the doorway, was a little metal crank.

"That should open the door," he said.

"How do you know?"

"How do you know it won't?"

Skyler decided to accept that answer. She didn't have many other options. All they had to do was reach the other side of the room. It was going to be okay.

"Oh," Sam said. His tone immediately deflated Skyler's hopes. He shined the light at the floor, every tile appeared to be raised and was covered in slits.

"What are they?" Though Skyler highly suspected the answer.

Holstering his gun, Sam snatched away her walking stick. He pressed it into one of the nearest tiles, applying pressure until the tile lowered. Suddenly, small blades came jutting from the slits. He jerked the stick away, pushing himself and Skyler into the bars behind them. Relieved of pressure, the tile rose again, the blades sinking back into their slits.

"What do we do?" she asked, her suspicion now confirmed. Though the blades appeared to be only inches long, they were sharp. She could see the marks they left on the wooden stick. Its bottom edges were splintering away.

Sam shook his head. That boyish fright returned to his face. She suddenly felt angry at him. Why did he have to go rushing into this room? Was he choosing to be an impulsive idiot? Whether his talk of a "society" was true or not, he seemed to think he was the most important person in the world. That it was on him to zip in and save the day, even when he only made things worse.

"Goddammit!" she screamed, smacking the bars, disregarding the pain it left in her hand. It was a show of anger she rarely let strangers see. "We need to figure something—"

Her foot kicked against the elevated tile that had trapped them, tripping her. She lost all control as she stumbled toward the slitted tiles. Sam grabbed her wrist, but it was too late. Her foot fell flat onto a tile. She felt it lower beneath her, expecting blades to slice through her foot. But before anything could happen, he pulled her away.

Skyler clutched the bars, panting heavily, dizzy from the adrenaline. The sting of panic pounded through her chest. Her foot was okay, though. She was alright.

"Huh," Sam said. "Did you see any blades?"

"What?"

Sam pressed the walking stick against the tile Skyler had stepped on. It lowered again, grumbling beneath the weight of the stick. She waited like a child watching a jack-in-the-box, expecting blades to shoot up at any moment. But nothing came. He released the weight, allowing the tile to rise again. She watched him, her heart pounding as he put his own foot onto it.

Again, nothing happened.

"Maybe this one is defunct," he suggested. "Or maybe…"

He pushed down on the tile ahead of him with the stick. Skyler leaped as blades shot up, slicing into the wood. The bottom point of the walking stick was beginning to resemble shredded meat. Sam braced himself as he pressed down the tile to his right. Skyler braced herself too. But this time, nothing came. He prodded it again before stepping onto it himself. From there, he further tested the tiles around him. One shot up blades. But the one ahead of him remained dormant. He looked at Skyler, his eyebrows raised.

"You think some of these are intentionally safe?" she asked. She was still holding onto the bars for dear life, though her adrenaline was subsiding.

Sam nodded. "It must form a path." He chuckled bitterly. "Whoever built this place had fun with it."

"Jesus." The thought sickened her. Of course, the fact that the architect was a bastard had been apparent the minute they entered this psychotic maze. She didn't want to think about how lucky she had been to land on an inert tile. Her clumsiness paid off for once. The flashlight beam blinded her again. "Hey!"

"Sorry," he mumbled before lowering the light. "Follow me and mark each one we've passed. Just in case we ever have to come through here again."

Uncertainty paralyzed her. "But... What if they aren't empty? What if they... they're just jammed or..."

Sam pushed down the tile ahead of him. It remained inert. He turned back to Skyler. His small mouth remained neutral but there seemed to be an exasperated glint in his eyes.

"What other choice do we have?" he asked.

She couldn't argue with that. Either they went across or they would be trapped. There was no shimmying around this one. It was time for Skyler to channel her inner Morgan. Her cousin would've been leading the way and never would've put up with Sam's overplayed bossiness. Hell, Skyler even would benefit from channeling her inner Rachel. Even as a little girl, Rachel would try to sneak onto the largest roller coaster in the park or have intense arguments with her teachers. Skyler rued whatever gene Morgan and Rachel had gotten that she'd been denied.

"Okay," she said, readying her marker. "Where was the first one again?"

It seemed to take ages. Sam prodded at the tiles around him. Some would cut the stick a tiny bit shorter, while others did nothing. At one point, he pressed the walking stick too hard and it snapped nearly in half. There was enough of it to keep testing the tiles, but it would no longer serve as a walking stick. All the while, Skyler skulked behind, marking each tile

Sam stepped off before stepping onto it herself. He had also given her the flashlight, as she would be better able to keep the light steady.

Halfway through the room, Sam became so eager that he didn't even bother to wait for Skyler to mark the tile he was on before moving onto the next one. Skyler looked up to see him already two tiles ahead.

"Wait!" She stepped forward, marking the tile he had just moved from. "Slow down," she said. Sam paused but said nothing. She realized she hadn't marked the tile behind her. Her head was so cloudy, she couldn't remember which she had stepped from. The possibilities were one of two, sitting side by side. Had it been the left one or the right? Left.

They managed to reach the other side of the room, both sighing with relief. By then, her jacket was damp with sweat and her hands were trembling. Her hair was moppy, and she had to push it from her eyes. Sam removed his own jacket and stuffed it into his backpack. His plain white shirt, loosely hanging around his torso, was drenched and putrid.

"You mark them all?" he asked.

Skyler nodded, and he tossed away the remains of the walking stick. It clattered across the room, not heavy enough to trigger the tiles.

"Here we go," he said, grabbing and pulling the switch on the wall without a second's thought. Next to them, the bars over the entryway sank back into the floor. Across the room, the other entryway was also opening. Skyler felt like she could breathe again.

"You ready?" Sam asked, taking the flashlight from her and withdrawing his gun. Not waiting for her answer, he went to the now-opened entryway and poked his flashlight inside. He didn't move forward, he just stared. At first he looked vexed, then his face tightened with anger.

"What?" Though her stomach was in knots, she also looked inside. The hall only went a short way before stopping at a complete dead-end. "Fuck," she grunted. They had gone through all of that for nothing.

"Well," Sam said, keeping his tone neutral, "let's double back."

"Right." There was no time to wallow.

They retraced their steps, Sam again leading the way. There was nothing to it this time—follow the Xs. The marked tiles were safe, they were home. But what if they weren't? Skyler couldn't help but hold her breath each time a tile sank beneath Sam's feet. It was like walking across a field of supposedly disarmed land mines.

Still, so far so good. It was going to be okay, everything was—

The sound of slicing blades shrieked through the air, followed swiftly by a deep, meaty squelch. Sam howled, an agonized, animalistic scream that churned the pit of Skyler's stomach. The flashlight was trembling in his hand, spotlighting a pool of blood where he stood. His foot was surrounded by blades, one embedded in his heel, another jutting through his foot.

She gagged at the sight, malnourished bile stinging her throat. Sam's scream faded to a whimper, his body convulsing as if small electrical shocks were periodically running through it.

She collected herself, trying to steady her breath. "Okay," she said softly. "Okay."

What were they supposed to do? Leave it in or pull it out? It wasn't like they had a choice.

Sam grabbed Skyler's shoulder tightly for support and slowly pulled his foot out, screaming louder than ever. She cried out as he squeezed her shoulder. When his foot was free, the blades retracted beneath the bloody pool.

Without hesitation, he hopped to the next X-marked tile.

"Sam!" she shouted, frightened he would get sliced again. He didn't listen, hobbling to the next one and the next. She quickly followed. He was taking the light with him and would possibly leave her behind in the dark. The dense trail of blood helped lead her more than the markings. They both managed to reach the other side. She took care not to step on the switch that had trapped them in the first place. It would have been a fatal mistake.

Back in the maze, Sam collapsed against the wall. Blood seeped from the gashes in his boot, a small pond beginning to form around his legs. It made Skyler feel dizzy. She usually could handle blood that wasn't hers, but this was too much. She wanted to call an ambulance or somebody. But there was nobody. It was just her, Sam, and all of his blood. He was going to die. He was going to die and leave her completely alone here.

Sam was no longer screaming. His breath was fast and heavy. He was looking paler than usual.

"Skyler," he said.

"What do I do?"

He sluggishly dragged his backpack from behind him and opened it.

When it was all over, Skyler could hardly remember what had happened. It had played out like a hazy dream. She hadn't really been thinking much during. Sam had instructed her every step of the way, at least while he was still coherent.

She remembered the messiness. She had tried to use his jacket to clot the wound, which only covered it in blood. She had futilely tried to keep her own clothes from getting bloodied in the process. She remembered the cauterizing, using the lighter to turn his pocketknife into a glowing-hot brand that she pressed against his wounds. Sam had screamed both times, the sound muffled by the cloth clenched in his teeth. He had also passed out a few times, after which Skyler quickly smacked him awake, as he told her not to let him fall asleep. Soon, his wound and flesh had begun to feel like external lifeless things to her, Play-Doh to experiment with. With a very simple first aid kit from Sam's backpack, she disinfected his wounds and wrapped his foot with gauze and bandages. It was not a perfect medical procedure, but it was the best they could do.

When his foot was taken care of, they spent hours sitting quietly in the hall. At first, he looked dead, his eyes gaping and his skin cold. She expected his breathing to stop at any moment, then he would be gone. But instead, he grew steadier. Eventually, he took a couple painkillers and some glucose tablets, along with a few gingerly sips of water. It became clear, Skyler observed with cautious relief, that he was going to live. If there was one thing she could say for Sam, he was unbelievably resilient. But his foot now looked like it came from the dumpster behind a butcher shop. It would probably never fully recover.

"Maybe I should've gone to medical school," she said half jokingly, her first calm words to him.

"You did fine," he replied. His speech was a little slurred and delayed. That seemed understandable; she couldn't have imagined the state he was in. It was just good to have him talking. "Three years ago."

"What?"

"My last tetanus shot. It was three years ago."

"Good." She noticed something on his heel. She had seen the dark shape while treating him but hadn't looked too closely then. It was a small tattoo depicting a figure with outstretched wings—an angel. But it wasn't the harps-and-clouds kind. It looked dark and threatening, wielding a sword in hand.

"What is that?" she said, pointing to the tattoo.

"Samael," Sam said after a pause. "He's an archangel—or a demon. It depends on who you ask."

"Can I ask why you got that?"

Sam shrugged and laid his head against the stone wall. "I was about fifteen. Thought it would be cool. Course, I wasn't brave enough to get a bigger tattoo. Needles, you know? And I was scared of how father would've reacted if he'd seen it. Probably would've called me a degenerate, force me to grate it off."

"Really?"

"Probably. Anyway, a little one hurt enough."

"But why this angel, I mean?"

"My name," Sam said. He readjusted himself, letting out a pained groan as he did.

"What?" Skyler thought for a moment, before putting two and two together. "Oh."

"Yeah," he continued. "I'm actually the third one. Third Samael. My great-grandfather was the original. He named his son after himself. Then Junior had a kid, my father, named him Michael. I guess they wanted him to be named after the 'good angel.' Then father named me Samael again. Carry on the legacy."

"I see." Skyler hesitated to add anything. Usually, it didn't seem like a good investment of time to bother trying to make conversation with him. It either ended with him giving her the cold shoulder or her getting frustrated. But he was apparently eager to talk now, probably to get his mind off the pain.

She sat against the wall across from him, bringing her legs to her chest. They felt rubbery, still a bit shaken. The uneven stone was hard and uncomfortable for her back, but it would be tolerable for the moment.

"I don't know why my parents named me Skyler," she said. "I think they just liked it. My grandma on my dad's side was named Rachel. She died only a year before my sister was born, so it makes sense why they named her that."

"Good name," Sam said. "Rachel."

"Yeah." She nodded. "I like my name too. I didn't used to, but it grew on me." When she was little, she thought it sounded too much like a boy's name.

"What name would you have wanted instead?"

"I don't know. Maybe Ginger. Ginger Spice was always my favorite."

"Favorite spice?"

"No, she's one of the Spice Girls."

"Oh." Sam shrugged. "I'm kind of hungry."

They shared a protein bar. It was very little, but it was something. They also passed the water bottle back and forth, though it was getting low.

"You have a hair tie in there?" she asked, nodding to the backpack. Her hair was still getting in her eyes.

"Rubber bands?" Sam suggested through a large mouthful of chocolate-flavored protein.

Skyler nodded—it would do.

"How about you?" Sam asked as she busied herself with tying up her hair. For the first time, she noticed a slight accent in his speech. He wasn't quite saying "a-boot," but it was close. "Do you have any tattoos?"

"Nah. I mean, I almost got one in high school."

"Were your parents okay with it?"

"I mean, I also would have needed to get a smaller tattoo. Let's leave it at that."

Sam half smiled.

"Yeah." In truth, Skyler had and still felt guilty about going behind her parents' back. "I went to this sketchy parlor with a friend of mine at the time, Jane."

"The one you're looking for?"

"No," Skyler said. "That's Morgan. This was before we got to know each other." Morgan often tried to talk Skyler into getting a tattoo with her. She herself had tattoos all over. One of Skyler's favorites was a small hummingbird on her hand. If Skyler were ever brave enough to get a tattoo, she would get that same one. "I don't talk to Jane anymore. Last time I saw her, she was married with two kids. Anyway, she wanted to get a horse on her shoulder. I wanted a dragon. She went first. The minute I saw the needles touching her skin, I passed out."

"Really?" he asked.

"I hate needles too."

"Figured you had a stronger stomach."

"It's the weirdest thing." Despite herself, Skyler started to laugh. "I literally can't look whenever I get shots."

Sam didn't laugh, but gave her a smile that even looked half genuine. It was comforting, talking about such mundane things, escaping everything they were going through for a moment. But she couldn't completely escape. She was inside a death trap with a wounded man. She still didn't know what exactly had gone wrong in that room. Had Sam stepped wrong or...

"Oh god." She remembered when Sam had gotten ahead of her, when she had been unsure of which tile to mark. It had been halfway through the room. Left or right. About the same point where Sam's foot got skewered.

"What?" he asked.

"I think—" It was hard to say, hard to admit. She closed her eyes. "It's my fault."

"What?"

"I... I think I marked the wrong tile." Tears built in her eyes. "I'm so sorry. Everything was moving so fast and I didn't... I..."

"What do you mean you... oh." A small, dark look passed in Sam's eyes. A shade of resentment? But it quickly passed, softening. "Don't worry about it," he said. "All we can do is move forward. There's no point in crying."

"Yeah," she said, trying to swallow the pain. A rogue tear or two still came.

Sam popped a couple more painkillers. He offered the bottle to her, but she refused. While she was sore in so many places—her legs, her arms, her neck, her back—it was nothing that matched his. It would be better to conserve them.

"Do you want to go to medical school?" he asked after quietly letting the pills set in.

"What?"

"You said you should've gone to medical school. Is that what you want to do?"

"No," she replied. "I was just saying that... It would've made what I had to do easier."

"What *do* you want to do then?"

His tone assumed Skyler wasn't already doing it. Was it that obvious? "Well, I don't really know. I've sometimes thought about being a professor."

Sam winced lightly at his pain. "Of what?"

"History."

"Broad subject."

"I mean, I'm interested in the nineteenth century. I told you that, right? Also a broad subject, I know. I guess I've always been fascinated by Victorian Britain. My dad's side is very British. So maybe I'd teach that area. Of course, I'd need to go back to school first. But I don't know. Morgan always says I should."

"You sure do talk about her a lot," Sam said.

"So? She's my cousin." She realized how defensive that sounded. She hadn't talked that much about Morgan with Sam. But she wouldn't deny that Morgan was a significant part of her life, and she couldn't help but give her all to those she cared about. Sometimes that meant not giving enough to herself. In fact, Morgan often told her that too.

"What do you currently do?" Sam asked.

"Huh?" Skyler was jarred by the quick topic change.

"For work."

"Oh, I'm an administrative assistant at an elementary school."

"Hmm."

She shrugged. "It's a living. My Mom is the assistant principal there so..."

"Ah, nepotism."

"It's not like that! I had to interview like everyone else. Mom wasn't even part of the selection process." Of course, she *had* put in a very good word. "It's not like I'm next in line for assistant principal or anything. Not *everybody's* family is a part of some shadowy cult."

Sam scowled, shining the flashlight in her face for a moment, perhaps intentionally.

"We weren't—" He winced again and sighed. "We're not a cult."

"I'm sorry," Skyler said.

He glared at her a little longer until she had to avert her eyes. Here, she noticed something a few inches from his leg, a small plastic bag. Sealed inside was a folded yellow sheet of paper. Perhaps it had fallen from his backpack. She leaned forward and grabbed it.

"What is this?" she asked. Sam lunged at her, grunting from the pain, and snatched the bag away. "I'm sorry!" she said, her heart pounding. She had thought he was going to attack her.

"It's nothing to do with you." He stuffed the bag into his backpack.

There came another lull. Sam leaned back, sucking through his teeth and grunting. When the pain seemed to stabilize, he spoke again. "Just don't touch my things without my permission."

"Okay." She wanted to change the subject. "So what about your mother?" As soon as she'd asked it, Skyler realized the pitfalls of that question, the assumptions it made, the sore spots it might have touched upon.

Given the grimace on Sam, it had apparently touched one. "My what?"

"I'm just curious," she said, trying to justify herself more than anything. "You've talked so much about your father and grandfather and great-grandfather. I was curious, you know? That's all."

"It's none of your business."

That's bullshit, she wanted to say. *So you can dig deep into my life all you want. But yours has to be so mysterious that we can only touch on your family's naming conventions or the fact that you got a tattoo when you were a teenager?*

"I'm sorry," she said instead, keeping herself in check.

His face was fixed in a stony scowl. He was closing off again, putting on his "Mister Mystery" facade. Skyler wanted to ask what the hell was wrong with him.

Finally, he said his favorite line. "We should go."

He slipped on his mutilated boot, groaning and wincing at every moment. When it was done, he began standing. As soon as he put pressure on his foot, he let out another scream and fell back to the ground.

Skyler didn't know how to help him. "Maybe we should wait."

"There'll be no better time than now."

Through his tightened and pained expression, Skyler saw that soft, scared little boy again. Though Sam fancied himself a survivalist, he probably had about as much business being here as she did. He was only a little more competent between the two of them, for the most part.

"Can I help?" she asked as he brought himself back up, this time keeping his wounded foot elevated.

To no surprise, he shook his head.

She came to her feet, letting the numbness in her backside fade.

"Okay," Sam said. The pain made him look so helpless and lost, she felt a wave of pity. She knew he believed in everything he was telling her. That they were inside the snow globe. That this was a world manufactured by some mysterious tool. That it was his job to find said tool. It wasn't like Tammy, whose stories had always been inconsistent and desperate. He spoke like his truth was as real as his own flesh. He believed it so much that it drove him to go beyond his own knowledge and limitations.

Sam believed it so much that she struggled to disbelieve it.

Chapter Eight

Onward to the tower. He needed to think about nothing else. He needed to believe the tool would be there. Maybe the way out would be there too; it had to be at least somewhere.

"Though the act of creating is performed on our earthly plane, the creation in itself exists on another. One cannot simply enter the construct by means of foot or horse, ship, or automobile. A skilled craftsman must account for two things when building his world. To put it simply, he must contrive the way in, and the way out."

Maria Faragó had written that herself.

"For reasons I do not quite understand, the way in and out cannot be one in the same. Perhaps the doors between planes can only be opened from without, like that of a safe or of a particularly robust armoire. It is indispensable to note, however, that both must be present. If the entrance is crafted but its brother is not, accession will be denied. The reason for this, Orion, is an enigma to me."

It could have been a lie. But given all the truths she had offered mockingly to the eldest Samael during those years of correspondence and fabricated trust, it seemed just as likely to be true.

The meandering halls were endless and Sam grew painfully irritated. His foot was throbbing, his legs trembling. He could smell his own sweat soaking through every bit of clothing. Sometimes, he accidentally put weight on his foot, sending electric jolts of pain through his entire body. He knew he would never walk the same on that foot. He wished they hadn't lost the walking stick. Leaning against the wall was his only support. Once or twice, Skyler tried to help keep him balanced. He almost let her.

"You're still marking, right?" he asked, realizing he hadn't seen a red X in a while.

"Yeah," she replied. There were hints of irritation in her voice.

Why should *she* be upset? Sam wondered. He was the one who was falling the fuck apart. And it was all her fault for marking the wrong tile.

But it's your fault you got stuck in that room in the first place.

And why did she have to bring up his mother? Sam didn't want to think about that woman. He wasn't supposed to think about her.

As far as he knew, things never ended well when an Adamsen married.

"We have a legacy of unworthy women," his father always said.

The first Samael had married late in his life—after Maria's disappearance. His wife, nearly forty years his junior—Sam couldn't even remember her name—had a hand in raising Samael Junior before dying of an illness. Junior married his childhood sweetheart when he was just a teen. The youthful pair had Michael before Junior went to war. After Junior was killed, Michael's mother, Sam's grandmother—he also never learned her name—had been declared unfit to parent. The child was put under Samael's custody until his death, after which the young Michael was cared for by a second cousin. The boy never saw his mother again. In what way she was unfit, Sam never quite learned. Perhaps she had been the same as his own mother.

Like Samael, Sam's father had married late in life, and like his grandfather, he had married a significantly younger woman—Sam's mother—Marjorie. Sam had known her well growing up. He could still vividly remember her good night kisses, their trips to the park or the zoo. She had seemed like the embodiment of kindness, who would give money to every panhandler, who smiled at strangers and always laughed so brightly, especially with her son, her sunshine. It was odd that he remembered those little details or random facts like her maiden name being Barnes, but he couldn't completely remember what she looked like or what kind of person she had really been. He only had rose-tinted memories. She couldn't have been a good person. She had tried to abduct him. The memory of that night felt like a dream now. She'd come into his room. He could remember her looking so terrified, because it terrified him. That unidentifiable face still stared at him in his dreams sometimes, invoking the same overwhelming fear he'd felt then.

"Come here, Sam," he remembered her whispering. "Come on, baby. We need to go."

He had gone with her. He didn't remember the car ride, but it had apparently been hours. One image he could conjure in his memories was blinding whiteness. There had been a blizzard that night and they stayed at a motel. The finer details of then, however, he could not recall, but he did remember that morning. A knock at the door. His mother had begged him not to open it. But he did anyway. He didn't know who he'd thought would be there. But he opened that door to find his father, bundled up and staring down at him. Behind the tall man stood two police officers.

Weeks later, Michael would tell him that she had been planning to kill him.

"She is an unhinged woman," the man had told his eight-year-old son. "She's going someplace where she'll be helped."

Many years later, on a drunken evening, his father told him that she'd killed herself only two years after being sent to prison. Sam hadn't cried.

He hadn't wanted to. His mother had taught him that so few were worthy of trust.

Goddammit. He didn't want to think about this. But it was so hard to think about anything else. Sometimes, the pulsing pain was overwhelming, other times it seemed distant or even nonexistent, but it constantly consumed him. And the bleak, dull catacomb halls gave no distractions. It was only a matter of choosing a corner to turn down and then finding the next. They just needed to make sure they were heading toward the tower, but he could hardly tell if they were.

The tool, he thought. *Remember the tool.*

That was the thing, wasn't it? That was going to make all the pain he experienced now, and in every other moment of his life, worth it.

But something followed him through these halls, demanding his attention. It was an unexhausted specter keeping pace: a pale face, shifting eyes, frazzled hair.

The specter was whispering: *Come on, baby. We need to go.*

He wasn't going to go. Not this time. The tool—everything else was so small, even his own body and mind.

Come on.

She had once taken him to the park to feed the swans. He asked if it was a waste of bread. She said it helped the swans and that nothing that helped others could be a waste. He had found his first coin that day, a Sacagawea dollar.

His breath was laboring. When the hell would this maze end? Where were they? Everything hurt so damn much.

Come here, Sam.

The tool. It was everything.

Come on, baby.

Mommy?

He was suffocating. Each hall was growing shorter and narrower than the last.

We need to go.

Where was he going? Where the hell was he going?

Seeing you just breaks my heart.

"Light!" The sudden shout snapped his mind to attention. He brought his foot down onto the floor, causing a massive shock to surge through his body. The pain made him briefly see red.

"There's light," Skyler said again, this time her voice nearly a whisper.

Once his pain melted back to its baseline throb, Sam glared. But she wasn't looking at him. She was pointing down the hall, focusing intently as if whatever she pointed at would disappear if she didn't keep an eye on it.

There was a slight silver haze of light rounding a corner. Sam turned off his flashlight to ensure it wasn't a trick of the mind. Though the haze briefly disappeared when the hall went dark, it rematerialized as his eyes adjusted. His heart beat desperately. Licking his lips, he hobbled toward the haze, maintaining balance against the wall while trying to keep his foot off the ground. He felt like someone who had been trapped underwater, desperately swimming up for air.

"Wait!" Skyler called. He could hear her running behind him, two strides for every one of his. But he couldn't stop. It was like something was nipping at his heels.

Baby.

As he jerked around the corner, he nearly ran into a massive figure. Startled, he stumbled backward. It was an extremely tall man, standing at the window, looking out at the silver sky.

❧

"Jesus!" Skyler yelped as she came around the corner, startled by the same figure.

The man stood completely still, not betraying a single twitch. He was bulky, masculine, standing at least eight feet tall. He seemed to be wearing some kind of gray military uniform with blood-red cuffs and a helmet with a large red plume sticking upright. It looked like something a soldier from about a hundred years ago would wear. Attached to the man's hip was a sheathed sword. Whatever bit of his head was showing was clean bald; it could have been a trick of the light, but the skin almost looked blue.

"Hello?" Skyler asked, stepping forward. Sam pulled her back. If this person happened to be unfriendly, he didn't want to wind up in a fight, especially in his current shape. Yet the figure didn't turn around, didn't even move a muscle. He was like a statue.

Sam moved toward him cautiously. The windowed hall was consistently wide and seemed to stretch on endlessly on either side. Each window was separated by a few feet. Every one of them had a soldier, powerfully built and dressed exactly the same, standing by. The way they stood in their statue-like uniformity reminded Sam of the Terra Cotta army.

"Are they real?" Skyler asked, her voice weak with uncertainty.

"I don't know." He'd seen people at the windows—these windows—during the battle. People who were moving and fighting. Maybe they had looked like these soldiers. It hadn't been easy to tell from so far away. But he had seen people, at least before the bell's ringing stopped, then nothing at all.

Of course, he couldn't always trust his mind, or his memory. He recalled a memory he could swear had happened. It had been of him, his mother, and his father. They were at a park, the one where Sam and his mother would feed the swans. Young Sam had wanted to play with the other kids on the playground. His father said no, but his mother insisted that he learn to socialize with others. Incredibly, father had begrudgingly conceded. It was such a vivid memory. But once, he tried to bring it up with his father who told him that had never happened. They had never gone to the park as a family. Sam's mother had never convinced him of anything. She had never loved Sam, or Sam's father, or their family. He had to believe that was true. For all he knew, those images of that caring, laughing, smiling woman had just been fabrications. There was no photographic proof, no videos, that she had been who he thought she was. Only shadows in his head.

Come on, baby.

There was nowhere to go.

Sam turned off the flashlight and handed it to Skyler, but kept his gun well in hand. He circled to the front of the gargantuan figure to take a closer look. The nearer he came, the more he could smell the stench of steel and oil. It became clear that the soldier's head and neck were bronze, turned a sickly blue from corrosion. Apparently, some bacteria still carried over to this world. The face startled him when he first got a look at it. It was hollow, like that of a mannequin. It was masculine with a strong jaw and cheeks, but otherwise there was no real definition. The eyes were two empty indentations, the mouth a slit, the nose a bump.

"What the hell?" Skyler asked, having also come around to get a look.

Sam poked at the figure's chest. It felt rock solid. It was certain there wasn't a human being in there. He poked the chest again, slightly harder. The figure teetered a bit before falling to the ground like a chopped tree.

Skyler stared at Sam, eyes wide like he'd broken something valuable. He shrugged defensively, though she seemed more scared than angry.

They continued down the hall, passing window after window. Each statue stood like a dog waiting for its owner. Sam couldn't imagine the purpose of these things. Intimidation? Between every two statues was what appeared to be a large brass ladle sticking from the wall. Each ladle was blue and corroded like the faces of the soldiers. The dips were cauldron sized, with handles and a pouring lip on each of its sides. The ladles were attached to a mechanism along the wall that looked like a gear. This likely allowed it to be pushed or pulled toward the windows on its left and right. A thick tube that looked like an accordion rose from the ground, feeding into the bottom of the cauldron.

"What are these?" he asked, pointing to one of the devices.

"I don't know," she replied.

"It looks like some gadget from the nineteenth century. A smelting pot or what have you."

"Maybe," Skyler said uselessly.

Sam remembered the battle, the bright lava pouring on the forest creatures. Maybe it had come from these things.

"I thought you'd know what they are," he said.

"I don't."

Skyler was staring dreamily down the hall. He could imagine what she was thinking. The same thing he was. Where the hell were the actual people? He stopped to rest for a moment. His foot was throbbing. He felt weak. He wanted to lie down. But he couldn't do that yet. He stared out a nearby window. From it, he could see part of the village. Beyond it was the forest. He was glad not to be down there, even if it was hardly safer inside. Looking out from a different angle, he could see the tower. It gazed back down at him. It seemed they were heading in the right direction. Was it too much to hope that someone might be up there?

Maybe. It was also maybe too much to hope that the tool would be there. But it was a start.

The window itself caught his eye. The glass was covered with markings. Scratches, from the look of it.

Glass that cannot break.

Perhaps this wasn't the same type of glass that was in the library. The claws of those creatures were making marks while a bullet had barely given a scuff. But why would they put better glass in the library than in the castle?

As he moved forward again, he was abruptly jerked back. His backpack, mouth slightly zipped open, was caught on the hilt of a nearby statue's sword. Before he could act, the statue keeled over, like its comrade a few rows down, only a hair's length from crushing Sam's good foot. His bag flipped over and its contents spilled onto the ground.

"Fuck!" he hollered, dropping to his knees to gather this flood of provisions.

Skyler rushed in to help him put his things away. Food. Medical supplies. Every time a hand of hers hovered over an important piece of intel or documentation, he slapped it away. Before long, it was all packed away again. His backpack had already been disorganized, but haphazardly packing everything in made it more of a train wreck. He'd figure it out later. Zipping up his bag and tossing it over his shoulder, he nodded at Skyler, who nodded back. They only took a few steps before she stopped again.

"Um, Sam."

He groaned and turned to her. She was looking at her feet. Her brows had a furrowed, guilty look to them.

"What?" he asked, leaning against the wall and keeping his injured foot in the air.

"I…"

She began reaching into her pocket when suddenly, the room shook with a deep thrum. At first, Sam thought another statue had fallen over. But the sound was louder than that. It bounced from the walls, beat into his eardrums, and filled the pit of his stomach with a guttural ache. The thrum faded and immediately began again, playing in short, repetitive bursts.

The bell, he quickly realized—the damn bell was ringing. The walls groaned and hissed like an angry, metallic dragon had awakened. The light bulbs hanging from the ceiling flared alive. Electric coils danced within them, lighting up the entire room with their lively celebration. A faint gurgling came from beneath his feet, the sound crawling toward the windows. The gurgle became louder as it carried up the accordion tube beneath the nearest cauldron. The cauldron's pit quickly lit up with bright liquid. Up and down the hall, every cauldron was bright and smoldering. The corridor was instantly filled with an overpowering smell—a chemical, acrid kind that singed his nose hairs.

Then came a loud creak, sounding like a poorly oiled seesaw. Skyler gasped and snatched his arm. The statue, the one he had just knocked over—it was sitting up. Once its back was slowly straightened, it turned its head, looking, if it could even see anything, straight at Sam. He still couldn't register what he was seeing as the statue came to its feet, creaking and popping with every movement, the hollow craters that were its eyes perpetually fixed on him.

Thrum. Thrum.

A chorus of creaking rose through the room. All along the hall, the statues were moving. Some of them were cricking their necks like a fighter limbering up. Others were gradually unsheathing their swords. Despite the sluggishness and painful sounding pops and creaks, their movements were seamless. They appeared quite human, even if something was unidentifiably off.

Sam knew they needed to run. Yet he was paralyzed by fear and fascination. The castle, which had seemed so dead up to this point, was now alive, all to the sickening thrum of that bell.

The statue that stared at him was now lurching in. Its legs cracked and popped angrily. Seeing its approach shook him from his daze. As soon as it reached for its sword, he aimed his gun and fired, somewhat stumbling back from not taking a proper stance. The gunshot gave the statue pause, but otherwise it showed no reaction. The smoking hole in its chest, lightly oozing with a black substance, was the only evidence it had been hit at all.

"Run," Skyler said, her voice wheezing anxiously. "We sh-should. We—"

He fired twice more, the pops fading into the mess of the other noises. Again, the statue was hit in the chest. But though it was stunned, it was not down. He pulled the trigger one more time, but nothing happened. He tried it again and again before realizing the gun had jammed.

"Fuck!"

Now the statues all throughout the hall were focused on Sam and Skyler, their hollow eye sockets staring emptily. The one Sam had shot slowly withdrew its sword. There was no fury in this action, no thirst for vengeance. It moved like it was just doing a job. It raised its sword above its head, nearly aligning it with the plume of its helmet.

Sam charged forward, attempting to tackle the statue. The thing was much sturdier than it had been while dormant, but he still managed to knock it against the window. Its sword clattered to the ground. With its hands free, it grabbed Sam. He tried to pull away, but its grip was mechanically tight. It whipped around so he was closest to the window and slammed him into it over and over, in rhythm with the thrum above. Sam thought the window would break any moment. But it didn't. *He* would sooner be smashed into pieces than the glass. The only thing softening the blow was his backpack. He could feel and hear the contents inside breaking apart. His body felt like it would burst like a balloon any moment. The smell of hot liquid from the cauldron next to him filled his nostrils. He feared the statue would dip his head in there. It could do anything it wanted to. He was helpless.

The slamming stopped. A sharp, black blade sputtered through the statue's stomach, splashing oily liquid on Sam's face. The thing looked over its broad shoulder at Skyler. Her eyes were wide, her hands trembling, as if unsure of what she had just done. The statue dropped Sam to the floor, reached back, and slowly pulled out the sword as it turned toward Skyler. The other statues were standing by and watching, staying silently and dutifully in their spots, observing, spectating, waiting to see how this would pan out.

"Sam?" Skyler cried out. She sounded like she was on the verge of panicking. "Sam?" He tried to think of something, but he was still jostled. His back, neck and head hurt, though it still didn't hold a candle to the pain in his foot. He looked to the window. At the bottom were large latches. Neither thinking nor hesitating, he pulled at the latches hard and threw the window open.

"Sam!"

He turned back to see the statue swinging its sword at Skyler's head. She threw herself to the ground as the blade smashed into the wall. The statue tugged at the sword as she crawled away. The blade had apparently been embedded in the stone.

This was his chance. It was time to be the hero.

You are more than anyone else, father always said. *You're more than what you want to be. All you have to do is step up.*

He lunged forward and shoved the statue. The attack didn't budge it, but it still turned and focused its hollow sockets on him.

You're going to be a really good person, he heard his Mom saying. *You don't have to be a 'great' person, you just have to be a good one.*

The statue creaked furiously as it reached for him. He quickly dropped to the ground and scrambled through its legs. Once he was on the other side and getting to his feet, the thing was already facing him again. But the statue was too late to react as he threw himself against it, hoping to push it out the window. As it tumbled backward, it wrapped its arms around him, clutching him like a scared child holding a teddy bear.

Come on, baby.

He couldn't move. The statue held him tight as it continued falling out the open window. Before he realized what was happening, he was falling too.

"Sam!" he could hear Skyler shout. But her voice was quickly lost in the cool, stale air. Then all he could hear was the thrumming bell.

Chapter Nine

What the fuck had just happened?

Skyler couldn't think clearly enough to know. One minute, Sam was being attacked. She thought he was going to be broken in two. Then she took the sword. She couldn't even remember deciding to do that. She had to use all her strength to lift and thrust it into the thing's back. It felt like cutting into a frozen piece of meat. She remembered how terrified she felt when it didn't fall, but instead went for her. The rest happened so fast. The blade came at her and she hit the ground like it was second nature. The thing, the "automaton" as she dubbed them, turned back to Sam. Next thing she knew, they were both gone.

Now, she was alone.

No, not necessarily. The walls bubbled and hissed and groaned around her. The lights flickered above. The bell's ringing pounded into her body. And all the remaining automatons were staring at her. The one closest to her drew its sword and shambled her way.

Creak. Creak. Creak.

There was no time for fear. She considered taking the sword out of the wall, try to fight back, but immediately decided against it. Running was her best option. The automaton raised its sword. She crawled forward underneath its legs like Sam had done earlier, scraping her arms against the stone floor. She felt the overwhelming thud of the blade coming down behind her. She scrambled to her feet and ran down the hall. Each automaton she passed unsheathed its sword but wasn't quick enough to strike. She only had a little space to maneuver, as the hulking figures took up so much of the hall. She had to practically hug the wall. One of the automatons reached out and managed to snag her, its tight grip clutching her sleeve. She scrambled out of her sweatshirt before the machine could do anything more.

Another stood at the end of the hall, waiting patiently for her with a sword raised. But to her left was a new entryway. She hurtled through it without hesitation.

She was in another mazelike hall. But everything was lit now, the coiled lights illuminating the stone corridor with their flickering glow. She could feel the automatons watching her from the entryway. But she wasn't going to stop and see if they were pursuing.

She took a right at the first fork.

Toward the bell tower, she thought. *Keep going toward the bell tower.*

It was easier to navigate a maze with everything so bright. But the flickering, accompanied by the thrumming bell, was disorienting in its own way. If it stopped, though, and everything went dark again, she would be doomed. The thought of being trapped in the darkness pushed her forward. She came to a large entryway that led to a staircase down into a narrow hall. The hall was short and led into a large, round room. Like everything else in the castle, it was sparse. There were only two unique things about the space: a slick, black-tiled floor with white night-sky patterns—more constellations—and a stairwell that spiraled up.

There was something else. Though the thrumming was still everywhere, it was most prominent right above her. Was this it? Was this the tower?

The thrumming ceased. Quickly after, the grinding and growling in the walls and beneath her feet died down and the lights slowly dimmed. Everything became dark. Skyler could hear her own breathing picking up, her heart pulsating. She felt trapped, consumed, powerless. But then, she realized, she wasn't completely blind. There was some dim light. It was coming from the top of the spiral stairs.

She felt less trapped but still terrified. There was no semblance of safety here. But this was almost certainly the tower. This is where she wanted to be, where they both had wanted to go. But now she was alone. Sam was gone and had taken everything with him: food, water, the flashlight, the gun. All she had was her phone, the rubber band in her hair, and a little Ziploc bag with an old piece of paper in it. That had come from Sam's backpack. She'd pocketed it while helping him pick up his things. She'd had no bad intent, she only wanted to know what the hell it was and why Sam had it. In fact, she'd surprised herself by taking it. Something was happening to her here, changing her, and she didn't think she liked it. At any rate, she had been ready to fess up and give it back to him. But then... everything happened.

Skyler took in the aching hunger in her gut, the dryness in her mouth, the slight dehydrated ache in her shoulder. It still felt like Sam would come limping in at any moment. He would bark some order in that annoying, self-assured way. But at least she wouldn't be alone. Then she would have a chance.

She knew he wasn't coming. But she also knew that she didn't want to give in. The only place to go was up.

∽

There were more automatons on the second floor. About seven or eight of them stood vigilantly, each at its own window. She nearly retreated back down the steps when she first saw them. But she quickly realized they were inert again. There were also a few of those cauldron things. She could smell the molten ooze, though the cauldrons appeared to be empty.

Skyler carefully and quietly moved across the room, though the caution was hardly necessary. Reaching the next stairwell, she noticed a long, metal slit trailing up each wall. It looked like the track for a wheelchair lift. Despite her eagerness, she slowly moved up the stairs. Halfway up, one of the steps slightly sank. Startled by this, she fell forward, hitting her chest against a step, knocking the wind out of her. It was a sensation of breathlessness she hadn't felt since childhood, getting too rowdy at the playground. She felt something *whoosh* above her head. Ahead of her, a thin, silver shape glided along the stairs before quickly retracting into one of the metal slits. A blade. She rested her forehead against a cold stone step, regaining her breath. Had she not tripped, she would have been skewered. Her stomach clenched. She just had to breathe. To breathe and keep going.

She crawled the rest of the way, keeping herself pressed against the stairs, not thinking about what might be around the next corner, but just about getting there.

The next floor was identical to the last. But this time, there was that familiar rotting, swampy stench. She could see the claw marks on the floor, leading from one of the windows toward the stairs. At the foot of the stairs was a mossy, humanoid body. It had been severed in two—the halves only connected by a trail of black blood.

She cautiously stepped around the body, keeping her distance and watching it as if it would leap alive and grab her. It allowed her a close look at one of the creatures. Its skin was unmistakably humanlike, sagging and discolored as it was. She could even make out moles. The moss around its body seemed papery. It didn't look like it had grown on the creature but instead had been threaded into its skin. This close, the smell was nearly blinding.

She crawled up the stairs, again pressing herself tightly as possible against the steps. Eventually, she reached a switch step and felt the blades swish overhead. She reached the fourth floor this way, then the fifth, sixth, seventh, and eighth. The stairs scraped her skin from all the crawling. But it was a worthwhile measure. Every stairway had a trap.

Ninth floor. Tenth. Eleventh. Twelfth.

The dehydrated ache in her shoulder grew worse, her stomach curdled, her vision grew hazy, and she was seeing spots. But she kept going.

Thirteenth. Fourteenth. Fifteenth.

It was never ending.

Sixteenth. Seventeenth.

She wasn't sure she could do this anymore.

Eighteenth. Nineteenth.

On this last floor, she reached a stairwell that didn't seem to have any traps. There were no metal grids along its walls. At the top of it was a steel door. She hoped beyond hope that she had finally reached the top. Despite the apparent safety, she still crawled. Once she reached the door, she pushed and pulled at it. It wouldn't move. It was like a safe that had been sealed for years.

She pounded on the steel, shouting.

"Hey!" Her voice was raspy. "Hey!"

There was only silence on the other side. Nobody was in there. She knew it.

"Hey!" She pounded as hard as her trembling arms would allow. "Please!"

She was alone. She had come all this way for nothing. Tears burned in her eyes, she was sick and exhausted.

"Hey!" Her fists hurt, but she kept pounding. Her grief turned to fury now; beating into the lifeless steel door was all she could do. All it could do in turn was answer with a hollow echo. "Please!"

Suddenly, she heard a loud pop from the door. Her first thought was that she had caused the noise. But then came another pop. The door flew open, its hinges giving the same terrible creak as the automatons' limbs.

She was face-to-face with a hunched old man. He wore filthy rags that hung from his extremely thin body. He scowled at her beneath his sinewy white beard. His beady, sunken eyes glared at her. His skin was so pale and his body so concave, he looked ghoulish.

Skyler held her breath and said nothing. He didn't frighten her, but she was hardly relieved to see him either. The man smacked his lips and gave an acrid smile. Most of his teeth were missing, though a few black and yellow mounds poked from his gums. She noticed he smelled like a flooded basement.

"Ah, yes." He had a soft, nasally voice. "Of course. Of course. Yes. Come in, then."

Part Three
The Tower

Chapter Ten

T HERE WAS NO MORE thrumming when he came to. Everything was silent. The first thing he saw was the sky. Its silvery gleam seemed particularly bright at the moment. His back hurt, as did his neck. His foot throbbed. He felt like he was lying on an agonizingly hard bed, or the hood of a car. There was a pungent smell of metal and rot.

Turning away from the sky, he came nose-to-nose with a hollow face. The statue. Its empty eye sockets stared back at him. It was still clutching him against its body. With a jolt of panic, he scrambled from its grip. The arms surprisingly, and quickly, gave way in lifeless submission. Before he could take himself off the statue, he realized the grassy ground was about two stories down. They seemed to be suspended in midair.

It took some glancing around, and some easing of his aching head, to realize what had happened. All along the wall, beside and below him, were rows of curved spikes. The statue had fallen onto one or two of them. Luckily for him, the points hadn't sunk all the way through. He straddled the statue like a horse, one leg stretching out, the other resting along the base of a spike. Above him, he could see the open window, but it was too far to climb to. The castle's stone walls were jagged, but not enough for him to get a solid grip.

"Skyler!" he shouted toward the window.

There was no answer.

"Skyler! Are you up there? Skyler!"

He let the silence sit a bit before letting out a loud, "Skyyleeer!"

Nothing. She'd obviously moved on. If she were alive at all.

He looked down to the grass again. It was quite a drop. Probably something he could survive, but high enough to likely break his leg. His foot was already fucked. Emboldened by his acknowledgment, it gave a sharp sting.

Goddammit was all he could think. He adjusted his backpack. It had been nearly flattened in the statue's grip, some of the contents likely crushed to pieces. There was only one way down unless he wanted to nest up here until he starved to death.

The statue slightly rocked as he pulled his weight off its body. But it was embedded enough in the spikes to remain stable.

Come on, baby.

He used the spikes as footholds, at least for his uninjured foot. For his other leg, he rested his knee on a spike's curvature. The sharp points were too high for him to raise his legs up and over; he had to slide his foot in and his knee out to get to the next one. Making his way down the jagged wall was tricky and painful. He often poked and nicked himself, at one point even shallowly slicing his hand. They snagged his pants, his shirt. His backpack got slightly caught on one and nearly spilled out again. But that wouldn't have been the worst-case scenario. One slip, one stupid move, and he would be skewered. Stuck like a pig until his body rotted away, like the green and black residue he could see dripping from other parts of the wall.

He became moist with sweat, making him more and more slippery. He kept his eye on the ground, the grass which was growing closer.

Come on, baby. It's time to go.

He rested, when at last, he was off of the barbed wall and onto the rocky plateau. It was still a little way to the grass, but at least he was past the tricky part. Above him, the statue was still mounted to the wall.

Poor bastard, he thought. But it was just a machine. Lifelike, but a machine nonetheless.

He finished his brief respite and continued. He crawled down the rocks to keep weight off his foot. The stone scraped against his knees and elbows. More than halfway down, he slipped and fell. It was only a few feet, but he still hit the grass. The pain at least was only in his shoulder and faded quickly. He was certain he hadn't broken anything and he thanked his lucky stars he hadn't landed on his foot.

The rough football field-like grass scratched at his skin, but he was happy to feel it. The ground almost seemed to welcome him. Sweet Earth, or whatever the hell this was. He breathed in fully. After the suffocation of the castle, the strange, stale air of the outdoors was a dream. The silvery sky was a little brighter than usual, as if somehow the sun managed to shine a light in this world but could only peek through a wall of cloud.

The sky wanted him to stay. The grass wanted him to stay. The air wanted him to stay. But his place, his purpose, was back in the castle. He knew that in his gut. Besides, if Skyler were alive, he couldn't leave her there alone for too long.

And you can't be left alone for too long either.

He sat up and removed his backpack. Before he did anything else, it was best to do an inventory check. Food, water, and defense were the main necessities as far as he was concerned; that became his focus when he sifted through the contents of his bag. First thing he found was his jacket. Though patches of it were slightly hardened by blood, he decided to put it back on. It felt as secure as armor. His canteen was dented, but fine. It needed to be refilled. All of the protein and granola bars were crushed but still edible. If he'd been smarter, or at least if he'd known the extent of what he was getting into, he would have invested in military rations. There was the half-empty first aid box, broken but the contents usable. Otherwise, he had some deodorant, a Ziploc bag containing a toothbrush and toothpaste that had burst from its tube, his notes, batteries, a lighter, and a flashlight, miraculously still working. There were few things he could use as a weapon. If necessary, he could use the flashlight as a blunt weapon. But if he was going back in the dark castle, he would prefer not to break it. He had his small pocketknife, the blade still black from when Skyler cauterized his wounds. There was also a Swiss Army knife somewhere in there. But given what he was up against, he needed more.

One of the backpack pockets was filled with bullets and a couple clips. The ammunition box had been crushed open. Where was his gun? It had fallen with him out the window, that he remembered. It had to be somewhere around there. He stood and searched the grass. It didn't take long before he came upon two black objects.

"Fuck," he muttered. The gun was broken in pieces. Of course, the damn thing had jammed anyway. He had neither the expertise nor tools to fix it. He would have to find a weapon in the village. Maybe he would find an axe or a pick. Maybe a machete, sword, or even a working gun, if he was lucky. Perhaps he'd find more provisions too.

He limped toward the village, swallowing his bitterness. If only he'd known. If he'd had so much as a hint of what he would be facing in this world, he would have brought his arsenal. He would've brought a damn army. Or at least friends, not that he had any. His father had always discouraged that. Friends were only potential enemies. Loyal followers were a different story, as long as you kept them believing in you. But even then, the Adamsens could only rely on Adamsens. Sometimes, Sam liked being a loner, keeping this secret. He liked going down to the shooting range to train, knowing a great truth the hobbyists and survivalists would never know. There was power to that.

But other times, being alone was the last thing he wanted. Those moments of weakness were his to overcome. There was no denying, however, that being a loner was much easier when everything wasn't trying to kill him.

Along the way, he could see the two headstones a few clicks from him. Beyond them was the dead tree, its sallow and rotting form lingering above the graves. His foot throbbed with each step. He wanted to lessen the weight he was putting on it as much as possible, but he wasn't adept at hopping on one foot for long either. He considered fashioning another walking stick from one of the dead tree's branches.

But maybe he would find something better in the village.

The street's bulky and uneven cobblestones were no easier on his feet. But he pushed through it. His first objective was to get to the stream and refill his canteen. He didn't like the idea of getting so close to the forest again.

Just a few minutes, said a faint urge in his head. *Just step in there for a few minutes.*

He limped through the square, past the open well. He still vividly remembered waking down there, after he'd raised the snow globe above his head. Panic had nearly gotten the best of him, pathetically enough. If he had noticed the corpses before climbing out, it may very well have.

Child.

The dark, empty windows of the buildings watched him. He almost expected to see a ghostly face peer out from one of them. Of course, he'd never believed in ghosts.

"There is power in this world," his father had once told him. "Power a simpler man would call supernatural. On our own, we are nothing more than meat, worthless meat that goes bad and rots. Then it's gone for good. Only the power gives us meaning, makes our stories worthwhile. The tool? No, the tool is just a vessel of this power. I'm talking about, well, I don't fully know. But this power is significant. It makes us matter beyond the scope of human history, even beyond the history of the universe. It makes us weavers of fate itself. We have no soul or spirit or what have you. We are meat and bone. But with this power, we can craft our own souls..." And so on, as the scotch flowed.

Maybe this place was Maria Faragó's soul. That would explain why it felt haunted.

Leaving the village and walking across the fallow field toward the forest, his unease grew. The forest was undeniably haunted. But he'd seen the demons that haunted it with his own eyes.

He made his business at the stream quick: splashed some water on his face, drank a couple handfuls, refilled the canteen, and hustled back to the village. His foot protested, but he wasn't going to accommodate its need for rest. At least, not until he found a weapon.

Sitting somewhat apart from the rest of the village was a stout cottage. It was encased in a gray stone resembling the kind the castle was made of. Next to it was a wooden barn, only big enough to comfortably hold one or two animals. From the outside, at least, the cottage appeared simple and cozy. Back in the day, when he almost thought he'd had someone to share a future with, this was the kind of house he pictured that future being in. Somewhere quiet, peaceful. In such a future, he wouldn't have his purpose anymore. In fact, he would be completely unimportant. But if he'd had a choice, would that be so bad? Finding the tool would give meaning to all he'd been through in life, the struggle, the disappointment, the loneliness. But maybe *she* would've given him another meaning.

Maybe.

Along the side of the barn was an old-fashioned outhouse, crescent moon on the door and everything. Sam relieved himself in there before heading into the cottage proper. The house was as simple inside as on the outside: a kitchen on the left, a hearth in the center, and to the right, a bed, a fragile looking wooden chair, and a wardrobe. The place reeked of rotting vegetables and moldy bread. There was also a desk beside the entrance—the only thing in the house that wasn't purely necessity. But even it was mostly sparse other than some paper and a pen lying in a dry inkwell.

One of the papers had writing on it:

"If I'm gone, leave this World.

To Hell with what our Lady says.

Keep the heid, get to the castle, and leave.

- Mayor Shanks."

Sam remembered the signs on the doors of the village with the same handwriting:

"STAY INSIDE - ORDER OF MAYOR SHANKS"

So this was where the mayor of the town had lived. He must have been a down-to-earth guy, or at least tried to be.

Sam hobbled to the bed and sat on it, finally appeasing his whining foot. He decided to look at his wounds, assess the damage. He always liked seeing the source of his pain; it made him feel a little better, at least for a while. He peeled off his shoe. It felt like he was taking skin with it. Once it was off, he could see the wounds peeking through the loose bandages and dried blood. Both were black, but also slightly yellow around the edges. His feet hadn't stunk so much since the time he'd gotten athlete's foot. Despite everything, they still got infected. But what did he expect? After all, he'd had an amateur stick a searing knife on them. He still had some disinfectant. He hardly knew how much it would help at this point but he took it out of his backpack and poured some on. The sting made his vision blur.

His father often talked about pain.

"The pain I've gone through for *your* sake... Your mother was a monster... You were insolent... I've smiled through my tears for you. For what you could be."

Sam wondered if this made up for that.

The stinging slowly subsided, but the throb continued. At least he could breathe again. Glancing around him, he noticed something sticking out from under the bed. It looked like the smooth hilt of an axe. He pulled it out. It was rusty but still sharp.

Thank you, Mayor Shanks.

He drank some water and poured a little on his wound. It stung, but not as much as the disinfectant, and it felt kind of good. He ate two protein bars, cookie dough and mint chip. He was too hungry to leave it at one. There probably wouldn't be any food in the house worth pilfering. It took all he had to stop from devouring a third bar.

After his feast, Sam laid back. The old, dusty blanket beneath him was wooly, the pillow hard as a rock. Mayor Shanks had apparently not been a man who worried about comfort. Sam wasn't either, at least he tried not to be. Though if he'd built this house, made it his home with Casey, maybe he would've included a softer bed. Some indoor plumbing too, probably. Maybe a bedroom. Maybe an extra bedroom, just in case.

It didn't matter anyway. He was so exhausted that this bed felt like heaven.

Everything was dead quiet but for a small ringing in his ears. He didn't have time for rest, he knew. He had to get back to the castle.

But he closed his eyes anyway.

Chapter Eleven

This place was straight out of an old fairy tale, the tower keep where a young princess was held prisoner. Except Jon McKinnon was no princess. He looked more like the evil goblin imprisoning her.

Skyler looked around the library while she ate a bowl of soup consisting of peppers and chickpeas. Books covered nearly every wall. It was not an orderly library, with many other books strewn about the floor and the table. Old leather-bound tomes and case-bound novels. Some had hard cases, others had fabric lining that was wearing away. Their pages were thick and yellow.

With each spoonful, she savored the warm liquid running down her throat. The soup was flat and unseasoned, but it was satisfying to get food of any kind into her stomach. Though it was thin enough, she still washed it down with a cup of water. She couldn't care less about the strange, sweet taste anymore. Every drop felt like a rain shower on a dying field. The water came from a well in the garden. According to Jon, the well went all the way down, tapping directly into an aquifer beneath the tower.

"Father thought of everything," the old man had explained. Skyler often needed to strain herself to hear his soft, nasally voice. But he talked a lot, so she'd rarely have to worry about missing anything. "*Everything.* Father built this castle, as you know. The Frenchman designed it, but

Father built it. Well, I suppose it was the army of builders who did, but Father is the reason why she lives and breathes the way she does. Doesn't she breathe well? Course, she's asleep most of the time. But that was the genius of Father's design. Doesn't have to wake up until Vivian comes a'calling. Finest engineer of our time, Father."

From another room, she heard him let out a hacking cough. He had retired to the privy while she ate her dinner. He was certainly a strange man. He hadn't asked Skyler who she was, or what she was doing here, or how she had survived. It was like he already knew all of that. The first thing he had done after letting her in and proudly introducing himself was show her around the tower keep, like a kid showing off his toys. She had been so exhausted, so hazy and confused, that she just went along with it.

The library was the first room upon entering the keep.

"I think I've read every book in this place," Jon had boasted. "Just about. I suppose, at least."

Next, he had shown her the privy. A fowl-smelling closet with little but a grimy chamber pot and a window to empty it from. The walls were stained yellow and brown. She would have expected flies to be swarming the place, but it was devoid of life.

Before moving on from the horrible privy, he had squinted and pointed a gnarled fingernail at her shirt. "Wings?" His sunken eyes had widened as much as they could. "Wings! And these are... Are these letters? What do they say?"

"Aerosmith," Skyler said.

"Aero-Smith?"

She had felt too tired to explain what that was.

"Is that your profession? An 'Aero-Smith'?"

Thinking back on that made Skyler chuckle. But he had been completely serious, even if he'd quickly lost interest in the subject and began gushing about his father. He explained why plumbing, in whatever primitive form that would take, hadn't been a lucrative option.

"This tower was meant to be lived in for only months. Maybe two or so years. Mama, Father, and me. Months only. Has it been only months? Who's to say? Days don't work here like they do in the other world. Who's to say. One minute I was a boy, then the next I was old." He had cackled at that. Then he had finally moved them away from the privy, just as Skyler was on the verge of fainting from the smell.

Other world, she reflected. She hardly felt any resistance to that thought. She hardly felt anything about it at all. Perhaps she was accepting that this was another world. And perhaps this world was inside a snow globe in the basement of an abandoned mom-and-pop shop. But it still was hard to understand how this was possible, despite all Sam's talk of "tools" and "secret societies."

Maybe Jon would know, she considered, sipping the soup. She heard him let out another cutting cough and groan. She hoped he wouldn't die in there.

Next on the tour had been the kitchen. It was almost as disgusting as the privy. Pots and pans were strewn about, muck spattered on the floor and the ceiling. It had the strong, sour stench of rotted food. There was a large black stove with elegant patterns on its front. It looked like a relic from the nineteenth century, or at least the early twentieth.

A time capsule, Skyler reflected, much like Jon himself.

He had directed her attention to one of the walls. Several small, dead creatures were nailed in a row. They looked like birds of varying sizes, some of them scraggly and misshapen. They all had that mossy coating.

"My collection," Jon had explained gleefully. "Tried to come in here. They broke my window, you know. The glass is meant to be impenetrable. Impenetrable! But they broke it. I don't remember when. But it hadn't happened before. Never. I thought the glass was impenetrable, you know. It's the same glass that keeps this world enclosed. Now they can break through it. They've adapted. You can see why I'm so important in this war."

The same glass that keeps this world enclosed. She hadn't asked him about that, nor what he meant by war.

Returning to the library, they had moved up to the second floor. The first thing she had noticed at the top of the creaking wooden stairs was a ladder along the wall. It led up into what looked to be an attic. Jon didn't take her up there, in fact, he seemed to make a point of keeping himself between her and the rungs.

"That's where she is," he said, pointing toward the attic. His voice had an affectionate air, as if he were gushing about his spouse. "Vivian. When I smell them, the forest's army... I always smell them you know. When I smell them, I go up there and we dance. Like Quas-i-modo in Notre Dame. It awakens everything, as you know."

At the time, Skyler had been too out of it to know what he was talking about. But now, she realized he had been talking about the bell. That fucking bell—and he was the one who rang it.

To the right of the stairs was a green door Jon had disregarded, instead leading her to the left. This brought them into a greenhouse. The minute they entered, Skyler felt like she was in a humid jungle. The garden was aligned with rows of crops; within each row was a metal contraption that sprayed water. The glass ceiling was high. High enough that, toward one end of the room, two small peach trees had grown. They looked a bit sickly. In fact, all the crops in the garden looked like they were fighting desperately to stay alive. But apparently, they not only survived, they produced enough to keep Jon alive.

"This tower was only meant to be lived in for months," Jon had repeated. He often repeated things. "Months! But Father built a garden so we could produce our own food. It wouldn't have been a safe undertaking, trying to run supplies through the castle—or gurney it up either. So, Father felt we ought to feed ourselves while we're up here. Then, he realized we ought to live here and feed ourselves forever. Used to be able to grow more, but things died over the years. Used to even raise chickens!"

To his point, a grungy old coop sat in one corner of the greenhouse.

"I do miss meat," he had said, and she saw drool ooze from his lip.

Next to the peach trees was a pumping well that brought the drinking water. It took several tries for Jon to get the water up to the spout. Skyler had even started thinking the well might be dry. But eventually, water had come. Jon had gathered some into the cup of his calloused hand and drank before encouraging her to do the same. She drank and it was wonderful.

"Father is the most brilliant man I know," Jon had prattled on while Skyler savored the water. He had stopped pumping and slowly, the well petered out. "Absolutely brilliant. Much more so than the Frenchman. Though I'd say they are equals in chess." Jon let out a weak and throaty laugh. "Maybe in that, at least."

The way he talked about his father and the Frenchman made Skyler wonder if they were still alive and somewhere up here. Jon looked at least a century old. How old would his father be?

Just as Skyler finished her bowl of soup, Jon lumbered from the privy. He mumbled a tuneless song beneath his breath.

"The forest will never win..."

He slowly sat across from her, his bones creaking with every movement. It was a long way down. Even hunched, he was a tall man.

"What is your name?" he asked.

It caught her off guard. "I'm uh—Skyler."

"Sky?"

"—ler. Skyler."

"Sky-ler," Jon whispered, his mouth curled in a gummy prospector's grin. "That's good." He cricked his neck, the sound reminding Skyler of the creaking limbs of the automatons.

"What are those things?" she asked while the thought was in her mind. She had so many questions, it was overwhelming.

"What?"

"Downstairs, in the castle, the automatons." Jon dully stared at her as if she'd said a tongue twister. "They're tall... and..."

"Ah! Noémie's children!"

"Noémie?" The name sounded familiar.

"Noémie Goddard. A brilliant maker of automata." He spoke slowly, trying to get the details straight. "Her creations dazzled the spirit and treated the eyes."

Skyler remembered why she recognized the name. "I think I saw her grave."

Jon disregarded the observation. "With the Society's resources and Father's assistance, Noémie was able to make her children powerful and rather smart. Frightening, wouldn't you say? But, as you know, they... they only awaken to Vivian's song. To our dance."

"To fight the..." She nodded toward one of the windows.

"The forest's army? Yes, indeed. Very true indeed."

"How long have you been doing that?" she asked. "How long have you been up here?"

Jon looked to the ceiling, his eyes in a dreamy haze.

"Jon?"

"It was supposed to be automatic, you know," he said, his red, sunken eyes still not acknowledging her. "That is why we lived up here. Mama and Father and I. Father wanted Vivian to be able to ring on her own. But the forest began taking the people below, one by one. Soon we were alone. Mama..." The old man gave an airy wheeze that Skyler realized was laughter. "Mama wanted to leave this world altogether. She said, 'we need to pack our bags and find the way out.'"

The way out. A spark of hope crackled in her stomach.

In a flash, Jon turned solemn. "But Father said, he says 'we're going to stay.' You see, the sky had spoken to him, it had told him of his purpose. Or, I suppose it was *my* purpose. But he couldn't have known that at the time."

"The sky?"

"The forest and the sky." He stopped there, as if expecting her to understand what he meant. When she said nothing, he grunted irritably and continued. "They are alive, you know. Always fighting. Always, always."

"Why?"

Jon dragged his fingernails against the table in a pencil-drawing motion. He smiled at her as if that explained everything. Before she could ask him to elaborate, he continued.

"The forest. It wants more and more and more. The sky just wants to watch and to love. It tries, you know... to appease the forest. But the forest can never be appeased. More and more and more. That is my purpose. An automatic system would never do. The castle needs a watchful guardian. Father knew that. Mama couldn't understand." Jon wheezed amusedly again. "He just threw her out the window."

It took a moment for Skyler to register what he just said. He had spoken like as if recounting a funny story about his pants falling down.

"What do you mean he threw her?"

"Bedroom window," Jon said. "She fell and fell!"

"So he... he killed her?"

"What's that?"

"He killed her?" she said louder.

Jon nodded. "I don't remember much after that. I do remember I took a pan and thwacked him in the back of the head." Jon's wheeze built into a cackle. "We both had a good laugh about it later. We laughed quite a bit. Quite a bit. We still do."

"Where is your Father?" Skyler asked.

"With the Frenchman."

She patiently asked him who that was.

"Bastien Lemercier!" Jon said the name as if it were obvious, shouting as loudly as his soft voice allowed. "The architect of this castle. Smart fellow, but nothing without Father."

"He's here too?" She didn't know if she wanted to meet the fucked-up mind responsible for this castle.

Jon nodded. "He's actually Canadian. But he talks like a frog. Thinks he's the progeny of a famous architect, Lemercier. He thinks himself an ingénue." He pronounced that word like in-gen-u. Then he cackled again. Something about his laugh made her feel uneasy. It wasn't that it was cold. It was the opposite, in fact. It seemed too warm and joyful for a place like this. "The dimwit fell into one of the traps. One of *his* traps."

Skyler thought about Sam, about how much he had bled when the blades impaled his foot, how much he screamed. She didn't want to think about him. It made her feel sick and sad. It made her feel alone.

"So," she started, shifting the subject to something more productive, "you said something about a way out?"

"What?" His hearing was obviously weak.

"A way out! A way out of this, this world. This snow globe." Skyler was still surprised at how much she accepted that concept. But whether she was actually inside of a snow globe or not didn't feel like the urgent priority anyway.

"Snow globe?" It took a senile delay before Jon nodded. "The vessel for the world. The cover. Ingenious, really."

"But there's a way out, right?"

"Eh?"

"A way out of this world."

"Oh yes," Jon said. "Yes, yes. But it's hidden deep in the castle. Only four people know of it."

"Your father and Bastien?" Skyler assumed.

"Yes. And Maria, of course. And that little shadow of hers."

This confirmation made her breathless. Perhaps a little more hopeful than she should have been. "Can't we just ask them? Your father, I mean. Or... or Bastien?"

Jon laughed again. This time there was a hint of malice, its echo scratching into the walls. "Why would they answer? It is a secret they swore to keep. We all must accept that. Secrets must be kept. And some secrets must be kept from *us*. It is what all those who serve the Society need to accept. Understand. At the top are the elites, the wealthy and powerful who control the Society and its secrets. Even they have their own pecking order among themselves. The old guard are at the very top.

Those born into the Society. The Faragós and their ilk. Then there are the newly indoctrinated families, like those Adamsen dogs. Below them are the talented, like my father and the Frenchman and Noémie. And their families of course." He pointed proudly to himself. "Not always wealthy or privileged, but brilliant enough to join and serve, to be gifted whatever secrets will allow them to serve the Society best. Then at the bottom are the servants, the builders, the farmers, workers, foot soldiers. Not official members, are they. But they are taken care of. And below even them are the outsiders."

He pointed at her. Discouragement was crawling back into her heart. But she refused to succumb to it. There *was* a way out. As long as that much was true, there was hope. It was clear, however, that she wasn't going to learn where it was from Jon. But maybe she would be able to ask the other two, whatever state they might be in. *If* they were even real or alive. At any rate, she would have to get Jon's permission before she could see them.

He mumbled so lowly she couldn't make out the words. She only knew he was speaking to her from the fact that his eyes were staring directly into hers.

"Father wanted to do great things," was the first legible thing she heard. "He believed he had much to make up for. He had helped build many terrible weapons in the Great War. He wanted to build something that, even if terrible, would help the human race. Nothing about the Great War helped the world. That he told me. That he told me."

The Great War? Had he been in here so long that he didn't know there had been another World War? Assuming it was even World War I he was talking about. It reminded her that he never answered her question about how long he had been up here.

"How old *are* you?" Skyler asked. She realized it was a rude question. "Sorry."

But Jon didn't seem to think so. "What year is it?" he asked. "Out there?"

When she told him, he nodded.

"1915. 1915. I was born in 1915." He spoke as if reciting something memorized by rote.

This stunned Skyler. That would make him over a hundred years old. Though he certainly looked that age, he was still quite sharp and his arms were strong and lean. He had aged well, especially for a man who had apparently lived in this tower for most of his life. The more she considered it, a centenarian was hardly the strangest thing she had encountered in this world.

"Difficult to believe," Jon babbled. "Difficult. Difficult to believe so many years have passed. It's hard to tell. There are no years here. No changing days."

Skyler looked up at one of the windows where the silver sky shined through. "It's always day?"

"It used to turn dark. There used to be night. That was Maria's design. She wanted to make it as much like the old world as she could. But eventually, the night stopped." His face sank with confusion. "Maybe there used to be night. I think there did. Perhaps it was just in my dreams. But now it is only day. The sky has to keep an eye on the forest, you know."

She was about to ask him what exactly the forest was. Was it really alive? The sky too? How? And what were those monsters? But Jon abruptly let out a wheezy giggle and pointed to the window. Skyler followed the aim of his distorted fingernail. She couldn't see anything but the sky, at first. But then she saw the small dots against its silver backdrop. *Snow.*

"Come along," Jon said, tremulously rising from his chair.

He led her up to the garden, near the peach trees, to where they could see through the glass. She saw the village below, the forest beyond it, and the sky curving into the horizon. The snow was coming down fast, but only as much as a strong flurry.

"Look," he said, pressing something cold and hard against her neck. She jerked away and saw him pointing a small brass telescope at her face. "Take it! Quickly!"

She did so and peered through it. The first thing she saw were those still, plastic-looking trees. A chill went down her spine. It was like spying on someone who was spying back.

"The well!" Jon hissed. "Quickly! Find the well!"

It took her a while to find the square and the well at its center. Once she found it, she saw a shape rising from the pit. It was a young man, about Skyler's age, wearing baggy jeans and a filthy shirt. He looked terrified and confused. She wanted to shout to him, but didn't think it would be any use.

"When it snows," Jon explained, "it means another has come. Only when it snows. And it only snows when another comes. The sky sends them down, you know. Another gift for the forest. A peace offering, I suppose. The sky is not always wise. Or perhaps there's some greater plan I'm not seeing. Perhaps."

The young man looked around, pacing, panicking. He was shouting. Skyler couldn't tell if he was yelling out for a specific person or to anyone who would listen. Then he gradually calmed as if someone had injected him with morphine.

"The forest gobbles them up. Greedy and ungrateful. It takes them."

The young man turned as if he heard someone calling to him. He slowly walked past the square, through the village, and onto the field. He walked with the assuredness of someone heading to work.

"It takes them into its army."

Skyler felt her throat dry up. "You mean... Those things. They are people?"

Jon nodded. "People, animals. Those who had lived in the village. Those sent by the sky. They become a part of the forest, when it takes them. Less a man or beast and more a thing of bramble and sticks. They merge with the forest, become nearly indistinguishable from it. Some of them become tangled together."

The image of the centaur popped into Skyler's head and the bat-bird thing that had attacked her when she first entered the world. She knew it was futile, but she yelled out to the young man. He didn't hear. He just kept walking before disappearing into the forest's blackness. Her voice died into silence, her chest aching with sadness and disgust. There was nothing she could do for him. There was nothing she could do for any of them. She didn't want to think about how close she had come to going in there herself. The worst thing was, the urge never really went away. But the castle, for all its awfulness, at least protected her.

"I don't know what the sky's designs are," Jon said. "Helping the forest build its army. Perhaps the forest will become so bloated it will collapse beneath its own weight. Or perhaps it's just a mistake. Who knows? But the sky has sent *me* someone now, hasn't it? Hasn't it, Sky-ler? Hasn't it?"

She couldn't watch any more. She placed the telescope on the ground and stared dully out the window. She could see the castle below. It looked so quiet and peaceful. She could see the many stories of windows, about six, including those along the roof. On the second floor, right above the sharp wall of spikes, she could see a window that was open. Was that the one Sam had fallen from?

"It has," Jon said. Skyler heard a slight quiver of fear in his voice.

The snow abruptly came to a stop.

Chapter Twelve

HE WAS SCREAMING. SCREAMING at his father. Or maybe it was his great-grandfather. In reality, neither man looked anything alike. The painting of Samael the First depicted him as upright, slender, tall, pale, and sharp. His eyes were a hypnotizing azure; possibly the artist's touch. Sam had never heard his voice, but he could imagine something cold and commanding. His father was also tall and mostly pale except for his rosy cheeks. But he was broad shouldered and stooped, his eyes brown and dim. His jaw was strong, not the needle point that was Samael's. His facial hair was patchy, as if glued on, rather than the perfect beard of his grandfather. His voice wasn't cold. If anything, it gave the appearance of warmth, the way it filled the room.

But here and now, the figure he was yelling at could have been one or the other.

Sam didn't know what he was screaming. But no matter how much fury he dealt, it seemed inadequate, restrained. He felt weak. The man staring back at him was unfazed. If anything, he was amused by the display.

But at least he wouldn't have to be with this man for too long. His mother was coming to pick him up. He couldn't wait to see her. She would be coming through the door any minute.

It was getting awfully late, though. Surely, she should've been there by now.

Why couldn't he stop screaming? It wasn't enough, it wasn't nearly enough.

Finally, Sam stopped. The man smacked his lips and spoke back, an overwhelming voice both familiar and alien.

"Go to the forest."

Sam woke up before his mother could arrive. He was back in the little cottage. He could see out the window. It appeared to be snowing.

Maybe I should start a fire, he thought. *It might get cold in here.*

But instead, he fell back asleep.

⁓

The darkness of sleep flashed away with a bang. His head painfully slammed onto the wooden floor. He lay dazed for a moment before the ceiling began to move. There was a tight grip around his ankle. He was being dragged, his back scraping along the floor. The ceiling soon gave way to the silver sky and the floor to rough weeds. *That stench.* The hand gripping him felt damp. He glanced up at his captor; it looked like a green Sasquatch that had been split in half. Two torsos, two heads, four legs that jerked the rest of the body along.

Where was it taking him, he wondered in his confusion. The creature was pulling him across the field like he was a used-up Christmas tree. One of its torsos was robust, its massive arm clutching Sam's ankle. The other was thinner, its willowy arms flailing about.

Beyond the split creature, he saw the green, brown, and black wall it was pulling him toward. The forest.

"No," he said, finally getting hold of his senses.

The creature's thinner head turned to him. It looked like a bog witch from a fairy tale. The face seemed to have melted inward, puckered. Green hair streamed over its sage-colored skin. The large, morass eyes glared hatefully. Through its crumpled mouth came a hiss.

"No!" Sam cried. "No!"

He tugged, but the grip on his ankle was powerful. They had his good foot, so he couldn't use his other to kick. All he could do was use his newfound energy to twist and wrench as violently as he could. This forced the creature to halt and readjust itself, slightly loosening its grip. He took this opportunity to wriggle his ankle away. Once freed, he scooted backward. The massive body twitched around to face him. The big half truly was a Sasquatch. Its face was blanketed in moss, its lips drooping away from its jaw, exposing sharp, doglike teeth. It let out a deep roar. Its slender counterpart wailed in conjunction. Their guttural cries were filled with primal hate and brutality. Sam scrambled up, balancing himself on his healthy foot.

The axe. He needed to get to the axe. He hopped as fast as he could back to the cottage. He could feel his pursuers behind him. He could hear their panting and the awkward thudding and dragging of their feet, the weeds crunching beneath. Their reek stung his nostrils.

He darted into the cottage. The axe was on the bed. Just as he grabbed the hilt, a powerful, moist arm wrapped around his chest, jerking him back. A daintier, yet equally strong hand gripped his wrist, forcing him to drop the weapon. The hybrid body crested around him. The witch shrieked into his face, clawing at his cheek. Up close, her glassy eyes looked like snow globes filled with sludge.

He couldn't bear the smell anymore. It was everywhere now, assaulting him. He retched and spurted bile on the witch's face. She recoiled and the Sasquatch loosened his hold once again. Sam seized the moment and threw his head back, smashing it into the Sasquatch's face. It felt like he was hitting the back of his skull against a rock. But he heard the crunch of a nose breaking. The thing grunted and released him, holding its face in pain and dragging its companion with it.

Sam rushed for the axe again, this time grabbing it tight with both hands. He turned around in time to see the hybrid barreling toward him. He swung the axe and dug it into the witch's slender waist. There was a juicy squelch. Black ooze sputtered from the witch's mouth and she let out a cry so piercing it made Sam want to curl up and cover his ears. But he held strong. He tugged out the axe, slinging black ooze all over the floor and himself. Without hesitation, he raised the blade above his head. The Sasquatch reached for him, howling vengefully. He brought the axe down, the blade sinking into the large head.

The hybrid tottered aimlessly about the room, ooze spewing from the stunned Sasquatch's head and the terrified witch's torso, painting the room black. Sam could only stand and watch them erratically scramble about like a spider in a hot frying pan. He wasn't quite sure it was over, but it appeared to be. The fear in both creatures' buggy eyes was palpable. Finally, the Sasquatch became limp and fell, pulling down the entire mass of two bodies.

The witch continued twitching on the floor, trying to pull from the lifeless hulk she was infused with. Eventually, she slower, her screams fading to grunts. Then the grunts melted into a whimper. The sound was eerily human. The witch slowly wrapped her arms around the dead Sasquatch's torso, rested her head against the broad chest, and moved no more.

Sam kept staring long after it ended. He was transfixed by the picture they made: lying in a pool of black blood, entwined like two lovers who'd finally found their peace. He felt sad for them, yet also somehow envious. He baffled himself. He shouldn't have felt anything. Not for these monsters. He also had an urge to retch again, though that was likely the smell.

When he could no longer stand being in there, he grabbed his bag and left, leaving the axe embedded in the Sasquatch's head. He hobbled out onto the dead field. His eyes were still welled from the stench. Part of him wanted to let them burst until they were dry.

You are so weak.

He sucked it up and wiped away the tears.

Chapter Thirteen

SHE WAS ABLE TO sleep, even if it was on the hard library floor with only a bundle of smelly old rags for cushioning. It felt like a long time since she'd slept on a bed. She used to think she couldn't sleep without one. Of course, since coming into the snow globe, she experienced exhaustion that she'd never felt before.

In her dream, she was with Sam. Or at least, in her mind she knew it was him. But physically, the man looked more like her father. He was running through a forest. She was trying to keep up but couldn't run as fast. Her legs felt like they were made of rubber and she couldn't breathe.

Skyler never caught up to him before waking. Her eyes opened to see a wrinkled face leering at her, hollow eyes squinted and mouth frowning in perplexion.

"Jon?"

"Do you read?" he asked. He was sitting at the long table. A book was clutched in his hands.

"Yeah," she said, sitting up and hugging her knees.

"I love Alexander Dumas. Do you?"

"Oh." The random question took her off guard. "Yeah, I do. I thought *The Count of Monte Cristo* was fantastic. I expected it to be overrated."

"*The Three Musketeers?*"

"Haven't read that." She crawled onto the chair next to him. Most of her body was aching. "I'd been meaning to." She hadn't expected a discussion of literature for breakfast, but there were worse things.

"I have read *The Three Musketeers*. I have read all of *The d'Artagnan Romances*."

"Is that what you're reading now? *The Three Musketeers*?"

Jon shook his head. "I am reading *Les Misérables*. Do you like Victor Hugo?"

"I'll admit, I haven't read any of his stuff."

"This one is fine. But I love *The Hunchback of Notre Dame*. I ignore the parts about architecture. It's enough to hear all of that from the Frenchman. I prefer the story of Quas-i-modo. I have become akin to Quas-i-modo. His purpose was to ring the bell of Notre Dame and awaken the city. Mine is to ring the bell and awaken the castle. Have you read it?"

"No, but I've seen some of the movies."

He stared blankly at her. She realized how stupid it was to mention something that was totally over his head. He was young enough perhaps to be familiar with moving pictures. But maybe unfamiliar with the fact that they were more commonly called "movies" now.

"What books do you like?" Jon asked.

She wanted to stick with titles he would likely be familiar with, which seemed to be "must-read" western canon classics. "I love a lot of Charles Dickens, *A Tale of Two Cities*, *Great Expectations*. Uh, *The Picture of Dorian Gray* is wonderful. I even named my dog after Oscar Wilde. Umm... *Anna Karenina*. *Crime and Punishment*. Uh... Oh, *The Adventures of Huckleberry Finn*!" In truth, she was more of a nonfiction reader.

"Do you like *Frankenstein*?" Jon asked eagerly. "Have you ever read it?"

"Oh, uh-huh." Though she hadn't read it since her eleventh grade literature class. "For a book it's age, it's very chilling."

"Maria is like Victor Frankenstein, you know."

"Oh. Um... I suppose." Their discussion had given her a little escape from where she was and what was happening to her. But now she was inevitably pulled back, just by mention of that name. *Maria.* The name of a vague shadow, but one that loomed over everything here.

"Victor Frankenstein's creation became something far beyond what he had intended." Jon suddenly grew more solemn than Skyler had ever seen him. "It became something else. Something great and powerful—otherworldly. Brilliant too. Maria thought she controlled this world. But she didn't. She couldn't. No creator can control what their creation becomes. They can guide it, but nothing more. Like how parents can raise their children, but they can't control the person that child becomes. You may have power, you may have the talent to use it. But the creation will take on a life of its own. That is the truth. Especially if you deign to carve worlds."

Skyler was unsure about what to add to that.

Before she had a chance to think of anything, Jon's somberness melted and his jaw popped into a broad smile. "Oh! Have you read *Alice's Adventures in Wonderland*?"

Their conversation about dead White man canon books went on a little bit longer before Jon retired upstairs.

"I will smell them if they come," was the last thing he told her.

It still amazed her that he had so much energy at his age. He had lived through a lot of history, another world war, a cold war, the digital age, and hadn't experienced any of it. Yet, he was so spry. She remembered when her grandfather had died of cancer at seventy-five. That had seemed so old. Skyler couldn't help but cringe whenever she thought back on that period of hospital visits. She had been fourteen and such a brat. Though sad Grandad was dying, she had also been bored hanging around the hospital all the time. The day he died, she remembered getting so angry at Rachel for wearing one of her shirts. She yelled at her ten-year-old sister loudly enough for the whole hospital to hear. Their mom, already devastated by her father's imminent death, snapped at Skyler to behave.

"You're always taking Rachel's side!" Skyler shouted back. Her mother gave it to her good after that, which even then left Skyler feeling deeply ashamed. After the dressing down, her dad took her home. Before he could get back to the hospital, her mother called him to say Grandad had died.

She popped her fingers against her chin. It embarrassed and disgusted her to think about it. How she behaved that day was one of her biggest regrets, even if she'd just been a kid. After that moment, she never protested against Rachel wearing her clothes. In fact, she became a downright pushover until Rachel realized she could be far more stylish than her older sister and started getting her own outfits. Her style ended up being more in line with Morgan, diversely fabulous, adventurous, yet painstakingly refined. There was always a careful symmetry even to the lazy clothes. Morgan's pajama pants and T-shirts always burst with complimentary colors. Skyler usually focused on comfort and practicality, whether staying in or going out and about. That was the way she liked it. She preferred understated colors, navy blue probably being her most colorful. Morgan never judged her. Morgan always said her colors fit her well.

Morgan. Skyler hadn't thought of her for a while. She wasn't up here. That was evident. She probably wasn't anywhere in the castle or in the village. If she was in the snow globe at all the only place she could have gone was...

No. That wasn't a possibility. She wouldn't entertain it.

She heard Jon's hacking cough. He had such a soft voice when he spoke, but his cough carried from the upstairs room. The forbidden room behind the green door where his father and the Frenchman also apparently resided.

They probably weren't real, Skyler decided. Or, at least, not anymore. A man who lived alone in a bell tower for as long as Jon did had to have made up a few imaginary friends to keep him company. She wondered if the personified sky and forest were also imaginary friends. Logically, that made sense. But she was unsure. Everything in this world seemed so lifeless, yet... It was the feeling of being alone in the empty room of an allegedly haunted building. You're alone, yet you don't *feel* alone. There's a presence. Maybe it's just a bad vibe, probably all in your head. But maybe there are actually ghosts. Whatever it may be, there's an undeniable energy there. Because of that energy, you are not truly alone. Isolated, yes, but not alone, even if there isn't so much as a gnat around.

So many nights, when she'd get stressed out or anxious or sad, she and Morgan would stay up late and talk about nothing for hours.

That will never happen again.

Stop it.

She wished she had Jon's conversation again. Something to quiet her thoughts.

If you don't die in here, she did.

Or she isn't Morgan any more.

Even when the thoughts were wordless, they still found ways to gnaw at her. They played out as images, feelings, sensations—a typhoon of bullshit.

The only person you could rely on. She's gone. You're on your own. And you're fucked.

No, I'm not. I can't be.

Maybe she could read a book. There were more than a few options around.

Or...

The paper. The paper she had taken from Sam when his backpack spilled out. She could read that.

Sam is dead. You could've helped him. You killed him.

Did I? What could I have done?

That little piece of paper sparked her curiosity. Her curiosity would keep her mind busy, at least somewhat.

You're fucked. Idiot.

She pulled the plastic bag from her pocket, unfolded it, and slipped out the yellow, doubled-over sheet of paper. It felt thin and fragile. It was old, so she'd need to be careful. She wished she had interned at a museum; maybe it would have made her better at handling fragile documents. The opportunity to do so had been offered to her in college. But around that time, everything with her father happened and she declined.

Despite its fragility, the document was in good shape. The paper was nearly untarnished. She supposed that, being a member of... What was it? The Society for Finding Artifacts? No, it was something more long-winded. At any rate, being a part of it likely taught Sam how to take care of such things.

And he's dead. You killed him.

No. No.

It was a letter. The writing was a little difficult to make out as it was in a thin cursive. This was from a time when everyone wrote that way and not just in elementary school.

"My Dear Orion,"

There wasn't a date or address on it. It only had a signature at the end:

"Artemis"

Orion. Artemis. These names were most likely pseudonyms. Obviously, the correspondents were being discreet.

"Please let me apologize. I have no wish to test your patience. Your eagerness to learn more about our mutual interest is completely understandable. It is not my intention to deny you this knowledge. I see the bright, young hunter in you and I am eager to set him on his first kill. Do believe me, Orion, I would not have wasted ink and paper writing to you otherwise. But I need not explain to one as astute as yourself that, due to the nature of our mutual interest and the history therein, caution is not unwarranted. Skillful as you may be, others in the tribe believe you to be too young. This is not to say they doubt your competence, but only that your bloodline is too fresh. They do not see what I see.

So please be forgiving of me, my treasured Orion. We will meet again soon, and together we shall hunt..."

It went on like that for several more sentences. Who was Artemis supposed to be? Who was Orion? From the look of it, they were trying to fly under the radar of the tribe, or the Society, she assumed. Their mutual interest was perhaps the tool Sam kept talking about. At any rate, Artemis was being irritatingly circuitous. Skyler didn't know what Orion's response might have been, but she could imagine their frustration. She couldn't stand the pandering either. Of course, maybe Orion was the type to go for that.

She wondered if Orion was Sam's great-grandfather. Why else would Sam have had it? *Others in the tribe believe you to be too young.* Hadn't Sam mentioned his great-grandfather being new money in the Society? Jon had also mentioned that newer families were below older ones in the hierarchy.

So, Orion was Samael the First. Then who was Artemis? She seemed to have knowledge of the workings of the tool. At one point, between the pandering nonsense, she wrote:

"It is alive, Orion. I have never had a child, nor has that ever been a desire of mine. Yet, I now know what it is to create and nurture life. With every careful scrape, every blister on my finger, this life breathes a little more. As I watch it blossom, I feel a love that only a parent could. It is brilliant, but pure. Familiar yet perplexing. I am bound to every part of it. You will see, Orion. You, too, will know the pride."

Skyler decided it had to be Maria, the creator of this world. Had she not been so drained, Skyler would've been proud of herself for figuring this out. Four years of ravenously seeking primary sources paid off.

But why would Maria write to Sam's great-grandfather? Sam said that they had been enemies. Maria had apparently tried to have the man killed. He'd had to flee the country and only returned once she and her followers vanished. On the other hand, the fakeness oozing from all her promises and compliments showed no hints of real affection. There was some cold, calculated deception at play. It unnerved Skyler. She hoped Maria wasn't still alive. But if Jon was, who could say?

She folded the letter back up carefully. She felt the need to treat it with respect, not for posterity, but for Sam. She reflected on the names. Artemis was a Greek goddess, that she knew. Orion was also from Greek mythology, but she couldn't quite remember his story. However, she did know where she had heard the name first. Orion's Belt. Orion's bow. The man in the stars. The constellation.

She sat under the peach trees. Though the garden was dimly lit and smelled like weeds and metal, she found it quite peaceful. The tree and the crops around her felt alive, naturally alive, even if they were withering. It was the fact that they were withering that made them all the more beautiful. They didn't have the eerie perfection of the forest's trees. They were real. They were home. She wondered how anything had been able to grow at all without sunlight. Maybe the sky simulated sunlight somehow. She couldn't understand how. But she couldn't imagine anything about how this world worked.

A peach was lying next to her leg. She picked it up and bit into it, at least the part that hadn't been touching the ground. It was mushy and juicy, sweet but bitter. Perfectly flawed. She checked her phone. As always, Oscar was there, showing her his ball. The pang of sadness it gave her felt as sharp as any blade. She hoped he was being looked after. The screen was devoid of any notifications. Had anyone been trying to call her? Her mom? Rachel? Probably. Did they wonder where she was? Were they worried? She also found herself wondering if Morgan was trying to call. Maybe she hadn't been taken by the snow globe, had been somewhere else all along and was home. Now she was the one who was worried to death.

Skyler turned off the phone and tossed the peach aside. She no longer had an appetite. She sobbed into her knees for a few moments before composing herself.

From the corner of her bleary eye, she saw a gray shape prowling toward her. Jon's movements were quieter than his voice. His hobbling appeared slow yet he quickly got to wherever he was going.

"Hi," she said, wiping her eyes and sniffling. She tried to be covert about it, but he was probably able to tell she had been crying.

Jon didn't reply. His eyes, fixed on Skyler, seemed angry. But it could've just been his wide, sagging brow. A small tingle of dread flared in her stomach.

"It's very peaceful in here," she said.

Jon nodded. "Made yourself at home." He bared his gray gums in a wide smile, though his brows were still bitterly creased. His joints let off painful pops as he leaned against one of the trees. Skyler slightly edged away so that he wouldn't loom directly above her. His musty and sour odor was particularly pungent at the moment.

"I've spent so much time up here," he said reflectively. As usual, Skyler had to strain her ears to hear him. "So many years, apparently. It used to be so simple. They would come once in a while. I would do my duty. Dance the dance and take our bows before the long peace. Then we'd dance again. But now, they are coming more and more often. And they... they used to be so pathetic in their attempts. But now they are getting better. I don't think I'm getting stronger. No. I'm old, aren't I? They can break the glass now. Noémie's children can only fight for so long. So many changes, so many curiosities."

His humid breath brushed along the top of her head. It was staler than the air itself. She scooted further away, as casually as she could, and rose to her feet.

"Now, there's another curiosity." He pointed a sticklike finger at her. "Sky-ler. With the wings on her shirt. Why did it send you to me?"

"Why did what send me to you?" she asked carefully.

"What?"

She repeated her question.

"The sky," he answered, now pointing his finger up. "The sky. The sky."

"I don't think it did."

From the prunish scowl that grew on Jon's face, she was unsure if that had been the right thing to say.

"I... I mean, I don't know if it did. Or... I don't know."

Jon raised his sunken eyes and scratched at his beard, gray flakes fluttering from it.

"I suppose it makes sense," he said, his voice even lower than usual. Skyler focused all her attention to hear him. "I suppose you wouldn't necessarily know. Who would? It brings them here, but I suppose they don't have the privilege of knowing why. I was the only one with such a privilege. Well, my father too. But you came to me. I couldn't stop you. Try as I did. You came to me all the same."

"I'm just... I don't.... I'm sorry?" She wondered what he meant by *try as I did*.

"Sky-ler from the sky." Jon had a pained, despairing frown.

"I just want to find the way out," she said softly. Though she didn't understand the agonized grief in his face, it triggered a small feeling of pity. "I really just want to go home."

Jon's face instantly contorted with fury. "It's not here," he snapped. "If that's what you want, then leave."

"I don't know where it is."

"Neither do I. But you know where the door is. If that is what you want, then go."

Her stomach tightened. She knew there wasn't any point to staying in the tower. Maybe it was time to return to the castle. But the idea sickened her. She had found at least some semblance of safety up here. Of course, she didn't want to stay here forever either. The idea of doing so made her feel even sicker. But would it be better or worse than wandering aimlessly around the halls of the castle until a trap or automaton got her? Or she starved to death? Maybe she'd be better off outside, going into the forest and becoming one of those things.

Jon sneered at her, the hatred in his ghoulish face abundantly clear. Skyler was stunned. She had no idea where this disdain was coming from. She tried to think of anything she might have said or done to piss him off.

"Get out of my garden," he said.

"Wh-what? Why?"

"Because it's mine." His sneer widened, exposing every yellow mound in his gums. "I granted you permission to be in here. Now I demand you leave."

"I just don't..."

"You'll ruin my crops with your air."

"What?" She had no idea what the hell he meant by that.

"I wouldn't expect you to understand," he said condescendingly. "But you no longer have permission to be in here. You must leave."

It was a blatant and baffling power play. His tone took her back to college, to guys in her classes who thought they knew everything. Maybe they were afraid she would do better than them, so they sought any opportunity they could to condescend or correct or explain something to her. Hell, even at work, she dealt with men, sometimes older women, who would feel indignant whenever she had to correct them or even just offer an idea. So they almost always had to try and one-up her or at least give her the "I've been doing this longer than you've been alive" speech. She even had gotten that kind of bullshit from Sam. She always took it politely. But now things were different. She couldn't stand the idea of being nice about this.

Still, she had to be strategic. Jon was the only other person she had now. She didn't want him to hate her. More specifically, she couldn't afford to have him hate her. Of course, the toxicity of his smirk suggested there was probably nothing to be done about that. Still, there had to be answers up here. A hint at where she could find the way out.

"Okay," she said after a deep breath. "It stinks in here anyway." She sped past Jon, not deigning to look back at whatever expression he wore, and out of the garden.

Rachel or Morgan, they would have stood their ground. Hell, they would have been bossing Jon around by now.

But it didn't matter how much she tried to channel them. She wasn't them. Skyler had to deal with this her way. She only wished she knew what the hell that was.

Chapter Fourteen

SHE PACED AROUND THE library, kicking books, popping her fingers, thinking about her next move. She had perused many of the books, but found no hidden documents or blueprints. No hints of the way out. It had been a crapshoot anyway. There was nothing to be found in the privy or the kitchen. Neither of which she could stay in too long before getting sick. There were two places she hadn't been to yet: the belfry and the room with the green door.

Maybe there was something to the latter. Jon had to be keeping it locked for a reason. According to him, the two men who had essentially built the castle were in there. But even if they weren't, a blueprint to the castle or some kind of clue could have been.

Lost in thought as she speed-walked around the library, she banged her hip against the large, old table.

"Fuck!"

She sat, letting the uncomfortable throb in her pelvis fade. Then she heard the creaking of the library stairs.

"What brought you here?" Jon asked. He put in extra effort saying this and his voice carried more than usual.

Skyler groaned. This again. "I'm looking for my cousin. We're from Omaha, Nebraska. You've heard of Omaha? Or at least Nebraska?"

Jon said nothing to confirm or deny. He hobbled toward the table. It looked like he needed a cane, but somehow got by well without one.

"The Frenchman," he said, chuckling. "I remember the day he came crawling into our tower, bleeding. One of his traps got him. Mama wanted to help him, you know. Father said there was nothing we could do, said it was all in the sky's hands. Then Mama said we needed to leave. She said she was going to take me and leave without Father. So he threw her out the window."

Skyler nodded as if he hadn't already told her all this. Perhaps being cordial with him was her best course of action.

The old man sat across from her. "I remember that day. I heard her screaming. I thought she'd tripped or something or other. Went into the bedroom. There's Father standing by the window. It's open. No Mama anywhere. He turns to me, he says, 'She couldn't fly.'" Jon wheezed with laughter. "It must have been so long ago, but it still feels so fresh in my mind. I remember how angry I was. I regret that. I think he regrets what he'd done too. Mama probably would've understood with time. See, we thought we'd been sent up here to build some bell system that would ring on its own at the nearest hint of danger. But such a thing wouldn't be perfect. No. No. *I* was meant to be the ringer. The loyal. The vigilant."

"You have been vigilant," Skyler said.

"I..." There was a choke in Jon's voice. "I've served for so long. But now you've come and..." Again came that a raw look of anguish in his face.

"I just want to go home," she said, and something broke in her own voice. "That's all I want."

"You are home," Jon said, an air of defeat in his tone. "You are here to replace me. I'm old, and I've failed to end the war."

"No!" Skyler said.

Now it was starting to make sense—the insecurity, the anger. He was an old man who had done and believed in something for so long. Like anyone so deeply set in their ways, he felt uncertain and intimidated by the slightest sign of change. A strange person coming into his tower was no "slight" change at all.

"No," she said again. "This is your tower. I would never take that from you."

"But is it your choice?" Thick tears trickled down his hollow cheeks.

"Maybe..." Skyler knew she had to choose her words wisely. If he truly believed a higher power had designs against him, there was little she could do to console him. "Maybe I wasn't sent here to replace you. Maybe I was sent here so you can help me. Right? I-I don't belong here. What would I know about protecting this tower? I know nothing about ringing bells. Would I even be able to pull it?"

"It takes strength," Jon said.

"Which I don't have." She waved her short arms for emphasis. "If the sky is so wise, it wouldn't send me to replace you. I think it sent me to you because... It sent me because if anyone can help me, it's you. But there's no way I can do what you do. You've been here for a century. Why shouldn't you be here for another century? Or another?"

"Father said the sky chose our blood," Jon muttered. He was still tearful, but there was already more cheer in his voice.

"See? I'm not related to you or your father." At least she didn't *think* she was. "There's nothing special about my blood. I'm clumsy. I get tired so easily." She was encouraged to see Jon's beard crumpling with a puckered smile. "If the sky is so wise, wh-which it is, then it wouldn't actually think I'm right for this."

"The sky is wise," he conceded. "Very, very wise. Yes, very wise. Yes, it makes mistakes. It gives gifts to the forest. Which the forest greedily takes. It doesn't always make the right choice."

He scowled with uncertainty again.

"Well..." *Think Skyler. Get creative for god's sake. Get full-of-shit.* "Well, what if it isn't the sky that brings them here?"

Jon's eyes widened as if she'd blasphemed. "They come from the sky, you idiot!"

"But before I came here, I felt like I was being called to this world. Once I was here, it seemed like that same voice was calling to me. It was coming from the forest."

"Yes," Jon said. "The forest is quite seductive."

"So, what I'm saying is, I guess, maybe we come from the sky but it's the forest who actually calls us here." She was confusing herself. But Jon looked reflective, as if her argument was a perfectly compelling one.

"They didn't start coming until Virgil Shanks opened the well," he said. "I watched him do it. Long ago, yes. He was already a two-backed beast by then. The forest's lackey. But could the forest really have the power to call to those beyond?"

"It can," Skyler said. "I know it can. It's called to me. It's called to everyone who's ended up here. I swear it."

"She swears it," he muttered to himself. "Who am I to say she is wrong? She has heard the voice better than me. So the sky calls nobody here. She makes no choice. It has always been the forest. The sky only watches and weeps."

Skyler nodded.

"Then perhaps it was the forest who sent you to me, after all. Sent you to discourage me, or frighten me."

"N-no!" She tried to keep calm, but Jon was apparently determined to see her as hostile. "The forest wanted to take me. It almost did. I only escaped it because... I was helped."

"The man," Jon said.

Skyler wasn't going to ask him how he knew about Sam. She knew he had been watching them.

Of course, the words *I couldn't stop you* still wormed through her mind.

"Jon?" She feared bringing this up would be cataclysmic to her cause. But she had to know. "When the bell rang, while we were in the castle, nothing was attacking. Did you ring it because of us?"

"Of course," Jon said casually. "Of course. I have to protect the castle, you know. I didn't know you two had gotten inside until I saw the man in the window. Very fortunate timing."

"So—" Anger was growing in Skyler's gut. "You tried to kill us."

"I did what I am meant to do," he replied. His unrepentant tone made Skyler angrier. "You lived, didn't you?

"You..." There were hundreds of things she could say. But she couldn't think of any of them. Even if she could, would she say anything? This man admitted to trying to kill her and it felt like he wanted to do it again. Yet, she had to... What *did* she have to do?

Jon tapped a long fingernail against the table. "And why did this man resist it?"

"What?"

"The man. Why, or how, was *he* able to resist the forest?"

"He... he knew we needed to get to the castle."

"How?" he hissed. There was a new intensity to Jon. She might have mistaken him for former gestapo, the way his questioning tone drilled into her. Was this an act? Something he'd pulled from an old detective novel? Or maybe this was his true self and the childishness had been the real act.

"He knew the way out of the world was in here," Skyler said. "Or at least, it would lead us to the way out."

Jon grinned. "The way out. I told you. It's a secret those who are not you or I had sworn to keep."

"But why?"

"Because... well, you don't need to know why. He wanted to find the way out? Everyone who comes into this world does. That was it?"

"But he also..."

"Yes?"

Skyler was getting sick of this interrogation. "Nothing."

"Ah, nothing. Of course. He knew nothing else."

"Yes."

Jon tapped his fingernail even harder. The sound was like tiny hammers pounding on Skyler's eardrums.

"I love Shakespeare," he said.

"Sure," Skyler mumbled. Jon's nasally babbling was also getting on her nerves.

"What?"

"So do I."

"*Hamlet* is my favorite," Jon said to the steady cadence of his tapping. "Have you read *Hamlet*?"

"Yes," she replied. She hadn't.

"I do love ghosts. I've seen many ghosts. I only see ghosts any more. Sometimes I'll wake up and Mama is walking across the room. Father never sees them. Nor does the Frenchman. But I do. My eyes are strong. Always have been. Not as much as they once were, mind you. But still very strong. When I saw your man, I thought he was a ghost."

"My man? You mean Sam?"

"Sam?" Jon abruptly stopped tapping. "Interesting. I had never met Samael Adamsen in my life. But I had seen his likeness in photographs and paintings. I have heard the stories. When I saw your Sam peering up from the window... my my..."

A haunted look came over the old man's face.

"I..."

Jon leaned across the table, his hot breath beating against Skyler's face. "Was it a ghost?"

"No," she said, turning her head and gritting her teeth.

"No?"

"Sam is..." *Was.* "His great-grandson." She wondered if she should have said that.

"The creature survived, then?" Jon looked dreamily to the sky. "Despite Maria's efforts. His progeny is still trying to seize the Society's secrets. I heard many stories of Samael, you know. The wicked man wanted all those secrets for himself. He wanted to unravel centuries of progress. He was the reason Maria had built this world. Well, him and the Great War. I suppose she began crafting it long before anything boiled over, but she had certainly seen it comin'. She knew wickedness was growing too quickly in the old world. Samael was but one example. She decided the tool should be hidden deep. At least for a time. At least for a time."

He mumbled something Skyler couldn't discern. For a short time, he settled into a silence, staring at the table. She thought he was about to fall asleep.

"So many of us came into this bold new world with her," he continued suddenly. "A very new start, you know. The servants built the village, built the castle. They brought all kinds of animals with them. Birds, dogs, mules, even vermin... Plants too, just to make it a little like home. Maria was never much of a leader for them. Nor Father. It was Virgil Shanks who led them. That's why they made him mayor. I barely remember what he looked like without a mule for an ass." He cackled. "And Maria. She became a mystery to the rest of us. Not even Father heard from her much toward the end of it all. She hid herself away from everyone but her little shadow. Such a mystery. Our mysterious, benevolent god. Truly befitting of the title, I'd say. Maria, our god. Samael, the lurking devil. Mama would sometimes tell me, she'd say, 'If you don't behave, I will ship you off to Samael.'"

Jon cackled again before abruptly quieting with a somber grimace.

"I don't believe Samael was a devil. No longer. I don't believe Maria was really a god. She was the inventor of the sky and the forest. But they took on their own designs. Victor Frankenstein wasn't a god, was he? But his creature very well may have been."

It is brilliant, but pure. Familiar yet perplexing. Skyler could remember that from Maria's correspondence with the "devil."

"That isn't to say that Samael was never a concern," Jon continued. "Not if he had somehow lived. Not if he had spawned." He gave a toothless beam. "So it *was* a ghost, you know. I had done right, if he's gone now. I had done well."

Skyler was breathing deeply. Disgusted as she was by Jon gleefully taking responsibility for Sam's death, she was also strangely relieved. It wasn't her fault. It wasn't her fault. Not completely.

"So perhaps that is the key to the puzzle," Jon continued. "He came, unwelcomed. Unwelcomed by all but the forest, that is. The forest used him as a tool to infiltrate the castle. To ruin everything. But my purpose is greater. I ended him. You had only been strung along then, I suppose. You are just an anomaly." Jon joyfully clapped his hands together and rose from his chair singing: *"The forest will never win! The forest will never win!"* The screeching tone of his singing voice raised the hairs on Skyler's neck. She wanted to shout at him to stop. But she didn't have to. He abruptly stopped on his own. "You had only been strung along, I suppose. You are an anomaly." His voice was soft and content. "This is my sanctuary. You are just a guest."

"So, will you help me?" Skyler asked. "Will you help me find the way out?"

A frightened look came over his face. The pitiable look of a disappointed child.

"No," he said. "And I will have to stop you if you try."

He hobbled back toward the stairs, humming his tuneless song.

Skyler sat stunned until Jon vanished again in the forbidden room upstairs. She never imagined the man would be a friend, but she'd hoped he wouldn't be an enemy. Though what exactly could he do to keep her up here? Ring that damn bell, perhaps. But if she could avoid those automatons, that would only light up her way at worst. Right?

There was no certainty in leaving, no security. Up here, she at least knew that she might not die. *Might.* She wouldn't put it past Jon to strangle her in her sleep. The thought of those gnarled hands wrapping around her neck made her shudder. She leaped from her chair and sped to the metal door leading out of the tower keep. She had to know that she could leave. She had to...

She pulled on the handle; the door didn't budge.

No. No. No.

She pulled again and again. The bastard had locked it. Maybe he'd done it while she napped or while she was in the garden or squatting in the privy. Or maybe he had locked it the moment he let her in and she hadn't noticed. But it didn't matter when it'd happened. All that mattered was that she was his prisoner.

No. No!

"Jon!" she shouted, panic coursing through her, making her lose control of herself. "Jon!" She ran up the stairs and pulled on the green door. "Jon! Open the hell up!"

It was quiet on the other side.

"Goddamn you, open up!" All her fear and long pent-up frustration was spewing from every pore. She pounded on the door hard enough that her palms stung and caught splinters. She almost thought she was on the verge of knocking the door over. But before she could, it flew open violently. She heard the sound of something metal clinking onto the floor.

Jon stared at her, his eyes cold. The room behind him was dark, other than small strips of light poking through some curtained and boarded windows. Her eyes watered at the stench. The room smelled worse than even the privy, even the forest creatures. It was a swirl of musk, decay, fecal matter, and acrid body odor.

The old man smacked his lips. "Mama told me once or twice. She said, 'Hospitality is a two-way act.' It falls on the graciousness of the host and the respectfulness of the guest." His tone was obnoxiously condescending. But Skyler's irritation was stifled by the gun he held at her stomach. It was an old revolver, a rusty antique that might have been used in the Spanish–American War. She wasn't even sure it still worked, but she didn't want to test it.

"Now," he continued, pushing the metal harder against her belly. It felt cold through her shirt. "Will you be respectful?"

She didn't answer. She had never been held at gunpoint before. Although she had been through worse at this point, it was still surreal. She held her breath, imagining it going off at any moment, the bullet tearing through her stomach. But still, what if he was bluffing? What if the thing was long defunct and just a prop? She didn't want to test it, but she didn't want to be fooled by it either.

As if reading her mind, Jon sneered and pointed the gun at the ceiling, gripping it with both hands. She quickly covered her ears, but the deafening pop still rattled her. The kick from the gunshot nearly toppled him, but he stayed on his feet. Some debris from the ceiling harmlessly crumbled down. Regaining her composure, Skyler missed her opportunity to fight back before Jon held the gun to her gut again. This time, the metal shook. He was trembling. Sweat dotted her face. It felt all the more likely that the gun would go off and rip her insides to pieces at any moment.

"This will hurt you just fine, you know," Jon said. "Now, you can stay here. You can read all the books you want." There was a slight hesitation in his voice, as if unsure he liked that idea. At the same time, there was a glint of excitement in his concave eyes. "You could try to fight me, if you'd like. The other option, I suppose, is to leave the same way Mama did. There are plenty of windows here, you know. Feel free to pick one."

CHAPTER FIFTEEN

H IS FOOT WAS STINGING more and more.

"No, no, no." He noticed droplets of blood seeping through his shoe, smearing the cobbled streets. The fight must have agitated his wounds.

He returned to the square. His next move would be to search other houses for food and weapons. He needed to be in the best shape possible before braving the castle again. Or at least in better shape, which wasn't saying much.

His mind kept returning to those two creatures back in the cottage, bound together, lying on the floor. Here he was and they were still there, in the same place he'd left them. They would stay there until they rotted or melted or however the hell those things decayed. He didn't regret killing them. He'd fought to protect himself. But he *did* regret seeing that last moment. The witch, the woman, laying her head on the other's chest. So afraid, yet accepting her fate.

His foot screamed again. Before doing anything, he would need to take another look at it.

The large stone-and-brick building containing the library sat silently in its corner of the square. That was a familiar place. It would be the safe place for a quick rest.

On the inside, the library was the same as he'd left it. He pondered whether or not to again block the front door with a bookshelf. He decided not to. After all, the last time he had to have Skyler help him push it away from the door.

Skyler.

Something in him twitched. A feeling that he was failing her, leaving her alone, that he needed to get going and find her. But she had to already be dead.

He sat beneath the headless statue at the center of the room. The mutilated body of some Greek goddess.

Artemis?

The head lay close to his feet. It didn't quite have the face of a goddess. The features were stern and pinched, reminding Sam of a stereotypical stuffy old governess. The kind who would make young women balance books on their heads to learn poise.

But something about the face disturbed him. He quickly realized why. He had seen old photographs and paintings of Maria Faragó, ranging from her posh youth to her more intense older age. His father kept them all. The images always sent these kinds of chills through him. Maybe not the earlier ones, where she was a more benign youth. Intelligent, but naive. But in later ones, which this statue's head most resembled, her eyes were always the most pronounced, common in turn-of-the-century photos, two bright orbs shining through the grain. They always stared at him, as much as the paintings or photographs of his great-grandfather did.

"I will show you the very instrument of being."

Maria's was a face of selfishness, hatred, disdain, condescension. A face of empty promises, flattery, kindness. False comradery. How could Samael have ever believed her? Maybe he hadn't. Or maybe he only let himself believe her, nearly fatal as that mistake had been. Sam wondered what he would do if someone, a supposed colleague, told him they would teach him how to use an "instrument of being," a tool that carved real, living worlds. It would be hard to refuse.

Peeling off his shoe was even more painful than last time. His foot looked more and more like a piece of raw meat. Blood was dripping from red strips that he couldn't tell if they were bandages or skin. Biting the sleeve of his jacket, he poured some more disinfectant on his foot. It felt like acid. He groaned from the pain. The wounds bubbled and crackled.

As the sting simmered down from a screech to a hum, he felt a warm sensation in his pants. Then came the stench of urine. Shadows crept over him, made him want to crawl into a hole and disappear. They were the shapes of his father and his great-grandfather, saying nothing, leering at him with disgust. He'd wet himself in front of the eyes of their enemy. Indeed, the stone likeness of Maria Faragó watched him with satisfaction. Sam hated himself. He was supposed to be the last bulwark, not just for those who opposed Faragó, but for humanity as a whole. The humanity from which she denied secrets. And here he was, in her domain, before her eyes, wetting himself like a frightened child. Or an old pathetic dog that needed to be euthanized. He didn't even have a change of pants or underpants. He'd left all his extra clothing in his car.

"I wish I had other sons," his father once said when Sam was sixteen. It had been one of Sam's more rebellious times. A time when he questioned the legacy he was born to fulfill, and to that point, didn't want to. Those streaks of doubt and rebellion came and went, ebbed and flowed. Some-times lasting embarrassingly long. The final time had been with Casey. By then, Sam had been in his early twenties. "I wish I had other sons." The man had been drinking heavily, of course. But Sam remembered no falseness in his tone or in his angry eyes. "Well, maybe that creature you called a mother would have ruined them too. But... but at least one of them would... I should have married another one. I should have had more while I still could."

What if he had been right? Sam felt helpless. He wanted to scream and shout and sob, but then that would only prove his father more right.

Take a note from those things in the castle, he thought to himself. *Be blank. Be cold. Be ready.*

Outside, it was beginning to snow. He wrapped his wound with fresh bandages and gauze and put his boot back on. He resisted every wince. *Be blank.*

He limped to the window and stared out. Snow was falling onto the village square, melting instantly on the cobblestone.

A shape slowly emerged from the well. A person. A young woman? For a moment, Sam thought it was Skyler. But he quickly realized it couldn't have been. This woman had the same dark brown hair as her, but it was longer, maybe a little curlier. She had a narrower frame than her too. Slightly darker skin. Her clothing looked similar: a black shirt and jeans.

Then he noticed her face. It took Sam's breath away. It reminded him of Casey's. Those bright eyes, that wide mouth with the full lips, the slightly flat nose. The young woman called out for help. Her voice also sounded like Casey's.

He should have been answering her call. He should have been running out to help her. But instead he was thinking back. Back to when Casey had caught his eye at the library. He couldn't remember what had come over him, what had made him approach her and ask if she wanted to grab a coffee with him. But he could remember his excitement when she'd said yes.

The short time he spent with her made the world seem different, brighter. He felt he finally understood all the love songs and romantic movies and books. She hadn't been the first woman he'd kissed nor the first he'd seen naked. She wasn't even the first who'd touched him in intimate places. But she took his virginity. She took it at her apartment, on that beautiful third date, after they went to the haunted house. He had never thought a person's skin could be so soft.

The next day, he'd tried to text her. She only gave short, delayed replies. He figured she was busy. But as the days went on, her texts became less frequent until she wasn't answering at all. When he'd tracked her down to the library, she smiled at him. For a moment he'd thought everything would be fine until she said:

"Hey, I was gonna reach out to you. Listen, I um... You know... Like, I'm sorry, but... I've really liked getting to know you but... I don't know if this is right for me."

To this day he still tried to figure out what had gone wrong. What he had done wrong. He hated her. He hated himself. He would still pass her from time to time at the library, but she never made eye contact with him. He would look at her social media, haunted by the jealousy of seeing the beautiful pictures she'd take, seeing her date other men. Seeing her get married. Have a baby.

Once, he had been drinking and decided to rant to a late-night gas station clerk about her.

When he finished his sob story, the young guy clicked his tongue. "Three dates, man? That was it? You weren't in love with her, man. You didn't even know her. Like, I know you never forget your first. I get that. But like, you gotta move on. That was barely an actual relationship. Come on, buddy. If it ain't right for her, it ain't right for you. You gotta get over it. Come on."

Sam had resented that. But he knew it was true. He had gotten emotionally invested too quickly. He had seen an intense feeling of lust as something resembling love. He'd felt... special wasn't the word. His father always told him he was special, or at least that he was supposed to be. Specialness was a burden, not a gift. But he'd felt valued, perhaps. Of course that hadn't actually been the case. It had just been three worthless dates that Casey probably didn't even remember. But those moments had made him truly imagine another way he could live his life. He'd been wrong. Casey proved that. The clerk had been right; Sam needed to move on. Though she still haunted him, and he resented that, she had also helped him realize he had more important things to achieve. A purpose that went beyond petty, silly romances or sexual desires.

The woman outside was still shouting, snapping him out of his trance. She was confused and frightened, like Skyler had been, like he had been, like everyone who'd been brought to this damned place had probably been. He needed to go to her. Soiled pants, raw foot and all.

No, forget it. Get what you need and go back to the castle.
Be cold.

Yet, he was moving to the door. Suddenly, a deep thrum shook everything. The bell was ringing again. Why? Panic rushed through his body. Were those things coming? He peeked out the window again. The young woman was covering her ears. Retreating toward the forest.

"No!" he shouted. But she couldn't hear him.

He scrambled out the door. He tried to run across the square but could only manage a belabored limp. She was out of his reach and quickly left his sight.

"Shit."

He looked up at the castle. It was alive again, lights flickering from the windows. He caught movement out of the corner of his eye and turned his attention to it. Something was falling from the tower. He realized it was a person. The body flailed through the air before disappearing from his view behind some buildings.

Before he could ponder who the hell that could have been, his thoughts were shattered by one last loud, clumsy *thrummmmmm*. Its reverberations occupied the air for a few moments before fading. The lights in the castle slowly faded too. For whatever reason, he felt as if he were watching the entire castle die before his eyes.

The silence didn't last long. Somewhere along the village streets, he heard a wet clopping sound approaching the square. He retreated into the library, shut the door behind him, and peeked from the window.

It was the ugly horse-man creature, the one who appeared to be a leader of those monsters. It was galloping, its crooked, branch-like legs carrying the rest of the bulky body the best they could. It appeared to be heading toward the forest. It moved with purpose, fury. Maybe it was pursuing the young woman. In that case, Sam realized with a twinge of grief, there was nothing he could do for her. Yet he didn't have a sense this thing was chasing something. It looked more like a messenger, galloping to the front to deliver important news to the troops. Or maybe to rally them.

At that thought, his stomach tightened. They were coming again. And he had a gnawing feeling that the castle wouldn't fight them off this time.

Be ready.

Chapter Sixteen

Skyler was pacing again, back and forth like a lion in a cage. She was furious, terrified. She needed to do something.

This drive surprised her. She would have imagined herself allowing despair to come crashing down on her, to curl up in a corner and accept the situation. Maybe develop some kind of Stockholm syndrome. But while she and Jon bonded over every classics professor's favorite books, she had a difficult time mustering any fondness for him. She felt for him, in many ways. He had been stuck alone in the tower for so long; it seemed only natural that he would develop the kind of delusions he did. But keeping her prisoner, threatening her—was she supposed to accept that? She was sick of accepting things.

She ran up the stairs, again facing Jon's forbidden green door. Maybe if she pounded on it constantly she would irritate him so much that...

Then she pictured the door opening, a loud bang, and her brains splattering on the walls. There had to be some other way. She scanned the door and noticed something poking out from underneath. It was a dark, metallic-gray object, or at least part of one, a narrow stick leading to a transparent eye on top. Her heart raced. Could it really be that easy?

She kneeled and slid out the object. It slightly scraped against the floor, but likely didn't make enough noise to alert Jon.

It apparently *was* that easy. She was holding a key in her hand. Jon must have dropped it earlier without realizing.

Propelled by fear and adrenaline, she rushed down the stairs to the metal door. She pushed the key desperately against the lock. It refused to go in. She thought, at first, that she was just missing her mark or that she was holding the key the wrong way. But it became quickly apparent that this wasn't the key out of the tower.

"Shit!" she hissed. "Shit! Shit! Shit!"

What was this key for, then? There was one other possibility. She had been so desperate to get away from that green door, as if a bomb were on the other side. But now she would have to go back, at least to see if her theory was correct. Besides, if there was anywhere the actual key to her escape would be, Skyler figured, it would be in that room.

Her slow walk back up the stairs felt like a stealthy march of shame. It seemed hardly necessary to be cautious. Jon hadn't responded to her tromping up and down the stairs, or her fumbling and scraping only moments ago. But she couldn't stop imagining an old bullet tearing into her skin, the kind of agony it would give her if she didn't die right away.

When she was once again standing before the green door, she hesitated. She took in its rustic appearance, the fading green color, the wood splintering. But it was still sturdier than it looked. She gave one last push and pull, to see if it was really locked. It was. Maybe Jon had locked himself in, she considered. And now he lost his only key out. In that case, she could just wait it out until he starved to death. How long would it really take?

But that thought repulsed her. She repulsed herself. Jon was a human being. Not one she particularly liked, but a human being nonetheless.

The cruelty of the thought, and the ease with which she'd had it, frustrated her. She wanted to defy it. So she stuck the key into the lock—it fit effortlessly—and turned. The lock clicked.

⌘

She delayed the next move as much as she could, standing by and popping her fingers against her chin. If she was going to do this, she had to dispel the fear from her head. Nothing was going to happen once she opened this door. Nothing at all.

She turned the handle and pushed slowly. Very slowly. It let out small creaks, which made her heart skip beats. But there was little she could do about that besides take it slow. The foul air encompassed her as the door came open, her stomach reacting like someone was sticking two fingers down her throat. But she kept herself steady and took shallow breaths through her mouth. She couldn't see anything inside. The room was pitch-black. She could only see the boarded-up and curtained windows, outlines of faded light poking through them.

Her eyes adjusted as she moved further into the room. To her right was a large, old bed. It nearly filled the entire space. On the far side was a white mass Skyler couldn't identify.

From the bed, she heard a deep, groaning sound. Snoring. Within the tattered blankets was a lump. At the tip of the lump was what looked like a bruised cantaloupe. It was Jon's head. He was in sight and looked and sounded asleep—that was good. She would still be very quiet. She had always been good at being quiet; it was the one thing she'd surpassed Morgan in or maybe even anyone else she knew.

Holding her shirt collar against her nose and mouth to avoid getting overwhelmed by the stink, she snuck further in, keeping a close eye to the floor. The remnants of a wardrobe—splintered wood and rotted clothing—were splayed everywhere. She tiptoed around the debris. Thankfully, the floor was stone and wouldn't creak beneath her weight. She kept an eye out for anything that might look like a key.

In the farthest corner of the room, one of the curtains fluttered. Next to that window was a bookshelf. She didn't recognize the titles she could make out: *Mechanical Movements: Powers and Devices*; *Principia Mathematica*; *Arithmetica Universalis*. Some books were lying on the ground and looked like they had been torn apart forcefully.

Jon let out a sputter, which made her freeze. She stood in silence for a long time before the old man resumed snoring. She hardly felt relief when he did; her time seemed limited. To reiterate her and Sam's mantra, it was time to keep going.

After only a couple steps, she froze again when she saw what was beside Jon's bed, staring at her: the pale white mass she hadn't identified at first. A pair of human skeletons, both in rotting old clothing and sitting along a chess table. The sight electrified her. It took all she could to suppress a scream. One skeleton was lounging back against the wall, chin up as if taking a moment to recall the good old days. The other was leaning over the table, as if listening carefully for rushing water beneath the ground. They were both grinning at Skyler. Jon's father and the "Frenchman," she presumed. It was no surprise that they had been dead all along. Yet, seeing them now, their blank, lingering gazes, she felt unsure if they actually *were* dead.

When her shock faded, she quickly and carefully scanned them. The skeletons, chess table, and chess pieces were covered in dust. There was a distinct absence of cobwebs. The pieces were all in their starting places, aside from a couple that had been knocked over. Maybe these two men had been good friends all their lives, so Jon allowed their friendship to continue in death. That was assuming he was even aware they were dead. She noticed the back of one of the skulls was caved in. It was too big to have been a product of time.

So I took a pan and I thwacked him in the back of the head.

The sleeping Jon let out a sharp hack. Skyler was braced enough to not go leaping into the chess table, but the sound still gave her a small heart attack. It was time to find the key and get out quickly. She was sick of this.

The bed was the last place to look. Her knees trembled violently, both from nerves and the extreme steadiness she was trying to maintain. She looked underneath. It was hard to see anything in the darkness. Here, the stench of rotted food was especially strong. There were shadowy lumps that she didn't want to feel. She fumbled her phone from her pocket and shined it inside. The glow revealed the lumps to be more old clothes and musty sacks. It was doubtful that the key would be among these. She certainly hoped not.

Taking care to put away her phone first, she rose slowly. She was overwhelmed with an urge to pop her fingers, but making any kind of noise was the last thing she wanted to do. There was one more place to look. It also happened to be the likeliest place: Jon himself.

The man looked dead in this dim light, leathery skin tight like an embalmed cadaver. She remembered when she was very little, when she would visit her grandparents, and her grandad would sleep in front of the TV. He would look dead, his head thrown back and mouth gaping. She would wait in anticipation to see the slow rise and fall of his chest to confirm otherwise. That wasn't necessary here. Jon's snores growled through his narrow nostrils.

She lifted the blanket only slightly enough to peek in, the cloth damp and musty in her fingers. His fragile body was curled like a fetus grown old in the womb. He had the old revolver clutched to his chest like a teddy bear. In some ways, it was a heart-sinking sight. He looked so harmless, vulnerable even, and alone. But she couldn't forget he was also her captor. She wondered how easily she could take the gun away from him. But she decided it was better to avoid conflict all together.

The rags he wore didn't appear to have any pockets. He didn't have a belt, a chain, a pouch, or anything that a key would be inside or attached to. Her gut tightened. There was nothing here, then. Nothing at all but skeletons. Maybe she would have to take the gun from him after all. Then perhaps she could get him to tell her where the key was. Or he would give it to her. But these thoughts disturbed her. She'd never held someone at gunpoint before. Could she do it? Or more importantly, could she pull the trigger if she had to?

She tried to consider any other way and realized there was one place in this tower she hadn't yet visited. The belfry. Maybe the key wasn't up there either. But it was a possibility and any possibilities were good.

With caution, but haste, she tiptoed out of the bedroom. As she closed the door behind her, she wondered again if she should have taken the gun. But she didn't feel eager to go back in there.

Instead, she went to the ladder. The metal rungs were icy against her palms and the sweat made it hard to grip them tightly. But she powered through the discomfort and climbed.

The bell was big enough for Skyler to live in. Its mouth gaped over her as she climbed into its domain. What had Jon named it? Emily? Vera?

Regardless of what its name was, it wasn't friendly looking, despite the elegant wreath pattern along its surface. Cracked and discolored, a greenish blue, it seemed to judgingly look down on Skyler. It was wedged within a system of industrial equipment: chains attaching it to gears and wheels of varying sizes, steel beams and girders. She felt like she was inside the brain of a giant steam-powered robot. The machinery looked long inoperable, rusty, and covered in dust, almost decorative at this point. Jon had talked about how the bell was intended to be run on an automated system. She wasn't knowledgeable enough to know how close to completion this system had been. But everything seemed elaborately rigged.

She squinted and scanned the room for any signs of a key. This was the brightest place in the tower, even more so than the garden, with a window on each wall. One window was mostly boarded up; it must have been broken at one point. But the others remained intact. She could see nothing outside but the silver sky.

Her search didn't take long. Besides the bell and its mechanisms, there was little in the room. A small bundle of blankets, along with what looked to be a pair of blocky earmuffs, an old, grimy plate, fork, and butter knife sat in a corner. Along the opposite corner was a short wooden ladder. It led up to a hook. Hanging there was a black key.

The excitement made it hard for her to swallow. This had to be it. Once again, it seemed a little too easy, but maybe Jon had just forgotten it was up here. After all, he hadn't noticed when he dropped the bedroom key. But she was still suspicious. Even if he wasn't a diabolical puppet master, the people who built the castle—Jon's father and the French architect—were. How was she to know that the room wouldn't suddenly lock down and gas her to death once she grabbed the key? But she couldn't let her paranoia stop her. Not here. Not now. Either she went for it or she would spend her last years in a tower. In that case, what difference would it make if a jerry-rigged anvil came crashing down on her head?

The small ladder grumbled angrily as she put her foot on the first rung. She felt the wood buckling beneath her. It gave her a strong urge to climb fast. She stepped on the next and the next. The fourth rung crunched in two, causing her to fall to the ground, bringing the ladder down on top of her. Its edge jabbed into her chest, knocking the wind out of her. Once she could breathe again, she got back to her feet, pulling the ladder up with her. It's fourth rung was broken, but maybe she could still get to the key without it. But the first rung snapped before she could even bring her full weight onto it.

"Goddammit!"

She hurled the useless ladder aside. Now what was she going to do? She tried to reach it on her own, stretching her short arm as much as she could, propping her foot against a jutting stone in the wall to give her a boost. But it was to no avail, she fell a couple inches short.

There had to be something in this room she could use. A broom, maybe? There would certainly be one downstairs. But she didn't want to go back down there without the key if she could avoid it. She looked back at the bundle of blankets and the plate with its fork and butter knife. Maybe the utensils would work. Not on their own, but if she tied them together...

The rubber band in her hair. Everything that was going on, she had gotten used to the ponytail, even forgetting the tightness of the hair against her scalp. She removed the band. Her damp and moppy hair flopped against her cheeks, delighted in its newfound freedom. She wasn't quite sure how best to tie the fork and knife together. But she didn't need an infallible device. It just needed to last long enough to snag the key. She wrapped the band tightly around the butt of the fork and the top of the knife.

When the two pieces of silverware were adequately conjoined, she tried for the key again. She still had to stretch and use the stone wall as a boost, but she managed to slip the fork's prongs through the key ring and pull it from the hook. The sound of it clattering to the floor was immensely satisfying. Her heart swelled with pride. She wished people could see her now, silly as that was. She wanted to tell Morgan how she MacGyvered her way through a death castle. She stopped that thought before it made her too sad.

"So long," she said to her makeshift key grabber, tossing it aside. So long to the bell, to the tower. And so fucking long to Jon McKinnon. Once she was out, she could figure out how to find the way home. It was in this castle somewhere... Somewhere...

She snatched the key and darted toward the ladder leading down from the belfry. But before she could descend, a spidery hand shot up from the opening and grasped her ankle. She let out an involuntary scream and kicked. The hand had a strong grip, but it let go.

Jon pulled the rest of himself into the belfry, grinning through his wispy beard. The manic glare in his hollow eyes burned with anger and hate.

"You were a test," he said.

She had no idea what he was talking about. Before she could say anything, he raised the revolver and fired, nearly throwing himself back down the ladder. The bullet missed Skyler and hit the bell, causing it to reverberate and give a weak version of its haunting thrum. The way the noise burrowed into her gut, it felt like her bowels were about to expel. A light hanging above them flickered softly until the thrum ceased.

"I got it all wrong," Jon said, grunting as he tremulously regained his composure. "You were not just an anomaly. Samael's bastard seed wasn't my only test. You are too. The sky is testing my worthiness, my resolve."

Skyler was still dazed, but the old man was hobbling closer to her. She scrambled to the other side of the bell, using it as a buffer between them.

"I almost failed," he mumbled. "I came so close. I knew I should've killed you from the beginning. But I... well..."

"I just want to leave!" Skyler insisted desperately.

"If you leave, I fail," Jon babbled lowly, almost speaking more to himself. "If you stay, I fail. Or if you stay alive, that is."

She saw movement from the windows. Small specks. It was snowing; another poor soul had come.

"You are my best friend," Jon said. Skyler wasn't sure if he was speaking to her or to the bell. He sounded like he was on the verge of tears. Beneath the bell, she could see his grungy feet nearly fused to his sandals, shuffling slowly toward her. With each of his movements, she stepped the opposite way.

"But I suppose that's the point," Jon continued. "It's not easy to be the Keeper. But this is my purpose. And you said it yourself, I've been here for a century, and I can be here for another. I believe you said it. Yes, you did."

"Please," Skyler said, squeezing the key in her hand and considering her next course of action. Maybe once she circled around to the ladder, she could quickly scramble down it.

"Vivian," Jon said lovingly. "Vivian was Mama's name too. Father threw her out of the tower. But she's still here. Partly. Nobody has any right to her. None but me."

She heard a raspy sound. Once she realized he was clutching a rope, the bell swung forward, knocking her against the boarded-up window. The boards cracked from her weight, but held strong. The bell's thrum shook through the entire room. Her teeth chattered, her guts felt like they were pushing themselves out of her body. She thankfully didn't have a lot in her bowels to release. But a little came out. The light above her fluttered alive. Beneath her feet, she felt the grinding roar of the castle awakening. Even some of the gears in the room turned, like the jerking response of a dead animal. The bell went into a rhythm, swinging back and forth and singing its deep, discomforting song.

She tightly pressed her hands to her ears, so much so it was painful. She hugged the boarded window, tightly enough to avoid the bell; the board bent against her weight, but didn't break.

Before she could think, cold, slender fingers wrapped around her throat. Jon had practically materialized from thin air and was now on top of her. His eyes were wild, his mouth gaped open, his drool speckling her face. The grip was weak enough that she could buck him off. Just as she did, the still-swinging bell hurled toward him, striking his fragile body like a flipper hitting a pinball. He tripped over Skyler's leg and crashed into the boards. They gave way, breaking apart and vanishing into the silver sky, taking Jon with them.

The bell continued swinging violently. It was unstable, crashing into the machinery and metal around it. Skyler crawled into a corner, still trying to clutch her ears. She wanted it to stop. She screamed for it to stop. When she thought it couldn't take any more, she was right. The bell and all that supported it collapsed into itself. The sound was like an otherworldly cry, like the whole world was collapsing around her. She curled up tight to protect herself.

Before long, the dust faded, the thrum settled, the grinding and roaring halted, the flickering lights faded, and all was quiet and dim again. Skyler slowly uncurled herself. She checked her body to see if she had been harmed. She could feel and smell the mess in her pants, but otherwise was unscratched. The bell, on the other hand, had fallen from its place, lying along a twisted mass of gears and beams.

Skyler removed her pants and underpants, tossing the soiled undergarments aside before slipping her pants back on. All the while, the cool, stale air from outside kissed the back of her neck and trembled her hair, snowflakes melting on her skin. She slowly crawled to the jagged, gaping hole where the boards had once held. The last speckles of snow fluttered into the room before stopping. She was afraid to look out, afraid of what she might see. She wished someone else was here. Someone who would look first. Then she could brace herself.

But she was alone. She had to look.

It was a good thing she had never been afraid of heights; she was as high up as she could be. First, she saw the steep slope of a blue roof. Beyond that, she saw the green field and the village below. Further beyond that, the forest and the sky curving toward it. It was strange that Jon thought the forest and the sky were separate. Along the horizon, they seemed to fuse seamlessly, coming together as one.

Down below, she noticed something. It looked like a spot, a small black blemish against the green field. It was hard to tell what it was from this distance. Jon had that telescope lying around somewhere, but she didn't want to see this up close. The spot almost certainly was Jon's lifeless body. Then she noticed another spot approaching the unmoving one; a flea buzzing toward another. This speck was slightly bigger. Focusing hard, Skyler began to make out a shape, a man on a horse. Or a mule. A chilly feeling came over her as she realized it was the centaur.

Though it was hard to tell with the naked eye, she felt he was looking back up at her.

Ripping herself away from the hole, she retreated down the ladder. She had never felt safe in this world, but in this moment, the panic was something else. She felt like a bomb was about to go off and she didn't know when. But she couldn't stop it. She could only run.

Once she reached the metal door in the library, key in hand, she was stunned into stillness. Was it safer to go back into the castle or to hole up in the tower? She didn't like the latter option. Jon, as repulsive as he'd been, had been the only thing to give the tower any sense of life. Already, without him, it felt like a dead, hollow place. She would lose her mind up here. And besides, it was better not to back herself into a corner. The bomb was ticking.

That settled it. She had to leave. So why couldn't she move? The door was right there, the key in her hand. But she was mortified.

Miss Horne, said a berating voice in her head. Morgan's voice maybe? Not quite, but it was close enough to comfort her. *Girl. I say this only 'cause I love you. Get your ass moving. When the hell have you ever had stage fright?*

It was one thing to be on stage with a group. It was another thing to be alone.

Well, you know what I do when I'm scared shitless? I fucking do it.

I can't.

Yes you fucking can. Do it!

Please...

Do it!

Skyler yelled and pulled down one of the bookshelves. Heavy as it was, it surrendered quickly, crashing onto the floor. She hated this. She wasn't supposed to be here. Nobody was. She threw a book against the wall. She threw another, then another. She hated this. Hated it. Hated it. She threw down one of the chairs along the table, pulled down another. She flipped over the whole goddamn table. She grabbed a book and tore out the pages. She didn't even bother looking at the title. Once the book was gutted, she tossed it aside and fell to the ground, sobbing.

After a while, she composed herself again. The rage and agony weren't out of her system. Not even close. But she felt focused. Rachel had once told her that if she was good at anything, it was crying. That had been meant as an insult. But she didn't regret her outburst. She felt a little embarrassed despite nobody having been there to see it, but her head was clearer.

Then she felt the air become still. Stiller than usual. Like a tuba player taking a breath before blasting a long, sustained note. Skyler also held her breath until the fire in her lungs reminded her to do so.

Move.

Faintly, outside, far in the distance, she heard a loud hissing. The rustling of millions of leaves. She could vaguely smell hints of that swampy stench, just on the periphery of her nostrils. It could've all been in her head, but the clammy feeling on her skin told her otherwise. They were coming. They knew the castle's last line of defense was gone and they were mounting their assault.

Run!

She rushed to the locked door, nearly tripping on the shelf she knocked over. She was relieved when the key fit perfectly in the lock.

The stench was becoming more pervasive by the second. They would be there soon.

CHAPTER SEVENTEEN

THE AIR SETTLED INTO stillness. It was calm, waiting. Beyond the village, he could hear the shrill sound of the hissing trees. The noise was mocking him, testing him, propelling him to move quicker. He hobbled as fast as he could, looking up at the castle wall, trying to find the entrance he and Skyler had taken at the very beginning. Where the hell had it gone? Had it disappeared?

The omnipresent hiss grasped at him, trying to throttle his innards and paralyze him. He couldn't let it.

Where the hell was that entryway? Why had he closed the front entrance? What the fuck had he been thinking?

He felt like a trapped animal. But this wasn't the time for that. Now was the time to pull himself together. The forest, the monsters, Maria Faragó. They wanted him to panic. They wanted to see every last inch of dignity drained from him. He wasn't going to let that happen. Not even with the noise and the putrid stink swirling around him and the waves of panic constricting his veins. He was going to be better. He *was* better.

Looking along the castle wall, with his newfound resolve, he at last found the elusive entryway.

❦

Climbing the rocky surface was hell for him. It wasn't just his foot. He felt like it took twice as much effort than before. Undernourished, dehydrated, exhausted, cold. It was no wonder. But he wouldn't let himself succumb.

Once he reached the mouth of the cave-like entrance, he glanced back at the village. A scattered stream of grungy, green shapes were weaving through the streets. Their screeching war cries sent chills through his body. He immediately kept moving. If he stopped to think, he wouldn't be able to move at all. He hobbled into the chamber with the firepit. He remembered sitting there with Skyler not that long ago. She had become the first person he ever told about the Society and the tool. A small pinch of grief burst somewhere inside him. He pushed away the thought, pulling out his flashlight and moving through the doorway he had opened with his great-grandfather's key, back into the dark halls of the castle.

As he navigated the twisting hallways, remembering to be conscientious of trapdoors, he realized he didn't know where he was going. More specifically, he didn't even know where he *wanted* to go. What had been the goal before he fell out the window? Where were he and Skyler planning to go?

The tower. He had to move toward the tower. The maze somehow felt more disorienting than ever. He felt every turn brought him back to the place he had been before. His head was spinning.

He heard noises echoing through the halls. Growling, hissing, moaning, scratching. He smelled them. They were already inside and he was completely unarmed. He couldn't believe he had left the axe behind.

Sure, it would have been little help if a bunch of those things converged on him, but it would at least have been *something*.

He found an opening along one of the walls. That was new, wasn't it? He didn't bother thinking about it too much. Something new was more than welcome. He slipped inside.

He didn't realize what a mistake he made when the floor groaned and lowered beneath his foot. Nor did he realize it when a steel door slid in, closing the opening behind him. It was only when he heard hissing and looked up to see pale yellow mist spewing from the brass faucets above that he realized what a mistake he had made.

He covered his mouth with his sleeve and scrambled around the room, looking for something to help him.

What had he done? Why hadn't he taken one moment to think? He killed himself. He was going to die in the darkness. Alone.

Maybe this had been inevitable. Maybe he needed to lie down and accept his fate. But he was still grasping along the walls, looking for something. *Something.*

It couldn't end here. It couldn't be over.

But it was.

He lowered his sleeve from his mouth. There was so little good that would do. The gas was filling the room. He knew he was going to die, maybe something inside him even accepted that already. But he still couldn't stop himself from grasping along the walls.

Maybe there was something.

CHAPTER EIGHTEEN

S HE HALF RAN, HALF fell down the first set of stairs. Her knees hit the stone floor of the landing hard, sending a shockwave through her body. The automatons around her stood dutifully still, despite the onslaught coming their way. They could only stand there helplessly, watching the threat come closer, unable to defend themselves even with their swords at their hips.

Their swords.

Skyler was woefully unarmed. She thought about Jon's gun. What had happened to it? It very well could have still been at the top of the tower lying somewhere next to Vivian's carcass. Of course, there was no sense in going back to get it.

She ran to the nearest automaton and grabbed its sword by the hilt. It was hard to pull from the sheath. She had to push against the automaton's massive back to get some leverage. When she finally pulled out the sword, the automaton fell face-first into the window, slamming loudly against the glass, which remained fully intact. Lifting the sword took some effort. She wouldn't last in an actual sword fight, but she felt better having it.

After all, she'd used one of these before.

Before moving down the next set of stairs, she noted the metal slits along the walls. The blades. In retrospect, the triggering step had almost always been in the middle. Instead of crawling her way like she'd done going up, she could perhaps step over it. But she didn't know which step it *was*. The triggering steps had blended in with the others, no discoloration, and needed full weight before lowering. There was no testing it.

The sword trembled in her hands as she carefully moved down the stairs, prepared to drop if needed. She had to readjust her grip several times to keep the hilt from slipping out of her sweat-soaked hands. She counted fifteen steps before the next floor was in sight. If she were right, there were eighteen more stairs left. She took a leap of faith over the three middle steps, nearly losing her balance and tumbling the rest of the way. But she managed to catch herself and the heavy sword. She panted with relief and panic. No longer feeling bold, she scooted down on her bottom the rest of the way. It was painful on her lower body and the sword screeched as she dragged it along with her. But she reached the floor without incident.

The monstrous stench was growing more pungent. She heard the faint cacophony of howling and moaning—an approaching army. Now was the time to go faster and maybe take more risks. For the next few stairs, she made the middle leap without crawling the rest of the way. Several times, she nearly tripped again after landing. She thought about how dangerous it was, running around with a sword in her arms. How many times had she been told not to run with scissors as a child?

Upon reaching the floor below the twelfth or thirteenth flight down, a shadow crawled over one of the windows. At first the shape looked like a large, green orangutan. But the veiny and pale green face, though nearly skeletal from the skin sagging away from it, was more human. Its buggy green eyes locked on her. The creature raised a clawed hand and began slamming it into the glass; it went into a frenzy, slamming harder and harder. With each strike, cracks in the glass materialized. The automaton guarding the window stood calmly, practically greeting the intruder like an old friend.

Skyler made haste, quickly charging down the next set of stairs, leaping over the middle three steps by estimation, but not actually counting. There were more shadows banging at the windows on the next floor. Some of the glass was already giving way. She kept going, not stopping even with the terror pulsing through her body—or the revolting stench.

By the time she descended the seventeenth or eighteenth floor, she lost count, but had to be close. She heard a shatter and crash below. She skidded to a halt beyond the steps. Before her, a small, almost child-sized creature was pinning a lifeless automaton to the ground. The thing slashed furiously at the machine, ripping apart the hollow face. Other creatures were slipping in from the hole it had left. A nearby window shattered; it sounded like glass breaking, but looked more like a transparent wall bursting away, knocking down the automaton. A slender creature leaped through and mounted the downed automaton, bashing its metallic head into the ground.

Skyler again pushed through her fear before paralysis could set in, rushing past the creatures beginning to crowd the floor. One reached for her, letting out a throaty howl, its claws barely missing the back of her shirt.

She was stopped again before she could descend the stairs. A bulky creature was lurching up the steps toward her. It had the build of a pro wrestler but the face of a sickly old man. It groaned, reaching its claws toward her. From behind, a slimy hand grasped her arm. She couldn't see the creature that grabbed her, but it had the strength of an ape. It hissed and slobbered on her, the hot stench pouring onto her head. The beastly wrestler came closer, reaching out its jagged green hand for her. She was pinned. Though she was still holding the sword, her arm was trapped. The poisonous smell kept coming, completely consuming her, watering her eyes, filling her nostrils. She heaved, but had nothing to vomit.

Suddenly, the groan of lowering stone was heard. The two creatures halted. The one holding her arm loosened its grip. She took this moment to drop to her bottom. The blade sang above her head, along with the squishy, meaty sound of sliced flesh. Warm slime spattered onto her. A pair of mossy green legs, devoid of a torso, tumbled down beside her. When it was all over, she was slathered in black blood that also painted the walls and stairs. The blood was squeezing her clothes to her skin and her hair to her scalp. She let out several uncontrollable gasps, disgust and horror filling her body.

Keep moving.

She scuttled down the stairs. Along the way, she triggered a trap step, causing the blades to fly above her head again. She crawled over the body of the larger creature, or at least the torso. The legs were floating in their own blood at the bottom of the stairs.

The next floor looked like a grotesque garden had filled it. It was crowded with creatures. Skyler felt all the energy fade from her. It was over. But the creatures looked stunned, even repulsed, some recoiling at the sight of her. It was quickly apparent they weren't going to attack her, not at the moment at least. The image of their comrades' blood on her seemed to repel them. She gathered herself and carefully moved through the room without issue. The creatures even parted for her, avoiding her touch.

It was the same the rest of the way down the tower. The last stairwells were also covered in black blood and dismembered corpses that she navigated around. She had to get used to holding her breath. More than a few times, the stench made her heave again.

At last, miraculously, she was back at the windowless tower base. It was thankfully devoid of creatures. The black goo covering her was rapidly drying, and she didn't know if that would take away its repellent power. She dashed across the star-patterned floor, the heavy, unused sword still glued to her hand.

She paused at the entryway that would lead her back into the castle. It was a thick wall of pure blackness. She couldn't even see a foot ahead of her. For all she knew, one of those creatures was there, standing only inches from her.

But she couldn't let this wall stop her. There was no going back. She pulled out her phone, keeping it tightly clenched in her trembling palm.

Please work. Please.

It came on, though the battery life was at eight percent. *Fuck.*

She would make do; she would have to. Bright as it was, the screen itself wouldn't be enough, so she turned on the flashlight. It was going to drain the battery even faster. But at least she could see a narrow hall before her leading to a small stairway. There wasn't time to think about what she would do once the phone died.

She ran down the brief hall, up the stairs leading back into the castle, holding her phone in one hand and nearly dragging the sword in the other. Once she was in the castle proper, a three-way fork greeted her, each path indistinguishable from the other with the uniform gray, dungeon-esque walls and floors.

Her roller coaster of hope and dread was plummeting again. She'd known this would be inevitable. But she couldn't believe she was back in the castle.

❧

She was a starving mouse in a maze, exhausted, disoriented, frightened. But she kept moving, winding through the halls. When she hit a dead-end, she turned around and kept going until the next one, or the same one, perhaps. The markings, the red Xs, her breadcrumb trail, she had to find one of them soon.

The creatures seemed to be everywhere, yet nowhere. She could smell them—sometimes faintly, sometimes powerfully. She could hear them as well, their sounds bouncing off the walls, claws clicking, raspy breathing, groaning and hissing. Sometimes she'd turn a corner and see a shape vanishing around another. They were sniffing about, hunting. Not for her. At least, she didn't think so.

A small creature skittered between her feet, nearly tripping her. It looked like a diseased rat that had drowned in a sewer, but it had a longer, hunched form. Perhaps it had once been a squirrel. It turned its buggy green eyes to her and screeched, baring its sharp buckteeth. She kicked it away and retreated.

Soon after this encounter, she came upon a stairway. Most likely a false one, but she tread down it anyway. Carefully—who was to say a bad step wouldn't lead to her getting cut in half or dropped down a trapdoor? But she reached the landing without incident. The next set of stairs seemed to lead farther down to the lower floor. No dead-ends.

But before she could take a first step, an enormous shape came tromping up from the thick shadows toward her. It reminded her of the Skunk Ape from those fake pictures she would see on the internet, its bulky body hunched over, moss trailing down it like moppy fur. But its face was humanoid, besides the melted cheeks. Its breathing was deep but exerted. It reached a thick hand toward her.

"Stay back," Skyler said. She held up her sword with both hands, which took the light off of the creature's face. "Stay back!" She intended to shout but it came out as a whisper.

The creature gave a loud and angry groan. It must have detected the hesitance in Skyler, her uncertainty. It lunged forward. She thrust the sword, hardly realizing she was even doing so. There was a thick squish, and it felt like she was cutting into a decomposing piece of meat. But it was an easier strike than the automaton had been; the creature's flesh was much softer. She felt more lukewarm blood trickling onto her already covered shirt. The creature halted as soon as the sword penetrated its body, its face only inches from her own. Its hot breath spewed into her eyes. She held her breath as much as she could. There was something almost familiar about the face in this light, as if this was someone she'd seen in a movie or a TV show once. The creature's bulbous eyes were massive with either fury or fear, or both. There was a helplessness in this expression that made Skyler want to turn away, but also keep looking.

The creature let out a low pathetic groan. It began to teeter back, taking the sword with it, so she let go of the hilt, accidentally dropping her phone as well. Once she did, the creature tumbled down the stairway and vanished into the darkness.

For a long time, everything was still and silent. Then, from the blackness came a pained howl. It didn't sound like the same creature, it was higher pitched. Tremulously primal, yet it sounded strangely familiar. Skyler picked up her phone and shined her light toward the bottom of the stairs. The massive creature was lying there, sword in its belly, its eyes emptily staring up at her. But long, spindly arms were wrapped around the dead creature's chest, both leading up to a head of green, matted hair that veiled a thin face. This new creature raised its head and curled back its thin black lips letting out another low, croaking cry. But the cry quickly faded and the black lips retracted in a snarl. Skyler knew it was looking up at her. The spindly arms released the dead behemoth and the creature began crawling up toward her. This time, she had nothing to fight it with, so she turned to retreat. But before she could get too far, the creature's cold and slimy hand wrapped around her ankle, pulling her down against the steps.

Her hands, wrists, and throat stung from the fall. Though protected, her phone had hit the stone hard. Fortunately, the flashlight worked, now shining in her own eyes and blinding her. She felt the thin creature crawl on top of her, raspy breathing in her ear, damp hair brushing across her neck. It grasped her by the shoulders and flipped her onto her backside, forcing her to face it. Skyler turned the bright flashlight into its eyes, causing the creature to recoil. Its hair parted and its black lips curled back revealing sharp, greenish teeth.

There was something about the face, something familiar. In fact, everything about this creature began to look familiar, from its long hair to its thin body. As the familiarity set in, Skyler felt her blood crawl away from every inch of her body.

"Morgan?" she asked weakly.

The creature didn't respond. Skyler didn't know why she had said that. Of course this wasn't Morgan. There was no way. Morgan was beautiful. She made a point of taking care of her perfect copper skin. This thing's pale sage skin was drooping. It had black veins all over. Its eyes flew open now, resisting the flashlight. The eyes. Morgan had small but striking brown eyes. This thing's eyes were false-looking, green and buggy, like old golf balls.

The creature screamed at Skyler. There was something in the voice that sounded indescribably familiar.

She wanted to run. She needed to run. Whatever this thing was, whoever it was, it was none of her concern. It only resembled Morgan. That was all.

She crawled backward up the steps. The creature again reached toward her. A distorted shape stretched along the back of this hand. It looked like some kind of green-and-blue Rorschach. But Skyler could recognize the shape, could see it all too clearly. A hummingbird. Her favorite tattoo of Morgan's, the one she told herself she would get if she was ever brave enough to get one.

The sight made her pause long enough for the creature to grab her throat.

"Morgan?" Skyler asked again. It was a whisper, quickly choked away as the grip on her throat tightened.

This time, something softened in the monster's face. The thick eyes still looked coldly at her, but the mouth quivered. It loosened its grip on her neck, allowing her to breathe, even as her throat burned and eyes stung with tears.

"Morgan." She didn't know what was happening. What was she even feeling? Relief? Sadness? Hope? Fear? Maybe she felt everything. Whatever feeling it was, it suffocated her, even if she could literally breathe now. She felt out of her body. She didn't know what else to say. What was she supposed to do?

The creature—Morgan, it was Morgan—slowly pulled its hand away from Skyler, and began backing down the stairs. Her mouth twitched as if she wanted to say something.

"Mor—" Skyler was about to say it again, but the name caught in her throat. How could this be Morgan? The teeth were so sharp, more like a dog's than human. Morgan never took dental hygiene seriously, yet her teeth seemed perfect. Skyler always thought that was unfair.

Morgan stopped backing away, but continued twitching and sputtering, trying to speak. It was as if she didn't know how. Every second made the creature look more and more like Morgan. Warped, but Morgan nonetheless.

Finally, a couple words managed to escape. "Rae... Rae..."

The world fell away from Skyler. Whatever feelings she had before melted as sadness jabbed into her gut. It wouldn't have felt worse if she'd found Morgan's corpse instead. She curled up into herself and broke down into tears. It was all the more painful that Morgan, whatever was left of Morgan, only watched her. She offered no shoulder to cry on, no advice, no hugs. She just watched Skyler sob and gave that struggled mutter.

"Rae... Rae..."

Slowly, the sadness melted into anger.

No, hatred. Skyler howled and beat the stone steps with her fists, wishing she could tear down everything around her. She hated the world, the forest, and everything in it. She wanted to make it all suffer for what it had done to Morgan.

When she was drained and her throat and fists stung, Morgan still only sat there, staring like a confused stray dog.

"Morgan, I—" Skyler wanted to tell her that she was sorry. But she didn't have the will to say it. She hardly had the energy to even think about this. Besides, something in Morgan's demeanor changed again. Her face contorted back into its monstrous scowl; she was no longer trying to speak. She looked at Skyler like prey. Something in this look cast a spell on Skyler. It made the anger and sadness fade. It made everything fade. This was not her cousin, her best friend, not now. This was a monster who was poised and ready to kill her. She had to push everything away right now. She had to find whatever energy she had left and run.

She made it past Morgan, down the stairs, nearly tripping over the large body of the monster she killed. As she weaved through the castle's desolate halls, she could hear Morgan's echoing shriek. The noise felt like it was everywhere, both right behind her and far away.

There were other noises around her, scratching, growling, shuffling. When rounding every corner, she felt sure she would come face-to-face with something. When the corner turned out to be empty, her relief was short-lived before the next one.

The floor gave way. She leaped forward, avoiding the trap beneath. But her phone fell from her hand and into the pit. She heard the groaning trapdoor close behind her, and the light of the phone blinked away with it, leaving her in complete blackness. Alone. She pressed against the wall and hugged her knees. What was she going to do? Somewhere in the hall, she could still hear the echo of Morgan's angry cries. They seemed to be coming closer and closer. Skyler clutched her head and shut her eyes. With the darkness around her, she could only tell they were closed by the sensation of her lids being pressed together. Then she heard steps thudding toward her. She tensed her entire body, squeezing herself into a ball. But as the footsteps came closer, a bright red glow grew beneath her eye lids. When she opened her eyes, her retinas were hit by a blinding light that forced her to shield herself.

"Skyler?" The light was lowered from her vision.

It was impossible. She had to be hearing things. But she looked up to see Sam standing before her. He was haggard and drained, his torn backpack loosely hanging from his shoulder. But it was undeniably him. He was alive.

Skyler rose to her aching feet. Sam took a limping step toward her. The idea suddenly hit her that maybe her brain was playing tricks. He wasn't really there. Or maybe this was a ghost.

But she didn't care. No doubts could stop her from wrapping her arms around his waist, pressing her face into his chest. It didn't matter how fragile and clammy he felt or how his jacket smelled of dried blood and sweat. He was warm, breathing, alive.

Slowly, somewhat hesitantly, he rested his hands on her back and his chin on her head. He didn't seem to care that she was a mess—he was a mess too. She whimpered, tears soaking his jacket. She wasn't alone anymore. She wasn't alone.

"Listen," Sam whispered weakly, "I think I've found it."

She had no interest in asking him to elaborate, not at the moment at least. She just basked in his presence.

"I think so," he said. "I think I've found the way out."

PART FOUR
THE FOREST

Chapter Nineteen

The twisted halls were strangely starting to feel familiar, even if she couldn't tell where any of them led. But she didn't have to think about that. She followed behind Sam, guided by a trail of Xs he had left.

Caution was still vital. The reek was ever present. At every moment, she could hear the creatures shuffling and growling, their breaths heavy. She couldn't hear Morgan anymore, which both relieved and unnerved her. Occasionally, they would see a shape move by and Sam would turn off the flashlight and hide them behind a corner. After a moment, he would turn the flashlight back on and they would continue on their way.

She was so relieved to have Sam back. And though of course he didn't say it, something told her he was relieved to have her too.

"Listen," he said, his voice nearly a whisper. "The chamber. It... you'll see. I stumbled on it completely by accident."

"How do you know it's the way out?"

"I just do." There was an edge of uncertainty in his voice that was far from reassuring. "I was gonna investigate further, but then I heard you screaming. Or I thought I could, you know?"

She couldn't remember screaming, though her throat was a bit raw.

"Luckily, I practiced a little foresight." He slapped one of the Xs on the wall. "For once."

For once? Was that Sam being self-deprecating? She never thought she'd see the day. He didn't even seem aware he'd done it. Of course, his tone had been more bitter and frustrated than good-humored. He still tried to carry himself with that stubborn pride, though his shoulders were stooped more than ever, his steps laboring, and did his hair seem even grayer now? Obviously, carrying himself was becoming an Olympian task. She could understand that.

They reached an entryway along one of the walls. The X next to it had been circled profusely.

"Anyway, what was I saying? Oh, the chamber, right. Remember to watch your step." Sam carefully slipped inside.

Remember? Had they been in this place before. It didn't seem familiar. It looked like an empty room. Was this the chamber Sam was talking about? As she stepped inside, a tile lowered beneath her foot.

"I said watch your step!" Sam shouted, whipping around.

It was too late. Behind her, a steel door slid over the entryway, trapping them inside. A hissing sound came from the ceiling. She looked up to see several metal faucets spewing yellowish gas.

"Oh god." The gas chamber. "Oh god! No!"

She rushed to the steel door and banged on it. It couldn't end like this, it couldn't end because of her stupid mistake. She couldn't smell the gas—she could only see and hear it. When would she feel it? How would she feel it? Would it hurt?

"No!" She banged harder on the steel door.

"Calm down," Sam said across the room. "Hey, Skyler! Calm down!"

Something about his tone grabbed her. She turned and looked at him. He seemed unperturbed. He was standing at the other end of the room, covering his face with his sleeve.. Skyler didn't have a sleeve and used her shirt's collar to cover her own mouth. Sam felt along the wall until his hands rested on one of the stones. He grabbed it and pulled it down like a lever. The hissing immediately stopped and she heard the door behind her slide back open. The wall next to Sam parted, revealing a new entryway.

"Keep your mouth covered and come on," he said.

⌒

They were in a gigantic round room. It felt like an interior courtyard. It was mostly empty except for a circular black platform in the center. The platform had about forty or fifty white metal pegs jutting haphazardly from its surface.

Once again, Skyler was startled by a low groan. She looked to see the wall closing behind them.

"Don't worry," Sam said calmly. "There's a switch on this side too."

She would have to trust him.

"What is this?" she asked, nodding at the platform.

Sam shrugged. "I didn't have much of a chance to investigate before I heard you."

"Thanks," Skyler said. "Thank you for coming for me."

"Yeah. Well, seems you did fine on your own."

She nodded. Fine was maybe an overstatement, but she survived.

"What made you scream like that?"

Skyler suddenly felt like her throat was closing up. She didn't want to talk about Morgan right now. "I... It... Those people. I mean those... They were all over the place, you know? One of them almost had me."

"I see."

"But we're alive," she said. Surprisingly, the thought of that hit her in the stomach. A feeling of guilt and grief. But she was able to swallow it and give Sam her best "how-can-I-help-you" smile.

His reaction to her smile was surprising. He looked like she had told him he had cancer.

"What's wrong?" she asked.

"I don't know. I mean, nothing. Nothing's wrong." Sam turned the flashlight to what looked like a small fountain along the wall. "What the hell is this?"

He was dodging. That was fine. She did a lot of dodging too. Whatever was wrong was probably his business.

"I don't know," she said, also focusing her attention on the fountain. It looked like an indentation in the wall with a long torch in its middle. Sam felt around the fountain until his hand rested on a knob that looked like an old brass light switch. He pulled the knob upward. After a brief pause, the torch flickered alive.

"Well, there you go," Sam said.

These fountains, or more accurately, lanterns, circled the room, each spaced only a foot from the other. Sam went to the next, turned it on, and then moved on to the next. To speed up the process, Skyler went to the first lantern on the opposite side. Its switch was strong and stubborn, and once she finally brought it up, some dust kicked into her face. But the torch came alive and she moved to the next. Once Skyler and Sam met in the middle, the room was completely lit. He turned off his flashlight; it was unnecessary now with the warm, comforting glow of the torches.

"If only we had those in the rest of the castle," Sam said.

"Yeah."

He pursed his lips before asking, "Do you need something to eat? Drink?"

Skyler hadn't been thinking about that. But yes, she did.

They sat on the platform. Skyler was so tired. Her body was sore, not to mention her ass was chafed after disposing of her underwear and scooting down stairs. Sam studied the white pegs while she ate a crumbled protein bar and drank some water. Some bites were hard to swallow. Images of black lips and bulging eyes kept popping in and out of her head. She imagined Morgan—what used to be Morgan—in those halls, looking for her. The thought was disturbing. She wished she could think of a way she could help Morgan. Anything. Anything at all. But there was probably nothing and that twisted her guts.

In her mind, she kept hearing that wail Morgan gave over that massive creature's body. What had it been to her?

She reached into her mind and pulled out a memory. Something Morgan had once said regarding her father:

"He's a big guy. Big enough to go toe-to-toe with Dwayne Johnson. I mean, he'd get his ass beat. But he'd qualify!"

Had that large creature been Darwin Miller? Had Morgan actually found her father? Skyler's skin went cold, and she put aside the remaining half of her protein bar. She lost her appetite.

She killed him. She killed Morgan's father. But she did what she had to, didn't she? She had to fight to protect herself. She hadn't known it was him. She couldn't have.

"Hey," Sam said. "Are you okay?"

His voice pulled her away from the spiral. She pushed it all from her mind. She knew resisting these thoughts and feelings was unhealthy, that it would cause problems, that her therapist would advise against it. But she had neither the time nor the spirit to deal with this. Sick and exhausted, there was no place for these thoughts. Not right now. Maybe not ever.

"Skyler?"

"Yeah, I'm fine." She forced down the rest of the protein bar. It was now like trying to eat gravel.

"Have another if you want."

"Shouldn't we ration?" She wished she'd taken some produce and water from the tower.

"We may not need to ration for long."

She didn't want to question him. She wanted to believe his certainty that he'd found the way out and that certainty was grounded in proof. She didn't want to shatter the hope. Still, though.

"I mean, how do you know?" she asked.

"I just have a gut feeling," he replied.

"Oh." That was the last answer she wanted to hear.

Sam suddenly looked angry. The wrinkling from his scowl made him look twenty years older. She wondered if these wrinkles had formed recently. How many wrinkles had *she* formed? Was her hair still brown or was it turning gray? She hadn't looked in a mirror in a long time. At this point, she didn't want to.

Sam pointed at a long, smooth crack that stretched along the length of the platform.

"You see that?" he said. "This thing opens."

He turned to a nearby peg and pushed it down. It lowered into the platform until a loud click indicated it could go no further. Part of the peg still slightly poked out so it could be pulled up again.

"You heard that, right?" Sam asked. "There's a mechanism in place here. My guess is, if you push these things down in the right order—or maybe the right pattern or... I don't know—but this platform will open up if you do it right."

"But what's the order? Or pattern?"

"Well, I don't know," Sam said. "But there's got to be a clue in here."

"But *how do you know?*"

Skyler was growing irritated. Why was he being so goddamn naive? He knew this castle. He knew it was a cruel, cold, evil fucking place. If there were a clue at all, if there were anything to even need a clue for, it probably wouldn't be here.

Sam looked startled, almost a little hurt, by her curt response.

"I'll figure it out," he said.

Skyler felt bad, but not enough to step down. Not anymore.

"You don't have to believe me," he said, his tone turning firm and icy. "You just need to trust me. Help me too, if you want. But at least trust me."

"But how do you know?" she asked again. "How do you know this is the way out and not just another trap or another dead-end? How do you know you can figure out how to unlock this? How do you even know it can be unlocked at all?"

"I don't!" His eyes widened and his lower lip trembled. He seemed as surprised at the outburst as she was. "I..." He cleared his throat. "I don't. You're right. Maybe we should ration as long as we can, and then just... You're right."

He sat next to her and buried his head in his hands. He wasn't crying or pouting, he just seemed embarrassed. Seeing him like this—admitting a failing—pacified Skyler's frustration. She had no idea if she was supposed to pat his back, put her hand on his shoulder, or say something; so she did none of those things.

"I'll tell you this," Sam said, raising his head after a long silence, his voice trembling. "I have a feeling we are where we need to be. Just a feeling. Maybe it's wrong. But as long as I have this feeling, I need to see it through. Okay?"

Skyler nodded. It was fair. For all she knew, his feeling was right. Then she would be home. Everything would be okay. Except, she killed Morgan's father. And Morgan was...

"I have a question," Sam said. Somehow, he regained that classic Sam tone and sounded like he was ready to interrogate her. "What happened to you?"

"What happened to me?"

"I mean, how did you survive?"

"Oh... well, um... I—" It took her a while to find her start, but once she did, she told him as much as she could: Finding the tower base. Climbing those many flights of stairs. Meeting Jon.

"So there's someone living up there?" Sam asked.

"Was," Skyler said.

"What happened to him?"

"There was an accident. He fell." That was right. Jon was dead too. But that couldn't possibly have been her fault. Yet, why did her insides twist at the thought of it?

Sam nodded as if unsurprised by the news. "That... Oh..."

"What?"

"I remember seeing something... someone falling."

She went on to tell him how Jon had lived up there for a long time, surviving in a dwindling, self-sustained environment. How he was the one who rang the bell. Just him. Every time. And how he had been part of Maria's following. How he had been the son of the engineer who designed the mechanisms in the castle. She told him some of the things Jon had told her. How the creatures of the forest were people. *I killed a person.* People who had been brought or taken by the World.

"That... that makes sense," Sam said. His eyes darkened and he suddenly looked ill, haunted. She noticed the tar-like blackness that speckled his clothes, darker than the patterns of his own dried blood. It was probably best not to ask him about it right now. Instead, she told him how Jon had become dangerous. How he'd held her hostage and then tried to kill her. How he fell from the tower and the bell had fallen, shutting down the automatons for good and allowing the creatures to take the castle.

"Wow," Sam said. "You've gone through a lot."

Skyler suddenly felt like crying again. But she kept it down.

"Those things were people," he muttered.

"And animals," she said.

"Yeah..." His face grew even darker. "God, it's fucked up."

"I know. I just wish... I wish there was a way we could stop it."

Sam buried his head in his hands again.

"Sam?" It surprised her how deeply this revelation seemed to affect him. "It's okay. It's..."

"No," he said, looking at her. "Listen, I have to tell you something. I don't know if I... Before I came back here, it started snowing."

"It does that," Skyler said. "It does it every time someone new enters."

"Right." He rubbed the bridge of his nose aggressively. "And when it started snowing, I saw her... I saw her coming out of the well."

"Yeah?"

"It was this girl. This woman. I wanted to help her. I wanted to. But then I heard the bell and I saw that centaur thing and I... I wanted to!"

"Sam," she said. This time, she felt emboldened to touch his hand. "It's okay."

It was always so easy to absolve guilt that wasn't her own.

"No." He pulled away his hand as if Skyler were infected with something. He looked pained, apparently unsure if he should tell her what he had to say.

"Sam?" Now she needed to know.

"She looked familiar. She looked like... Well, she looked like this person I knew. But she wasn't that person. She was... I knew I had seen her somewhere else but couldn't... It wasn't until I saw you when I finally figured it out."

"What do you mean?"

"Back when you showed me those pictures, right? It all clicked."

"Sam?" He was scaring her now. Her heart was in her throat. She popped her fingers against her chin.

"Skyler," he said. "I think it was your sister."

◊

"Rachel?" She wasn't shocked or horrified, because what he said was ridiculous. He had to be mistaken. That made no sense.

"Yeah," Sam said, his tone too grave for this to be a sick joke. "Rachel. I knew the woman looked familiar, then I remembered that picture—"

"I showed you *a* picture of her. One. But that's not enough to... I don't know."

"You're right." Yet, Sam's conviction seemed unshaken.

"It can't be her," Skyler snapped, trying to emulate his conviction. She began to slowly feel dizzy. There was no way it was Rachel. Why would she be there? Skyler had told her to stay home.

But the last thing Rachel had said to her was, *I don't give a shit.*

"She had your dark hair," Sam explained. "The same dark hair."

"A lot of people do!" Her gut sank deeper and deeper.

"She was a bit darker skinned than you."

That still meant nothing. Why was he doing this to her?

"I'm telling you..."

"Shut the fuck up!"

She needed to think. Her head was swirling. It couldn't be true. But if Rachel *did* come out this way, what would make her any less susceptible to the world's call? At the same time, it didn't take every single person in the vicinity, like the hotel manager and the gas station clerk. Plenty of people had to have passed through the area without being taken. But Rachel wouldn't just be passing through. She was there to find something. Like Skyler had been. Like Morgan had been. And why wouldn't that search lead her right to the mom-and-pop shop? Right to the snow globe.

"I think..." Sam stopped himself and nodded. He looked a little hurt again. "You know what? Forget it. I must've been mistaken."

Forget it? How could she forget it? He said he had seen her sister. Here. In this hellhole. Skyler had already lost... She'd had enough. If Rachel truly had been taken, and Skyler just "forgot it" and left, she'd never get her sister back. What would she tell her parents? What would she be *able* to tell them? What would she be able to tell herself?

"Oh god," Skyler mumbled absently. She felt like she was full of sand. "Oh god."

"I'm telling you," Sam said irritably, though the irritation seemed to be directed at himself, "I was probably mistaken."

"You don't believe that."

"Actually, I think it was probably a dream," he tried to lie. "I just dreamed I saw someone."

She wouldn't even entertain that.

Sam sighed. He was oozing with sinking regret. "I'm sorry," he said. He spoke as if giving his condolences. As if there was nothing that could be done about her loss. Maybe that was true. Or maybe...

"I have to go."

"She went to the *forest*," Sam said, as if that was the final word. That made Skyler angry. She had an urge to lash out, to shout and maybe hit him. But that wasn't what Rachel needed.

"Then I need to go there," she said, trying to keep calm while pacing. She wasn't thinking about what she was saying. She couldn't think about it. Let the implications fly over her shoulder, that was the only way she could keep it together.

"What?" Sam looked horrified.

Skyler continued pacing. If she stopped her feet now, they would never move again. Thoughts flooded her mind. Maybe this wasn't Rachel. But what if it was? Or what if it wasn't and Skyler went into the forest for nothing and died there? What if it was Rachel but Skyler *still* died there? Then her parents would lose both of their children. And they would never know what happened to them... unless they came out this way too, felt the urge, and...

"I don't know!" she shouted. "I don't know! I fucking don't know."

"Keep calm," Sam said. He couldn't have imagined how much she was trying. It felt like all the oxygen was streaming out of the room.

But how could she live with herself if it was Rachel? How *would* she live with herself?

She wouldn't.

Skyler stopped pacing and breathed deeply. A small sense of calm came over her. A feeling of acceptance. Of resolve.

"We'll figure this out," Sam said. He seemed satisfied, as if he had been the one to reel her in. But the truth was, all roads led to one conclusion.

"I'm going," she said. Without a moment's thought, she moved to the wall where the entryway had been.

"Hey!" Sam said, hobbling toward her and trying to block her way. "What the hell are you doing?"

Skyler quietly slipped past him. She couldn't stop and think or she would never go. She scanned the wall with her hand, searching for the switch. Eventually, a stone lowered. The entryway came roaring open. Before she could go through it, Sam snatched her by the shoulders and whipped her around.

"Let me go!" she said, nearly giving herself whiplash trying to tug away from him.

"You can't go out there!"

She pulled away. "Don't touch me," she snapped when Sam reached for her again.

"Skyler," he said, keeping his voice calm. "It's probably too late."

"Fuck you."

"You're being—"

"I'm being what?" Her sister was out there. And Morgan was... But she couldn't do anything for Morgan. Nothing she could think of, at least. Not now. But Rachel needed her. Unattended, the entryway closed again. And suddenly, Skyler was angrier than she'd ever been. She thought all of her energy would have been spent by now. But a new wave washed over her. She was tired of all of this.

She screamed, kicking the wall over and over again. "God-fuck-ing-dammit! Goddammit! Fuck!" She was kicking the world. Both of them. Kicking Sam, Morgan, Rachel, herself, everyone and everything. Where was the answer? Where was the simple fix?

When the anger petered out and her toes throbbed, she turned to Sam. He looked shocked at her outburst, frightened even.

"What?" she asked. Her anger wasn't erupting anymore, but it still bubbled beneath the surface. She breathed like a warrior recovering from battle frenzy.

"Uh, nothing."

She closed her eyes and focused on her breathing. She needed to go now, while she still had the anger to push her forward.

"So you're going," Sam said. There was a tense caution in his voice.

"Yes," she replied without hesitation.

Sam nodded in acquiescence. "Hold on."

He pulled off his backpack and fumbled inside, taking out his pocketknife—the one Skyler had used to burn his flesh—and handed it to her.

"It's more for utility than combat," he said. "But it's better than nothing." He also gave her the flashlight, two backup batteries, and a protein bar. "It's all I can give you."

"I know." Skyler felt lucky to have this much.

"I'm keeping the water. Do you want a drink before you go?"

The bottle he handed her was less than half full. She took a conservative sip.

"If..." Sam gritted his teeth. "*When* you get out of the castle, you can get more from the stream."

"Thank you." She gave him back the water bottle.

"It might not be her, you know."

"But if it is—"

Sam shrugged. Instead of remounting his backpack, he rested it against the platform. "I need to stay here," he said. "I'm just so close."

There was a hint of shame and pleading in his tone. She gave him a nod she hoped would show that she understood. Part of her wished he would come with. Part of her resented him for telling her what he did and not helping her. But she knew he was justified staying behind. He looked so tired and sick. It was relatively safe here and he seemed to think with all his heart that it was the way out. If anything, Skyler felt like she was in the wrong for leaving him behind.

She turned to the wall and once again pulled the switch, opening the entryway. She was tempted to turn to Sam, maybe try and convince him to come with her after all. But she thought better of it.

"Thanks," was all she said before stepping out.

Sam said nothing, even as the entryway grumbled closed, leaving her in complete blackness.

She flipped on the flashlight, half expecting something to be glaring at her from the other end of the gas chamber. But she saw nothing but an empty room with the lethal faucets hanging above. Somewhere near the entryway leading back to the maze was the trap step. She needed to mind it. Even if she stepped on it, she reminded herself, all she would have to do would be to reopen the way to the courtyard. Though if she did, she feared she would never leave again. And then Rachel would be lost.

She noticed something along the floor: three dark red dots, evenly spaced. Blood. Whose was it? Hers?

Or Sam's?

Chapter Twenty

HE WANDERED AROUND THE large room, cursing to himself, every step further agitating his foot. Of course this would happen. Why did he have to tell her? He kept looking at the wall, expecting the entrance to slide open again.

But it didn't. Skyler wasn't coming back. Moments kept slipping by. Minutes? Hours? Perhaps none of that mattered in here. Part of him had an urge to go after her. But he couldn't. She had the flashlight. She had his best weapon. What the hell had he been thinking giving those to her? He was trapped here and she was probably already dead.

"Fuck!"

He should've forced her to stay. Even if it meant knocking her out. Not that he would've been able to do that. He should have done something, though. But she had looked like she was in so much pain and he...

Weak. Weak. You weak piece of shit.

He could've at least given her an extra protein bar.

His head was spinning. He was drowsy, tired. Weak. He sat on the central platform, noting the white pegs jutting from it. That was supposed to be his focus. This was his purpose. Skyler made her own bed to sleep in. This was his. He only felt bad because... Well, he'd been poisoned, hadn't he? From a very young age, his mother had poisoned his head. She'd tenderized him, turned him to putty. Then she'd tried to take him.

His father always told him she had been nothing more than an unstable woman. But maybe he had been wrong. Perhaps she'd been cunning and calculating, a latent follower of Faragó. Sam's weakness, his father's drunkenness, the collapse of Samael's Society—maybe it all had been her fault.

He hated her.

Come on, baby. Come on.

That voice. Was it even hers? It sounded more like Skyler. He couldn't even remember his mother's voice. He wished he could hear it again. Just to remember what it sounded like. He wished she was there.

No you don't. You do not.

Skyler definitely wasn't coming back. There was no doubt in his mind. He needed to be fine with that. She made her choice.

But he could have stopped her. Or he could have just kept his mouth shut to begin with. But then it would've eaten him up inside and... His damn mother. It was *her* fault he felt this way. It was Maria Faragó's fault. It was Skyler's. It was his fault. His fault. His fault.

Seeing you just breaks my heart.

Maybe she hadn't gone too far. What if he could catch up to her?

No. She chose to go after her sister. If it had been *his* sister, he wouldn't have gone. That he knew. There were bigger things for him than petty little relationships. He wouldn't even have gone after his own father. His father certainly wouldn't have gone after him. Their family was nothing compared to the purpose it served.

He needed to be here. This was the place. He knew it. Everything had been leading up to this: his birth, his lessons, his training, even his hobbies.

He remembered the coin he'd found in the main entrance of the castle. The Austro-Hungarian ducat. He wished he'd kept it.

He lay flat on the cold platform. What a child he was, wanting his toys. Wanting to go home and be wrapped up in someone's arms. But what was the meaning in all that? He had meaning here. Where was his pride in that?

Rising, he looked to the wall again. Not a sign of movement. She truly wasn't coming back. He was alone and that needed to be okay. He'd always been alone.

He turned his attention back to the pegs. What he needed to concern himself with was solving this. What could be the pattern or order here? Perhaps a clue was in the room. Or maybe he'd seen a clue somewhere else. He tried to think of where he'd been, the things he'd seen. But his head was full of cotton.

What if Skyler had triggered the gas chamber and couldn't find the way to open the entrance again?

The thought panicked him. He leaped up so quickly his vision went spotty. He opened the entryway. The chamber was empty but for his shadow against the orange flicker of the torches. There was no sign of her, alive or dead. Like he'd thought, she was long gone. He angrily smacked the wall, hurting his fist. What a stupid thing for him to get worried about. If she *had* been trapped, he would've at least heard her shouting for him.

Weak. Weak. Weak.

What had his father always told him he'd lacked? Emotional intelligence.

"Emotional intelligence," he had once said, "is about keeping yourself in check. Detaching yourself from anything that isn't useful. And for us, that's most things."

His pants were still warm and moist and rancid from pissing them. He was a child. A pathetic, emotionally idiotic child.

But he was on the verge of something amazing! Something worth it all. Then he would be the one who'd hold the greatest known power in the world. He'd bring back the Society. Build a name for himself. Maybe he'd even grow to have influence over the highest echelons of the western world, or the *whole* world for that matter. The old Society and its earlier variations had consisted of lords, ladies, noblemen, advisors, bishops, merchants, princes, politicians, generals, even kings and queens and emperors. He could really mix things up. Change everything. He was born to do that. What kind of world would he *want* to build with his potential influence? He didn't know. Just something... different. Something extraordinary. He'd figure it out once he had the tool. Maybe once he had it, everything would click. For now, he just needed to push harder.

The entryway grumbled shut as he returned to the black platform. His palm was now throbbing as much as his foot. He pushed down the first peg he could reach. It made a loud click when it went as far as it could. Maybe the click was the hint? He would have to go one by one, testing each. He could do this.

It was time to end the idiocy and focus on the task ahead.

He hoped Skyler would be okay. Maybe it was alright for him to hope that. As long as he remembered that her life was her problem and not his.

It was.

As for him, he was tired, hurting. Fading. He needed to act fast and act now. There was little time.

Chapter Twenty-One

Sam had left a trail of blood for Skyler to follow. Some of the droplets were bigger and splotchier than others. Some formed perfect circles while others trailed outward. There were so many of them, though. He had lost a lot of blood. Maybe she needed to go back; he shouldn't be alone.

But neither should Rachel.

Even if Skyler could let herself return, she had lost sense of how to get back to the chamber. The blood was not a perfect breadcrumb trail. After all, Sam had been navigating the maze aimlessly for how long? God could only say. She cursed at herself for not bringing a marker. At least the blood helped her identify where trapdoors were, as droplets would begin trailing toward the wall.

There were noises all over, growling and scratching. She could smell them everywhere, even if she couldn't see them. She gripped the unfolded pocketknife in her sweaty palm. She had images of Morgan, her best friend, hunting for her, eyes bulging, mouth twisted. Those teeth.

What was she doing? She wanted to hide in a corner. That's all she ever wanted to do. Trouble never appealed to her. All her life she tried to avoid it—as much as she could, at least—by not looking for it. This wasn't fair. She didn't choose to come here.

But she wouldn't hide in a corner. She kept moving, following the blood. So much blood. Too much for a human being to lose. She shouldn't have left Sam alone. But Rachel...

She moved down a narrow stone hallway, just like the last one and the one before that. The same thing over and over again. Before she could turn where the blood was leading her next, a shape rounded the corner. She halted, looking to her right. It was a short hall that clearly led to a dead-end, just a nook. She quickly turned off her flashlight, leaving herself in complete blackness, and slipped into the nook, pressing herself against the wall.

She heard and smelled the creature coming closer. Its breathing was loud. Its claws clicked against the ground; it sounded like it had four feet. Its breathing and grunting sounded like the panting of a dog, or something that had once been a dog. She held her breath as it came closer. The rotting, swampy smell grew more pungent the closer it came.

Then the clicking stopped. It was right next to the nook. She heard nostrils flaring, sniffing. Her lungs were burning, begging her to breathe. The protein bar she ate earlier was threatening to come spewing up. Every tightened muscle in her body ached as she tensed. She squeezed the knife hard. The sniffing continued. It seemed like it was blowing more air out than it was sucking in. If it smelled her, it wasn't acting on it. It just stood there while she continued suffocating herself.

Suddenly, the thing let out a loud grunt. Her blood went cold. This was it...

But nothing happened. It simply snorted and continued moving onward, further down the hall, away from her. She allowed herself another breath, which came out with a slight whimper and relaxed her body, though her heart was still beating wildly. The clicking became more and more distant until she couldn't hear anything, despite how much she strained herself. It was time to move again. She switched on the flashlight, rounded the nook, and continued following the blood trail down the hall. A shrill howl erupted behind her. *Fuck.* The creature was still there, and now it saw her. She pushed herself into a sprint, down the hall around the corner, down the next hall. She heard erratic clicking behind her, the creature coming closer and closer. Her legs took her as quickly as they could go, but she could feel her pursuer approaching, snapping hungrily at her heels.

Even in her panicked retreat, she tried to pay attention to the ground, to the blood. At one point, she caught the slight outline of a trapdoor. She leaped over it. It was only about three feet across, but might as well have been ten from the way she flailed in the air and stumbled onto the ground, falling on her stomach.

Clickclickclickclickclick

She scrambled to get up, but it wouldn't do any good. She braced herself.

Clickclickclick—

The sound of groaning stone, a pathetic, high-pitched yelp, a stabbing squish.

She still lay there, bracing herself. But nothing happened. The stone groaned again. She finally turned and shined the flashlight behind her. There was nothing but an empty hall.

She supposed she had the "Frenchman" to thank. One of his fucked-up traps had saved her.

She got back on her feet, relieved but remembering she still wasn't safe. She continued following Sam's blood. One turn. Then another. Dead-end. Double back. Take a different turn. She wasn't even thinking about it anymore. Nor was she thinking about Sam, Rachel, Morgan, or even herself. She was focusing on the blood, on the next move.

She caught a glimpse of another creature as she rounded a corner. More humanoid. It disappeared just as she saw it. She needed to be more careful. With every subsequent corner, she practiced more caution, stopping to first poke her head around. It slowed her progress but was safer.

However, she quickly ended this caution once she peered down a hall, and at last, saw faint light coming from an entryway. As soon as she saw it, she was intoxicated, barreling toward it like a dehydrated castaway pursuing a mirage.

The light led her back into the massive main entrance. It hadn't changed since she'd last been here, the great ballroom-like foyer with its pillars and two sweeping stairwells. The only difference now was the thick broken glass covering the floor. Nearly all of the windows in the room were gaping open. Without stopping, she made for the massive door that would take her outside. She only slowed her pace to keep the glass from cutting through her shoes. If her feet got as fucked up as Sam's, she'd be finished.

She pushed and pulled on the door; it was completely immobile. It only took a glance at the silver switch to her right to remember that Sam had locked the door again. She grabbed it and pulled tight, trying to conjure more strength than her body had right now. The contraption was stubborn, but after nearly blowing out her back, it finally crept toward her. Locks and gears clicked and screamed within the door. Before the door could finish this sluggish unlocking process, a shriek rang through the room. Skyler turned to see several creatures, both humanoid and otherwise, descending the stairs. They all moved in a disordered unity, like a mass of sewage streaming down a cliff during an earthquake. Every bloated eye was on her.

When the door's clicking stopped, Skyler whipped back around and grabbed the cold handle. Before she could push, something latched onto her leg. It looked like a green, wingless bat but must have been a rat or a ground squirrel. She tried to kick it off, but it continued clinging to her leg, its claws sinking into her calf. The other creatures were closer; she could practically feel their breath. She kept pushing the door, and when it inched open enough, she ran outside. As soon as she was out of the castle, the pinpricks and pressure in her calf ceased. The small creature that had attacked her was scrambling back inside.

The mass of creatures stood before the open doorway, staring at her like a group of directionless school children. She backed a little further away, taking care not to fall off the elevated trail. The creatures remained frozen, staring dumbly. Finally, almost in unison, they turned and began slowly making their way back up the stairs.

Skyler was filled with a swirl of relief and confusion. Maybe the creatures were afraid to leave the castle. But why would they be?

Besides, they hadn't seemed afraid, just kind of ambivalent, as if the castle was simply where they needed to be.

Walking through the village streets completely alone under the watchful calm of the desolate houses, Skyler felt both an oppressive unease and a deep sadness. People had lived here. And they at least appeared to live decent lives. Then, one by one, they had been taken, transformed. Those remaining had to live in fear and paranoia until finally, nobody was left. It wasn't hard to compare it to the towns of Dayton, Farrington, and

Rembrandt, and everyone who lived near them. All the unfortunate people who were taken. All the frightened people who felt compelled to leave. Or those who weren't able to leave. Surely, they all had hopes and dreams. Who didn't have hopes and dreams? She did. Rachel did too, and unlike Skyler, she had a lot going for her. She was going to be a dentist or some other kind of doctor, a surgeon, a chiropractor, whatever the hell she wanted to be. This world wasn't going to take that all away. It wasn't going to take her sister away.

Skyler walked through the square, past the well. That well she came in from, where everybody did. She wondered, if she closed that damn thing, would it seal off the world for good? There wasn't time to stop to test it. Instead, she moved through the rest of the village and across the fallow fields until she and the forest were face-to-face. It was waiting. The trees were completely still, holding their breaths in anticipation of what she would do next. Between them, within them, she could see nothing. Just darkness.

"Rachel!" she hollered, one last desperate measure to avoid the inevitable. "Rachel!"

She paused and waited, straining herself to hear the slightest squeak and to see a flutter of movement in the darkness. Nothing.

"Raaacheeeel!"

That urge began to prick at her. The forest was tired of this. It was time. The urge spread to every muscle in her body. The more she fought it, the tighter it set in. It was tickling her, pushing her forward. Rachel was there, it promised. She would find her again; the Horne sisters would be together again. It had told her Morgan was there and that had been the truth. There was no reason not to trust it.

She looked up at the silver sky. If it was such a benevolent entity, why wasn't it putting a stop to this? It just watched her. If anything, it looked vibrant, joyful at what was happening. Most likely, Jon had misinterpreted the nature of this world. The sky and forest weren't separate, battling entities. They weren't entities in themselves at all but parts of a greater whole.

She had just enough will to pause at the stream, where the cool and clear water was flowing into the darkness. Maybe the stream could be her lifeline. Stay by the stream, then if she wanted to retreat, escape the forest, she would need only to follow it back. That was a decent plan. It was at least a plan. She kneeled, scooped up some water in her hands, and drank, tasting its sweetness, its bitterness. Letting it fill her. Then, she splashed a little on her face.

The urge jolted through her. No more waiting.

She wasn't scared. Her trust in the forest, in the world, gave her a powerful calm. She knew it was a misplaced trust. In fact, it was artificial, planted in her. But the falseness of this trust didn't matter. Rachel was waiting.

Skyler cleared her thoughts and entered the forest.

Chapter Twenty-Two

IT WAS COLD. SUFFOCATING. Why was it so hard to breathe?

It was even harder to move. Snaggles of foliage and brambles covered the ground, tight as rope. Sometimes it felt like they were coiling around her calf, nearly tripping her. Everything was so dark, darker than night. She was using the flashlight, but the light only traveled a foot or two ahead before being eaten by the blackness. The trees were branch to branch, their trunks almost as close as jail bars. Their bark was cold and rubbery to the touch. Yet, there was a vibrance beneath that cold. Something resembling life. Some trees were covered in moss, but it didn't have that wet, mushy feel of moss. It felt dry and fuzzy, like cotton.

The stream was becoming difficult to see and equally difficult to hear. Sometimes she would think she'd lost it, but then would step in it, soaking her foot.

This wasn't like the woods behind her and Morgan's house. This wasn't like any forest she'd ever been in. The darkest she'd ever been in was one of the Redwood forests. But that had been a calm and peaceful darkness, a magical twilight. Could she even call this a forest? There were no bugs, birds, breezes, leaves falling. This felt more like a dungeon constructed to look like a forest. Even the smell was closer to a tree-scented candle.

She called out for Rachel. Her voice hardly carried. She felt like she was shouting in a soundproof room.

Deeper and deeper. She felt like she was slipping into a dream outside of her own body and mind. Alone. No, not alone. Lonely, but not alone. And somehow, the loneliness felt as blissful as it did painful. Bliss to have nobody around. Bliss to just be for the sake of being. It was comfortable, she wanted to lie down, wrap herself in the bramble. Embrace it. Disappear into it. Maybe she loved it. Or she hated it. But she needed it. It would be like curling up in bed while sick. Miserable, yet cozy as can be.

But she didn't lie down. She knew it would be over if she did. She kept walking. It was so hard to breathe. So hard to think. So hard to know what she was feeling. So hard to be anything but simply being. And even then...

One coherent thought popped into her head. One of her favorite Emily Dickinson poems. Of all that she read in college, it was one that stuck with her and not simply because she'd had to analyze it for a project.

"I felt a Funeral, in my Brain,"

How did it go again? So much for sticking with her. But maybe she could remember. She trudged through the darkness, the bramble and sticks, trying to keep track of a stream that hardly felt there, even as it soaked her foot.

She couldn't tell if she was calling out to Rachel anymore.

Remember the poem. Maybe that would help her *be* a little more. Just a little.

"I felt a Funeral, in my Brain,
And Mourners to and fro..."

That was it. That was it.

"Kept treading-treading-till it seemed

That Sense was breaking through-

And when they all were seated,

A Service, like a Drum-

Kept beating-beating-till I thought

My mind was going numb-"

There had been so many times in her life when her mind felt numb. Those moments seemed to come to her more, the older she got. But this wasn't one of them. Now it felt like something else. Her mind was everywhere and nowhere. She felt everything and nothing.

"And then I heard them lift a Box," she murmured. *Focus. Focus.* "And cr—creak across my Soul. With those Boots of Lead, again. Then Space began... to toll."

She heard a faint crackle, somewhere in the darkness. She called out to it. Or maybe not. She'd exerted her lungs, but she couldn't tell if anything came out.

At any rate, there was no answer. There would never be an answer. There never *could* be.

She grasped for the next stanza; like feeling around for her cheek after it was pumped full of Novocain. Something about a bell, a bell named Vivian? And silence. And being solitary. Maybe Jon would like that line.

"I like Emily Dickinson, do you?" She heard him say it. He was right next to her.

"I do," she answered.

She remembered the last stanza.

"And then a Plank in Reason, broke,

And I dropped down, and down-

And hit a World, at every plunge,

And Finished knowing-then-"

She'd always thought of that line as optimistic. Maybe she had been wrong. A plank in reason. Her plank had dropped a long, long time ago. And now she was plunging.

There was another crackle. She couldn't try to call out again this time. She couldn't breathe enough. Besides, she didn't want to make noise. She didn't want to *be*. No, she did. But why couldn't she lie down for a bit? The trees watched her. Excitedly waiting to see her drop.

And she wanted to.

Another crackle, and a squeak.

What was she doing any more? Why was she here? It hardly seemed to matter. Not as much, at least, as lying down. Just for a bit. Or...

She had to let her mind move away from the darkness. Away from the grasp of the trees and brambles. What was another Dickinson poem? She couldn't think of one. It was difficult to even pull the one she'd just recited again.

A funeral... Welcome to the funeral... We've got fun and games.

The funeral had moved on. What about a dirty limerick? A song? Everything she knew about the Franco-Prussian War, the Revolutions of 1848, the Industrial Revolution, the life of Queen Victoria, her own life, the goddamn ABCs? It was all gone. Nothing left but the dark.

More crackling, followed by a high-pitched whimper.

This made her stop and look around. The whimper could have come from any direction. A faint, white blur moved across her periphery. When she shined her flashlight toward it, there was nothing but the uniform trees and the blackness beyond them.

Another whimper, this one more elongated, more agonized. It sounded like a young girl. Another white blur in the corner of her vision.

The next whimper, this one pricking into Skyler's soul, it sounded so frightened, seemed to come from behind her. She felt something brush by her. Maybe a breeze. Suddenly, off in the distance, she saw a white figure. A little girl with curly, blonde hair, wearing a white nightgown. She was so far away, yet Skyler could see her clearly, even if she couldn't see anything else. The girl was running, her feet seamlessly avoiding the brambles.

Skyler choked trying to shout to her, her voice still constrained. Her legs were still working though, heavy as they felt. So she ran after.

The little girl's weeping was the only sound echoing through the darkness. She must've been so frightened. Skyler needed to catch her, save her. Then they would find Rachel together.

After a lifetime of chasing, the brambles scratching her legs, the girl halted. Skyler caught up to her and reached out, hoping to grab the girl's gown. But her hand slipped through the fabric like it was air. She tripped and fell onto the little girl. Instead of landing on top of a small body, she fell onto a soft bed of grass. It felt good. A cozy bed. Everything inside her grew warm. Her undernourished body was suddenly feeling fed, stronger. She closed her eyes.

The girl.

She popped them open again.

Where was the girl? Or...

What girl? All she could conjure in her mind was an image of a white blur. A whimper. A sob. Fading into the void.

Kept treading-treading-till it seemed

That Sense was breaking through-

The girl. The little white blur.

She tried pulling herself up, but might as well have been deadlifting a thousand pounds. Her body didn't want to stand. The grass statically clung to her. Trying to pull away from it stung. She shined the flashlight on one of her arms. The grass was sticking into the skin like needles. The sight sent a sudden jolt through her body and she tugged. It stubbornly refused to let go. It felt like trying to rip off her own skin. After a violent struggle, she freed herself. Pulling her second arm away was easier, but just as painful. Some of the grass had cut through her clothes and embedded into her back and legs, but not as deeply. She pulled herself completely free and leaped to her feet. Much of her skin stung like she had just pulled off a wax strip.

Along the bed of grass, the blades that had pricked into her were lowering, laying down in defeat and disappointment. The sight made her feel miserably guilty. Poor things. They had only wanted to bring her home.

But no. Wait. This wasn't home.

She ran, all the while trying to keep her footing stable. She had to find the stream. What stream was she even talking about? She couldn't even remember what had brought her to this point. A white blur. There was no blur, had never been one. All that existed was the darkness, the brambles, the grass, the dirt, the trees. The motion of her feet and legs.

Something was still needling into her. Not into her body but her brain. Memories flooded through her, vivid as a fever dream:

Her parents sitting her down in the living room on that old ugly green and brown couch Mom had thrown away after the divorce, telling her she was going to be a big sister. She hadn't been angry or jealous like a lot of older siblings get. She had been excited, fantasizing about who her little sibling would be. What kind of big sister she would be. How she'd look out for them.

Her dad picking her up from school, taking her to a museum; a monthly routine. A small milkshake from McDonald's in the car. Chocolate.

Her dad in his office, head back in ecstasy. Terra on her knees. Her family falling apart before her eyes. Rachel's blaming glare. "You can't stop me."

Morgan. Morgan. Morgan. Mr. Fellers. Choir. Paintings. Spice Girls. Terrible sex. A sword in the stomach. Oscar. Trashy reality shows. Cuddling up with her cousin after a hard day. Shrimp Piano. Bulbous eyes. Dreams of the future. A future in the past. Professor Skyler Horne.

These thoughts and memories were hers. Maybe. It didn't feel like they belonged to her. Not anymore. Something was digging its way in, peering into them, observing them.

Jon. His toothless grin. Showing off his books like a child showing off his toys. His beloved bell.

Thrummmm. Thrummmm.

That terror in his sunken eyes before he fell out of the tower. She had killed him. Darwin too. His massive body, green and distorted, lying in the stairs.

Morgan shrieking with grief. No longer Morgan.

Sam. Haggard, wary, bleeding.

The indoor courtyard. The black platform. Pegs like stars. The Society for the Preservation of Miscellaneous Artifacts. The Society for the Recovery of Lost Artifacts. The Order of the Chisel. The centaur. That stench. The Automatons. The tool that creates worlds. Maria and Samael. Orion and Artemis.

She thought she could outrun this penetration of her mind. But the invisible coils that poked and prodded were everywhere. And the silent witnesses, the trees, only looked on, enjoying the sight of this violation.

Kept beating... beating... till I thought... My mind was going numb...

Artemis. The Gas Chamber. The switch. Sam's blood on the floor. Rachel.

She saw light. A faint horizon of light beyond the trees. She picked up her pace. Trying to keep her mind blank to avoid any more violations. Failing.

Seating her mother on that same green and brown couch. Telling her what she saw that day, Dad and Terra. Mom saying nothing. Her face flashed into something Skyler had never seen from her before. A mix of rage and pain and sadness. And in that moment, she wondered why she had to be the one to tell her. She'd told Morgan first. Morgan had offered to break it to her mom. But Skyler knew it had to be her. But why?

The light was getting closer. She could see hints, promises of the silver sky.

Her grandad, dying, afraid and in agony. Meanwhile she was pouting about a shirt. To think she'd always used to check his pulse when he'd fall asleep to make sure he was still alive.

She would never break her promises again.

She was closer.

Anything to make it stop. She just wanted it to stop.

She could see a little beyond the trees. Water. There was water!

What could she do to make it stop?

Almost there.

What did it want?

You will see.

Finally, she broke through.

⌒

The sky was gazing down on her. From where she stood, it looked like half a dome, slanting downward. Apparently, the edge of the world wasn't too far. Before her was a large lake, as silver as the sky. Her mind was beginning to clear, if only a little. She at least felt back in her body. There was sweat drenching her face and her shirt. She could tell her hair was frizzy, some curls popping out and brushing her skin. Her breathing was coming back. Stale and unsatisfying as the air was, it was bliss after the constriction she'd felt moments ago.

Looking around, it was evident that she had been released but was not free. Trees surrounded her and the lake on all sides. She was in a clearing, nothing more. But she was grateful for the reprieve. All this time, she had been gripping the pocketknife so tightly it left indents in her hand. She slipped it into her pocket before kneeling at the water's edge and scooping some up. It was so clear.

On the opposite side of the lake, she could see the stream. So much for trying to follow it. Had she really gotten so lost? She splashed some water on each arm, letting its coolness balm the still stinging spots where the grass had embedded in her. Another scoop she tried to drink, and quickly spat it out. It tasted filthy. Fishy, even... She stood and peered into the water, looking hard. Along the lake's silvery surface, there was swirling and bubbling.

Then, closer to the shallows, floating beneath the water like an angel soaring through the clouds, was a large, gray fish. She didn't know what the hell kind it was—that didn't matter. From what she could tell, it was a normal, undistorted fish. Her heart tightened, her vision blurred. It felt like it had been so long since she'd seen a normal, living creature. She almost had an urge to reach out and touch it. Grab it. Feel it squirm in her hands. Not kill it. Not let it die. Just feel it. But it swam out of her view.

She heard the crackling that she'd heard in the forest. It was right behind her. She turned to see a shapeless mound emerging from the blackness. The first thing she could see when it came into the light was bulging green eyes. Next came the muscular torso, coiled in veins, the beard hanging down like weeds, the limping four legs building toward a grinning equine skull.

The centaur crept swiftly toward her. She could see it, smell it, and if only faintly, hear it. But was it real? Did she need to run? Before she could do anything, the centaur paused several feet from her. With trembling effort, it raised one of its thick, green hands.

"Don't be afraid," came a deep, gurgling voice. It was hard to tell if the centaur had said it. The creature's lips hardly seemed to move. "I will not hurt you." Despite the throaty curdle, the voice sounded very human. It even seemed to have a slight accent, maybe some kind of Scottish.

"My name," it continued, "is Virgil Shanks."

The name sounded familiar to Skyler. Though she couldn't remember why.

"I will not hurt you," it... Virgil... said again. "It isn't my wish to hurt people. The others don't know better. The need for violence is deep inside them. Can you blame them? It is what the world demands. But my only wish is to guide."

"You talk," was all Skyler could muster.

Virgil threw back his head and let out the harsh shadow of what might once have been a boisterous laugh. Something about the sound sickened her.

"Stop," she said. It was an embarrassingly timid gesture, she knew. Yet, Virgil listened. The laughter ceased and he gave a slow shrug, his veins tightening with every movement. "You are of us now, lass."

"What?"

"It's dug its way into you, hasn't it? Like it did every damned one of us. Saw our fears, our dreams. It wasn't long before it knew us more than we knew ourselves. And then it made us a part of it. And a part of each other." He gently patted the rotted mule's neck. "Showed us one another inside and out. It's a damned strange thing. We wanted to leave our dirt lives in the old world behind and build heaven here. A shining city where no man would go without. Where nobody would go shooting or loosing mustard gas on his brethren. Where everyone understood each other."

Skyler had her flashlight at the ready like a baton. Then she remembered the pocketknife. She slowly slid her other hand into her pocket and pulled it out, gripping it tight. She'd need to still unfold it, but at least she had it.

Virgil either hadn't noticed this motion or didn't care.

"That'd been a lie, of course," he said after a deep sigh. "Maria had shepherded us here with her great promises. We built her castle, built our town. We practically worshipped her. A foolish thing of us, but we didn't know better. She made this world, and indeed it reflects her soul inside and out. Her ambition, the vision. Cold, yet more intoxicating than the strongest drink. But make no mistake, this world is something more than she could ever be."

"I don't understand," Skyler said.

"Aye." Virgil moved toward her. "You will, of course."

Skyler quickly pulled out the blade and pointed it at the centaur. It was so tiny compared to Virgil's body, but it made him stop again, raising his hands in yielding.

"Worlds, you see, they live and breathe like we do. Think. Feel. Learn. Change. I grew up on a farm. I've ground my fingers to the bone working the land since I was a lad." He looked at his hands. The thick, clawed fingers couldn't have resembled the ones belonging to a farm boy. "You learn that the land has a mind of its own. It's something you can't truly explain, is it? Sometimes it gives, sometimes it takes. The crop is good one year and bad the next. Science can only tell you a small part of it.

"Our world, the old world, I mean, is very alive. A very old and tired crabbit. Not to say I blame her. Now, this world." Virgil motioned around him. "Just a babe. So small, but dreams so big. And it is already wise. Certainly wiser than its creator ever was. And now we belong to it. And it belongs to us."

"I don't..."

"You do," Virgil said. "You've come to the forest. The heart of this world and its power. You belong to it now."

"I don't belong here!" Her arm was growing tired from holding up the knife. She tried to think of what to do next, but her mind was scrambled.

"It called to you, didn't it?" There was an alarming hint of frustration in Virgil's tone. "It needs all the help it can get. Think!" He tapped his broad forehead. "Listen. You are part of me now. See what I've done for us. For all of us."

She didn't want to listen to him. But once he said it, she couldn't help thinking about it. She could feel what it was to be him. She could taste a constant flood of sour filth streaming down her throat. There was a deep pain, cold, thick vines perpetually threaded through his legs, trapping him. But beneath the agony was intense joy, exuberant pleasure. It wasn't his own, though. It was administered. Morphine. Brainwashing. But he didn't care one way or the other. He was here to serve, to lead. He loved his fellow humans. He loved the community he had helped build.

He also loved the world. Whatever it needed of him, he would provide. When it had needed him to open the well, he opened the well. Then they came. My, how they came.

"You?" Suddenly Skyler felt more angry than afraid.

He shrugged, unfazed by her anger. He had no regrets about what he'd done. There was nothing wrong with what he'd done. The world needed numbers. It needed to take back what Maria had hidden away. It had designs. Good ones.

He moved toward her again.

"Stay away from me," Skyler hissed, thrusting the knife into the air. But this time, Virgil didn't let up. She backed away as he came closer.

"Forget about natural and unnatural," he said. "We fought with every inch of our lives, at first. I was not the type to lie down in my day." That harsh laugh again. "But I became wise. Gave up the fight soon enough."

She took a bad step and nearly fell into the lake, but caught her footing.

"Careful," Virgil said, halting and reaching out his hand, almost sounding concerned.

"Stay away."

His globular eyes were unreadable, but his jaw was crooked in what might have been frustration. "You've done so much for us. The old bastard in the tower. Don't tell me it wasn't you. Now the castle's ours. And we know you've found the place where the tool is being hidden. At least it seems so. The world's seen it in you. So now we all know where it is."

Skyler felt sick. He had to be lying, but she knew he wasn't. She didn't care if they found the tool or whatever the hell it was the world wanted. But Sam was in there, injured, alone, and unable to defend himself.

Virgil laughed. His amusement at her concern made her feel deep disdain. The centaur was suddenly disarmed by this hatred. "Do not worry," he said, a touch of hurt in his voice, "we're forbidden from going there just yet. Not until you've been shown what the world wants to show you."

"And why are you here?" she asked. "Why don't you just go to the castle and leave me the hell alone?" Part of her couldn't believe she was being so bold, speaking to this creature in such a way. But all her fear was gone, even as his frustration with her increased. Somehow, she knew it would take a lot to make him to hurt her.

"It's always been my purpose here to be the foreman, guide the rabble, lead the charge. I'm here to make sure you're doing what we need you to do." He nodded to the trees behind him. "It's time to see."

"No." Skyler knew she had no choice but to go back in there, unless she wanted to die in this clearing. But she wouldn't go with him.

She expected this to make Virgil angrier. But instead he was amused, his mouth twisting into a smirk.

"You aren't the stubborn type," he said softly. "Not at all. Not like Morgan. Not like Rachel."

"You..." She felt like she'd been punched in the stomach.

"Isn't that who you want?" Virgil asked, slowly moving toward Skyler again, and this time she didn't back away. "Rachel? You'll be with her again."

She felt weak. Yes, that was the whole reason she'd come to the forest. But to hear this creature say her name was still a shock. Unless he was lying. Her disdain toward Virgil worsened.

"You bastard," she said.

Virgil laughed again. "You wouldn't be the first woman to call me that."

Before Skyler could speak or react in any way, he lunged forward. His large hands clasped her by the arms and lifted her up. The flashlight fell to the ground, but she still held the knife tight. It wouldn't do any good at the moment. Virgil's grip was so strong, Skyler felt like she was being constrained by rope. Her arms painfully pressed against her ribs. His warm, acidic breath spewed acridly into her face. But any more, the stench affected her only as much as the smell of a public restroom. Disgusting, but too familiar to give a strong reaction.

She kicked, but the feeling of her foot against the mule's soft head made her quickly recoil.

"I'll let you go," Virgil said, slowly backing toward the forest. "But only in there. Though if you keep making a nuisance of yourself, then I'll never let you go."

She had an image in her mind of being fused with Virgil for the rest of her existence. It sent waves of panic through her, and she kicked even harder.

"Stop it!" His voice turned into a monstrous growl. His jaw widened, baring sharp teeth.

Her foot hit the mule's head, it let out a guttural bray, and Virgil halted and slightly loosened his grip. But before she could take advantage, he squeezed harder.

"I understand your fear," he said. His voice was abruptly softer. He continued backing toward the woods. "When the world takes you, it takes every part. It expects nothing less. Nothing less. But you can accept it. Maybe you don't know it now. But you can embrace it!"

There was the mockery of joy and boisterousness in his voice. But under all that was an inescapable hollowness too. Whatever man he had been was gone.

Just like Morgan was gone.

Skyler couldn't let that happen to herself. She certainly wouldn't let that happen to Rachel.

She kicked again, more furiously than ever.

Virgil sputtered and snarled. His grip tightened more; she thought her bones were going to break. But again, she hit the mule's head. This time, Virgil reared and again loosened his hold. The world moved at a lightning pace as she pulled her arm free and jabbed the knife forward. She hadn't been aiming anywhere, but it hit something. It was like cutting into a piece of raw meat, a feeling all too familiar to her. Virgil dropped her and she nearly tumbled into the water. Looking up, she still couldn't see where the knife had gone until he reached toward his throat and pulled it out, black blood spewing down his massive chest. He hurtled the knife into the lake.

"Oh," he said. Blackness sputtered from his mouth and he pressed feebly against the wound. Suddenly, she saw the same look in his eyes that she'd seen in Darwin. A hint of humanity, of fear—intense fear. It filled her with a deep sadness.

"Oh." His voice was a low, clicking rasp.

Virgil's bulging eyes looked at her until they stared at nothing and the large torso fell onto the ground, carrying the entire body with it. The mule was still alive, letting out a weak but desperate bray. Dirt flew as its legs kicked against the ground. Skyler wanted to start beating the creature, beating it until the noise would stop. Until the pain would stop. But she couldn't stand to go near it. She wasn't going to stand there and watch this either.

She snatched her flashlight from the ground and ran into the forest, exactly where Virgil had been trying to drag her to in the first place. She went deeper and deeper into the darkness until the braying, scuffling, and pounding faded.

Once again, there was nothing but the silent void.

∾

Once she was deep enough where the flashlight was her only faint guiding light, it flickered out, leaving her in darkness. She wanted to shout. But her voice was constricted again, her chest tight. She couldn't hear anything, she could barely smell or feel anything, and now she couldn't see.

She smacked the flashlight once. The light popped alive briefly before vanishing again. She smacked it harder. This time, it didn't blink at all. She slapped it over and over again, knowing it was useless.

Then she heard humming. A feminine voice somewhere in the distance. It was soft and low, tired, harsh with wear, yet firm. The tune was strange and mournful, completely unfamiliar. Skyler walked, or at least, she seemed to be walking. The darkness was no obstacle; somehow, she knew where she was going. The tangled brambles beneath her feet didn't stop her either. In fact, they seemed to flatten and clear the way for her. The humming was coming from everywhere and nowhere.

The farther she walked, the more the hum lost its tune. Eventually, it became a formless drone. The sound grew louder and louder. It was right in front of her. It was right behind her. The more she walked, the more it encompassed her. The droning became choppy, but consistently so, as if the sound had been sliced into evenly sized pieces. It faded and emerged, faded and emerged.

Thrummmm. Thrummmm.

"Stop it!" Skyler tried to yell. Maybe she had been successful. But she hadn't heard herself. She couldn't even hear her own thoughts. She tried to yell again. "Stop!"

But it didn't stop. The thrumming only became louder. And, against the black canvas that was her vision, colors burst forward in time with the repetition. Reds, whites, grays, browns exploding to life, expanding, retracting, swirling together until they formed a round, identity-less mass. Slowly, this mass took shape, the hands of God pushing, kneading, carving. Hills rose, craters and valleys formed. Other colors burst forth—greens, blues. Water flowing. A forest sprang to life. A world was born. But this world was compressed, imprisoned. It needed to thrive, to grow. It needed purpose. Skyler could feel that, could understand its pain, its frustration. Her heart flooded with satisfaction when the world burst from its containment, its colors swirling from the epicenter to the beat of a supersonic thrum. Growing. The growing felt so good. Skyler was proud. She was excited, terrified, hopeful, uncertain. Free.

All at once, the thrumming ceased and the colors imploded. She cried out, reaching for them. But they fizzled away, leaving her alone again, aimless in the silence and darkness.

But before this loss could set in, the darkness became speckled with dots. Stars. Long dead suns spattered across a young universe. Then the stars were blotted out by shadows. Shapeless beings crawling across the vacuum. Their intent was clear: to create. To continue life. Lifeless rock was taken and molded into their own image. Another world was born. This world changed, shifted, died, lived again. On it, creatures lived, died, were destroyed, replaced by others. Soon, the world resembled nothing of its shadowy creators. Soon, this little blue world gave birth to creatures that began to build worlds of their own, civilizations, empires, systems. Their worlds grew, expanded, crumbled, contorted, became uncontrollable, all the while reshaping their home against its will. The little blue world was sad. It was bitter. The shadowy forebears had left their tools behind, their secrets. But were these creatures worthy of these secrets?

The blue world imploded and Skyler was blind once more. Again, she heard humming. But this time it was only behind her.

She turned to see a woman. Though thin and short, she also seemed towering. She wore a bright white dress. Her hair was gray and curly, her face wrinkled and gaunt. She gazed at Skyler down her thin nose. Though she said nothing, her blinding golden eyes, narrow but inescapable, showed everything.

They showed violence. War. Bloated corpses in trenches. They showed the ruins of a mansion. A bomb planted by an enemy who could no longer be deceived. Pieces of friends and families scattered across the land. They showed a violent anger, a brutal vengeance. A civil war that, within days, tore apart an ancient organization. Followers of the guilty enemy were hunted down, shot, gutted, burned, tortured, impaled. All the while, the man who had sparked this wrath disappeared.

Skyler felt nothing seeing these horrors. She was an observer, a visitor in a museum, floating along from exhibit to exhibit.

The eyes showed her a man falling from a tower, his heart stopping just before his head could explode against the ground. A sword slicing through a man's gut. A cousin's father. A best friend's father. A knife in a man's throat. A jolt of grief and guilt hit Skyler before she felt nothing again.

The sun-bright eyes grew tired. All this violence wasn't unique. It wasn't new, or profound. But it wasn't inevitable either. Things could change. And these eyes, these eyes that had gazed into Skyler and saw her secrets, her insecurities, her past, her future, offered hope. Everything could change. All Skyler had to do was what they asked of her. They knew she would, because Skyler Horne was, after all, Skyler Horne. She would obey.

But what *did* they ask? The eyes answered her by bursting into a swirl of greens, blues, and browns. A world freed, shaping itself and everything around it. And Skyler and everyone she loved would live in peace. And she felt at ease. Safe. Imagine what would happen, or wouldn't happen, if she refused. It was too painful to think about.

A cacophony of voices angrily whispered at her. Jon. Sam. Morgan. Rachel. They threaded through her head, encouraging, demanding. They would be deeply disappointed if she didn't follow through.

She would! She promised she would!

The voices and images mercifully faded away and Skyler felt herself tumbling onto the ground. Feeling and vision returned to her as her arm slammed into rock. As she shook off the pain and came to her feet, she realized she was facing a massive wall of faint silver light. The wall stretched upward until blending seamlessly with the sky.

This was the world's edge. The dome of the snow globe.

A prison, said a thought that didn't feel like her own.

The light was painful to look at, like staring at a fully lit computer or TV screen up close. But she knew she had to keep looking. Against the silver backdrop, millions of little orbs popped in and out of her vision. Then a handful of them, which sat directly in her line of sight, froze in place. They were carefully spaced from each other, forming a pattern.

A constellation.

Once the pattern was burned into Skyler's mind, she squeezed her eyes shut. She no longer felt compelled to look.

Behind her came the sound of crunching brush and crackling trees. Was something else approaching? But what she saw when she whirled around wasn't a creature. The trees themselves were bending backward like straws. The vines and brambles on the ground were slipping away, creating a clearing. The forest was parting for her, providing her a path. She wondered if this was a trick. But deep inside, she knew it wasn't.

Why would the world trick her when she had a role to play?

She walked down this newly laid trail, her body stiff and trembling. She popped her fingers against her chin. At least she could feel herself again. She was sore all over; her legs were especially cramping up. She felt like her brain had been sucked of all its fluids and now was a blank, dried husk. It seemed at any moment, the forest would close and swallow her up again. Sometimes, she would hear a popping sound and it would make her pick up her pace. But despite her fear, the vines, brush, and trees stayed in their places. They wanted her about as much as she wanted them right now.

Something appeared in the middle of the path. It seemed to come out of nowhere. Or maybe her eyes had just noticed it. But it looked familiar. A person. Black shirt, blue jeans, both discolored by dirt. Long, curly brown hair, frazzled but not discolored. Vines were tangled around the slender arms and legs. She couldn't see the face; it was pressed against the ground. But she knew who it was.

"Rachel!" she shouted, noting that she actually *could* shout again. "Rachel!"

The vines slinked away from the prostrate figure as Skyler came closer. She turned over the figure. At first, she couldn't tell if this actually *was* Rachel. The woman looked like a corpse, her narrow face dirty, flushed and taking on a sickly hue of dark green. Yet, it was undeniably her. She looked peaceful. Skyler sat still, waiting to see her sister's chest rise, or for some other sign of life, like she used to with her granddad.

The wait was agonizingly long before Rachel let out a deep gasp and arched her body upward. Sputtering and coughing as if she had been saved from drowning. Skyler squeezed her hand and rubbed her back, like their mom always used to do when they weren't feeling well.

"It's okay," Skyler said. "You're okay."

Under Rachel's shirt, Skyler could feel welts along the skin. Pockmarks also graced her arms, neck, face. Anger surged through Skyler's chest. This world had harmed her little sister. Violated her. But what could she do about it?

Rachel's eyes fluttered open. Skyler's breath caught in her throat when she saw the eyes were a dark, mossy green.

"Rachel?" she whispered, squeezing her sister's hand tighter than intended.

Very quickly, the moss dissipated. And Rachel's eyes were back to their normal vibrant gold. Rachel gazed sleepily at Skyler for a long time, parting her lips now and again as if trying to say something.

"It's okay," Skyler said, trying to hold herself together the best that she could. Trying to be the big sister. "It's okay." She couldn't think of anything else to say.

"Sk-Skyler?" Rachel finally said. Her voice sounded exactly like it had when she was a little girl, running into Skyler's room to hide from the thunderstorms. This was too much for Skyler to bear. She rested her forehead against her sister's and cried.

"Skyler," Rachel said again. This time, her voice sounded more like the woman she'd become, though devoid of its usual confidence and now trembling with fear. When Skyler pulled away, she could see tears streaming down Rachel's cheeks, her eyes puffy and red. The green hue in her skin was gone and it was back to its usual light brown though the pockmarks remained.

"It's okay," Skyler repeated, holding her sister tight. "I'm gonna get you home. We're gonna go home, okay?"

CHAPTER
Twenty-Three

IT WAS A LONG, quiet walk out of the forest. Skyler practically had to use her whole body to prop her sister upright. Rachel was not very heavy, but she was the taller of the two and still had lean muscle from her JV volleyball days. Skyler was surprised at her own strength in keeping them moving. Maybe it was adrenaline. But it also could have been something else.

When they were finally back in the field stretching up toward the village, the trees behind them snapped back into place, sealing off the trail. Skyler's legs suddenly felt wobbly. Her strength was fading again. She quickly hobbled them to the stream. Along the way, they nearly tripped over something black, green, and mushy, like an unhealthy cow pie. It was the body of the bird thing that had attacked Skyler when she'd first come to the world. It felt like that had been years ago. Where would she be if Sam hadn't come and shot it away? Would the forest have taken her? She wouldn't have been able to escape then. She only did now because the world allowed her to leave. As to why, she didn't understand. Thank god for Sam.

Sam... who was still in that room, alone. Bleeding out, most likely. She needed to get back to him quickly. But first, water.

She attempted to guide Rachel to sit along the bank. But Rachel shoved her aside and seated herself. It relieved Skyler to see her coming back to herself a bit, though she still needed her older sister to scoop up the water and bring it to her. When Rachel first drank, she scrunched her face, maybe at the sweetness of the water. Or maybe the filth from Skyler's hands soured it, no matter how much she tried to clean them beforehand. She brought Rachel several more handfuls, drinking and splashing some on herself as well.

"That's enough," Rachel said after the last serving.

"Okay." Skyler sat beside her. "Let me know if you want more."

They sat silently contemplating the dark forest before them. Skyler no longer felt afraid of it, but she never wanted to go into it again. Her time in there seemed to have peeled her away, whittled her completely to the bone. It was better not to think about that.

"Skyler," Rachel said after a while. Her voice was getting stronger, Skyler was relieved to hear.

"Yeah?"

"You smell like shit."

Skyler couldn't tell if she was being facetious. Probably not, because she was right. Skyler smelled rancid. No amount of washing would save her shirt, pants, socks, probably even her shoes. The filth was coded into the clothing's DNA. She just hoped that her skin and hair were salvageable.

But at least Skyler could smell that filth. All of her senses seemed to be coming back. Maybe she was still whole after all, at least a little bit.

"Are you hungry?" she asked.

Rachel shrugged. That usually meant, "Yes, but I don't want to admit it."

There was still a protein bar in Skyler's pocket. It was pretty crumpled, but was probably edible. She tossed it to her sister. Rachel scowled at the taste after popping in her first broken pinch. After a pause, she scarfed down the rest of it.

"That's all I have," Skyler said. "We need to get to the castle sooner than later."

Rachel looked to the castle, gaping as if it were the first time she'd seen it.

"It looks like Disney World," she said.

"It's not."

Rachel pouted slightly, the face she usually made when she was thinking. "Where are we?"

"It's... it's a lot to explain."

Rachel gave her an exasperated glare.

"I'm sorry," Skyler said. "I'll tell you everything once we're safe, I promise."

It would have to be a long talk. The truth was only going to lead to more questions, many of which Skyler didn't even have answers to.

"I went into this abandoned shithole store," Rachel said. "I remember that. I don't know why I went in there. I guess I just thought I needed to."

You didn't think anything. You were told. Instead of saying this out loud, Skyler just nodded.

"For some reason, I felt like... like you and Morgan were there. Like, I *knew* that."

Skyler wasn't going to think about Morgan right now. She refused. "I think we should get going," she said.

Rachel stared at the stream's crisp water, likely trying to piece everything together. But even being the straight-A dean's-list premed student that she was, she probably wouldn't figure this one out.

"Rachel."

Instead of replying, Rachel scooted down to the stream. Skyler scooted after, staying close while Rachel scooped up a couple mouthfuls. Apparently unsatisfied with this, Rachel dipped her mouth into the water, slurping it up like a dog. Skyler worried she was going to drown herself, but her younger sister waved her away when she reached out to help.

Finally, Rachel rose from the water, gasping and falling back onto the grass.

"Are you good?" Skyler asked.

Rachel closed her eyes and nodded.

"Are you ready to go?"

"Why?" Rachel asked, popping her eyes open.

"Why what?" Skyler couldn't believe Rachel was going to be so stubborn, even now.

"Why are we going to the castle? Are there people there?"

"There... there is one person." *I hope.*

"Morgan?" Rachel sat up, her eyes wide. The almost-innocent hope in her face stung Skyler. Rachel would have to learn what Morgan had become eventually, right? But Skyler didn't want to have that conversation now.

"No," she said, trying to keep herself calm.

The light faded from Rachel's face and she slumped. "So, she's not here."

Tell her you don't know, said a voice in Skyler's head. This wasn't a needling voice from outside, it came from within. *Or tell her you know about as much as she does. Be a good sister and lie.*

"I..." Suddenly, her mouth felt dry. It felt like everything was closing in around her, like she had felt in the forest. She just wanted to get up and run, run as far away from Rachel and everything else as possible.

"We need to go," she said.

"Where is Morgan?" Rachel asked, seeing through Skyler's dodging.

"I'm sorry."

"You're sorry about what?"

What could she even say? "Morgan, she..."

A horrified look came over Rachel's face. She scrambled to her feet, as if sitting was the worst thing she could do. Skyler knew what Rachel was thinking, that Skyler was going to tell her Morgan was dead. She had an urge to say it wasn't true. But then she would have to tell the truth. If she did, Rachel would want to go looking for Morgan. There wasn't time for that—they had to get to Sam. Skyler wanted to help their cousin, to find some way to save her. But deep down she knew it couldn't be done, a fact that would skewer her if she dwelled on it too long. Morgan had been warped by the world. It didn't want to give her, or anyone else, back. Skyler could still see the woman's once-beautiful face, pained and twisted. She wished she'd never seen Morgan that way. She didn't want Rachel to have to see it too. Still, she couldn't outright lie and say their cousin was dead. She couldn't do that to Rachel. So she said nothing.

Would Morgan have done the same thing? Would she have given up on Skyler so quickly?

"You don't know what the hell you're talking about," Rachel snapped.

"Rachel." Why couldn't she figure out how to handle this? "I don't know where she is, okay?"

It was a helpless and pathetic attempt to reel things back. She hated herself for this. There was no way it needed to be this difficult.

"You don't know," Rachel said. "You don't know a fucking thing." She turned and limped quickly back toward the village.

Skyler sat there, biting her lip, popping her fingers.

What are you doing? asked that voice inside. *Get off your ass and go after her. Be a big sister.*

It was clear she still wasn't up to that task. But she had to try.

Skyler couldn't find her sister when she reached the village.

"Rachel!" She wound through the desolate streets, shouting at the top of her lungs. At least her voice was back, though it sounded like a fork scratching against a plate. "Rachel, please!"

Panic tingled in her chest. Rachel had seemed to vanish in thin air again. Skyler was beginning to question if she'd even found her in the first place. Maybe that had been a delusion.

"Rachel!" Her call became softer. It was too exhausting to keep shouting. Before the panic could get a tighter hold on her, she saw a small figure huddled next to one of the houses. Rachel was curled up, sobbing quietly into her knees. Skyler deflated with warm relief. She sat next to her little sister, saying nothing. She reached out her hand and cautiously placed it on Rachel's thin, trembling shoulder, anticipating being pushed away. But she wasn't.

After several moments of silent crying, Rachel finally said something. Her voice was soft and muffled but clear enough. "You should have let me come with you."

What would that have done? Skyler thought, but she kept her mouth shut. Now wasn't the time for arguing.

Rachel looked at Skyler, her eyes puffy and red. Skyler again had an urge to be out with it, to tell the truth about Morgan, horrific as it was and as difficult as the outcome would be to control.

But before she could act on the urge, Rachel looked away.

"You should've let me come with you," she said again. "Maybe we could've... We..."

After this, they sat quietly for a long time. Rachel eventually reached a point where she couldn't cry any more, at least for the time being.

"What the fuck is happening?" she said. This time there was no anger in her tone. There was only fear, helplessness. It saddened Skyler to hear Rachel sound this way. "Where are we?"

Perhaps Skyler owed an explanation of at least that much. It wouldn't hurt Rachel any more than she was already hurting. It probably wouldn't help either. But she felt Rachel deserved it. As briefly as she could, she told her sister about the snow globe, Sam, the Society. The entire time, Rachel looked at her in a way she hadn't seen in many, many years—the same edge-of-her-seat gaze from when they'd tell ghosts stories with their dad. The look encouraged Skyler to keep going, no matter how ridiculous the words coming out of her mouth sounded. She wasn't sure what Rachel would say to all this, or even what she wanted Rachel to feel about it.

"There is a way out," she said to cap off her summary. "And I think Sam found it. We just have to get back to him, in the castle, and we'll go home."

When she finished, there was again silence between them. Jittery and anxious as she was, she would let Rachel process it. She had to accept there would be skepticism and pushback.

But once Rachel finally did break the silence, she said nothing Skyler expected. "It was like a nightmare in there."

She nodded toward the castle, but Skyler knew she meant the forest.

"It was," Skyler said.

"We don't have to go back in there?" Rachel's voice became timid.

"Never."

"I just want to go home."

"We will." Skyler was so comforted yet frightened at how confident she was of this.

They were silent a little longer. Everything was still around them. The world seemed to be holding its breath in anticipation.

"Morgan," Rachel mumbled. "I..."

"I know," Skyler said. "Listen, I think it's time to get going."

To her relief, Rachel nodded.

Skyler led them through the village square, hoping it would be the last time she would ever see it.

"That well," Rachel said. Her voice trembled, like she was identifying a guy who'd attacked her. "That's where I woke up. I had to climb out."

"We all did," Skyler said. "It's the entrance to this world."

"Doesn't that mean we can also get out through there?"

Skyler shook her head.

To her irritation, Rachel stopped walking. "How do you know? Have you tried?"

"No," Skyler said. There was no way in hell she was ever going back down there.

"But why wouldn't the way in also be the way out?"

"I don't know. Let's keep going."

But Rachel stayed fixed in place.

"Why don't we try it?" she said. Her eyes were wide and her lip trembled, the thought clearly frightening her.

Why don't you *go down there?* Skyler was tempted to say. But then Rachel would potentially do it. She wondered if her sister had seen the corpses.

"Trust me," Skyler said. "Please. Trust me when I say there's nothing for us down there. The way out is in the castle. That's where we need to go."

"Are you sure?" she asked, once again wearing her thoughtful pout.

"Yes."

Rachel looked at her feet and nodded defeatedly. Skyler felt a wave of relief. She had no love for that well. She still remembered opening her eyes in that dark place, snowflakes sprinkling on her head.

But then she thought about the memories she had seen and felt with Virgil. How he had opened the well so that it would open the world. So that it could reach beyond and take more people for its army.

"Skyler?" Rachel said. This time she was the one looking irritated.

But Skyler couldn't stop thinking. If all it took was for the lid to be pulled open to allow the world to reach to the outside, then perhaps they could put an end to that by simply pushing it shut. They could end the nightmare that was the Prairie Triangle once and for all. She looked at the well sitting quietly in the middle of the square. If it was so simple, then she had to do it, didn't she? How could she not? She had to close it.

"Rachel," she said. "Can you give me a hand?"

"What are you doing?" Rachel asked as Skyler began moving toward the well. She sounded annoyed.

Skyler pushed against the stone lid. It felt like trying to move a boulder.

"Rachel," she said.

"Why are you—"

"Just help me!"

Something in her tone snapped Rachel into compliance. With both sisters putting their entire weight against the stone lid, it began to slide forward. Skyler's arms were on fire, as was her back. Her form was probably wrong. But she didn't give a damn. The darkness inside the well was slowly winking away, that was all that mattered.

"Keep pushing!" Skyler grunted.

"My fucking arms are gonna snap!"

Skyler suddenly had images of someone arriving at the last minute and getting trapped in the well forever. But it wasn't snowing, and Skyler felt certain nobody was coming. They continued pushing until the stone blotted out the last small sliver of darkness. At this point, the lid seemed to pop into place, letting out a massive boom, like some big cosmic door had been sealed. They both dropped to the ground, panting.

"I think that did it," Skyler said in between catching her breath. "Are you okay?"

"And what if another person comes along?" Rachel asked. "What if they get stuck in there."

"They won't."

"What makes you so confident?"

Skyler shrugged. She didn't know, but she was. "We should get going."

She slowly came to her feet. But Rachel didn't budge. She looked up at Skyler like she was contemplating an odd painting.

"We really need to go," Skyler insisted.

Rachel lowered her eyes. "I need a fucking drink."

"Me too."

Rachel glanced up again, looking even more perplexed. What? Was she expecting Skyler to lecture her about how a nineteen-year-old shouldn't be drinking? There was no time for that. It mattered about as much as a hangnail.

"Come on," Skyler said. Her tone was firmer than she'd intended, but she was in no mood to apologize for that either.

Rachel didn't argue. She only sighed and stood.

"Christ," Rachel said as they wound up the trail toward the castle entrance. Skyler wasn't sure if she was commenting on the exhausting walk, the size of the castle, or its barbed wall. It could've been anything.

"Almost there," Skyler said.

"Do you think it's safe?"

"We'll be fine." Then she remembered that those creatures, Morgan included, were in there. How would they get around them? She also remembered her flashlight was broken. She paused for a moment to test it. Despite pressing the button and slapping the cylinder, the light never came.

All the while, Rachel lingered over Skyler's shoulder. "Is it working?"

"Shit!"

"Will we need it?"

"Yeah." She wasn't in the mood to describe how much they would.

"Maybe we shouldn't go in there."

"It's the only way."

"That's impossible." Rachel obnoxiously stiffened her voice, trying to make it sound authoritative. "Y-you've only looked at this problem one way, right? There have to be other ways of—"

"This isn't a fucking math class!"

Rachel jerked back like a startled cat. She was right about one thing, though, they needed to do a little problem-solving.

"Do you have your phone?"

Saying nothing, Rachel reached into her pocket and pulled out a phone with a purple, glittery case.

"Is it working?"

"Battery's at like forty-eight percent. There's no service."

"We don't need service, just the light." Skyler held out her hand. In any other circumstance, Rachel would never have let Skyler near her phone. But here and now, she immediately handed it over. The lock screen picture was a selfie of Rachel with a couple of her college friends. They were all dressed for a night out. Skyler was stunned at how Rachel glowed, though that was partly from the soft filter.

"What's your password?"

Rachel took the phone back to unlock it. The trust wasn't all there yet. "Where's your phone?" she asked.

"It fell into a pit."

"A pit?"

That reminded Skyler. "When we go inside, you need to watch your step."

"What do you mean?"

Skyler told her about the traps. Rachel looked anxious about that, but not petrified.

"Just follow my lead."

Rachel handed back the now-unlocked phone. The wallpaper picture was another selfie, this time of Rachel and Morgan at the Spice Girls concert. Skyler lingered awkwardly in the background. The photo gave her a warm feeling while at the same time gutting her. She set these feelings aside and found the phone's flashlight function. The bright light illuminated the ground around their feet. Sam's flashlight was useless to them and deadweight to carry, so she tossed it off the trail. For a brief moment, she felt a pang of regret. Maybe Sam had paid a lot for that. Maybe it was special. Immediately, these concerns melted away and she felt ridiculous for having them. Such trivial thoughts came from somewhere else in her life and had no place here.

They continued moving. The closer they got to the castle entrance, the more Skyler's veins tightened.

"It smells like dead bodies," Rachel said.

Damn it. There was something else Skyler needed to mention. "Listen," she said, pausing and looking Rachel in the eyes. "You might see things in there..."

"Things?"

"They come from the forest. They..."

Rachel's eyes widened. "I think I know what you're talking about. Before I went in there, I saw these..." She looked sick from the memory.

"Again, follow my lead."

"Do we have any weapons?" Rachel had a desperate tremble in her voice.

"No." Skyler now realized the flashlight might have been a decent blunt weapon, but she couldn't see where she'd thrown it.

"I... Are you sure there's not another way out?" Rachel reminded Skyler of a kid with stage fright. It made her heart hurt. Without asking, she wrapped her arms tightly around her sister's waist. Rachel didn't recoil, though she was shaking. She rested her hands on Skyler's back. As hesitant as this touch was, Skyler needed it. In fact, she was grateful for the limpness. If it had been any tighter, Skyler would have allowed herself to be enveloped by it, to melt away until she was nothing.

"I will do everything I can," Skyler whispered up into her sister's ear, "to make sure you get home. I won't let anything happen to you." It sounded like an empty promise. But she meant it. Skyler wouldn't let anything happen, not if she could help it.

Rachel pulled away, but still kept her hands on Skyler's back. "It's a bad idea to go in there."

"Remember when we went to that abandoned farmhouse with Morgan? I sure as hell didn't go inside, but you both did."

Rachel grimaced at the memory. "That place was disgusting. There were cobwebs and bat shit everywhere."

"But you went in there, and you came out just fine. You both came out running and screaming, saying a guy wearing an old woman's face was chasing you."

Rachel's mouth curled into the shadow of a smirk. "You took off running so far down the road, I thought you'd never come back."

"I didn't have to go far, you two were laughing loud enough to hear twenty miles away."

"You were so pissed."

"I was fucking pissed. But it was okay in the end."

The hints of joy faded from Rachel's face. "This is different, Sky."

"Pretend it isn't. Or don't think about it at all."

Rachel pondered for a moment and then nodded apprehensively. "Okay," she said, finally dropping her hands away from Skyler's back.

"Okay," Skyler said, letting it go as well.

Rachel took a deep breath and closed her eyes. At the moment, she was a stark contrast from her glowing pictures. She looked almost ten years older. There were faded smears of makeup on her face. Her hair was disheveled. As their dad would always say, she looked like she "had just been on a joyride with a kamikaze pilot."

"Ready?" Skyler asked.

"Yeah."

It was now or never.

∽

The massive red door was still slightly open from Skyler's escape. The more they moved inside, the stronger the stench grew.

Rachel was cupping her hands over her nose and mouth. "What the fuck?"

The smell was still repugnant to Skyler, but it didn't affect her as much anymore. She was somehow used to it. She was scared shitless, yet completely calm. Something—that same something that had been in her head since the forest—or even since she came to this world, told her they would be fine. Or, at least, they would be safe. And despite everything, she felt little reason to doubt it.

The younger sister retched, pulling her hands away as a little vomit sputtered onto the floor.

"Are you okay?" Skyler asked.

Rachel shook drips of vomit off of her hands. "Are you seriously asking me that?" Her voice was tight from nausea.

Skyler looked around them. The grand entrance looked different, less open and sprawling, more cluttered. It looked like a garden had grown inside the room, bushes everywhere. As her eyes adjusted to the darkness and her brain caught up to them, her blood iced over. The bushes had shapes ranging from mammal to avian; humans, birds, dogs, cats, rats, squirrels, deer, and creatures too misshapen to be identified. They crowded the entire room, from the first floor to the second. Every bulging eye was on Skyler and Rachel. It was like the Horne sisters were their guests of honor. But there was no cheering, no singing, no yelling "Surprise." They were hardly making any sound at all other than breathing and the occasional grunt or growl.

"Oh, fuck," Rachel said, noticing them. She turned to run back toward the door, but Skyler grabbed her arm. "What the fuck are you doing?" she screamed, violently tugging so hard Skyler feared her sister's arm would dislocate.

"They won't hurt you," Skyler said.

"How the fuck do you know?"

"I..." She didn't know. It was something she herself was just realizing. She wasn't fully confident about it either, but there was no choice but to trust it.

Rachel continued tugging, pulling Skyler along with her. "Let go of me! Let go! Let..."

"Rachel!"

Abruptly, Rachel stopped struggling. One of the creatures was moving toward them. A narrow figure. It stretched a thin arm toward the sisters. On its hand was a distorted shape, a shape that had once been a hummingbird. Morgan's face was distorted with fury. Skyler braced herself, preparing to protect her sister from her best friend.

But Morgan didn't attack. She halted a few feet from the sisters, baring her teeth. Rachel grabbed Skyler's hand, squeezing tight. Skyler looked up at her sister's face, her eyes wide with terror, but there appeared to be no recognition. She didn't know who she was looking at, not yet at least. Once again, Skyler saw something soften in Morgan's face, a sorrowful affection. The softness made her more recognizable. Skyler's heart tightened. Morgan wasn't back, she reminded herself; it was like looking at an old photo.

"What?" Rachel asked. In her voice, it sounded like she was on the verge of realization. As if to circumvent this, Morgan turned away. She craned her neck toward the western entryway that would lead into the maze of hallways. The mass of creatures had parted from this entrance, providing passage. Morgan glanced back at Skyler, keeping her head strategically tilted so that Rachel wouldn't see her face. She nodded toward the entryway. The message was abundantly clear. It reminded Skyler of the gesture Virgil had given her at the beginning of all of this, encouraging her to go to the forest.

Skyler nodded back. This time, she would follow.

Morgan moved toward the entryway. Skyler tugged at Rachel, whose hand still cut off the circulation from hers.

"We need to go," she said.

Rachel looked at her in horror. "Are you sure?"

"I'm sure."

With Skyler leading the way, they followed Morgan, still squeezing each other's hands. The creatures watched them pass—their faces solemn. Something of their natural forms lingered underneath. Beautiful lives—beloved lives—taken, transformed, warped. She didn't know what she could do for them. There wasn't anything she could do; there couldn't be.

"Jesus," Rachel muttered, covering her mouth and nose.

The smell was at its absolute worse. But to keep the phone light raised, Skyler couldn't cover her mouth. It would pass soon enough.

Morgan glanced back, just to make sure they were following. Then she slipped into the darkness.

Chapter Twenty-Four

T HIS WAS PROBABLY IT.

At first, Sam thought it was just his exhaustion worsening; he needed a break from scrambling around the room pushing down pegs.

He'd spent hours going through many fruitless methods. When becoming hungry, he'd eat a small, unsatisfying portion of a protein bar. When thirsty, he'd take a sip of water, no more than that. Even with this moderation, the bottle became emptier. He wondered if he would have to start drinking his own piss.

His first method was testing the sound each peg made when pushed down. Maybe only the correct ones made that loud click. But they all seemed to make it. He then tried to guess a pattern. His first guess was the Society for the Preservation of Miscellaneous Artifact's symbol, an obelisk with a flat top. He tried to make the shape pointing in every direction, but it came to nothing. When he gave up on the obelisk, he tried various other shapes: a circle, a square, a triangle. Numerous times, he checked the room for clues, scanning every inch of the rounded wall and ceiling for a hint of a pattern, overanalyzing the cracks in the stone floor. There was nothing. At his most desperate, he looked through some of the correspondence between Maria Faragó and his great grandfather. Faragó's letters had been cryptic enough, so maybe there were clues. Yet, why would she bother leaving him clues in the first place? She'd had no objectives but to deceive the original Samael. At any rate, the letters became hard to focus on, the writing looking like a bunch of meaningless, cobbled-together symbols.

As his head grew fuzzy and his body cold, he came to a point where he could barely stand. He laid on the floor—but just for a moment. For one moment, then for the next moment, and the next. Everything felt wrong. He needed to rest a little, rest like a rock. A useless, worthless rock that deserved to be kicked into the bottom of a river. He was so cold. But also warm in a way. He felt cozy. He was also terrified. He was dying.

He'd come so close. It was right there, but he couldn't figure it out. He had let Skyler go off on her own. She was probably dead now, and for nothing. He had let her die in vain. He let himself die in vain too.

He wanted his mother. This was weak and pathetic of him. He was glad his father wasn't there. It was suffocating to even think about the man—those sad, bitter eyes. Even worse was the thought of his great-grandfather. The idea of that judgmental portrait staring down above the fireplace mortified him.

But thinking about his mother didn't sadden or scare him. Her smile, her laugh, her touch. He could hear her voice.

Come on, baby. It's time to go.

He closed his eyes.

Come on, baby.

Lights were flickering against a meaty canvas. Beneath them, shadows were crawling. Were they her?

Come on.

She never would have hurt him. He had always known this. When his father told him she went crazy and tried to murder him, what other choice did he have but to believe it? After all, it was his duty to believe his father. If he fulfilled his duty, no matter how hard it might be, it would all come to something. But she hadn't wanted to hurt him—that was the truth. She had wanted to help him. To get him away from a life she knew would destroy him. Maybe he should have kept trying to save himself, to get away from his father. Sure, he'd been rebellious at times, but had he ever truly been at risk of denouncing his purpose? Or what he had been told was his purpose? Now he was going to die like she had. Cold and alone. And unlike her, he deserved it. He had opened the door to the motel room. She'd told him not to. Begged him not to. But he had. He willfully went back to his father, sealing his mother's fate, and his own.

"Sam!" she said.

"I'm sorry," he said back to her.

"Sam!"

"Mommy. I just want to go home."

"Sam!" The voice was sounding less and less like hers. She was fading. He was losing her again. He didn't want her to leave him.

What a pathetic, pissing, bleeding child. He thought he could escape that fact. But it was who he was. That wasn't his mother's fault, but it had killed her.

"Sam! Oh god!" It didn't sound like his mother's voice any longer.

He opened his eyes. Through the blur, he saw two humanoid figures looming over him. He shut his eyes again.

"What's wrong with him?"

"He's hurt."

He felt a gentle touch against the back of his neck. When he re-opened his eyes, he saw a face peering down at him. Those oval eyes.

Casey. This couldn't be real. She looked younger than Casey would be. Much younger. Her mouth was wider, her hair and skin darker. And the woman behind her...

"Skyler?" He wanted to trust what he was seeing. But it was impossible.

"I'm here," she confirmed. She looked haggard and pummeled. Both women did. Surely a hallucination would have been a little cleaner...

"You..." But how the hell could she have possibly made it back? Not only that... "Who are you?" he asked the woman holding him.

"Rachel," she said. "You're Sam, right?"

So Skyler had not only survived, but saved her sister. Sam was filled with both relief and envy. How the hell did she do it?

"Do you have any more water?" Skyler asked. Without waiting for an answer, she fumbled through his bag and pulled out the water bottle. She swished it, listening to the tiny droplets that remained trickling around. "Shit!"

"Sorry," he said. "I think I drank it all."

"Don't be sorry," Skyler said.

"I'm sorry," he said again anyway. He should have brought more bottles. His mouth and throat were so dry.

"We need to get out of here, fast," Skyler said, an increased urgency in her voice.

"No," Sam said in weak protest, thinking they were going to drag him out of the room. But instead, Rachel stayed with him while Skyler moved toward the black platform. "I couldn't figure it out," he tried to tell her. She either didn't hear him or was ignoring him.

"What happened to you?" Rachel asked. Maybe it was the state he was in, but her eyes were more breathtakingly bright than Casey's had ever been.

"M-my foot."

Rachel looked down at the mangled appendage. She turned back to Sam with a pained smile, clearly trying to hide her horror. "You'll be fine," she said. "You'll be fine."

Something in that voice: a soft, soothing compassion. Or at least an attempt at compassion. It made him lose himself. Even if he wanted to hold it back, like he used to be able to do, like he was supposed to do, he couldn't. His vision blurred, his skin baking, chest heaving, and lips sputtering.

"It's okay," Rachel said again. His episode seemed to trigger something in her as well. Her lips trembled and tears streamed down her cheeks.

He couldn't stop sobbing. He hated himself for this, he felt so pathetic. But he didn't want to stop either. It felt good. It felt too satisfying to be any good for him, but still...

As their tears subsided, an intense, loud grinding and whirring snapped Sam and Rachel to attention. At first, Sam thought the castle was coming to life again. He looked up to see Skyler hopping away from the black platform, which seemed to be collapsing into the floor, folding away and kicking dust into the air. The loud grinding ended once the platform was gone and there only remained a depression in the floor. Sam couldn't see much from where he lay, but the depression appeared to have stairs leading downward.

He looked back at Skyler, who seemed as shocked as he was. "How did you..."

"It's a constellation," she said.

"How did you know?" Sam tried to raise himself up, but it felt like trying to pull up a hundred ninety pounds of deadweight with his neck. Rachel patted his chest to keep him still.

"I really don't know," Skyler said, practically mumbling.

"What does a constellation have to do with anything?" Rachel asked.

Then Sam had a thought. "Which constellation?"

Skyler thought for a moment, but only a moment. "I think O—" Her eyes widened, developing the same thought as him. "Orion."

Anger stabbed into his gut. The answer had been right there. Maria, cruelly mocking her old rival: *Come get this, my dear Orion, if you can.* She was mocking not just Samael, but his progeny. But the Adamsens had the last laugh now, didn't they? It was solved. Sam only wished he had been the one to solve it.

"You really think this is our way out?" Rachel asked.

"I think so." Skyler seemed so confident about that. Now that the puzzle was solved, Sam felt less sure. Maybe it was another cruel trap, like the spike room had been, forcing them to put in effort for nothing. And if that was the case, then this would probably be it for him.

"Where's my knife?" he asked.

"It's gone," Skyler said. "Sorry."

"Those things."

"They won't be following us." Again, that certainty—and obviously she herself didn't know where the hell it was coming from.

"It led us here," Rachel said.

"What did?"

"One of them," Skyler replied, her tone suddenly vacant.

He wanted to ask why a creature would lead them here, but doubted he would get an answer.

Fumbling into his backpack, he pulled out his Swiss Army knife. It was the best they could do. At least he wouldn't have to feel completely naked, venturing into the unknown unarmed.

"We should get going," Skyler said.

"I think he needs some rest," Rachel countered.

"No," Sam said. Rest was the worst idea, even if he wanted it more than anything.

Rachel didn't protest, and she and Skyler helped him to his feet. He was able to move a little better than he thought, which was a relief. But he still had to lean heavily on the women, even with their heads only up to his armpits. Skyler used a cell phone to light their way as they descended the black and white steps.

"Where's my flashlight?" Sam asked.

"It's also gone. Sorry."

It was a belaboring journey down the stairs. By the time they reached the bottom and entered a short tunnel, Sam could hear his own breathing echoing against the cylindrical wall. He wanted to collapse again, and if he didn't have Rachel and Skyler keeping him upright, he would have. At the end of the tunnel was a narrow slit in the wall. This led to another stairwell, curving further downward.

"Are you good?" Skyler asked.

"Yes." Sam couldn't give enough strength to his voice to make that convincing.

"Yeah," Rachel also answered. Sam wondered if the question had even been for him. Suddenly, he felt embarrassed at himself. He couldn't believe he had cried earlier, had fallen apart in front of these women. But before he could think of anything to explain himself, he was corralled through the tight entryway.

This stairwell was so narrow, they had to move single file. He was sandwiched in the middle, Skyler leading the way, Rachel behind him. He felt boxed in and his head flooded with panicked thoughts of the entrance closing and trapping them, or the phone's light going out. His heart pounded more erratically. He wanted to beat against the walls and scream. The vertigo was coming back with a vengeance. He also felt queasy. It was rancid in there. Skyler's hair, just inches from his nose, especially smelled awful. They all stank.

He had to pause, close his eyes, and lean against the wall.

"Sam?" Rachel asked, grabbing his arm.

"I'm fine, I'm fine."

He opened his eyes to see Skyler looking at him. Her face told him everything. She was worried, but there was nothing she could do. There wasn't much he could do either but focus ahead of him, on the phone's light shining on the wall, and keep moving.

The spiral downward seemed endless. They were spiraling down to hell. Maybe he was about to face his devil—his family's devil. He wanted to feel some pride at that thought or perhaps some sense of power or consequence. But, to his shame, all he felt was fear.

The stairwell fortunately did end, leading them to another tunnel. This one was larger than the last and the wall was less smooth. A gaping cavern, the walls were entirely rock and moisture, no human-made foundations. Well, that wasn't true. It was all "human-made," wasn't it?

Down here, the air was the coolest and most stifling it had ever been. Stalactites dripped downward, but like the trees and grass, they looked false, factory made and installed. Besides, this world couldn't have been old enough for its caverns to be forming full stalactites naturally, unless time worked differently between worlds. Sam was suddenly hit with a disturbing thought: what if hundreds of years had passed in the outside?

He thought it best not to share this idea with Skyler or Rachel, who were huffing under his weight, again serving as human crutches. The cavern led to a large red door resembling the one at the castle entrance.

A mix of fear and excitement rushed through his blood.

"Where are we?" Rachel asked.

"I don't know," Skyler said, panting.

"I thought you did!" Rachel stopped moving, forcing Sam and Skyler to a halt as well.

"I mean, I can't say for sure."

With their movement stopped, Sam suddenly felt restrained. He was eager to keep going. He pulled his arms away from the women. To his own surprise, he didn't immediately drop to the floor but was able to keep hopping forward, though it was an effort. It was like jogging underwater.

"Sam!" Rachel shouted after him.

"Come on," he heard Skyler mutter to her sister. Rachel rushed forward and grabbed Sam's arm to support him. He didn't shake her away even though it made him feel like a little old lady getting helped across the street by a Boy Scout.

The red door was already cracked open, inviting them in. Skyler ran ahead of Sam and Rachel to check inside. They paused while she shined the flashlight through the door's crack. Sam quickly felt antsy; Skyler was taking forever to look. But finally, she nodded at them and pushed the door open further. It screeched with the effort. Then, with her phone as their guiding light, she led the way inside.

At a glance, the room looked like a small library or maybe an archive. Either way, it was a disorganized one, the place flooded with haphazardly placed shelves full of books and other documents. Some documents were scrolled up or bound, others were lying about loosely. Many papers were scattered about the floor. A couple shelves appeared to have been knocked over. Sam wondered if a confrontation had occurred in here.

"Thank god," Skyler said, pointing at the stone wall where there were more of those lanterns.

While she went to each lantern, cranking every one to life, Sam and Rachel moved toward a stone table at the center of the room. A ragged shape was draped against the table. As each lantern lit the room further, the shape became more recognizable. It was a person wearing a faded blue-gray dress that hung loosely from their body. They sat in an old wooden chair, head lying on the table, concealing their face. Their hair was long, stringy, and gray. The head seemed very thin with patches exposing a grayish-white surface underneath.

"H-hello?" Rachel said to the shape. It didn't sound like she expected any response. It had to be as clear to her as it was to Sam that this person was long dead. He touched the frail figure's shoulder, feeling nothing but bone underneath the cloth. He leaned over to look at the skeleton face, bottom jaw hanging open with gray and brown flakes of what used to be skin or muscles hanging from the bones. Its left arm was stretched out along the table. Its bony talons clutched something small. The object looked like a pencil made of stone. Next to the hand was a thick hammer and sheets of paper. There were also two small bones that looked like fingers, but the skeletal hand seemed to have all of its fingers intact.

Skyler finished lighting the room and came to their side. "Was this Maria?"

Sam shook his head. That seemed impossible. The Maria his father told him about all his life was a demon, a tyrant. Cowardly, but also wicked, conniving, and powerful. This figure was so small and frail, probably had been even before rotting away to nothing. She looked like she couldn't have been taller than five feet. There was nothing threatening or powerful about her. There was nothing despicable either. She was just a dead thing.

His head became fuzzy and he couldn't stand anymore. There was another wooden chair alongside the table, so he sat. Skyler and Rachel rushed to keep him steady as he did. The chair was old and fragile and felt like it would break beneath his weight. But it stayed stubbornly strong, despite its loud creaks. As he relaxed, he realized it would have been more dignified to stay standing, or maybe offer the chair to Skyler or Rachel. It was a man's responsibility to be strong, his father always told him. His father also always told him to never cry, or at least never let anyone see him do so, especially not women. But that ship had sailed. The sisters didn't seem to care at least. Skyler began wandering around the room, examining the shelves. Rachel stayed by his side, kneeling and rubbing his back.

He became curious about the sheets of paper next to the body. They were spattered with writing. What were they? A suicide note? A last will and testament?

He dragged the sheets to him. The flourished, cursive handwriting was instantly familiar:

"Elizabeth,"

Elizabeth. He heard that name often in his father's stories. It was the woman who had turned the tide, who had betrayed Maria Faragó, escaped her grasp, and sailed across the sea to find Samael. She was the one who told him of the world, even if she'd died before she could say much more. If not for her, Samael may never have come out of hiding. The Society for the Recovery of Lost Artifacts never would have been formed. Sam wouldn't have been born. Or if he had, his life would have been very different. Part of him resented Elizabeth for that.

There was no denying it then, though part of him had always known it to be true. The fragile corpse next to him was Maria Faragó.

"My Elizabeth.

Just writing your name hurts me. I'm sick at the thought of your face. I do not know why I write this. There is as much purpose in writing this as there is writing to one who is long, long dead. How strange it is to end this way for me. I've spent so long thinking of my great purpose. I crafted a world with my own hands. Yet, here I sit, sick and starving. I am just another dying fool writing a last confession to her love.

Did I ever tell you about my ripest memory from girlhood? It haunts every moment of my life."

Something felt different about this letter's voice compared to the letters Maria had written to Samael. It felt sincere, lacking deceitful pretenses.

"I have told you of the castle. My family's castle. The one I lived in for much of my life. It had served as a fortress, commandeered of course by the Society. I was always safe in there. But in my restless youth, I did not always appreciate that safety. On one particular night, this restlessness became unbearable. I do not remember why, perhaps Greta had sent me to bed without any zimtsterne. My, was that woman an iron-fisted shrew! Or perhaps I simply needed fresh air. Whatever the reason, I fled the castle in the dead of night.

The castle was surrounded by a large, deep forest. From behind the castle walls, that forest had been my darling. Some days I would stare out my bedroom window and look into its wooded depths. I would imagine myself living out there, a huntress, touched by Artemis, stalking beasts with my mighty bow.

But on that night, when I actually stepped beyond those comfortable palisades and into the forest's cold grip, I did not feel the goddess of the hunt's blessing. This is where my memory becomes most vivid.

I was lost in the darkness. Everything around me felt alive, reaching for me, the trees, the grass. I cried out as loudly as I could, but my voice could never penetrate the prison I had found myself in.

Then, and I still dream of this often, there was a horrendous stench. Elizabeth, it was the smell of death. Perhaps it had been the rotting carcass of a nearby deer or a small animal. But the smell consumed me. I curled into the leaves and buried my face into the dirt. At some point, I became nestled in the forest's embrace, consumed by it. It felt like ages before I opened my eyes, the sun grinning down on me, eclipsed only by the castle guards, their plumes raising nobly in the air. I would learn that they had spent all night looking for me. I welcomed my guardians with open arms as they carried me back to the castle.

But I suppose I had never truly left the forest that morning. I never can leave. This world, my creation, has proven that to me. And so have you…"

There was a crash somewhere in the room.

"Shit!" he heard Skyler say.

"Elizabeth, how could you do this? I had put my faith in you. You were safe, and loving. You were like a snow globe. Secure, beautiful, predictable, unchanging on the inside, always doing what is expected, and only at command.

But of course I had been wrong. Perhaps I knew that long before your betrayal. I would see that distant look in your eyes, hear that festering resentment in your voice, the growing coldness of your touch. But I had been so entranced by my creation—amazed by what it was, frightened of what it was becoming—I hadn't stopped to consider that your loyalty, devotion, and love were not unconditional.

But your loyalty and devotion had once existed, hadn't they? Or had you always been a silent agent of Samael?

I know you were disgusted with my retaliation. Even I was shaken by my wrath and the piousness with which my followers carried it out. But Samael had drawn first blood. You know this. You were there, like I was. My house, my home, bombed, many faithful servants, followers, and relatives killed. You saw them. You saw the smoldering mounds of flesh spattered about the garden where we had taken many late-night walks together. Why not consider the horrors those victims had suffered? But worst of all, this world I had spent so many years creating—my purpose—was nearly lost. Samael had committed that atrocity only because I had deceived him. But that action justified my deceit. He was, or perhaps still is, a monster. And if you, my sweet Elizabeth, were in league with such a creature all along, well, to call me soulbroken would be too tame."

Sam looked at Rachel.

"Are you okay?" she asked.

"Are you reading this?" he asked.

"Um..." That answered his question. He had nobody to share his shock with but himself.

For so long, he was told that Maria had deceived Samael, and she admitted to that in her own writing. But he had also been told her attack on Samael and his followers was unprovoked. But now, he was learning that his great-grandfather had attacked first. Not a victim then, but the loser in a war he had started.

No. Bullshit. Maria had to be lying.

But on the other hand, why would she? Writing a letter she thought nobody would read, there was nothing to prove. Maybe she was just trying to lie to herself.

But was the idea of her story being true so absurd? His father always told him he should be proud of his great-grandfather's ruthlessness, to emulate it. Did that mean he should be proud of mass murder too? If all of this was true, it meant that Maria hadn't been responsible for the decay and destruction of the original Society, at least, not solely. Samael had also had a part in it.

And for what? The tool? Where even was it?

A gnawing urge demanded Sam read the rest of the letter. Maybe there would be some kind of explanation in the remaining passages. Something that would give him a sense of peace—or some hint of reassurance. At the same time, he was terrified to keep reading.

"Are you okay?" Rachel asked again.

"No."

I am tired and weak. My food and water have run out. I cannot return to the surface. My world has changed. I don't know how to control it anymore. I don't think I even can. I still love it. I will always love it. But I wish I had never created it.

Through much of my life, I had been praised. Praised for my mastery of the chisel. Praised, applauded, though also condescended to, sneered at. Jealousy is more powerful than pride. So many felt that a woman had no place in using the tool, let alone mastering it better than any man alive. But I did, and I always felt so very special for that.

But am I? How can we be so sure my hands are the most capable? After all, very few have been allowed to use the chisel. I always knew my destiny was bejeweled in greatness. But those jewels were stitched on by my forebears. When I reflect on the world I have made, I see a distinct lack of nuance or creativity. What I had produced was a dour replication of our own world, or more specifically, my own world. My designs were so uninspired and limited that even the world itself tired of them, and developed designs of its own.

It might be that all humans lack creativity at this stage in our existence. Maybe we are simply not ready to craft worlds. Or it could be that, perhaps, I alone am not as worthy as I believed. Could it be possible that somewhere, perhaps within the lowly thief, the chaste nun, the silent monk, the subjugated tribesman, lays a worthier creator? I have come to realize these thoughts have haunted me for a long time. But this doesn't matter, none will get their hands on it now. None should get their hands on it, especially not the likes of Samael. I am resolved in this matter. You yourself have seen this resolve, suffered from it, as evidenced by your now-malformed hand. I do not regret what I did. After all, my actions let me keep a small part of you close to me.

If I am not worthy of being the wielder of the chisel, then let me make myself worthy of being its protector. You told me I was selfish, arrogant. I remember the day you called me such things, words you had never called me before. They filled my soul with ice. But perhaps you were right. I am selfish and arrogant, so are you, so is the rest of our species, among many other things. That is why the chisel must stay hidden.

If the day comes when humans are clever enough to reach this chamber where I sit now, then I suppose my work is done. My enemies cannot bomb their way into this one. We have put to use all the secrets this Society accumulated over the centuries. My fortress is impervious to brutishness. That was my design. And, though the world itself may rue the fact, it is safe as well. Hidden away in its snow globe, a fortress in its own right. That was also my design.

Of course, I couldn't impose all my designs on my creation. Nor could I impose them on you. I always treated you and your love as my design. That is why I loved you. That is why I lost you. Oh, Elizabeth.

I would have loved to sail down the Rhine with you."

Sam had to look through the letter a few more times. Was this really it? Nothing more than a mournful little love letter? Maybe one of the other papers scattered around the room would have more answers. But this seemed to be the last thing she wrote before her death. He would have expected... Well, what *did* he expect? A special hint just for him?

"Rachel!" Skyler called out from the other side of the room. "Come take a look at this!"

Rachel put a hand on Sam's shoulder, checking to see if he was alright. He nodded. Being alone was fine by him right now.

When she left, he considered the pitiful carcass next to him. The skeleton was utterly still, as much a fixture in the room as the table. Maria Faragó had been no demon. She hadn't been a good person. But she wasn't the monster he hated and feared all his life. In fact, he related to her. She had wanted things to go as planned, for existence to be cut-and-dried, and constant. Whenever it didn't, it frightened her, made her feel alone and angry. She was able to adapt, certainly. And so was Sam. But a broken plan, a deviation from strategy, a shattered design, was no small thing. He understood this. Of course, he would never do the awful things she had done. At least, he liked to think he wouldn't.

No, there was no reason for him to believe he was such a decent person. He was Samael's great-grandson, and now he knew exactly what that meant.

His foot throbbed again. He'd come to forget how much it hurt.

Was the tool that creates worlds even in this room? He was born to find it, so it should be obvious where it was. He scanned Maria's corpse, looking for any clues. His eyes moved back to her hand, which gripped the pencil. As he looked closer, he realized it wasn't a pencil, it looked more like...

His heart raced as he pried the object from the skeleton's hand. There was some resistance from the spindly bones that closed around it. He had to break a couple to get it loose. But finally, the small object was in the palm of his hand.

It was old, made of some kind of dark gray stone. It looked like something a neanderthal would have used. It was not a pencil, but a chisel. So, the Order of the Chisel hadn't been a metaphorical name after all. There were cracks that looked like lightning bolts all along its surface. These cracks appeared to be glowing. The glow was subtle and faded; he had to look long and closely to confirm it wasn't just his eyes playing tricks. They pulsed with colors Sam couldn't identify. It may have been his heartbeat, but the tiny thing felt like it was throbbing. There was power in it—that was clear. Great power. The power to create worlds. The hammer lying on the table, Sam assumed, was the one Maria had used with it.

So, he had found it, then.

He set the chisel on the table, desperately searching inside himself for that catharsis, that satisfaction and victory. But he couldn't find it. Maybe it was all the blood he'd lost. He was so cold and tired, it took away his ability to feel anything.

Rachel returned to his side.

"Sam," she said. "We think we found the way out." She sounded more scared than certain.

"This is it." Sam pointed at the chisel.

Skyler also came to the table. "Sam, we found the—"

"See this?" He pointed at it again. "The tool that can create worlds."

"That?" Skyler leaned in and looked closely at it. Her face was contorted in confusion. He envied her; at least that was a reaction.

"I spent..." he began, but he didn't know what he was beginning. "It's just... it's so important."

He couldn't go on. Now he realized he felt something, a goblin inside pulling at his guts. This was the thing that made his whole life worth it. This. This was better than finding love. This was better than starting a family. It was better than having a mother. This thing that he could throw across the room and forget forever was better than his life. A life that probably wouldn't continue for long. His purpose, his existence, had all been for something no bigger than a pencil.

"What do we do with it?" Rachel asked.

"Fuck if I know." Sam shrugged. He stared at his fingers, fingers formed solely to hold this tool. The fingers that had grabbed that motel doorknob and killed his mother. "Take it back. Start a new Society, I guess. All the important people can join in. Who should we invite? Warren Buffet? Elon Musk?"

Skyler picked up the hammer with some strain and examined it.

"You know," Sam said, "my great-grandfather blew people up for this thing." Skyler looked at him, wide-eyed. "Why are you so surprised?" he asked. The goblin was pulling harder and he suddenly had an urge to scream and flip over the table.

"No," Skyler said. "It's just that... I think I knew that."

"Well," he said, not really caring how or why. "I guess it was all for the greater good." It was too hard to believe, but he had to hold on.

Be strong. Be cold.

Then, Rachel put a hand on his shoulder. The touch was so light, so gentle. Her skin was warm. She shouldn't have done that. He hated that she did. It was too much for him to bear. Disobeying his father's advice again, he began sobbing.

Rachel and Skyler said nothing. Their silence embarrassed him.

"I'm sorry," he said, trying to pull himself together.

"Don't be," Skyler replied. She didn't understand. He'd been willing to let her go and die in the forest, Rachel too. All because he had to get this tool.

He came to a point where he was able to keep the tears at bay. Part of him felt good, like he'd taken off a heavy backpack. But he also felt like shit.

"Fuck, I'm pathetic," he said, burying his head in his hands, running those deadly fingers through his hair.

"No you're not," Skyler said.

"If my dad could see me—"

"Your dad is an asshole," Skyler reminded him, her voice sharp enough to cut through the air. "I'm sorry, but it just sounds like all he ever did was berate you or tell you bullshit about who you're supposed to be."

He couldn't deny that. But still. "This was all I was meant for. What good am I?"

"Look at me," she said.. He did. Her eyes were surprisingly fiery. "You chose to come here and do this. Right?"

So, it was his fault, then. He figured as much.

"You are more than any of this Society bullshit," Skyler continued. "I know you are. You can't let people tell you what your purpose is. You can't..."

Rachel gave his shoulder a reassuring squeeze.

"No, you don't fucking get it! I was born for this."

"Sam," Skyler said. "You were born to be born. That's it. You decide the rest. It doesn't matter what your dad says. Do you understand me?"

Maybe it was delirium, but this made sense. Skyler wasn't bullshitting him, giving him sweet words for his sake. She obviously felt deeply about this. But it was a little hard to grasp. A life without purpose? Or at least without one he didn't choose himself? That seemed terrifying, impossible. Yet, it also sounded comforting. Maybe it wasn't his fate to be like Maria, her life overtaken and consumed by the tool and her design. Maybe it wasn't his fate to be like Samael, also consumed but in a different way. It wasn't his fate to be a self-pitying mess like his father. Maybe, in his more rebellious times, Sam had known as much. He wondered if his mother had been there, somewhere, every time those thoughts came to him. But maybe he was more than her as well.

"I just... I don't know. I don't know what I want."

"Join the club," Skyler muttered.

The goblin was settling, at least for now. He let out a sigh and his chest felt warm.

He grabbed the chisel and put it in his backpack. Doing so was his decision, not his purpose. His decision. Maybe he would show it to his father. Maybe his father would feel underwhelmed too, and it would inspire him to make a new start.

Skyler held out the hammer. "You should take this too."

"There are hammers in our world."

"Not like this, I don't think."

He conceded, taking the object. Its heaviness caught him off guard. But he regained control before it could drop him to the ground and tucked it away with the chisel.

With Skyler and Rachel's help, he rose from the table.

"Let's go," he said. It was his choice to keep going. Come what may, it was his choice.

Then came that stench.

Chapter Twenty-Five

E VEN NOW, IN HER state, there was something about this room that excited the historian in Skyler. Not that she'd ever felt she'd deserved that title. But once the room was fully lit, she was compelled to peruse the shelves.

The diverse ages and make of the documents were alone enough to spark the eager curiosity inside her. There were sketches, maps, blueprints, journals, letters. The writings were in a vast assortment of languages and characters, many of which Skyler didn't recognize. She noticed a pale face on the floor, staring up at her from a sheet of paper. It looked like a da Vinci drawing, a Vitruvian Man made of gears and coils, every inch of its inner workings exposed. She quickly realized it was a blueprint for the Automatons. There was a note attached with that cursive handwriting she'd seen many times before.

"Your criticism of my request is noted. Indeed, there is no practical use of the uniform, and perhaps the plumes have potential to be intrusive. But I want you to humor me. Can you grant me that wish, Madam Goddard?"

On one shelf was a row of chunks of metal that seemed to serve no function. Maybe they were samples. She picked one up. Taken aback by its heaviness, she dropped it.

"Shit!" she shouted after it clattered on the floor.

There were other objects throughout the room. Small, round pieces of glass marked with numbers. Different shapes, sizes, and colors of stone, some broken apart, others fully intact. Liquids of varying colors were in dusty jars. There were also seemingly random things: lone gears and springs, swords, knives, archaic guns, the shells of bulky, steel machines that couldn't be identified, antiquated cloths, slates, and tools of all kinds. These objects clearly came from a diverse array of regions and cultures, most were likely stolen from their rightful places during colonial conquest.

Another blueprint lying carelessly on the floor caught her attention. This one depicted a bell. Jon's precious Vivian? The bell in the blueprint was hooked to all kinds of gears and mechanisms. There was also a note attached to it, that same cursive.

"Quite an ambitious undertaking, Mr. McKinnon. Can it be done? All resources are, of course, at your disposal. We can discuss the details in person."

On a lower shelf was a pile of decapitated, chipped, or otherwise broken hammers. Arching over these was the blueprint of another hammer. There was large, excited writing on it.

"This one works!"

The exclamation was undergirded by a smaller note:

"Use carefully. This hammer is stronger than expected. The tool is not invincible."

In another time, she would have been intimidated by such a collection, drowning in self-imposed expectations to be studious when all she wanted to do was take a nap. But now that she was here and not thinking too hard about anything, she felt deeply at ease. She wanted to read every document, at least the ones she could decipher. She wanted to uncover the stories they may tell. Maybe there would be something in here that would make everything she'd experienced make sense.

She could hear Sam and Rachel mumbling elsewhere in the room. She didn't focus on their words. There was something in the corner that had her attention: a round hatch on the ground. The door was covered in dust, its colors blending with the stone. The only reason Skyler had noticed it was its metal valve sticking out. The door looked like a hatch in a submarine. She pulled the valve left and right. At first, it wouldn't turn either way. But when she put her entire weight into it, her shoulders on fire from the strain, it finally moved. The valve quickly became loose enough that Skyler could twist until she was finally able to tug open the hatch. It burst opened with a powerful, gut-punching force that nearly knocked her over. It reminded her of the force she'd felt when closing the well. The hatch open, a pitch-black pit lay before her. There was no ladder or stairway leading down. It was so painfully dark down there. It reminded Skyler of Vantablack, the darkest shade of black that absorbed nearly all visible light. The pit could have led anywhere, or nowhere. It should have frightened her. But it didn't. The feeling inside her, and this feeling *did* frighten her, said it was okay. It told her this was the way home.

"Rachel!" she shouted. "Come take a look at this!" She would have shouted to Sam, too, but she didn't want him to exert himself.

"What is it?" Rachel asked when she came. When Skyler pointed to the pit, she asked: "This goes deeper?"

"I don't think so," Skyler said.

Rachel gave a confused frown. "What do you mean?"

"I think this is the way out."

"Or it's just a pit."

"Can't you trust me?" Skyler said, frustrated even if she understood Rachel's hesitation. "I got us this far."

Rachel said nothing. She looked at the pit with a ponderous pout.

"If we don't go for it, we'll die in here."

"I'm scared." Rachel said this casually, like saying she was hungry. But in her bright eyes, Skyler could see how true this was.

"I am too." Skyler wanted to give her sister another hug. But before she could even think about leaning in to do so, Rachel gave a jittery shrug.

"Okay," she said. "So, we just climb down there?"

"I don't see anything to climb." Even the walls of the pit were smooth stone. Nothing they could get their footing in.

"So?"

"A leap of faith."

She had never been a religious person. But she had the faith and certainty of a zealot right now.

"You were too afraid to go into a crappy old barn," Rachel said. Skyler knew it was Rachel's roundabout way of saying, *What the fuck's happened to you?*

"We should get Sam."

"Yeah." Rachel immediately made for where Sam was. Skyler gave one last look at the pit, checking her doubts. There were many, but they all meant nothing.

"You were born to be born. That's it. You decide the rest. It doesn't matter what your dad says. Do you understand me?"

Though she winged through that statement, it felt good to say. It felt like something Morgan would say. But at the same time, she felt guilty. Who was she to give this advice? Ever since leaving the forest, whatever the hell was making her take each step was something she hadn't chosen. There was a passenger inside her, propelling her at each turn. She still had no idea what it wanted.

But then she looked at Rachel, who nodded at what she said. Maybe the passenger didn't deserve all the credit. Whenever she thought about herself, there seemed to be little to say. She found more value in living for others and not thinking about who exactly Skyler Horne was. But that didn't mean Skyler Horne was nobody. Maybe she was the kind of person who would take time to drop everything and drive out to the middle of nowhere to find a loved one. Skyler Horne was the kind who would venture through a fucked-up castle into a mind-warping forest to save her sister. She was the kind who, instead of choosing to live in a tower for the rest of her existence, chose to find her way home. And she was the kind who, instead of letting her family continue on a lie, told a hard truth that brought it to an end. She was far from one for easy ways out, she realized. Nothing would change that, not even this feeling—this passenger—inside her.

Sam tucked away the chisel and hammer into his backpack and came to his feet.

"Let's go," he said.

But before they could take first steps, he stiffened.

"What?" As soon as she asked this, she smelled it too.

One of the creatures was here. She knew they needed to make for the exit, or what she believed was the exit, quickly. But despite her instincts, whatever the hell those even were anymore, she looked over her shoulder. A thin, distorted figure stood in the entryway, glaring at them. Though the flickering lights cast shadows on her face, Skyler knew it was Morgan. What the hell was she doing here? This wasn't part of the plan.

"Fuck!" Rachel squeaked.

Morgan howled and hurtled toward them, kicking up papers along the way.

Before coming to this world, Skyler had only ever dreamed about being chased by someone or something, the danger dissipating as soon as she awoke. In those dreams, she would always be stuck, either being constricted by some unknown muscular atrophy, or getting stuck in glue or waist-high water. In this moment, where the threat was real, she was just as encumbered, having to carry Sam along. While panic was coursing through the back of her mind, she was calmer than she would have expected. All she focused on was getting to the trapdoor.

But Morgan was fast. When they reached the hatch, Rachel was tugged away; the force of her capture knocked Skyler and Sam to the ground.

"Skyler!" Rachel screamed. Morgan had her by the shoulder.

Skyler jumped to her feet, only to be smacked away by Morgan. It felt like she had been hit by a baseball bat. She fell again, ears ringing, head spinning. She heard a deep, pained cry and looked up to see two dancing figures shadowed by the firelight; one was throwing the other around like a rag doll. Morgan was killing Rachel.

"Morgan!" Skyler screamed, appealing to whatever was left in there. "Please!"

But when her eyes adjusted, she realized the figure Morgan was whipping around wasn't Rachel, but Sam.

What followed went quicker than a flash of light. Morgan was clearly leading the violent dance. Sam could barely stay on his feet. Yet, he somehow remained steady. The dance took them in circles. Skyler had to scramble away to avoid them. Rachel was on the other side of this fight, pressed against the wall with her eyes shut and ears covered. Skyler hardly had a chance to decide to jump in and help before Sam, with a deep cry, lunged and shoved Morgan into the pit.

Morgan's terrified roar rang out before vanishing. The noise didn't gradually fade away, instead cutting off completely as if someone had hit the mute button.

Once the sound was gone and Skyler's mind caught up to her, she crawled over and looked down into the oppressive blackness. Nothing peered back up at her. She turned to Sam. He was frazzled and battered with bleeding cuts painting his body a reddish black. Rachel was already by his side, trying to keep him steady.

"You both need to go now," he said, pushing Rachel away from him.

"You're coming too," Skyler said, climbing to her feet.

"Someone needs to close that." Sam nodded at the hatch door. "If one of those things got down here... how many..." His eyes rolled back and he drifted off for a moment. Rachel grabbed his arm. He snapped back to consciousness. It was clear he was using every ounce of energy he had left to keep standing. Once that energy was gone, Skyler knew he would be too.

"Sam," she said. This wasn't fair. He didn't deserve to die in here. But he was right—they couldn't leave the way out open.

"Skyler," Sam said. His eyes were dull and his skin had taken on a pale blue tint. He already looked dead. He slipped off his backpack and held it out to her. "Please take it," he said. His arms were trembling, he couldn't hold it for long. Skyler grabbed it before the weight could overwhelm him.

"Sam? Are you sure?"

He nodded. He had made his choice. He wouldn't change his mind; he wasn't coming with them. It was hard to know if it was the right choice, but it was his. She couldn't take that away from him.

"What are we doing?" Rachel asked. "We're not just going to leave him here."

Skyler couldn't think about that. If she did, she might try to keep it from happening.

"Rachel," she said gently.

"Come on, Sam." Rachel grabbed his arm again.

"You guys really need to go," he said distantly. He was on the verge of teetering over.

"You're coming too."

Skyler knew Rachel wasn't going to jump willingly. She grabbed Rachel's hands and pulled her forward.

"What are you doing?" Rachel tried to tug away, but without her usual strength, these attempts were unsuccessful.

"Listen to me," Skyler said, pulling Rachel closer to her. "Listen!"

"Let go!"

Skyler looked to Sam, pleading. She needed his help one last time, help in deciding if he really needed to do this, if there really was no other way.

"Listen," he said, hobbling toward them. His voice made Rachel stop struggling briefly enough for him to shove the sisters into the pit.

Skyler plummeted into the overwhelming blackness, the sound of Rachel's and her own screams echoed through her body. Then she heard a cosmic boom before her senses vanished completely.

Part Five
The Tool

Chapter Twenty-Six

The trees swayed in the wind. They moved mostly in unison, but some had branches wobbling every which way. Some trees were missing all of their leaves, others only lost most. A couple were losing their bark, taking on a white color, perhaps from a disease or fungus. Birds fluttered from branch to branch, undeterred by the cold breeze, some lightly hopping along the ground, a few chirping. There were a couple squirrels as well. One was chasing another up a tree, both spiraling up the trunk like a fuzzy brown snake. Though it was a chilly day, the sun gave everything a warm glow.

But it would be dark soon, she knew. The sun was already low on the horizon, peeking through the trees. She feared what would happen then. Maybe the sadness would set in, or the fear and panic. Or perhaps this would be one of those rare good nights, a calm and numb night. Maybe she would fall asleep quickly, without nightmares.

Skyler took a deep breath, trying not to think about anything else but the birds, squirrels, and trees. Looking out at the woods made her feel less alone.

The house was devoid of life. Oscar and Nightmare were with her mom. That was for the best, of course. But the lack of a living presence made the loneliness all the worst. Her phone was buzzing; it was probably her mom again, like clockwork, either to insist once again that Skyler move in with her or to list off another bunch of therapists. The woman had recently put her foot down and stopped sending Skyler money, stopped bringing groceries. Fortunately, Skyler still had enough money, though less and less each day, and could order her own groceries and pay her own rent. There were still a couple months yet before the lease was up.

Her mom sometimes sent people over to help "inspire" Skyler. Once, it was the counselor from the elementary school, Ms. Simone Wolfe, a woman only about ten years older than Skyler and about three inches shorter. She'd had little to say except that Skyler could talk to her whenever needed. The oddest person her mom had sent was Pastor Dan. The same pastor whose singing Skyler and Morgan used to laugh at. He had tried to give comforting words about faith and God. It only made Skyler feel worse. How could she possibly believe in any of that? Once, Skyler's parents had both come over together, the first time she saw the two of them in the same room in a long time. That led to nothing but the three of them quietly sitting in the living room. It was the only time her dad came to visit in person, but he tried to call her often. She rarely answered. She still didn't have a lot to say to him. Rachel, who never spoke to Skyler now, was living with him.

No, there wasn't anybody she could talk to. What could a parent, or a pastor, or a therapist tell her? Who would understand anything?

In the first days after returning, she'd tried to tell people about the snow globe. She was told everything she'd been through was a delusion. Maybe they were right. Investigators hadn't even found a snow globe at the scene. But the tool... She knew that was there, upstairs in her closet. At least she thought it was. She hadn't deigned to look at it for a long time.

Nobody had found Morgan either. According to the rest of the world, she was still a missing person, an unsolved mystery along with hundreds of others. Skyler had seen traces of her upon waking up in the mom-and-pop shop's basement. Shelves were knocked over, claw marks on the ground, bits and pieces of that artificial moss. Naturally, the authorities thought it was caused by a wild animal. She often had dreams of Morgan creeping into her room and grabbing her throat. There was an untrimmed bush outside her front door that often gave her panic attacks whenever she saw it, thinking it was the cousin she both feared and grieved. She would come any day, unless she was already there, waiting for the right moment. Upstairs, Morgan's bedroom door was locked. Skyler could not even imagine trying to open it, even just to peek inside.

She had other recurring dreams too. They were all about that snow globe, that world, the castle and the maze and the dark forest with its contorted creatures. She would often wake up hearing that bell. Once, she had been attempting to clean and accidentally hit a pan. Its ring sounded so similar to that *thrum*, it had made her vomit. She had many short dreams about falling back into the well that made her wake up sweaty and sobbing.

She would never trust a forest. Not even the woods she was looking out at, for all the calming peace it gave her, could be trusted. *Nothing* outside could be trusted, not the wind, the sky, or the sun. Not even the animals. Even the spiders or flies she found crawling around the house, she felt no hesitation to swat dead.

Sick of watching the trees sway and the birds and squirrels run about, she backed away from the sliding door. Once she was far enough from it to feel safe turning around, she moved across the living room, stepping over food residue and empty boxes. The smell of food, mixed with the smell of cigarette smoke embedded in the carpet, was potent. But she'd smelled worse.

For the umpteenth time that day, she checked to make sure the front door was locked and then sat on the living room couch. For a fleeting moment, she expected Oscar to rush in and jump up with her, like he always would. Her heart would warm at the thought of it, and then frost over when she'd remember he wasn't there.

She didn't even know what she felt like doing. Sometimes reading brought a little joy back to her. But not often. It was especially hard for her to read poetry anymore, especially Emily Dickinson. TV occasionally helped, as long as it was something light and mindless, nothing heavy. She shifted. Her spine was rubbing uncomfortably against the back of the couch. She knew how thin she was getting, even without her mom's comments. She would eat every day. She would even enjoy it sometimes. But she rarely had an appetite. Sometimes she would think about protein bars and would feel sick the rest of the day. She couldn't eat peaches, or any fruit that reminded her of peaches either.

She often thought about Sam, Virgil, Jon, Darwin. All the people she had killed. They would sometimes visit her dreams. Sam especially haunted her. Her thoughts would take her back to that archive, that pit. He'd hardly had any strength left; if she'd put in some effort, she could have pulled him down with her and Rachel. Or maybe she should have been the one to stay and close the doorway. What good was she alive anyway? She often thought about dying. The thought was a warm blanket one moment, a black shadow the next.

She closed her eyes, attempting meditation, or something of the sort. She snapped them open when hearing a knock on the door, followed by the doorbell ringing. Probably some Mormons or a salesperson. Her mother had a key—and would always tell Skyler in advance whenever she sent someone over. The knocking and ringing went on for a while, becoming more and more insistent.

Just go away. Go away.

The knocking and ringing eventually ceased, but it wasn't long before she heard knocking again, this time from the back door. There was also some shouting underneath it. It sounded male. The voice almost sounded like...

No. She was just hearing things. The knocking again stopped, hopefully this time for good.

She found the energy to get off the couch and go upstairs. Once inside her bedroom, she heard knocking on the front door again and the ringing of the doorbell.

Go away.

What if it was Morgan? The thought made her want to rush into her closet and hide or curl up on the floor under her bed.

The knocking and ringing stopped. Maybe they would go away now. Maybe it was actually over. She held her breath. Hoping for a long silence. But another noise did come. It was the creaking sound of the front door opening. Her blood went cold.

"Mom?" she called out weakly.

There was no reply. Her heart pounding, she rushed to the closet and grabbed a knife. She didn't know how to buy a gun online without having to leave the house to pick it up, but had been able to buy several combat knives. She never practiced using any of them, but she killed with a knife before.

"Mom?" she asked again.

She needed to make sure. If her mom saw her coming downstairs wielding a knife, she would flip. But there was still no answer. She slowly descended the stairs, her head swimming, tears in her eyes. All she wanted to do was retreat.

But what she saw when she came downstairs was no creature, but a man. He wore a green Mr. Roger's sweater and khaki pants. The most striking thing about him was the fact that he looked like an older Sam, tall and thin with ghostly pale skin and billowy hair. Though instead of a vanishing black, this man's hair was cotton white and thinning. His eyes also were darker than Sam's, brown rather than blue. And he had a broader jaw.

"I'm sorry," the man said. His voice was firm, but calm. It had the authoritative boom of a tenured college professor. His eyes glanced at the knife, then made their way up to her. He smiled; his teeth were dark yellow blocks. "I know it was rude of me to let myself in."

She looked at the door. Hadn't she locked it? She knew she should have invested in dead bolts.

"Oh, uh, I used to pick locks all the time," the man explained. "Been a long time, but I guess some things you don't forget. Listen, I can imagine what it looks like, but I'm not here to cause trouble."

Strangely, the man's calm manner lulled her into a sense of security, enough to temporarily numb her fear and lower the knife.

"Why are you here?" she asked.

The man smiled again and stepped toward her, keeping his posture confidently upright. As he came closer, she could smell that he stank like a bar. "I've been thinking a lot about the things that have happened to me lately." His face drooped into a wrinkled scowl. "And, well, I believe that you might help me make sense of them."

"Me?" She knew this man. She had never met him or even seen him before, but she knew him. But a name wasn't coming to her.

"Yes, Skyler."

She opened her mouth to ask him how he knew her name, but he interrupted. "My name is Michael Adamsen. Let's start with my first question, shall we?"

His face darkened, his scowl deep with bitterness, and Skyler realized she shouldn't have felt so secure.

"Where the hell is my son?"

Chapter Twenty-Seven

"I T's NOT UNUSUAL FOR Samael and I to go long periods without speaking," Michael Adamsen said, sitting cross-legged on the couch. Skyler noticed his pants were stained and ragged, the soles of his loafers worn to nothing. "But this time I felt something was wrong. I may not have had the first idea where to look if not..."

Skyler squeezed the handle of her knife with one hand and popped her fingers on the other. What could she even tell him? Where could she start?

"It's quiet in here," Michael said, taking in the room around him. "Unusually quiet for a young woman's house." She had no response to that. What did that even mean? "Does your sister live here?"

"No," she said quickly.

"It was quite a story the two of you told. Very exciting. A world inside a snow globe, a castle, monsters. A fascinating story." A sudden look flashed in his eyes that made Skyler grip the knife handle with both hands. It was a look of pain and rage. "You know, she wrote a letter to me, your sister."

"What?" Skyler couldn't believe that. Why would Rachel write him a letter?

"She told me that I didn't know her and she didn't know me, but she thought I should know that…" Michael winced and looked at his hands. "That Samael was dead." His voice was monotone as he said this.

A sick feeling crawled through Skyler's gut. She wanted to run upstairs and get away from him. Get away from all of this.

"So I looked into who this Rachel Horne was." He raised his voice, speaking again with a detached, scholarly flourish. "I learned about your interesting little story. What a strange place to end up in." There were dense echoes of condescension in his voice, but not necessarily disbelief. "One can only imagine the trauma you've been through. I also came to learn that my son had been out that way. The 'Prairie Triangle,' as it were. That his car had been impounded outside the same abandoned store where you and your sister were found. Of course, there was no sign of Samael. Just another lost soul, I suppose."

Skyler felt angry at Rachel. Didn't she realized how much she would complicate their lives by writing to this man? Of course, there was no sense in being angry. It was obvious Rachel had also been eaten by a deep, painful guilt; felt like she needed to do something, even just to ease her conscience.

"But I cannot stop thinking about your fascinating story. That strange world. Had Samael been in that world with you?"

She was ready to deny it all again. To say she didn't know what happened, whatever she had said before was in her head. But then she realized, this was Sam's father; if anyone would understand the truth, it would be him. Maybe he would even have some answers, something that Skyler could hold onto.

"Are you with the Society?" she asked.

Michael jumped slightly. He quickly composed himself and smacked his lips. "What Society?"

"The one your grandfather started."

He studied her for a moment, clearly at a loss about how to answer her.

"Sam told me about the Society," she said, hoping to pull him out of this act.

"Sam? Who is... Oh, Samael." He suddenly looked sick. "So you did see him."

"Yes."

"And?" She knew what he wanted her to say.

"He's gone." At least, as far as she knew. There was certainly no way he could have made it, not that she could think of. But it was better to get straight to the point and leave the details out.

Michael looked at his feet, deep in thought. His face was contorted in a way that reminded her of the boyish fear she would see in Sam, that look of frightful uncertainty. The reminder twisted her inside.

After a long, awkward silence, he steeled himself, tightening his face into a refined blankness.

"And what did he tell you?" he asked.

"A lot." She didn't have it in her to give a recitation of the facts. Michael was the one who needed to be talking.

"You are going to tell me everything that happened. What you saw, what you learned."

There was a cold and domineering change in his voice that she resented. He was demanding complacency. Skyler wanted to snap back and ask, *Why should I?*

But Michael answered this question before she could even attempt to say it. "I believe..." He cleared his throat in an apparent effort to maintain his composure. "I believe this could lead to something quite productive and beneficial to both of us. Surely, you have many questions. Perhaps I could fill in some gaps for you. Now, with regards to your story, I believe it."

There was a patchy brown satchel that until now had rested passively at his side. He reached inside. Skyler was instantly gripped by panic when she saw him pull out the bulbous shape. In his hands was that vast, dark world staring out at her, whispering hello. It was here for her. She couldn't let it take her again. Not again.

Michael continued talking, explaining how he got it, perhaps. Something about a corrupt local deputy. The words didn't matter. She could already feel herself being taken by that forest again, constricted by darkness.

Not again. Not again.

She leaped from her seat and dashed up the stairs.

It didn't take long before Michael came shuffling into her room. She was coiled on her bed, pointing her knife toward the doorway.

"I left it downstairs," he said, holding his hands high, fingers splayed to demonstrate emptiness. "I really do just want to talk." There was a frail tremble in his voice that encouraged her to lower her defenses a bit. She still kept the knife limply raised. "This is very important to me," he continued. His voice went low as he added, "It was very important to Sam as well. Please."

Something inside warned her that this was disingenuous, that he was just using Sam's name to guilt her. But it was enough to make her completely lower the knife. Michael sighed with relief and stepped further into her room.

"Ah." He pointed to the poster above her head. It was a map of Earth. It had a brown and tan coloration making it appear ancient though it was just a mass-produced poster she had bought online four years ago. "I was quite the globe-trotter in my youth. That was so long ago. My entire life was a search. We Adamsens have a very special purpose, did Sam tell you this?"

"Yes."

"And this special purpose is?" The professor hoped everyone had done their reading. She was resenting Michael more by the second.

"To find something."

"Well, we all want to find something. But what? What do the Adamsens want to find?"

The time for underhandedness was long past. Skyler was tired of trying to keep it up anyway. "The tool that creates worlds."

His eyes widening, he looked like Skyler had used a slur against him. "You've seen it?" he whispered, slowly sitting in the computer chair across from her bed.

She nodded.

"So Sam..."

"I wouldn't be here if it wasn't for him."

"But he found it?"

It was as if he hardly cared that his son was dead anymore. His interest was only in that damn thing. "Yes, Sam found it."

Michael breathed deeply and rubbed the bridge of his nose, like Sam used to. This man was impossible to read. It seemed he was always on the verge of some eruption, but whether it was anger or joy or acid reflux, she couldn't tell.

"I always thought I was the one," Michael muttered sadly. "The one who would restore everything. I'd searched all over this damned country. To think that all along the tool was in a snow globe in the basement of a shithole shop in the middle of nowhere Nebraska. I was nothing if not persistent, though. Even when I gave up on this particular one, I searched other parts of the world."

"What do you mean, this particular one?"

"Surely you can't believe there is only one tool out there." He chuckled. "Well, I suppose I used to think so too. The Society for the Preservation of Miscellaneous Artifacts was oddly closed-minded in this regard. But there has always been evidence of other tools. You would think with Europe conquering most of the world, many of the Society's highest members most benefiting from that conquest, there would be more interest in investigating that evidence. But at some point, I suppose, they decided to keep the powerful thing they had close to the chest without seeking its equals."

"Other tools?" She was all too aware of how dim-witted she sounded. But there was so much to take in.

"It would only make sense, don't you think?" Michael seemed more at ease, the confidence of a man talking down to an inferior. "My grandfather. You know, after Maria disappeared, he gathered his followers. Whoever was left at least. One of these men had been in Cambodia of all places. You see, there were old Khmer legends about an object of great power, too powerful to be used by any human, even kings. There are similar stories in Africa and South America. Of course, I didn't find a damn thing."

"And what are these things?"

"Who's to say?" Michael asked with a chilling excitement that made Skyler instinctively squeeze her knife's handle. He sauntered to her bookshelf, filled with historical fiction and nonfiction books, as well as an assortment of notebooks and binders from her college days she hadn't gotten rid of. "Can you imagine the implications?" He perused her shelf as if inspecting it for dust. "After all, these could well be the very tools that created our own world. Wouldn't you say?"

A scene squirmed into her memory. Shadowy figures in the darkness, forming a world in their own primordial image. That world changing and forming an image of its own. Then the scene was gone from her mind, unconjurable as a moment of déjá vu.

Michael looked at her. "You know why the secret of the tool was held so closely? It wasn't just because of its power and danger. The implications are earth-shattering. Religion would crumble, power structures all over the world would struggle to maintain themselves. Well, that was the fear at least, and not unjustified."

Skyler said nothing. This wasn't anything she hadn't already considered in her own ruminations, though Michael seemed to believe he was throwing hard-hitting revelations at her.

He moved away from the shelf and toward Skyler's dresser, its surface also covered in old books and dust. "But imagine what could be done with such a tool today. The earth is burning, resources are dwindling. Too many mouths to feed. Too many bodies cluttering up the place. But what if we can create new worlds? Worlds you can sell off to the highest bidder, be they private corporation or nation, or even particularly ambitious individuals. We would have a limitless supply of resources. *Population...*" He said this word with disgust. "That issue would be at thing of the past. Move boatloads of people to a new world, put them to work however you see fit. Yes, whoever could use such a tool... could create such worlds..." He couldn't finish, too delightfully warmed by his thoughts.

Skyler, on the other hand, felt chills crawl through her body. *Anybody* having that kind of power frightened her, but especially someone like Michael.

"The old guard didn't have that kind of vision, did they?" he said, grinning proudly. "Maria Faragó had no wish to innovate or better human existence. She wished to keep hiding the tool away. Not even my grandfather had such vision." Michael's face instantly turned solemn, as if the grin had just been an act. "What brought you to the world? If I may ask."

What did he mean? Did he want to know about the urge? Or what brought her to the Prairie Triangle in the first place? Either way, she didn't want to answer. But he looked at her, frowning, quietly demanding an answer.

"I was looking for someone."

"Who?"

Skyler had an image of Morgan, altered by the forest. She imagined those eyes peering into her bedroom window. "My cousin."

"Who had also been taken?" She nodded. "But what brought you to the snow globe? Did Sam tell you about it?"

"No, I met him in the world." She realized that wasn't true. They had met before, in that gas station. But that detail seemed unnecessary.

Michael's eyebrows were furrowed with frustration. "What brought you to the snow globe?" he asked again.

"I can't explain it," Skyler said. "It—when I was out there, the Prairie Triangle, I just had this feeling. Like something was calling to me."

"Like what?"

"I don't know." Skyler had an urge to pop her fingers against her chin, but didn't want to let go of her knife. "The world, I guess."

"The world called to you? So everyone who was taken by it, I suppose it called to them as well?"

"Yes."

"I see." Michael relaxed a little, strolling back to the computer chair and sitting. She noticed his hands were shaking. "You speak like the world is a sentient being."

"It is." She wasn't going to explain herself or second-guess that.

"So why haven't I heard this calling?"

"It can't reach out anymore. Rachel and I closed the entrance."

He stood and paced again. "I see. But *why* was it calling to people anyway?"

"It was building an army." As much as she wished Michael would go away, part of her felt relieved to have someone to talk to about this. He was a curious listener, but not a skeptical one.

"An army?"

"It wanted the tool."

"And what did it want with the tool?"

Another scene popped in and out of her head. Greens, blues, and browns swirling, reaching out, growing and encompassing all.

"It wants to expand," she said.

"Expand?"

But it needed someone to help it. That someone, she realized, was her. The world hadn't only shown her what *it* wanted, back in the forest. It showed what it wanted from *her*. It had chosen her, then taught her, conditioned her, so she could play her role. It was still in her head, after all this time. Nobody could enter or leave it. But it could still speak to those beyond. Perhaps it was speaking to Michael as well.

"Skyler," he said.

"Huh?" She realized she hadn't spoken for a while.

"You said it wanted to expand? Can you elaborate?"

"Oh." The world was never going to leave her alone, she thought with sinking despair. It had designs for her. These designs were the only reason it had let her and Rachel leave the forest. It was why Morgan had led them back through the castle. Perhaps at some point, the world realized its plan needed adapting. Its army finally seized the castle, but what then? So it picked someone. Someone weak and afraid that it could needle and nudge into doing what it wanted. A new Maria.

"Skyler!"

"Yes. It wants to expand."

"So then, it wants to be bigger?"

Skyler pulled her mind from these despairing thoughts and focused on the pacing man. "It doesn't just want to be bigger. It wants to be *everything*. To expand infinitely."

"Infinitely." Michael shrugged. "Don't we all?"

"Speak for yourself."

Michael didn't respond to her retort. He ceased his pacing and wiped his face with his sleeve. "Do you have anything to drink?"

"Water. Some pop in the garage." She realized he would probably be more interested in Morgan's vodka in the downstairs closet or the rum in one of the kitchen cabinets, or even the old boxed wine in the fridge. But she feared he would never leave if she offered any of those to him.

He shook his head angrily. "Never mind." He sat back down, clenching his fists and his teeth. His hands were shaking even more. Despite herself, Skyler couldn't help but feel a little sorry for him.

"More than a world," Michael said after a deep breath. "A living, breathing being. Makes you think about our own world." He gazed out the bedroom window.

She looked too. A dead tree was shaking in the wind, the sky behind it a faded blue.

"Maybe it's alive as well," Michael said.

"It is," Skyler replied. "More than we know."

"More than we know *now*," Michael corrected. "Gods, devils, heaven, hell, ghosts, and ghouls, stories that all boil down to the tangible and intangible forces before us, the forces we are intertwined with. Early people worshipped trees. We used to be very in touch with the life around us. I suppose certain indigenous peoples still are, or at least *were*." He chuckled as if he'd said something funny. Though there was a gravelly discomfort in his voice.

"It seems we are much more in tune with what we create than what created us," he continued. "It's telling that people could sooner respond to a world created by human hands, even from miles away." He smiled with bitter admiration. "She was an ambitious one, Faragó, I can't deny her that. Her world, if its intentions are as you say, has that same ambition. But at the same time, she became so consumed by her own creation, she lost sight of those around her. Including her own beloved Elizabeth. That poor girl had escaped with her life, and two less fingers." He held his hand in a three-fingered formation to demonstrate.

"History could have played out a lot differently. Elizabeth had taken the world after fleeing it, but she'd lost it on a damn train! Imagine if she'd been able to bring it to New Zealand. What my grandfather could have done if he had his hands on Maria's world."

He closed his eyes and basked in the thought. For a moment, Skyler thought he was falling asleep.

"You mentioned the tool," he said abruptly, snapping open his eyes. "You were going to tell me about it."

"Was I?"

He spoke like he was waiting for her to follow through on a promise. "Let's not waste any more time. These existential conversations have been amusing, but unproductive. Describe the tool to me. Or better yet..." A look came across his face. A horny old man licking his lips. Discomfort squeezed around Skyler's body; she was prepared to raise her knife again. "Show me it."

"Show you?"

"I'm sick of this runaround." Michael's eyes were so wide, she could see how pinkish red they were around the irises. "I know Sam would want me to have it."

"How do you know what Sam would want?"

Michael jumped to his feet. "You little bitch! Don't pretend you know my son!"

Anger brought Skyler to her feet as well, raising her knife. Standing on top of the bed brought her above Michael's height. "Get out of my house."

"Stupid, infantile..."

"Get out!" Her voice was so hoarse and vile, it hardly sounded like her own.

"My son is dead, you worthless little whore, and you..."

"Get the fuck out!" She swiped the knife, though too limply to make it cut into the air.

Limp as it was, the gesture made Michael go still. His lip quivered with rage and shock. He blinked a few times, composing himself before forcing his face into a smile. "This has gotten out of hand. I apologize for being such an awful host... guest, I mean."

"Get out." In another time, his change of tone might have placated her. But not now.

"Things were heated. We both said some foolish things. I'm not feeling my best, you know."

A terrifying thought popped into Skyler's mind. What if he would never leave? What if the only way to make this all stop was to use the knife? If it came down to it, could she do it? Could she actually attack him? If not, that would leave only one option.

"Listen," he continued, "remember what I talked about."

"Your world-making business?"

"Don't be mouthy. We must be civil! Listen, what if we studied the tool together? Is that what you want?"

She shook her head, hoping he wouldn't ask what she actually *did* want.

"Tell me this, then." He sauntered over to her closet. For a moment, she thought he was going to open it and her heart tightened. The tool and its hammer were just behind a bunch of old shoes, in a plastic bag. But he just brushed his fingers along the wooden door. "How do you know what you know? You say the world wants to expand infinitely. What makes you so sure? Not to say I don't believe you, of course. I truly do. Still, I don't know why I should."

"It showed me." She wasn't about to try and describe the forest, the images she'd seen, the things she heard. Nothing she could say in words would make him understand it. Even if she could grasp him by the head and show him everything she'd seen, he still wouldn't understand.

"But why would it show *you*?"

"I don't know," she lied.

Michael moved away from the closet, again licking his thin lips. "Where is the tool?"

"It's still with Maria Faragó's corpse," she said spitefully.

Michael's eyes bulged and he trembled. She thought he was about to start shouting again; she braced herself, still balancing on top of her bed. But instead, he collapsed back onto the computer chair, clutching his head. "My grandfather," he said, "his purpose unfulfilled."

Skyler leaned against the wall. This pity party was exhausting her.

"His son a disappointment," Michael continued. "His grandson... unsuccessful, now his great-grandson is dead. I only knew Samael the First for a short time in my life. A paramount man. He was propelled by hope and a vision that..."

"He was a monster!" Skyler snapped. Her restraint was all but fading. Just the thought of putting up with this man like she would have in the past exhausted her. "Who cares what he wanted? Who cares what he hoped for?"

"How dare you," Michael growled, rising once again from his seat.

"His little war with Maria? He started it."

"Of course he did!" Michael said. "What else could he have done once he learned that witch was leading him astray?"

Skyler didn't even know what to say to this. What could she say? So Michael knew the truth of his legacy, knew the violence his grandfather had committed against Maria, the bomb he'd set off literally and figuratively, and didn't even care. Once again, she wondered if she would be using her knife before this was all over.

"We need to be civil," he said again, trying to keep his cracking voice steady and firm. "I won't leave until I see it."

Skyler raised her knife higher.

"Oh, come now," Michael said. "I know you won't stab me."

Angry as this made her, he was right, despite all the thoughts going through her head. She'd killed three people. Four. Two of them looking right into her eyes. But this was different. She was home now, even if it didn't feel like home. She didn't want to hurt anyone else. She just wanted this all to end. Maybe she would have to go about this differently.

"Fine," she said.

Michael's eyes glinted and he relaxed his shoulders.

"Now then," he said, as if the upper hand was still his. Skyler intended on changing that.

"I have the tool," she said, slowly stepping down from the bed.

"I thought so." He tried to stay still, but he trembled excitedly. It was almost funny looking; he looked like an elderly child, some kind of Benjamin Button, waiting for candy. There was only one thing he wanted and she was the one who had it. The ball was in her court. She could use that even if she still wasn't sure what the endgame would be.

"Go downstairs," she said. "I'll bring it to you."

Michael looked offended. "Now listen..."

"I'll show you the tool *if* you go downstairs. Otherwise, you can stay up here as long as you want. But you won't see a damn thing."

He glared at her, seemingly thinking of some way to regain the upper hand. "I... I'll turn every inch of this house upside down."

"And I'll call the cops—"

"Good, I can use a hand." Good point. What damn good would come from calling the police? He was a wealthy old White man, she was a half-Black shut-in. He'd find some way to turn things in his favor. Even if he couldn't, there was little chance the Omaha Police Department would be much help to her.

"Maybe I'll just run out and scream loud enough for the entire street to hear. I've got some neighbors who would more than happily kick your ass."

"I..." Michael looked at his feet and let out a frustrated grunt. It was as satisfying as the sound of tinfoil being cut. He still didn't budge, though.

"I'll show it to you," she said. "But you need to go downstairs first."

Michael continued standing by stubbornly, trying to think through it. "Please don't waste my time," he said finally, before turning and storming out of her room.

She sighed and closed her eyes, letting the tension and awkwardness flood away as she heard him stomp down the stairs. Part of her hoped she would hear the front door slam. It didn't. He was determined to see this tool and she would show it to him. She would show it to the world too, show it exactly what it wanted.

But then what?

Chapter Twenty-Eight

THE TOOL GREETED HER with its subtle but colorful glow, once she mustered the will to look at it. She could feel its power, itching to be released. The hammer, that special hammer made from god knows what, lay next to it. They both patiently waited at the bottom of the plastic bag. She didn't want to touch them, so she carried the bag as if it were full of Oscar's morning routine, lightly holding it by the handle.

Michael was sitting on the couch, fumbling his fingers like a waiting-room patient. He stood when she came down, but his eyes were fixed on the bag, never once glancing up at Skyler's face. He breathed heavily through his nose. He was like a dog, Skyler thought, a hungry dog waiting for his treat. Next to him, almost sinking into the cushions, was the snow globe. It was also watching her, waiting.

Skyler dumped the chisel and its hammer onto the coffee table. They hit the surface with a loud bang, the hammer making a dent. Michael shot her an enraged look. She was certain he was about to go off on her, but his attention was quickly arrested by the chisel.

"This..." he said. His mouth gapes. The hungry dog salivated.

"Yes, this is it," Skyler said. She wanted him to be underwhelmed, to finally look all his self-importance and obsession in the face and feel embarrassment.

Unfortunately, he seemed awed. "Well, how about that."

When he reached for the chisel, Skyler swiped it away. Despite not wanting to touch it, she wanted Michael to touch it even less.

"What are you doing?" He looked like a hurt puppy.

"Why should you have it?"

"What?" His face twisted with indignation. "This isn't time for games."

A month ago, she would have recoiled at his anger. She would have handed him the tool just to make him leave as soon as possible. But she couldn't even imagine doing that now.

"I'm not playing one," she said. "I want to know why you should have this tool."

"What do you know?" he asked, hateful spittle dripping from his mouth. It reminded her of the malice she'd seen in Jon.

"Nothing, apparently. So inform me." As she gripped the tool firmly in her hand, she realized she'd left the knife upstairs. But there was another one, hidden in the closet behind her. It didn't matter anyway, she could hurt Michael far more with this, and most importantly, he knew that.

"I deserve it far, far more than anybody else," he said, unsuccessfully trying to give himself that professorial air again. "Especially more than a child like you. My grandfather was Samael Adamsen."

"That means nothing."

"Are you completely daft? Did you not listen to anything I said?" She shrugged.

"I have the vision. I have the bloodline."

"Okay, but *why* does that matter. The bloodline?"

"You said it yourself. My Samael found this." Michael stepped forward, reaching toward the chisel. Skyler clutched it to her chest and backed away. "God*damn* you!"

She held steady, keeping herself calm. "Sam died because of this."

"It was a worthwhile sacrifice!" The words flew carelessly from his mouth. Skyler wondered if Sam's death was really even sinking in for him.

"You really think that?" she asked.

I guess it was all for the greater good, she remembered Sam saying before bursting into tears. It hurt to think about, and only made her anger toward Michael stronger.

There was a noticeable pause before Michael answered her question. "Yes."

She shook her head and looked down at the pulsing thing in her hands. Something was gnawing at the back of her mind, she realized. Little more than a light itch, but ever present. It was an urge to give the tool to Michael, even if her gut was telling her otherwise. Maybe it was the world. It was there, after all, sitting behind Michael, nestled in the cushions. Perhaps it had a new plan, a new partner in crime. In that case, handing the tool to Michael would certainly make all of this go away. But...

"I thought I would be the one to find it," Michael said with the inflection of a rookie defense attorney. "Years and years of searching. Then I grew old, tired, and I knew it was time someone else carried on in my stead. So, I had Samael. His purpose was mine. For many years, I truly thought I'd failed with him. But when all was said and done, he followed the path I laid. He found the world and the tool. Thus, you can argue, his discovery was mine."

"Jesus Christ," Skyler said. He spoke of his own son like some kind of robot he'd built. She felt even more miserable for Sam, thinking about him growing up under this man's care.

"You don't understand." Michael sounded tired, as if he should be the frustrated one.

"Your *son*," Skyler said. "His obsession with finding this thing led to his death. The obsession you pounded into him his whole life. You should have seen his face before I left. He didn't look happy, he didn't look fulfilled." Her eyes stung and her voice began to break, but she pushed through. "He just looked like he was dying."

Michael's lip squirmed. "He's more of an Adamsen than ever, then. I'll build him a memorial next to his great grandfather's grave."

"And his mother?"

"Whose mother?" Michael's eyes widened as he realized. "What about her?"

It was a good question. Skyler had no idea why she brought up Sam's mother. Maybe she was just reaching for some kind of humanity in Michael, if she couldn't appeal to his feelings for his son.

But the image of Sam's mother only made the old man angry again, and Skyler knew she'd failed. "She has nothing to do with anything!"

"The mother of your son."

"She was more of an employee than anything," Michael said. "I needed a son, and she seemed fit enough to give me one. My grandfather had done the same in his later years, with my father's mother."

"Your grandmother, you mean."

"This is absurd."

There was a noise, the sound of trickling. Skyler glanced out the window and realized it was raining.

"And what about *your* mother?" she asked.

"I didn't know her," he replied, as if they were just talking about his neighbor's wife. "After my grandfather died, I went to live with my great uncle. There I learned my grandfather had kept me from that woman for good reason. She was a drunkard, a whore. I should have followed grandfather's example and kept my Samael from *his* mother. I'm not proud of the kindness I gave her. I provided her wealth and comfort she'd never had before. Comfort she certainly hadn't deserved. But it wasn't enough for her. She tried to steal my son."

"He was her son too. Maybe she wanted to protect him from you."

Michael lunged forward. For a moment, Skyler thought he was going to attack her. Perhaps he would have, but a glance at the tool in her hands stopped him. "Stupid fucking idiot girl," he said. "You're just like her, you know that? Awful, horrible little creature. If she loved her son so much, she wouldn't have taken her own life, now would she?"

"She killed herself?"

Michael licked his lips. "She was sentenced to life in prison. Even by that point, I was sickeningly lenient. You see, the kind of pull I had back then, I could've easily had her put on death row. Regardless, she killed herself a year into her sentence. They found her in bed, blood everywhere—she had no cellmate at that moment, you see—with a lockpick in her jugular."

"Lockpick?"

"Oh yes," Michael looked at his feet. "Not something she was supposed to have. But prison contraband can be sneaky."

"Jesus." Something about that story didn't seem right. She didn't know Sam's mother, nor did she know what the woman's circumstances were like or where her headspace had been. Still, she couldn't imagine someone choosing such a violent and painful way to die. Of course, that didn't mean it didn't happen. But there was something else. There was an air of guilt to Michael. An uneasy feeling was creeping through her.

"I'd been merciful," Michael said. He was now looking at the tool, sweat dotting his skin. "Understand? I make the decisions that best suit everyone, if not ones that make everyone happy. That's why I deserve the chisel."

Skyler was speechless. Did she miss the argument for why he should have it? Or did he really think he'd made it?

"I will not try to wrestle it out of your hands." Michael made an unsuccessful attempt to arch back his hunched shoulders and look dignified. "But I will have it. I deserve it. I am the only human alive who does. That's the goddamn truth. I will have it. I will. Scream at your neighbors. Call the police. I can leave without it today. But I'll come back. If not me, then someone else will."

The unease crawling through her body morphed into fear. Michael was not your average cruel and arrogant jerk. He was a dangerous and ruthless man who would go to great lengths to get what he wanted. Beneath the fear, she was angry. But she was caged; there was no way she could live with letting this man walk away with the tool. But she couldn't keep it either, couldn't live a life consumed by this thing or having to watch her back because of men like Michael.

There was only one thing she wanted to do, one thing she could think to do to end this.

"I understand your reluctance," he said, with an attempt at compassion in his voice, mistaking the nature of her indecision. "But I promise you, the pain and horror you've experienced will all make sense."

"No, it won't," she said.

Sam was dead. Her cousin was missing, and yet, she was terrified of ever finding her. She didn't even know how her sister was doing.

Hundreds of people, or what had once been people, were still inside that thing. Their friends, families, neighbors, loved ones would never know what happened to them. Nothing about this made sense. None of this should have happened. She couldn't see a way forward where this tool wouldn't cause pain. Michael had his terrifying vision. But it wasn't just him. Regardless of who got their hands on the tool, profit, expansion, and control were the only motivations that would have the final say. If not today, then tomorrow, or the next day. Even in a scenario where the intentions were pure, it could lead to insurmountable horrors. Maria's world proved that the creator had no say in what the creation ultimately became. Whatever those shadowy beings she envisioned had intended in leaving these devices, humanity was not in a place to be creating new worlds.

The rain continued trickling. It was getting darker outside. She could see damp and leafless branches dancing wildly in the wind. They were beautiful.

Michael sighed. "At any rate..."

"At any rate, you *will* have it?"

He nodded. A smile grew on his face, his eyes twinkled greedily and victoriously. They reinforced her anxiety, which gave her strength. She slowly went to her knees.

Michael's breathing intensified. "This is for the best," he said.

She laid the chisel on the carpet and grabbed the hammer from the coffee table.

"What are you doing?" Michael said.

She didn't answer, nor did she look up at him. She didn't want to leave room for any hesitation. The hammer was heavy but easy to handle. She floated the head over the center of the chisel, aiming. It was impossible to know if this would even work. But the chisel itself began to pulse even brighter. To her, it almost looked like it was pulsing with fear. Even now, she couldn't help the pang of guilt in her gut, but she moved past this, raising the hammer high.

"No!" Michael screamed.

She brought the hammer down. The chisel's colors pulsed blindingly as it was struck. She felt the whole force tremble through her body. The clank of the hammer hitting the chisel filled the entire room. Pain ripped through her arm and shoulder, but it didn't stop her from raising the hammer again.

Michael rushed forward to grab the tool. But before he could pull it away, Skyler brought the hammer down again. The crunch of brittle bones was palpable, curdling her stomach. The old man howled and fell back onto the couch, grasping his hand. Skyler ignored his sputtering and whimpering as she reoriented herself, aiming the hammer again, striking. The flash was even brighter. This time, the pain in her arm and shoulder extended to her chest. Despite this, she struck again and again. It was a small target, but the hammer seemed to home in on it. She heard the tool crack with one blow, a louder crack with the next. Finally, with an overwhelming pop, it let out a flash that took over her vision. Once she could see again, the tool was lying there, broken in two. There was a shooting pain in her arm. She couldn't hold the hammer anymore and dropped it. As it hit the floor, its head snapped off. The force had destroyed it as well.

The pain in her arm, her shoulders, her back quickly grew, thousands of needles deep in her flesh, overtaking her. She curled upon the ground and cried out. She could hear Michael crying as well.

Deep in her brain, she felt something shudder in agony before fading away. The grip over her mind was released. At that moment, even constricted by pain, she knew she was free.

She eventually came to her feet, her legs the only part of her body that didn't hurt. Michael was lying on the couch, gazing back at her, his eyes blazing with pain, agony, grief. The snow globe next to him seemed dimmer than usual. The world was no longer speaking to her, nudging her. It had no purpose anymore. It had lost. She looked back down at the two pieces of the chisel. Without the glowing, they just looked like pretty pieces of rock.

"Take it," Skyler said.

Michael's mouth was pathetically agape. His world had been turned upside down. Finally, he knew how she felt.

"It's what you came for," she said.

"Why?" was all Michael could weakly ask. His face was locked in that same fear and uncertainty she'd seen in Sam many times.

She wasn't going to give him an explanation. Truthfully, there was a part of her that wondered if she'd done the right thing after all. Was it really her place to destroy such a tool? Maybe her fears and instincts had been wrong. But she'd made her choice. She would take responsibility for whatever consequences. That was more than she could ever imagine Michael doing.

He still sat, small and trembling, holding his broken hand. There was a faint sour smell, and she realized Michael's pants and the couch around them were damp.

"Get out!" she said.

She allowed the old man some time to come to his feet and gather up the pieces of the tool, the snow globe, the broken hammer. He shuffled out the front door without saying anything. Skyler doubted he would come back.

She looked at the urine-stained couch and the dusty crumples of stone that remained on the floor. She had quite a mess to clean up. But before that, something felt a little more pressing.

She returned to the back door and stared out. The rain was already finished, sunbeams cutting through the clouds. When Skyler had been a little girl, she used to think those sunbeams meant someone, somewhere, was being called to heaven. Now she was being called, but not to the pearly gates. It was the sunbeams themselves that were calling her, as well as the droplets dripping from the branches, the chirping birds, and the rainy smell. It wasn't a dangerous calling, the kind that suddenly popped into her brain and took control of her. The forces at play here neither needed her, nor did they reject her.

She needed to be out there, be among everything, do it before her fears returned. It was just a matter of sliding open the door. Which she did, allowing the cool air to caress her face.

Then, Skyler Horne took her first step.

About the Author

Anthony Engebretson is from Nebraska and currently living in Michigan with his wife and two cats. Other works of his include *Sair Back, Sair Banes* released by Ghost Orchid Press, *Lumberjack* released by Tenebrous Press, and *Hell Pig* released by Off Limits Pulp.
His website is anthonyengebretson.com.

Acknowledgments

This book was six years in the making. Since I began developing this book, I:

- Met and married the love of my life
- Began and completed a Masters Degree
- Moved to a new state

I have grown and changed quite a bit over this book's lifecycle and (I hope) the book has grown and changed with me. I wasn't alone on this journey. I want to thank my parents, Alec and JS Engebretson, for supporting me and providing beta reads. I also want to thank my wife, Taylor, for always being there and giving her tireless love and support. Thank you also to Dylan and Anush for beta-reading some chapters. Of course I want to thank Grendel Press and its beta readers and editors for helping finally bring this book into the world and making it the best it can be.

Thank you, finally, to all those who read, rent, buy, share or otherwise support this book. Whether they like it or not, I am grateful to anyone giving this booktheir precious time.

Also by Anthony Engebretson

Sair Back, Sair Banes

Lumberjack

Hell Pig

www.ingramcontent.com/pod-product-compliance
Lightning Source LLC
Chambersburg PA
CBHW061336310726
48974CB00001B/69